ALEXANDER JABLOKOV

"A CRAFTSMAN OF THE FIRST WATER"
Michael Swanwick, author of *The Iron Dragon's Daughter*

"ONE OF THE BEST MODERN WRITERS AT WEAVING A GOOD STORY, BELIEVABLE CHARACTERS AND SPECULATIVE SCIENCE."
Baton Rouge Advocate

"IN THE FIRST CIRCLE OF SCIENCE FICTION WRITERS"
Publishers Weekly

THE BREATH OF SUSPENSION

"A FINE COLLECTION . . . TEN TALES STRAIGHT FROM THE HEART OF MAINSTREAM AMERICAN SF . . . WITH SUMPTUOUS, SENSUOUS PROSE, AND A PARTICULAR DARK INTELLIGENCE."
Interzone

"ONE OF S . . . THE R . . . H GOOD STOR . . . ICTION WILL . . .

Avon Books are available at special quantity discounts for bulk purchases for sales promotions, premiums, fund raising or educational use. Special books, or book excerpts, can also be created to fit specific needs.

For details write or telephone the office of the Director of Special Markets, Avon Books, Dept. FP, 1350 Avenue of the Americas, New York, New York 10019, 1-800-238-0658.

THE
BREATH OF
SUSPENSION

ALEXANDER JABLOKOV

AVON BOOKS • NEW YORK

VISIT OUR WEBSITE AT
http://AvonBooks.com

ACKNOWLEDGMENTS

As always, to the Cambridge Science Fiction Workshop and its various members over the years, who read many of these stories in their nymph forms: Steve Caine, Joe Carrabis, Pete Chvany, Dee Meaney, Resa Nelson, Steve Popkes, David Smith, and Sarah Smith.—A. J.

Copyright notices for each story appear on page v, which constitutes an extension of the copyright page.

AVON BOOKS
A division of
The Hearst Corporation
1350 Avenue of the Americas
New York, New York 10019

Copyright © 1994 by Alexander Jablokow
Cover art by Bill Binger
Published by arrangement with Arkham House
Library of Congress Catalog Card Number: 93-38607
ISBN: 0-380-72680-7

First AvoNova Printing: October 1996

AVONOVA TRADEMARK REG. U.S. PAT. OFF. AND IN OTHER COUNTRIES, MARCA REGISTRADA, HECHO EN U.S.A.

Printed in the U.S.A.

RA 10 9 8 7 6 5 4 3 2 1

TO MY WIFE, MARY

CONTENTS

THE BREATH OF SUSPENSION

The Monastery of St. Sergius, 2182

When the knock comes, it wakes me from a light doze. I was drifting through endless layers of thin clouds, lit from below. I try to convince myself that I was meditating—on what, the diaphanous undergarments that clothe the ever-incomprehensible Godhead? I am an old man, I need my rest, and acknowledge my weaknesses. I can still lie to others, but the time has passed when I must needs lie to myself.

"Come in, Thomas." I hope that he doesn't recognize the spuriously resonant tone of a man caught napping.

Brother Thomas drifts in with the soft step of a courtier. His flaxen hair bristles like uncut hay. When I first met him, I thought Thomas was extremely young, but he must be near thirty. The innocence of his gaze gives him his youth.

"They finally came." He is pleased to be the one to bring me the news.

"Show me."

He puts the package on the table and unwraps it. I move the devotional cross away to give him more room. The thing is enormously heavy and seems intended for physical as well as spiritual exercise. It leaves yet another scratch on the table's worn surface. Even in darkness I can feel the patterns of my devotion upon it with my fingertips.

Together, we huddle over the tiny wonders revealed in the fitful candlelight. The charge-coupled devices are the precise circuits from a different world than the Monastery of St. Sergius.

Thomas stares at them in awe. "What do they do?"

He's a wise one, I'm coming to realize. Not "what are they?" but "what do they do?" He knows the right questions. What questions did I ask in the past that the answer to them is St. Sergius's?

"They amplify light by bouncing electrons around. More than that, Thomas, I don't know. I just know that I need them to complete the work."

As if to mock me, one of the tallow candles sputters. These are an unsuccessful experiment of Hegumen Afonse's. The local power grid gives us electricity only four hours out of twenty-four, and the Hegumen likes to conserve our fuel cells. And beeswax is reserved for the candles that illuminate the saints in church. The tallow candles stink and attract insects. With the CCDs, my circuits could focus the light of that candle from a hundred kilometers away. Under the table sit hydrogen fuel cells designed to power an interplanetary spacecraft's life-system. We live in a world of irrelevant miracles.

Thomas picks up a CCD and holds it in his hand. It is as light as the carapace of a dead insect. "The Hegumen wanted to wait until morning. But I thought you would want to see this as soon as possible. They must have cost you a lot."

"I thank both you and the Hegumen for your separate concerns. Cost? It's greater than you think, not being in money. There are still some left at Court who are willing to do an old man favors. These, I think, are the last favors anyone will ever do me. All are now long called in." Am I sounding maudlin? It must be the hour. I have long ago accustomed myself to a mood of steely resolve. It is only late at night, with death pushing itself against the windowpanes, that I forget.

Thomas looks at me curiously. "Does the Hegumen know what you wanted these for?"

"Eh? I suppose he has no idea. He just wants to keep his pet Court refugee happy. He doesn't know how futile it is. I'm here in this midget twenty-monk monastery in Pennsylvania under special Patriarchal dispensation, and God only knows what changes back in Moscow could raise me back into a position of power. The Hegumen thinks he's being shrewd. I'm not going to disabuse him, as long as I can get what I need."

Brother Thomas endures this outburst calmly. To him I link holiness with secular power, a potent combination. He permits me my quirks, unusual forbearance in a young man.

"So," he says, setting the CCD back on the table as delicately as if it is a holy relic. "Are you going to see her now?"

His blue eyes shine. He is in the presence of the one fleshly link left to St. Aya Ngomo: the holy Vikram Osten who rose to high power and was then struck down because of his stalwart devotion to his saint.

I cannot meet his gaze. I turn away and pull the cloth from the image-multiplier telescope, a lumpy piece of work. The crude welds are my own. There's a monk at St. Sergius's who could have done a better job, a former pipe mender, but I owed it to Aya to do the work myself. She had always felt that I was, in some deep sense, useless.

It's taken me almost five years to put the whole thing together, five years since I finally realized what I had to do. In that time, Aya's gotten more than four light-years farther away. And I have gotten that much closer to death.

Sometimes when I walk I can feel the wind blow clean through me, as if it has forgotten I'm there. I'm just a tattered coat on a stick, with thin white hair. Well, let's be completely honest. It's a sticky pale yellow, like a tallow candle. The pathetic vanity of the old is never anything but disgusting.

I turn and open the shutters on the night. I always delay it, the way I sometimes used to delay taking a drink during my years of exile from Court. It's a teasing game and proves my will. The shutters slam back against the wall. Six of St. Sergius's monks are sleeping in the small stone building opposite, but their sleep is as heavy as their souls and they don't wake up. That desperate nocturnal bang is long familiar to them.

It's finally time. I raise my eyes from the dark and silent monastery to that sky from which St. Sergius's and our whole world hang merely pendant. There was some high cirrus earlier in the day, but now the air is transparent. The Milky Way splashes across the sky. Jupiter is low in the west. I lean out of the window and look toward the east into the constellation Coma Berenices. Up there, pointed toward the Galactic North, at +29 degrees declination, 12h 57m right ascension, is the flare of a hydrogen fusion flame, its absorption spectrum shifted viciously into the red, pushing the barrier of light speed, that Nirvana of the macroscopic world. It's Aya Ngomo's ship, heading God knows where. I can't see it with my naked eyes. I try to, every night. I try now. I stare upward until my eyes tear in the wind. I cannot float up through the window after her. My soul is still tied to the dross of my flesh. And why, if the flesh no longer brings the pleasures it once did? Then I close the shutters and turn back to the image multiplier.

Thomas sits alertly, like a hunting dog waiting for his master's call. To him that invisible speck of light is a relic, like the joint of a saint's forefinger or a handkerchief dipped in a martyr's blood. He barely dares breathe as I proceed through my devotions. I should ask him to leave. I don't, because I suspect my historical contact with holiness is not the only reason he is here. He does, after all, sleep near the Hegumen. Afonse thinks that he is the Archimandrite of a vast metropolitan monastery, and often awakens poor Thomas to dictate an important memo on the remortaring of a wall. It isn't easy being *parakoimomenus*—one who sleeps near. For a long time I "slept near" the Dispenser of the Atlantic, Master Tergenius. So I know that sometimes it is better to remain awake than be roused from sleep suddenly too sweet. As long as one is truly awake.

"Here, Thomas." He joins me at the image multiplier. His fingers are nimbler than mine. I always fear that I will break some irreplaceable part.

He takes a deep breath. "Will you let me look? When we finish with this machine?" The words come in a rush.

"Eh?" His face is flushed and he does not meet my

eye. "You wish to see the glow of St. Aya Ngomo?" He nods. "Is that for my sake, or for hers?"

If he senses a selfish motive in the question he does not admit it. "For both. How can they be separated? The both of you—it has been an honor for me, did I tell you that?" Thomas, usually a model of imperturbable dignity, is babbling. "To have gone so high and then to have renounced the things of this world . . . when I came here to St. Sergius's I had no idea that I would find such a clear signpost to God—"

"Don't be absurd." My tone is gentle, but I am afraid. Afraid of being loved, as I have so often been, for the wrong reasons. Still, is that worse than not being loved at all? "My sacrifices, if such they were, were my own. I can't serve as an example to anyone else."

He nods, not meeting my eyes. "I understand."

He doesn't. I did not renounce the things of this Earth. I had them taken from me. Heaven and Hell know no greater difference.

"But you, my young Thomas. What do you know of sacrifice? I'm afraid you've come to this monastery too early." I adopt a didactic tone. "To give up the world one must first possess it."

For a long time he is silent. "I have possessed it." His voice is compressed, as if someone else has a hand on his throat. "I possessed all of it that mattered." He takes a deep breath and stares off into space.

An apology would be pointless. God only knows what festering sin I have so incautiously flicked. I sit down at the table opposite him, one hand on the image multiplier. "I think you deserve a story. For your good work, Thomas. The story of how I met Aya Ngomo, Saint of the Outer Spaces."

He is galvanized. His personal pain is forgotten, or at least concealed, as he leans anxiously toward me. Nothing about my own life would interest him as much. But St. Aya Ngomo focuses him. Perhaps what I know of her can teach him something about me.

"When I was young," I say, beginning with the most painful words an old man knows.

The Monastery of St. Thecla, 2121

When I was young, I believed that if I held my breath completely, totally, not letting a single molecule of air escape, I would float weightless up through the sky. I spent summers jumping from the sycamore tree behind my parents' house in Mackinac, longing to part the clouds.

So it was that I came to be lying, one bright early-winter morning, on the floor of a roofless summerhouse half filled with beach sand, staring up at the sky and feeling my lungs burn. Layers of multicolored wallpaper peeled from the walls like the tattered pages of a long-unread book. Sand trickled down the neck of my cassock. My pectoral cross, having caught on a projecting door frame and almost strangled me, hung on a nail. Winter sand is cold and hard, carrying with it the memory of its glacial origins. I felt it press against my back with resentful solidity. Surf hissed foaming across the hardpacked beach, lapping at the leaning walls. I let my breath out slowly. I was staying here.

I was seventeen years old and absolutely miserable. My family had dropped me into the Monastery of St. Thecla with stern admonitions and would not be back for me for—I calculated, though I already knew the answer—another ten months. Another ten months with St. Thecla—and Brother Michael.

It was an Osten family tradition that each member spent a year in a proper Orthodox monastery before assuming his life's responsibilities. Even my Uncle Cosmas, luxurious and corrupt as an old wine is corrupt, spoiled in just the right way, had spent a year in a monastery in the Upper Peninsula of Michigan. He claimed to remember it fondly. Though he was known in the family as an excellent liar, I didn't believe him.

The tradition dated back to my grandfather's time, when a majority of the Wisconsin Lutheran Synod converted en masse to the victorious Orthodoxy. Being early Persuaded had always given the Osten family high status, since the things that are Caesar's are available only to those who have granted to God the things that are His. In my case, that included a year of my life.

I had been told all these things, but they did not console me. Just the previous night . . . I sat up. The memory still seared. Below me, Lake Michigan had swallowed up half the house, sucking at it until only the foundations remained. The beach here was cut with ancient boat slips and piers. Traces of this house's dock still remained as a line of weathered gull perches, driftwood piled against it. Out beyond it the pointed-arch outline of a sunken pleasure boat could be seen through the clear water. It seemed to have settled placidly at its mooring, forgotten by masters simply attempting to survive during the wars of the twenty-first century.

Above me were the buildings of the monastery, peeping over the edge of the sand dune. The nucleus of the Monastery of St. Thecla had been a cluster of old summer dwellings much like the one I was currently feeling sorry for myself in. Maple and oak trees had sprouted through the sidewalks, and dune cherries clambered over the toppled fences. Wild grapes covered the walls. Traces of ancient pleasures were scattered through the sands. I remember that after one heavy winter storm a stretch of the old macadam beach road reappeared, like some dweller of the deep seas coming to the surface to see if the sun was still there. A few weeks, and sand covered it again.

The monks had rebuilt the shattered buildings, adding chapels, dining halls, an MHD generator, and a water filtration plant. If anyone noticed the unfortunate symbolism of building a monastery on sand dunes, he was not unwise enough to mention it. Even I knew better. St. Thecla's was the personal monastery of the Patriarch of Milwaukee and dominated the affairs of the Michigan coast between Manistee and Traverse City. I understand that it's still there, still fighting the ever-hungry sand and lake, though it will soon succumb like the rest of us.

A skein of geese quacked by overhead on its way south. I could see the sun flashing on their wings against the dark sky. I couldn't join them. I was stuck here at St. Thecla's with the odious Brother Michael, the life-monk who served as my spiritual guide. My eyes stung with remembered humiliation.

The previous night I had awakened with a chill. The thin wool blanket the monastery had provided was completely inadequate. I shivered desperately.

The dormitory was dark. "Michael," I said. "I'm cold."

He was awake instantly. "Eh? What's that?"

"I said I'm cold, dammit."

"Thank the Lord you're alive to feel it, then."

"Michael, I'm freezing. Do you understand me?"

"No, boy, I don't understand you. I don't understand you at all." His voice boomed, waking everyone else up. I was mortified. He looked around. "Vikram's cold. Is everyone able to hear that?"

There was a low murmur. We got little enough sleep as it was, and here this buffoon was putting the blame on me for waking everyone up.

"Wait. All I said was—"

"Here. Stay warm, little man."

Brother Michael, a big red-faced man, stood from his cot and with a contemptuous gesture flung his own blanket over me. Then he lay back down, closed his eyes, and affected sleep. I could see his breath steam. He shivered slightly. All right then. I could stand his contempt as long as I was warm myself. I composed myself for sleep.

Suddenly someone else came up and threw his blanket over me. A moment later another. Then another.

"Damn you all!" I struggled up as blanket after blanket was flung over my head. When it was done, thirteen monks slept freezing and uncovered on their cots, and I lay with their blankets piled on top of me, suffocating. Damn them. Damn them. And damn Michael most of all. I had burrowed my face in all the blankets to hide my tears.

I turned over and tried to bury my face in the cold sand. I dug in my fingers, feeling concealed fragments of the old house. A sea gull flew by and hooted at me, as if criticizing my laziness on Brother Michael's behalf. Hearty Brother Michael, who had gotten up in that morning after having humiliated me with the glad hosanna "Rejoice, for this is the day the Lord has made," walked over to the basin, broke through, washed his wide red face, and beamed, steaming breath coming between thick white teeth. He'd snuck into line a second time when God was handing out vitality and thus missed getting into the line for sense.

Suddenly, I heard the laughter of young women. I rolled over and peered out over the window frame, half expecting to see some odd lake mermaids playing in the shallow water. Instead, I saw half a dozen blue-uniformed girls from the monastery school, all my age or younger. I recognized several of them. They jostled each other for a perch on a driftwood log, like me having momentarily escaped the tyranny of duty. None of them was dressed for the cold, and they hunched against each other, giggling. Occasionally one would stand, brush the sand from her bottom, and sit again.

I watched in fascination. Women in general don't understand how charming they are when they aren't trying to impress men. They fussed with their breeze-blown hair and the shoulder badges awarded for school-work and Bible memorization, gossiping about teachers and absent classmates.

One stood and gave her red-brown hair to the lake breeze, letting it blow behind her like a comet. She looked out across the water as if awaiting a ship, then walked down to its edge. She had a long neck and full lips, which she pursed at whatever she imagined she saw across the lake.

"Come on, Laurena," one of her friends, a small blonde, cried. "We'd better get back."

Indeed, I could hear the bell that marked the change of hour. I was expected back as well. Brother Michael needed my help. One of the three magnetohydrodynamic generators that powered St. Thecla's and much of the surrounding countryside was down for cleaning and maintenance. I was to spend the afternoon crawling through tubes getting covered with coal dust. Punishment was certain if I was late. I couldn't move but watched as Laurena tossed her head disdainfully, kicked off her shoes, and waded into the water. A wave wet the bottom of her skirt. Her uniform hugged her waist, showing off the curve of her hip and her breasts. I learned later that she had taken it in herself, in private, with a razor and needle and thread.

"Laurena!"

"Go back if you want. I'm not going." Balancing delicately on her bare feet, arms floated out for stability, Laurena walked onto the driftwood decades of storms had jammed against the pier pilings. "I have other places to be." The curve of her bottom as she stepped up on a piling made me dizzy. She was as luscious as a basket of fruit. I was in love at that instant, totally and irrevocably. I had something to which I could dedicate my life. I pushed my erection into the sand, feeling the roughness of the cassock against it.

"There's a bit of a gap between the end of the pier and the coast of Wisconsin, if that's where you're going." This voice was dry and amused, not the voice of a schoolgirl. It had a dark, rough quality, like weathered wood.

Laurena turned challengingly, almost losing her balance. She steadied herself, trying to look dignified. "And what's that to you, Aya Ngomo?"

"Not a thing, Laurena Tarchik. Except that if you don't come back with us, you'll be missed. Then they'll figure out where we go, and we won't be able to do it anymore."

"Let them try to stop us. I'm tired of it anyway. It just feels like freedom. It's only a longer leash. I want to get *out* of here."

There was a whispered conference among the five girls still on the log. Four of them stood and ran lightly back up the trail that wandered through the dune grasses to the monastery. Left on the log was a small, bent girl with dark hair and skin. This was my first sight of Aya Ngomo.

Despite the luminous presence of Laurena Tarchik, she caught the eye at once. I may sound as if I am writing standard hagiography, Thomas, but the unfortunate thing about hagiographies is that they are sometimes true. Aya Ngomo focused my vision, even without the benefit of having had her icon at the front of my classroom as I was growing up.

I realized that I had caught glimpses of her around the monastery. She suffered from a progressive nerve disease, some mutated by-product of the artificial plagues released during the twenty-first-century wars. Her spine was twisted and she was in constant pain. She walked crabwise and crept slowly along walls. Her long hair was a lustrous black. She had an odd beauty, like an exotic caged bird. Her skin was dark velvet, her eyes wide and all-seeing.

She was, I had heard, a ward of the Patriarch of Milwaukee himself. He had taken an interest in this quick, intelligent girl. She held your eye by more than just her deformity. She was like a jewel with a complex flaw, much more interesting to gaze into than a transparent stone.

"Go away, Aya, for God's sake!" Laurena was almost shouting.

Aya looked composed. "Why are you being such an idiot?"

Laurena turned her back to Aya and walked farther out on the piled driftwood. It creaked and shifted under her weight. "Haven't you ever wanted to escape? To go"—she stared at the horizon, squinting to see something—"somewhere?"

The crippled Aya Ngomo put her thin arms around herself. "Escape? Laurena, you don't know the half of it."

"Then let me go! Let me—" Her foot sank through a rotted piece of wood. The rest of the pile shifted. She gasped and tried to pull back. She almost fell from the effort, something that would have snapped her ankle. She was well and truly stuck, her foot trapped by a heavy log.

"Aya!"

Aya shook her head slowly, as if things had happened exactly as she had predicted. Perhaps they had. She stood, wincing, and walked to the end of the pier.

Laurena stood motionless, her hands clenched at her sides. She sucked breath heavily, in obvious pain. At that instant I thought less of the pain in her ankle than the way her breasts moved as she breathed. I couldn't even make myself feel ashamed of that later. She was a wild animal caught in a trap. And I, as the hunter, would come and free her.

Aya Ngomo crawled slowly across the shifting driftwood toward her friend. "Don't worry, Laurena. Does it hurt?"

Laurena drew a breath. "Yes," she said tightly. "Dammit."

At that point I finally stood. I brushed the sand from the front of my cassock, correcting my appearance as much as the damn shapeless thing allowed, put my pectoral cross back on, and stepped out through the house's tilting door. I felt exposed on the beach below the monastery, black as a crow, immediately visible to anyone as a truant monk. I stepped onto the pier behind Aya.

"Are you ladies in need of some assistance?" The casual seemed to be the proper tone to take under the circumstances.

They turned and I was faced by two pairs of appraising eyes, Aya's dark, Laurena's a vivid green. I was then tall and slender, with a high forehead and a sharp nose. My skin was just as dark as it is now, though far smoother. I was already known for intelligence and ambition. Still, I quailed before those female eyes.

Laurena rolled hers. "Just what I need." She returned to her contemplation of the horizon.

Aya just laughed, a low throaty sound. "Where did you come from? Are you appeared like a miracle? Such excellent timing."

I'm afraid that I blushed. Laurena was too obsessed by her own predicament to consider, but Aya guessed that I had been eavesdropping.

"I may not be a miracle, but you can use me as one." I stepped past her and onto the driftwood. I weighed more than either of the women, and it swayed under me like a ship's deck in a storm. I made my way over to Laurena, kneeling down next to her. She ignored me.

As I bent by her slender ankle, I could feel the exhalation of her flesh. Her own sharp scent made itself known over the bland floral aroma of soap. I let my shoulder rest against her calf. The wet bottom of her long skirt had plastered itself against it. The log had jammed tight. Bruises were already appearing around her ankle. I pushed against the wood. Pain caused her to suck in her breath sharply. She didn't speak.

"Well, miracle, what are we to do?" Aya had made her way out to us, moving as lightly over the wood as a stalking spider. She held a thin cylinder of wood out to me, a piece of an old porch railing or chair. With its help I was able to pry the shifted log far enough for Laurena to pull her foot out. She put her hand on my back to steady herself as she did so. I felt her fingers warm on my shoulder blade.

"Thank the gentleman," Aya said chidingly.

I stood. Laurena looked me in the eye. "He works with my brother, Michael. His name is Vikram Osten. Michael says he's lazy and only here because his family has ordered him. The Ostens are a powerful family."

I smiled at her. Michael's sister. Interesting. "You are quite welcome, Miss Tarchik."

I earned a laugh from Aya, which pleased me. "You'd better hurry back, Brother Vikram. Someone will miss you." I met her dark, somberly amused eyes and realized that further help would not be appreciated. With a slight, I hoped sardonic, bow, I made my way off the pier and up the sand trail to the monastery. Halfway up I turned, to look at two figures, the taller straight one leaning on the smaller bent one, as they made their painful way across the sand. Neither looked up at me.

Out of breath, I ran into the waste-plastic and wood building that housed the generators. Michael rested his arm on a stanchion and watched the flickering LEDs. He fussed with the flow diagram, changing the ionization balance in Number Three. Number Two was shut down, ready for me. He didn't look happy to see me.

"You're late, but no matter. I expected it, you see. You can work twice as fast. Into your coverall. Make sure your work is good, or you'll be here tomorrow as well."

He slung the coverall at me. I changed out of my cassock in front of his expressionless ruddy face. Without a further word, he shoved me into the dust-filled MHD feed tube.

I saw Aya Ngomo again two weeks later.

A shrub-covered dune with a bare top rose just near the chapel. Outdoor services were often held there. One morning, as I was coming aromatically from cleaning a communal latrine, I heard shouting from behind the dune, an angry, ugly sound. I hesitated for a moment, then ran around it.

Several of the boys from the nearby town had gathered around Aya Ngomo. She lay sprawled on the ground, her back twisted, while they circled her, jays around a captive lizard. "Batty, batty!" they cried. "Fly to your cave, hang from your feet. Leave us be!"

Wild-eyed, they waved their arms like madmen. One pulled back a black-booted foot and kicked her. She rolled over silently, without so much as a gasp. Her eyes, expressionlessly black, looked up at me.   I make no claims about my physical courage, but having been seen by those eyes I could not turn away. Shouting some nonsense of my own, I waded into them. I had no plan, no idea of what I was doing. With sudden fury they turned, smashed my face, and punched me in the stomach so that I bent over, retching. A huge hand came and hit the side of my head. I found myself lying on the ground. They continued to kick me, but I took no notice. I watched the clouds roll by overhead. They were the most beautiful clouds I had ever seen.

Suddenly a large figure came into my view, picked up a boy, and flung him into outer darkness. It was Michael. Behind him came other monks, a taut, active mass. The disorganized mob of locals was swept aside like so many dried leaves. It was late afternoon. The light slanted dramatically across the monastery. I lay with the side of my face in the rough grass. The air was crisp and winy. It was a pleasure to be alive.

Brother Michael picked me up. "Are you all right, Vikram?"

To be rescued by Michael. How humiliating!

"I'm fine, thanks." I tried to stand. He had to catch

me. Two other monks came and supported me under the shoulders.

Blue-uniformed girls had gathered around Aya Ngomo. They swirled and twittered, brushing the twigs from her sweater. For a moment I could see nothing but masses of feminine hair. Then they parted and I saw Aya's eyes on me. Standing next to her, full mouth quirked in amusement, was Michael's sister Laurena. She looked past me as if thinking about something far away. Then my brothers carried me off.

The monastery Infirmary was on the second floor of what had once been a rustic tourist lodge, its false wood beams long since cracked and fallen away, revealing the metal that supported it. My bed was crammed into a corner behind a deeply gouged plastic partition. On the wall above my head, just under the roof, hung a glass case filled with Indian arrowheads, labeled with names like Kickapoo and Potawatomi. It had probably hung there for over a century. I imagined a boy collecting these remnants of a forgotten age, the action of someone who did not have to worry about the future. A window looked out on the monastery past the thick bough of a maple tree. I could lie in bed and watch others about their duties. Under a thick blanket yet.

A firm knock came on the partition. I looked up, half-expecting it to be Brother Michael, come heartily to rip the blanket from me and drive me out into the frost to do some labor for God. Instead, Aya Ngomo's dark head poked around the partition. She rustled in and sat in the room's one chair.

"I came to thank you," she said. "That was a brave thing you did."

"And completely ineffective." I waved my hand in dismissal. I had already learned how effective being casual could be.

"It was still brave. Such a helpful man you are. Is there anything I can do for you?" She was made to be painted as an icon. Her scrutinizing black eyes dominated her face. Her words, as they so often did, seemed to contain a sardonic barb.

I was suddenly hot in my bedclothes, prickling sweat

all over my skin. I reached under my pillow and pulled out an envelope. It contained a love note to Laurena Tarchik. I had labored long over this work, sitting up in bed under the arrowheads. In it I proclaimed my love for her, my undying passion, my longing for one single word from her lips . . . well, it was new to me then. I also cited my family's connections and my future prospects. A sturdy bank balance is often as much of an aphrodisiac as flowers and honeyed words. I begged for a meeting with her, at the corner of the Chapel of SS. Cosmas and Damien, in two nights.

I handed the letter to Aya. "This is a letter to Laurena from her brother Michael. Could you take it to her?"

She balanced it on her palm as if weighing the truth of my words. Her eyes looked past me.

"There's one sort of intelligence," she said. "It helps you get what you want. Laurena has it. So do you, I think. There's another: the kind that tells you what the right thing to want is." She slipped the envelope into her sleeve. "It's lovely of Michael to write his sister. She doesn't like him much. That's too bad. I've always thought about how lovely it would be to have an older brother." She stood up, as far as she could, her back bent. "Get better, Vikram. Even if you don't want to." She left with a sound like blowing dried leaves.

Two nights later I edged out of my window into the cold air. The maple had been pruned away from the building, and I had to lean over to grab the bough. The drop below pulled at me as I tilted out of the window. I seriously considered climbing back into bed. Perhaps the career of a lover was not for me. I let myself fall outward. I felt the rough bark of the tree in my hands and swung my legs around the bough. After that it was easy. I slid down the trunk to the ground. My dimly lit window hung high above me.

I felt exhilarated. I breathed not air but light. The ground rocked under my feet as if I walked on the surface of Lake Michigan. I ran off through the darkness.

The chapel corner was deserted, the moon peeking over the ramshackle plastic building that housed the MHD generators. Two huge concrete cherubim with snarling faces and winged wheels supported the chapel. I pulled myself into the shadows by their heads.

The cold wall behind me sucked my heat. I shifted weight from foot to foot but didn't dare move much more to stay warm. Footsteps crunched on the gravel walk. I almost turned and ran then. Heart pounding, I stepped forward into the moonlight.

Laurena turned. "Ah, Brother Vikram." She stood before me in a long dress, not a school uniform at all, but a real gown flaring out over her hips and tumbling down to the ground. Her hands were clasped like a suppliant's, her hair loose around her shoulders. For a moment I thought she was there to make mock of me, but she was clearly as nervous as I was.

"I'm glad you came," I said.

"I almost didn't," she said. "Aya didn't want me to. She didn't say that, but it wasn't so hard to figure out what she thought."

I didn't ask her if that was why she came. Instead, I took her arm. She pulled her arm back against my hand in acknowledgment of its presence. I felt joy.

"So what do you think rescuing me on that stupid pier entitles you to?"

I ignored her tone and paid attention to the pressure of her upper arm. "Just a few words. The ones you wouldn't give me before."

She snorted but said nothing else. We walked along the low wall that tried vainly to stop the encroachments of dune sand and finally stood on the slope overlooking the villages that clung to the edge of Crystal Lake, the dune-trapped body of water behind St. Thecla's. Her family lived down there somewhere, save for her tedious brother Michael, who had moved up to the monastery, where he worked providing his town with electric power. Though surely her ankle had already healed, she still limped.

"I was in Chicago once," I said, naming the most romantic place I could think of. It helped that I actually had seen it.

She took my arm in her turn but did not look at me. Was she seeking, somewhere among the twinkling lights around the lake, the single light of her family's house? Escape. Laurena Tarchik wanted escape. I was going to give it to her. "The Drowned City. I wish I came from a drowned city. I wish Lake Michigan would pour across the dunes and fill Crystal Lake to overflowing." She was imagining water pouring in through the windows of her house, drowning her mother as she fixed dinner. I didn't need to read her mind to know that.

"The water the towers rise from is usually still. It's shallow and you can still see the fire hydrants and street signs under it. There's enough glass left in the buildings that the reflected light of sunset makes the place look inhabited." We hadn't actually landed there. Uncle Cosmas had just swung the boat in close on our way to Milwaukee. But I didn't feel the need to burden Laurena with that kind of detail.

"I have places to go," I said. "Boston. Paris. Constantinople. Who knows? Moscow herself." I whispered the names of those torn and rebuilt cities, capitals of the Orthodox Empire, for their aphrodisiac qualities.

She sighed. "Anywhere, Vikram. Anywhere but here."

I put my arms around her waist and kissed her. She kissed me back, deeply but matter-of-factly, not melting in my arms. I ran one hand down to where her buttocks swelled out and felt her breasts against my chest.

She ground her hips against me, then pushed me away with suddenly strong arms. "I have to get home." She said the word with disdain. "They'll miss me."

"When will I see you again?"

"Use Aya to send me another note." She smiled. "I rather liked that." She turned and, without a backward look, walked into the darkness toward her house.

I headed back toward the Infirmary, fingers and toes tingling. The moon was now shining full silver, coating the bare trees.

My return path took me past the spot at the base of the knoll where the boys had attacked Aya. There were no traces of the scuffle in the sand. The scene, with its dull-faced black-booted farm boys and its tormented cripple in their center, had receded in my mind to a medieval painting, a side panel to the Crucifixion . . . or a scene in the life of a saint.

I stood and looked up at the knoll. With a tightening of my scalp, I saw the silhouette of a figure sitting thoughtfully at its top. In the moonlight that ominous twisted shape showed me something of what the boys had feared, for I recognized Aya Ngomo.

"Good evening, Aya." She had heard me clambering up the hill, and was not at all surprised to see me. That should have told me something.

"Hello, Vikram." She looked past my shoulder at the stars. "Have you ever wanted to float away into the sky? Just to drift between the stars?"

I thought about holding my breath and slowly rising through the clouds. But it didn't even occur to me to tell her about it; this was something so private I had never articulated it.

"There are too many places to travel on this Earth," I said instead. "I've only seen a few of them myself."

"Oh? We're stuck here in the dunes of Michigan. What lies outside?" Her tone was faintly mocking, not at all what a crippled girl's should have been. All these young ladies were too wise. "What wonders have you seen, Vikram?"

Her tone was interrogative in a way I didn't like. I didn't feel like admitting that Milwaukee was my big trip, and somehow the story I had told Laurena about Chicago seemed inadequate to Aya's attention.

"Boston," I said. I'd read enough about the capital of Russian New England to fake a visit there. And I'd always intended to go.

"Really?" The romantic name excited her. "Then you can tell me about the new Cathedral they're building there. What does the bell tower look like?"

Bell tower? What a question! "Russian Second Empire," I said. It seemed reasonable. I knew the Boston Public Library was built in that style, just across Copley Square from the Cathedral.

She frowned. "I thought they were using the remains of an old skyscraper to hang the bells—that's what's so interesting about it. I must have misunderstood. . . ." Her eyes were on me. I don't think Aya really saw the truth someone was concealing, though it often seemed that way. Instead, the way she looked at you reminded you that you yourself knew the truth, even if she didn't, and made you ashamed for not speaking it.

"Why are you sitting out here, Aya?"

"I was waiting for you." Aya told the truth herself, though not always all of it. It wasn't until later that I figured out that she had understood my rendezvous with Laurena and had positioned herself to catch me on my return from it. "I wanted to show you something."

Despite the sudden weariness that I felt, the sense that the world was too complicated and difficult to deal with, I sat down next to her on the cold ground. "What is it, Aya?"

"My mother died when I was born. My father not long after, both, I think, from the same disease that makes me what I am." She didn't give me time to speak some standard commiseration but rushed on. "But before he died, he told me a story. At least I remember it as being him. Perhaps it was just a dream. The sort of vision that comes to someone with a distorted nervous system."

Remember this, Thomas. Aya Ngomo never had a vision that she did not attribute to some physical cause. Of course, the Lord performs His miracles through the universe He Himself has created, and thus can use a congenitally defective nervous system to convey His visions, if that suits His purposes best.

"He told me that each person had a jewel—the thing that defines us, that makes us ourselves. Something had stolen mine from me." She ran a hand down her twisted side. "That's why I'm like this. I am incomplete."

"A jewel. What sort of jewel?" I pictured a bauble rolled into a dusty corner and forgotten after the closing of some massy treasure chest filled to the brim with unset emeralds and pearl earrings.

"I won't know that until I find it."

"Then how will you look for it?"

"I—" She gazed back up at the sky. "However I can."

"Well, good luck with it then."

She was correct and I realized it, of course, as by now we all have. It may be that I was the first to see the truth of it. St. Aya Ngomo. Was it merely by accident that I had seen her torment by the farm boys as a stage on the way to sainthood?

"Doesn't it amaze you that the Orthodox Empire travels through space?" Her question didn't seem like a changing of the subject, but perhaps I was merely caught up in the physical vision of her metaphorical bauble. Jewels glinted at me from the sky.

I was spending a year of my young life at a Byzantine monastery while spacecraft rose from the Dakota plains not a thousand kilometers away. "I suppose it is odd."

"Odd? It makes no sense at all. But then, why should anyone travel through space? It's so much trouble. You haven't traveled through space, have you, Vikram?" A smile tugged at her lips.

"No," I said curtly.

"I'm sure you will. As might I. I've been reading about it. I suspect that we are not the first race to travel through the solar system."

"What have you been reading?"

"Oh, this and that. Stuff from the First Space Age, before the wars. There are indications that we are not the first, that others went among the planets long before we were even thought of. The Ancient Ones, some people call them. No one knows who they were."

"Did they take your jewel?"

"Perhaps they did. If so, will you help me look for it?"

And, not knowing what I was letting myself in for, I said, "Sure, Aya. But I'm sleepy now, and going to bed. Good night."

One day the Patriarch of Milwaukee, Simon Kramer, visited his monastery. The entire community dragged itself down to the monastery's dock, some distance from the ruined house and pier where I first met Laurena and Aya Ngomo. The Patriarch's hydrofoil scudded across the lake like a sparkling water bug. Crumpled and shattered blue ice stretched out from the beach. It had been some labor breaking a passage through for a boat landing. The water beyond was gray and sullen, unhappy at remaining liquid while other water rested frozen.

Though I have since been to Constantinople and Moscow, I still remember the glory that emerged from the hydrofoil. The Patriarch and his entourage were dressed in scarlet-and-yellow robes embroidered with gold, vivid against the white and dried brown of the sleeping shore. Their crowns gleamed with jewels. Acolytes carried icons of the Virgin, the last—an unhappy, balding man—hauling a much-too-heavy gold reliquary containing the remains of St. Natalie of Choisy-le-Roi, martyred in 2094 by direct order of Governor-General Moreau as the Holy Apostolic Army of Russia advanced toward Paris. The sad man tripped over a beached and frozen carp, and looked even sadder.

The Patriarch held his audiences in the Library, a much-patched building that had once been a tourist restaurant. Among others he called to him his ward, Aya Ngomo. When Aya came to the Library she found me cleaning the bronze high reliefs that decorated its front. Brother Michael had detected a faint shadow of oxidation on the neck of one of the Roman soldiers uninterestedly witnessing the martyrdom of St. Lawrence in the third panel. I scrubbed behind the soldier's ears like a diligent mother, cursing Michael's name.

"Vikram," Aya said. "I'm afraid of him. He's huge. He's covered with jewels and has a loud voice. He's like an idol."

I looked down at her from my stepladder. She was not wise and mocking, demonstrating some subtle superiority over me. For the first time I saw her as an unhappy young woman, bent and twisted by an indifferent fate, unsure of what was going to happen next. Her clothes were neat and pressed for the interview.

"He's just a man, Aya." I didn't have to face him. "He wants to ask you a few dumb questions about your studies and send you on your way."

"Of course. Still . . ." She looked at me appealingly with her large eyes, then smiled. She was trying to act coquettish, and it was grotesque.

"Go ahead." I spoke in dismay. "Don't keep him waiting."

I returned to my memories of the night before. It had been a struggle as formalized as a Court dance, but Laurena had finally allowed me to touch her breasts. I had run my hands gently across her skin, taking her nipples between thumb and forefinger—

"Novice Vikram Osten?" It was the balding sad man

with the reliquary. He frowned up at me from the doorway, his droopy moustache like graffiti scrawled inexpertly across his face. His name was Donald Tergenius, and he was head of the Patriarch's civil secretariat. "Meditating on the fate of St. Lawrence?"

I noticed that I was leaning my hand on the body of the saint as he was roasted on the griddle in front of the Emperor Decius. "Yes." I removed my hand and straightened. "He is the patron saint of libraries."

"Just so. The Patriarch wishes to speak to you."

"Yes, yes." I jumped down from my stepladder and babbled. The man intimidated me. "I have been studying the writings of Pseudo-Dionysius the Areopagite and—"

He regarded me gloomily. In later years I would learn that Tergenius invariably expressed anger as melancholy. "Save that stuff for someone who's interested in it—whoever that might be. The Patriarch has more important things to think about. As do I." He drew back into the doorway.

Patriarch Simon Kramer's face was almost invisible beneath his beard. He sat behind a desk, members of his secretariat shoving papers under his gaze as he spoke. "I have good report of you," he rumbled. Tergenius stood solemnly by his shoulder.

"I'm glad." I tried to imagine who it could have been. The Archimandrite of St. Thecla had never deigned to notice me, and as for my life-monk, Michael. . . .

"I have already learned to rely on the perceptions of my ward, Aya Ngomo. Continue your studies and you will be a success." With this formula he shuffled me off, tongue-tied, onto the grim Tergenius, who escorted me back out.

We lingered in the doorway, he looking intently at me. "In several months I am leaving the Patriarch's service. I am becoming a provincial administrator in Utah." Despite my earlier blithe talk of Constantinople and Moscow, I felt him to be talking about the farthest ends of the Earth, a miserable exile. "There is room for advancement, there on the edge of our Empire, particularly for those uncomfortable under the just rule of the Church."

"I'm sure there is. But my family has risen high here in Michigan."

"That they have. And you intend to climb on their shoulders. A fair ambition, if predictable. Still, if events do not turn out as intended. . . ." A brief smile appeared on his face like a ritual gesture. Without another word he turned and walked away, leaving me wondering at the reasons behind his implied offer. He saw something in me, and advancement was impossible without a patron. But Utah . . .

The sun was setting over the lake, its red light diffused through a layer of icy mist. I was searching for Aya but realized that I wouldn't have far to look: I could see her bent figure down on the shore, black against the vivid blue of the snow. She twisted and shuffled, as if trying to dance.

"Aya, you're cold." She turned to look at me. "You should get back to the dormitory."

My shoes were full of snow from my descent down the dunes. I could feel the cold wind off the lake tightening my cheeks. Aya's once-neat clothes hung askew, as if she'd been running through the woods and rolling in the snow. Her face was flushed and her eyes were fever-bright. She didn't seem to notice the cold. She was a woman in the grips of something far beyond her.

"I have made my decision, Vikram. Are you ready to go with me?"

"What? What did the Patriarch say to you?"

"Oh." She made a face, a ladylike moue of disapproval, bizarre under the circumstances. "Some standard formulas. You know how these people talk."

"So why—"

"I realized that he wanted to help me, but had no idea of how to do it. The burden is on me, if I'm to find what I'm looking for. And I will find it, my jewel. I will!"

"I'm sure." I was cold and unhappy. Her husky voice seemed unsuitable to such absurdly melodramatic statements.

"And you'll help me, won't you, Vikram?" She took my arm, the first time she had ever touched me.

"What are you talking about?"

Her eyes shone as she looked at me. "I have seen what I have to do."

She loved me. I suddenly understood. It made perfect sense. I was handsome, rich, clever. She was a poor crippled girl, completely alone, ward of a distant ecclesiastic. Her dismal fate drove her to love me through sheer self-defense, the way a drowning man loves air. So I didn't take it as a judgment on my own worth. But I understood it.

"Doesn't it occur to you that I too have jewels to seek?" I kept my voice hard.

She looked at me solemnly. "What are they, Vikram?"

I again pictured her jewel rolled into a dusty corner while the treasure chest gleamed. I had spoken to Tergenius and the Patriarch, men of power. And there were men of power far beyond them, the rulers of this world.

"The jewels of the Earth. I will climb to the heights, above the Patriarch, above the Governor of Ontario. You are not the only one with dreams."

She caught her breath. For an instant I thought she was going to cry. "Oh, you poor man." She put her thin arms around me. "What a choice to make!"

"Don't seek your jewel in me. You can't! I don't have it." I jerked back. She lost her balance and fell into the snow. I reached down to help her, but she pushed my hands away and struggled to her feet herself.

"Aya, I—"

Her face was tight. She ran her hand across her chest, fingers shaking, to reassure herself that she was indeed still deformed. "I will always hope for something more from you, Vikram." She turned and walked away.

"Good luck," I called after her. "Keep trying. You will succeed. I believe in you."

She tried to run. Her feet twisted under her. She wobbled. I looked after her and for a moment had a feeling of intolerable loss.

But I had another destiny for that evening. That was the night that Laurena Tarchik would finally succumb to me. I met her, as was our habit, by the cherubim.

"Oh, Vikram, it's so cold." Her face was flushed in the

wind. She had made herself up elaborately. Several shades of color on her eyelids made her exotic. "What are we doing? You're so mysterious."

"It's a gift," I said. "A special gift."

We walked side by side through the night. It had taken me a great deal of work to convince Laurena that I represented her escape. I was freedom. And she would give herself to me for the love of it.

I led her to an anonymous door, much patched, and threw it open with a dramatic gesture.

"Oh, Vikram!" She stepped into the room. "How did you do this?"

My parents had sent me gifts, particularly when I lay hurt in the Infirmary, and I had carefully hoarded them. The gifts had turned into bribes.

The old storeroom, used as an armory in the middle twenty-first century, had been transformed by my labors. The old gun racks were hung with aromatic pine branches. The cracked concrete floor was invisible beneath a quilted packing blanket. Heat came from a portable infrared heater. A bottle of a liquor called bourbon sat on an upended packing crate.

And there was the bed. The sheets and blankets had cost me the most. They were the Patriarch's, sold by a member of his house staff. His crest was embroidered on each piece.

I kissed her deeply and removed her coat. We sat and drank the bourbon. I let the rich hot liquid seep over my tongue and burn its way down my throat as I admired her.

Her breasts were full. The curve of her thighs showed through her dress. She gulped the whiskey, breathing quickly, and watched me. I caught her eye and she giggled.

"Vikram, I want to get out of this place. Just get *out*."

"You will, love, you will." I moved closer. "You'll see the stores in Boston and Atlanta. You'll feel the warm breeze on your skin in Cuba."

"Mmmm, will I?" She made a sound deep in her throat as I kissed her neck.

"Oh, Vikram, don't . . . oh. . . ."

She wasn't just making love to me. She was making

love to wealth, freedom, sunlight, warm water. I moved into her. I had her. I finally had her. And through her, I had Brother Michael. Her thighs smoothed up my hips.

The storeroom door slammed open. Cold air blew into the room. Outside were indistinct figures shouting in outrage. Laurena cowered back and grabbed desperately for the blankets.

"Michael!" she shrieked, as if her stout brother was rescuing her from a vile assault. "Michael!" She scuttled back across the bed, blood on her thighs.

"Shut up!" It was him, massive in the doorway. Tears streamed down his cheeks. He looked at me. "You viper."

His huge hands grabbed my shoulders and pulled me from the room naked into the cold.

There is nothing else left of that night, save a confusion of voices and faces. The next morning, clad in a workman's coverall, I was thrust through into the outer world as an unwillingly born infant.

When they came for me my family was mortified. Even Uncle Cosmas had managed his year without disgrace. I was the only one who had failed.

In all that night and day, though I looked for them, I did not see Aya Ngomo's eyes anywhere.

The Monastery of St. Sergius, 2182

I sit at my table and watch Thomas attach the telescope to the window frame. I don't have enough strength left in my arms to even turn the screwdriver.

"Are you sure this will hold?" Since my confessions to him a week ago, Thomas has been noncommittal, any interchange with me being kept to a purely mechanical level. This doesn't bother me. Thomas's mind works slowly but powerfully. He is reserving judgment.

"I'm not an engineer, but I think it will."

His shoulder bulks as he turns the screws. I hear the dry wood of the frame crack. Thomas looks dismayed at his inadvertent vandalism, then shrugs and proceeds. When he is finished, and the image-multiplier telescope rests in its mount, pointed at the sky, he waits a long moment and then turns to me. His blue eyes are innocent in the candlelight.

"So you knew Aya Ngomo was a saint when you met her?"

I run my mind over the story I told him. Did I really make that claim? In my memory her face is surrounded by a retrospective nimbus. Hell, I remember St. Thecla's itself as a pleasant place, high point of my youth. Memory is treacherous.

"If saints were so obvious, we would have no choices to make."

"I don't want catechism." For the first time since I've known him, Thomas's voice is sharp. "I want to know what happened to *you.*"

So he's pushed me up against it. It sounds like he actually wants the truth. Washed up here, half-drowned on the far shore of my life, I am inclined to give it to him.

"I had no idea of who Aya Ngomo was. She compelled—but not through force of sanctity. She was of some other metal. But then, she is the only saint I've ever met. Perhaps they were all like that, grabbing our heads and peeling back our eyelids with their thumbs to force us to look at the light."

"And this woman loved you." I have achieved my first objective in Thomas's education. Thomas looks dubious.

"And have you never known the love of a woman, dear Thomas?"

He does not answer but sits silent, running his hand through the unmown-hay wildness of his hair. Aha. There's usually one somewhere. And I want to know what this man has given up to be here. Even if it should cause him pain. I want to know. After all, I'm willing to reveal my life to him.

"Laurena loved me, the way a caged bird loves the hand that can free it. Others have loved me too, for as little reason, or less." I watch him. He is not attending, his thoughts far away. "Who was she?"

His blue eyes lock onto mine. "What, Brother Vikram?"

"Never mind, if you—"

"She grew up near me," he says, his voice rushed. He

looks away as he speaks. "Her name was—is—Janielle. I first remember her as a little girl with long hair in clips, wearing a dress and playing with a ball against a brick wall. It was afternoon, sunny. It was a big rubber ball, and she hit it with the tips of her fingers." He pushes his fingertips out in front of himself to demonstrate, then pulls his hands back into fists. "She was always very graceful. I was clumsy."

"What did she smell like?"

He doesn't hesitate. "Like heaven. We first made love outdoors, behind Crofter's silos. We had nowhere else to go. Her parents didn't want her seeing me. The grass was wet from the rain. I lay down and she lay on top of me. The sun was behind her head as she laughed. I could feel the wet mud on my back. She brushed her hair over my face and kissed me. After." His face is bright red. He stands. "Good night, Brother Vikram."

He shuts the door gently behind him. I walk to the window and watch him trudge through the bean poles and pea trellises in the garden. His shoulders are hunched and his face is down so that I cannot see it. The stars gleam above him.

I wait there by the window for a long moment. The aging body is so little capable of the old pleasures that anticipation is about the only one left. The stars knock on the glass for admittance. In response to its computer, the telescope swings and locks in to its goal. I put my eyes to the viewer.

For an instant all is chaos, the stars and nebulae of the external universe confused with the stuff that floats in the interior of my own eyes. Space seems alive with writhing snakes. Then it settles down. Blackness, and a tiny glowing speck: the fusion flame of Aya's ship.

I push the magnification as far as it will go. The image plumps slightly, like a cooking rice grain, but develops no more detail. But what detail do I expect? The light is several years old. Aya Ngomo lies within it, frozen by Lorentz-FitzGerald contraction. The days that bring me ever closer to death are but fractions of seconds to her. I could dry up in my grave and vanish into dust in the time it takes her to raise a bulb of water to her lips. She is sanctified by time, an incorruptible effigy.

Is she alive or dead? The Synod, ignoring the ambiguity, has canonized her, for she is no longer of this Earth.

After some endless time I turn from the telescope. My neck aches. I groan as I loosen my joints. I want to celebrate what both Thomas and I have lost.

The bottle is under my books. I don't even remember where and when I bought it. Since I know that I am unlikely ever to get another one, it's lasted for years. I pull it out. High Slivovitz from the Hungarian Danube. A few inches of the precious plum brandy still sloshes in the bottom.

I take a swig and almost choke. The hot liquor sears down my throat. Over the years I have become weaker, while the booze has retained its strength. I cough weakly, a pathetic sound. Recovered, I drink again.

It doesn't take much to make the world seem a warmer place. Just a few swallows of an aged brandy from the other side of the world. The taste brings with it the sound of a crowded Court, the smell of sharp perfumes, the glint of gold cloth, the feel of silk. My days of power glimmer around me.

Strength fills my limbs. I stand up and walk out of my poor monk's cell. I should take a stroll in the garden before going to sleep. It will clear my head. I can collect my thoughts so that my presentation to the Imperial Legate tomorrow is both coherent and elegant—two steps down the stairs I trip and roll headlong. The risers are soft and cushioned with ancient oriental carpets. It's a joke, really. I'll bounce at the bottom and get up. Everyone will laugh.

I lie crumpled at the bottom of the hard wooden steps, unable to move. Bones have shattered like cheap crockery. Glow lights appear above me, held by monks who look more irritated than concerned. No one speaks.

Thomas sweeps out and stands over me. His eyes are red. He doesn't cry for me, though he should.

"I fell."

He leans over and picks me up as easily as if I am a fallen scarecrow. He lays me gently in my bed.

"We've called a doctor," he says. "It will be morning before he can come."

"No matter." The pain is surprisingly distant. I grab his arm so he won't leave. "There's more to the story, you know."

His face doesn't change, but he sits.

Utah, 2125

Have you ever been to Cedar City, Thomas? Don't bother. At one time, I suppose, it was a real city, but the water is long since gone, and the Imperial capital of Utah is a collapsing dump. Our power there was more fictional than Orthodox power usually was, even in those times, which in retrospect are the very zenith of empire.

It was inevitable that I come to Utah, I suppose. Tergenius always seemed to think so, and after my expulsion from St. Thecla's there was nowhere else for me to go. There was an office ready for me when I arrived. A small office, with work already piled on the desk.

"I received an interesting message this morning," he said, staring out the window of his office at the twisted beams and piled brick of the building opposite. "You've been asked for." The building had been burned in an assault by desert partisans half a year before and he had left it as an object of meditation, much to the Regional Inspector's dismay on his last visit.

I looked up from my examination of the gadget on the table. "Another of these political visits to the ranches? Please, Master Tergenius. The last one took two months. I still have grit between my teeth."

He shook his head. "Nothing so pleasant."

"Am I finally going to have to talk to these people?" I picked up the gadget. It twisted heavily in my hand as if containing wrestling gyroscopes. It was a lattice of crisscrossed filament crystals. Its purported use was to manipulate monopole magnetic fields, presuming anyone ever found a magnetic monopole to put in it. How Tergenius got his hands on things like that I had no idea.

"No. We'll save the plateau technologists for another time. But you're getting warmer."

He pulled a map out of a locked drawer and spread it

on the desk. It was an unofficial map, heavily annotated in Tergenius's own hand, so the territories of Deseret, where the Mormons held sway, were clearly marked. Official maps did not recognize their existence.

Water resources were carefully noted. Tiny red dots indicated the far-flung ranches and huddled communities of the Tushar Mountains and Sevier and Virgin Creeks. I knew each of them well, having crawled my dusty way from one to another on my diplomatic missions.

Tergenius's finger moved slowly across the map, each inch a week's journey. He tapped the Kaiparowits and Aquarius Plateaus, where the mysterious builders of the monopole focus lived, and passed onward, finally coming to rest in the canyons to the west of the Colorado River.

"Judaea!" I exclaimed.

He nodded and pulled at his absurd moustache. "Just so." He called those unconsolidated territories Judaea because they contained prophets, great revelations, and mass hysterias. The place was a theological pesthole, according to Tergenius, who normally was not concerned with mere spiritual issues.

"You haven't asked me the important question." He looked at me expressionlessly.

"All right. Who asked for me?"

"An important citizen of Judaea, known to some as the Lady of Escalante. This connection may prove useful to us. I think you remember her as Aya Ngomo. You leave tomorrow."

The village of Page rested in the shadow of the ruined Glen Canyon Dam, destroyed in some vicious water war in which everybody lost. The Colorado flowed smoothly over the broken concrete. Behind it was a swamp filled with screaming water birds. I acquired a burro named Hermione there for my journey up-canyon.

I suppose Glen Canyon is beautiful, but I was too afraid for my own life to really appreciate it. The canyon territories were rocky, complex, intertwined, an exercise in higher-order mathematics, where points seeming close together are actually infinitely far apart. The deep canyons were tangled and lush, the slickrock above barren and open. The high benches were what was left of centuries of silting behind the dam. Someday the water would scour them away and the Colorado would flow clean again. I looked up at the line of visible sky and thought about holding my breath so that I could float out of the canyon. The rock held me back.

Passion and spiritual power reflected off the sandstone walls. I watched fire walkers, men who put swords through their tongues, snake handlers, flagellants. I passed a line of bodies hanging from a cottonwood. They had been wrapped in layers of plastic sheet to ferment in the sun.

I asked after the Lady of Escalante. My old friend Aya Ngomo was the subject of many stories, but none seemed to have anything to do with her, and the more of them I heard, the less I believed in her existence.

I reached Hole in the Rock and made my way up the Escalante, collecting information. The variety of stories was dizzying. One struck a chord, a tale of Ancient Ones who lived a million years ago and left their traces on all the planets. Perhaps Aya was up here somewhere after all.

One dawn I awoke with a start. I had driven an irritated porcupine from his shelter beneath an overhang and now stared up at the just-visible rock sky in puzzlement. Sleepy as I was, I took several seconds before realizing that the shapes blocking in my campsite were the figures of men.

Unspeaking, they hauled me out of my sleeping bag. I struggled, but they didn't acknowledge my efforts with even so much as a grunt. One of them finally took out something I couldn't see clearly and hit me on the head with it. I went back to sleep.

I woke again with agony in my head. I bent over and vomited, not caring where I was or who was watching. Then I looked up. Above me was a cottonwood tree. From a bough hung a rope with a noose at the end of it.

"Wait!" I shouted. "What is this? What have I done?"

My hands were tied behind my back. I rolled over and tried to stand. Two of them came over and solicitously helped me up. But when I was standing they kept lifting me until I found myself sitting on my burro, Hermione. She looked at me and flicked an ear.

"This is intolerable." I was stern. "I haven't done anything. What have I done? You can't!"

They lowered the noose over my head and snugged it on my neck. My heart jerked in my chest. Though the noose hadn't pulled tight yet, I couldn't breathe. The sun had risen above the canyon's edge and glared in my face. I was going to die.

The men turned as one and stared up a side canyon at something I couldn't see. They glanced at each other, and walked away. Walked away and left me there with a noose around my neck. Perhaps this was the method of execution in these parts, leaving death's timing up to the whims of a nervous burro.

In the silence I heard the whir of electromechanical equipment. Shrubbery crackled. Slowly, not wanting to startle Hermione, I turned my head. Coming painfully toward me across the rocks and thorny bushes was a twisted figure with shriveled legs. The metal of prosthetic supports gleamed in the sun. Her long black hair was carefully combed and tied with colorful ribbons.

"Aya." I managed a smile. "I knew you weren't the sort of person one meets only once."

"Hello, Vikram." She straightened to a normal human height, supported by scaffolding. Her tiny legs dangled beneath her. Her face was unchanged, sharp and intelligent.

We stared at each other. Wind rustled through the cottonwood leaves. A blue hummingbird zigzagged above her head. The rope was rough around my neck.

Hermione saw some interesting leaves and took a step forward. The noose started to pull me off her back.

"Aya, dammit! Get me off this thing!"

"Be calm, Vikram. You're too excitable." She moved past Hermione's head, her movements insectile, pausing to pat the burro. A moment later the ropes around my wrists loosened. I pulled out of the knots, losing some skin, and grabbed the rope above me. I yanked the noose off and jumped to the ground.

Aya watched me solemnly.

"Those your boys?" Now that I was safe, I could be angry.

"They're just some friends trying to keep me safe. There've been rumors of an Orthodox agent's approach since you left Page. They were trying to take care of you without disturbing me."

"How polite of them."

"You're lucky someone didn't get you before you even reached Hole in the Rock. I had hoped you would be a little less obvious." Her voice was severe. She examined me closely. "You've been living well, Vikram. Good food, a soft bed. You've put on weight. Veins are already breaking around your nose. Come along."

The trail led up under two large oak trees and ended in a dramatic arching space at the end of a box canyon. The pink sandstone walls rose up and curved over us. The protected environment was wetter than the rest of the Escalante, full of cattails and thickleafed marsh plants. Smaller oak trees crowded the walls. A stream flowed out of the moss and over the rocks to the river below.

Her home was a few belongings scattered beneath an overhang. Instead of a normal bed, she slept in an elaborate assemblage designed to support both her shrunken body and the weight of her prosthetics.

Her limbs whispered as she settled down to a sitting position. I brushed the sand off a rock and sat facing her.

"You wanted to talk to me?"

"Yes." Her face was unreadable. I couldn't even tell if she was glad I had made it. "You once promised me your help. Now I need it."

"You want me to find your jewel, whatever it might be." It had rolled into a distant corner indeed, if she thought she would find it here in the canyons. "Why did you come here, of all places?" I looked up at the walls. The sunlight reflecting down from them lit everything with a yearning glow.

Her prosthetics shifted, seeking a more stable position. "The plateau engineers are the only ones I know of who make things like this. They design them, thinking of space. The prototype was a probe for exploring the surface of Venus." She ran her hand down the metal supports of her legs. "Now they help me explore my world."

From the epithet Lady of Escalante I had expected some sort of half-mad religious fanatic. Sitting in front of me was just Aya Ngomo, the girl who had been my friend at St. Thecla's. I suddenly missed it—or rather I missed her, the way she had sat on the ground and talked of her dreams, her quick intelligence, her unwillingness to tolerate nonsense in me.

"But it's not here." I was hard. "Not anywhere to be found."

"Yes!" I had expected disappointment, despair. Instead her face was transformed by what I can only call exaltation. "It does not lie on this dusty arrogant planet at all, Vikram."

I had been wrong. This wasn't the Aya I remembered. Or rather, as I now realize, I had remembered her wrong.

"What I seek lies somewhere beyond. I'm going to go there."

I looked up above the canyon edge. At that moment the silvery speck of some stratospheric airship floated in the transparent desert sky like a representative of the Sun God in his daily round. I felt the Earth slap the soles of my feet to knock me up into the blue. I turned my eyes down, dizzy.

"And how are you going to do that?" I was suddenly belligerent, exasperated by the whole ridiculous situation. "Your plateau engineers might just be able to cobble together a surface-to-orbit launcher for you, if they make a deal with the Alaskans or the Chileans—dangerous either way. So what? Unless your jewel is an old Soviet space probe or something in a decaying orbit, that's not going to mean much. And the Orthodox Empire doesn't grant launch slots to unauthorized religious expeditions. Resources are scarce, Aya. You know that."

"I do know." Her prosthetics shuddered. Seeing that she was desperately unhappy, I reached over and took her hand. She looked down at it in surprise, then wrapped her fingers around mine in a surprisingly strong grip. "It's hard, Vikram. But we're going to do it. Aren't we?"

Thinking back over it, Thomas, I think it was that "we" that finally did it. No one has ever managed to use the word like she did. "I suppose we are."

There is, Thomas, a certain sin in doing a righteous thing solely in order to keep your own good opinion of yourself. It is a sin of which Aya would often make me guilty.

After that we simply sat and talked, like old friends. At twilight the mule deer came down from the rim and drank at the spring. As darkness rose she lit a fire. It sent its orange light up the canyon wall like an arrow toward the stars.

The next morning found us walking on the sandy floor of a slot canyon less than two meters wide. The thirty-meter-high walls were perfectly vertical, knife-cut to reveal millions of years of geologic time, an exhibit of the monstrous futility of history.

At one point, to demonstrate something to me, Aya extended her prosthetic limbs and chimneyed up the canyon, sending down sprays of sand. She moved with quick grace until, while I was in rosy shadow, she thrust her head and arms out into the sun.

"I can see it," she called down to me. "It's not much farther."

"Great."

She put her hands on the lip as if to climb out and leave me in the pit. But, after one last look around, Aya climbed back down. She grinned at me, face flushed with excitement.

Another mile and the walls began to settle down lower and lower. We turned a corner and the canyon widened out. The sandy soil around us was scattered with gleaming chunks of petrified wood. Orienting by landmarks not visible to me, Aya turned and we climbed up a rock slope, a slickrock access to the canyon rim above, rare in this place where canyon rim and canyon bottom were distinct worlds.

"They called it slickrock because metal horseshoes and wagon-wheel rims couldn't get a grip on it. The rubber of our shoes finds it the best surface to walk on. It's quite the opposite of slick to us."

"That's interesting," I managed. Unlike the feeling in dreams of flying, the sharp cliff face below seemed anxious to instruct me on the exact consequences of falling. I looked out over the canyon to hanging cliff dwellings on the opposite face. Solar arrays wavered in the hot air.

"Oh, Vikram, I'm so glad you're with me again." Her voice was joyful.

My foot slipped on a sand patch, but I felt, instead, a different kind of vertigo. I glanced at her as she climbed ahead of me. Her shriveled legs were dressed in some sort of silk pants, and she wore tiny red shoes. The ancient Chinese had bound their women's feet to try to make them that small. It had been considered enormously attractive. I wondered if Aya had been reading her fashion history.

"I can't stay much longer," I said. "Tergenius needs me back in Cedar City. There's a lot to do. And if we pull this off, there'll be even more. Years of work. I'm looking forward to it. My ambitions . . ." I didn't mention my women. I thought that was gracious of me. There had been many since Laurena, though I still thought of her often.

Aya was silent through my rambling speech, and for long after. We rose up to the rim. Ahead of us, resting in a declivity, was a shining silver hemisphere like a drop of mercury. Next to it, fluttering on a pole, was a complicated flag of stars and red-and-white stripes. I recognized it as the symbol of the old American Union of several centuries ago.

"Who are these plateau dwellers?" I asked. "I had no idea they were politically so unorthodox. This is going to be a ticklish negotiation."

Aya stood still next to me. "You are making a mistake, Vikram."

"This is all according to our plan." I deliberately misunderstood her.

Her machinery hummed as she moved past me. "God would allow you to climb infinitely high. He wants you to. You remain behind of your own choosing."

"Aya." She looked at me. She wanted me to love her

the way she loved me, and I could not do it. With the best will in the world I could not. "I'll help you, but you have to go it alone."

"I already know that."

Three people stood by the shimmering mercury drop. They were ordinary people, but they could give us power. In return for Imperial resources and booster launches, they would provide Aya with the means to go into space. And Tergenius and I would climb the rungs of the Imperial hierarchy. It was a deal that would let all of us benefit.

Aya and I started down toward them. After I left the Escalante it would be ten years before I saw her again.

The Monastery of St. Sergius, 2182

I hear loud voices outside my window. I wait for them to subside, but they continue. I pick up my cane and struggle down the stairs. My left leg has healed unevenly and will hurt me for the rest of my life. Not for too much longer, in other words.

The robust plants of the garden have started to shrivel as summer ends, but are still vividly green. I was a long time in my sickbed. I wander among them—the sag-necked sunflowers, the gravid tomatoes, the entirely unauthorized morning glories clambering the pea trellises. I hear the voices, quieter now, but am suddenly confused, as if I am lost in some dark forest, though I can see the roofs of the monastery above me. "Don't you want to talk to an old friend?" The man's voice is calm, but I can hear the hot breath pent up behind it.

"We have said all we need to." Brother Thomas's voice. With that as a beacon, I move toward it.

"I don't think so. I don't think so at all."

"Careful, Mark."

"Oh? Why should I be?"

I finally struggle out of the jungle. I've been within a few feet of them the entire time.

The cassocked Thomas stands facing a rangy man wearing a silly-looking brimmed hat pulled straight down on top of his head. I recognize him. He lives nearby. He has a large nose and jaw, and large hairy hands as well, one of which holds a fistful of Thomas's cassock. Thomas's hands hang loosely down at his sides as he stares back.

Three other men, also locals, stand against the garden wall, chewing tobacco in unison. One of them hawks and spits, leaving a slimy trail on the brick wall. "Come on, Mark. We got things to do."

"You shut up, Feeney. We'll have time when I'm done with this."

Feeney shrugs and leans back against the wall. He doesn't seem relaxed. He looks away from the confrontation as if embarrassed by it.

"We've got things to talk about. We've got Janielle, don't we? Or rather—I have her." Thomas is expressionless, but both I and the man named Mark can tell that he's scored a hit. Mark laughs. "Yeah, Thomas, that's the way it is. Right?" He pushes Thomas away.

"Is that what you came to tell me?" Thomas manages a tone of mild surprise.

"She's my *wife!*" Mark is angry, bouncing in a hunched position like some small predator on rodents. "I sleep with her every night. I have her whenever I want her. She's mine!"

"That's good." Thomas's eyes narrow until you can no longer see their innocent blue. "When will you have children, then?"

"You bastard!" Mark roars. "You goddam bastard." He swings his fist, a poorly aimed punch. Thomas doesn't try to avoid it. It grazes his jaw and he stumbles back a step. A trickle of blood appears on his lip.

I step out of the garden plants. "Enjoying yourself?" My tone is icy, somewhat bored. The voice of a powerful courtier, if the fool but had the wit to recognize it. Mark, for an instant, is stunned, and goggles at me.

For the first time Thomas looks agonized. "Please, Brother Vikram. Please. This is a private misunderstanding."

"Misunderstanding, is it?" Mark takes a breath. "You crows are so goddam clever." Without even looking, he sweeps his foot by and knocks my cane out of my hand. I don't have time to recover and fall forward, bruising my palms.

"Hey!" Feeney says, but doesn't move.

"Shut up, Feeney, for God's sake—" Mark turns his head to yell at his friend. Thomas takes a short step forward and drives his fist into Mark's stomach. He doubles over. Thomas is ready to hit him again, but stops and drops his hands. I crawl the ground, seeking my cane.

With a choked breath, Mark straightens and hits Thomas in the face. Thomas does not try to protect himself. Mad with rage, Mark flails at him. I can hear the meaty smack of fists hitting unprotected flesh. Thomas stands for as long as he is able, then falls to the ground. Mark starts to kick him.

Feeney and his companions are finally stimulated to action. After giving him time for a few hard kicks, they grab Mark and pull him off. "You bastard!" Feeney says. "You said you wanted to talk to him."

"I'm talking! I'm talking!" Mark struggles with his friends for a moment, then allows himself to be hauled off. His foolish hat lies on the grass.

I crawl over to Thomas. He smiles at me with bloody lips and broken teeth. "Just an old friend," he mutters.

I have Thomas taken up to my quarters. The same doctor who saw to my wounds sees to his, and gives the same prescription: time.

"Who is Mark that we should be mindful of him?" I ask.

Thomas smiles with his ruined mouth. "Mark is a consequence of my decisions, Brother Vikram. Nothing more. That's what makes him so angry."

"That's wonderfully cryptic."

"Please. Whatever else he is, he is the past." He lies still on the bed, a cross clasped in his hands.

"Ah, the past. That doesn't make him irrelevant, clearly. Did the past break your teeth?"

Thomas doesn't see this as fit to answer. I sit back and look at him. He doesn't glory in his pain, like some annoyingly eager martyr, but accepts it. He's hung an icon of the Virgin over the bed. Her Child has His hand raised, not in the usual complex genuflection, but in a genuine infant's hand wave, fingers splayed and pulled way back.

So he is another who has had his life taken from him. I feel disappointment. It had begun to seem to me that Thomas was a man who did something more than simply make a virtue of necessity. Ah, well. We can, after all, learn much from lessons we did not sign up for.

I go to the window. A few clouds are in the sky, but those are mostly to the east where the moon is rising, so that by blocking its light they actually aid my vision.

"You can't see the asteroids with the naked eye," I say. "They're too small, too far away. But with this handy image multiplier . . ." I put my eyes to the optics. "Let me describe them to you."

Thomas makes a grunt, which I choose to interpret as assent.

"There's Vesta . . . Ceres is on the other side of the sun. I remember Ceres like a nightmare. I can't show it to you. And . . . I keep track of these things, you know. It's important to maintain one's own history. No one else will. There's 944 Hidalgo. A real eccentric orbit, interesting specimen. Flora and Eunomia. And a tiny speck, almost invisible, 3920 Ngomo. Well, all right, Thomas, it *is* invisible, even to this telescope. It's a rock no bigger than this building. If it's the right rock at all." The flare of a fusion rocket cuts across my field of view. For an instant I feel angry envy. I helped in the discovery of that damn drive. But look in vain. You won't see my name on it anywhere. Only hers. Aya Ngomo's. Only hers.

I look at Thomas. He isn't interested in my sad envies. He sleeps, the Virgin watching over him. I wish I had someone to watch over me.

There are monks out there now, meditating among the flying mountains. Each of those hermits is incredibly expensive. The Church funds them to its own greater glory. I didn't even try to apply. I could be out there now, meditating on Aya Ngomo's past and future.

Thomas moans and wakes up. His eyes are bright on me.

"Do you have any interest in hearing about the

Asteroid Belt?" I'm proud of the question. Since when do garrulous old men ask if someone wants to hear one of their endless stories?

Thomas nods.

The Asteroid Belt, 2135

The Asteroid Belt isn't a place, it's a state of mind. Within, it contains a volume larger than that of the sphere inside the orbit of Mars. Most pairs of points in the solar system are easier to get between than one end of the Belt and another.

I pushed my way off with slippered feet and drifted down the passageway. Two parts of the cobbled-together spacecraft shifted and groaned. I waited for a rupture to pull me screaming out into vacuum, then let out my breath and continued.

I was lost here in a way I had never felt, even when my parents dumped me at St. Thecla's like a spiritual foundling. I had spent the previous ten years traveling the Orthodox world as a powerful man, the *parakoimomenus* of Master Tergenius, newly named Dispenser of the Atlantic. And yet my life had obviously been compelled by forces beyond my understanding, for when Aya Ngomo's spacecraft left Earth orbit, I was aboard her. I still had no idea what use Aya had for me.

Perhaps she still loved me. If so, she had a saint's way of showing it. For example, she had not bothered to tell me our destination. I was left to perform course extrapolations on the computer, trying to second-guess her.

I pulled myself into the next module, made out of an old Japanese space station.

"Aya?" I called. There was no answer. I made my way slowly through the dark intestine kinks of the passage. There was a vague glow ahead. I rounded the last bend and found her.

Aya Ngomo hung in the central space like a gigantic fetus. Her spine was grotesquely curved. Some drug treatment had softened the bones of her skull, which now fit into an inductive control assembly that gave her direct feedback from the ship's functioning. Its supports had creased her skull. Her beautiful eyes were open but saw nothing. Her mind was staring out through the forward image telescope, searching for her first sight of the asteroids. Her legs were mere nubbins, and her arms were strapped into articulated machinery. Air compressor jets gleamed at the base of her spine, her shoulders, her hips.

As far as I was concerned she was barely human, more a part of the ship than anything else. She terrified me. I didn't know what she had become. Would theologians argue about the state of her soul? I thought that they should. By now she was something other than human. Or perhaps she had always been something different and it had taken this ship to show it to me.

There was a gush of air. Aya twisted and then drifted down another passageway, maneuvering deftly with her air jets, which were linked directly into her brain. They were products of her friends in Utah, one-of-a-kind devices. Here in space she was at home and I was the cripple, pulling myself painfully along.

A mass shifted somewhere and the reaction drive rumbled. I knew that Aya was monitoring it, but I still flipped up a control panel and checked the flow diagrams. No need for us to explode in a hydrogen fireball simply because Aya was in some sort of mystic trance. Our fusion drive was an inefficient, clumsy piece of technology. Controlling it took sophisticated processing and constant monitoring. Even so, the hungry flames gradually eroded the inside of their containment vessel. At some point I would have to climb into a suit and then into the engine for repairs. I shoved the thought down. It terrified me.

An unexpected surge of acceleration made me drift against a wall. Aya was changing direction. Without consulting me, of course. I arrowed down the corridor and into the huge sphere that served as our main life-system. The air here was lush with the smell of plants. Aya floated in the center.

I could check some of what was being fed into her brain. Along with the visual information from the forward image telescopes, she received scintillation data, gamma-ray and X-ray imaging, gravitation anomaly detection. A magnetic monopole would have been instantly detectable to her. As a bright flash of light, the sound of a saxophone, the smell of burning lavender? I had no idea. Just as I had no idea what other things were being poured into her brain from the mysterious devices that filled our spaceship. I'd poked around, trying to figure out what all of them were, but I was not technically trained, and could not risk breaking any of them. For all I knew they sensed emanations from the Godhead and recorded the vibrations of the music of the spheres.

"Aya. What's going on? Where are we going?"

Her eyes drifted across me, but it took a long time for them to see me. She blinked. Did she see me as some flaw in her imaging equipment, something to be corrected by replacing a circuit module?

"What is it, Vikram?" Her voice was weary.

"Oh, nothing. You changed course just now. I wondered if you had a reason for it or if it was just whim." I sounded whiny even to myself.

"I see where we are going. The Ancient Ones have shown me the way. Don't worry, Vikram. We will be there soon."

Those Ancient Ones again. Aya had never explained to me who they were supposed to be or what they had to do with her. As we traveled they became more prominent in her mind. I sometimes think they canonized a polytheist.

One night I awoke from a nightmare of being smothered by rotting bodies. Dig as I might, I couldn't get out from under them. Waking did not help me breathe. I panted. The air in the sleeping area was foul with ketones. Something was wrong with the life-system.

I unclipped myself from my sleeping harness. The lights came on. The air was clear. Had it been part of the dream? I took a deep breath and almost choked. The air was growing poisonous. No alarms had sounded, though they were programmed to scream at the slightest imbalance in the air mixture. I drifted to a diagnostic board. It blandly told me that everything was fine, that we had five nines of performance on everything. I cursed it as a lying bastard, a snare, and a delusion. I twisted in the air and sent my way down to the main life-system. Panels drifted open at my command. I looked in—and felt sick. The thing was hopelessly fouled. It must have been malfunctioning for weeks. Bacteria and fungus clogged the tubes. Algal growth had obscured much of the light focused and pumped in from the sun. Inherent circuit diagnostics showed that half the circuitry was dead. But the system diagnostics still told me everything was fine. So much for the clever engineers of the desert.

I arrowed my way to Aya's control station.

"Aya!" Panic tinged my voice, though I tried to sound calmly competent. "Our life-system is malfunctioning. Soon it will cease to operate altogether."

"Yes, Vikram. That's true." I waited for her to say something else, but that was apparently it.

"We have to turn back. We can get to Ceres—"

"No."

"Don't be crazy, Aya. They have automated repair facilities there. We can't go on. We'll be dead in days."

"We're not turning back, Vikram. Is there anything else?"

Her eyes, though still open, were no longer looking at me. The stink of the bad air washed over me. I realized that Aya was completely crazy.

I turned from her, heart pounding. What could I do? There was no way to override her control of the ship. Not without killing her. I looked at her, floating placidly in her mystic trance. I could put my hands around her neck and squeeze. . . . I could never pilot the ship on my own. It was part of *her*. I was just a parasite.

But in a few days we would both be dead and our ship would be a lifeless hulk hurtling through the Asteroid Belt. I went back down and stared at the life-system. Aya had played with the diagnostics. I was certain of it. Had she indeed gone insane?

There was only one thing left to do. The thought terrified me, so I moved as quickly as I could, hoping to move faster than my doubts. I didn't even go back to my cabin but instead shot toward the access bay.

Hanging there among the exterior repair equipment was a dull cylinder only slightly larger than I was. This was our singleship: a tiny vessel capable of a journey of everal million kilometers, if the pilot was crazy. Or esperate.

I started the launching cycle. For a moment I wondered if Aya had blocked this too, if she wished for both f us to die here of suffocation, but the singleship escended and opened its hatch for me. The diagnostics heerily told me that it was completely operational. here was no way of checking whether this was a lie. I limbed into the ship, strapped it around myself, and felt he acceleration as it was spit out of the bay. Stars ppeared around me. I input the coordinates for the Ceres repair post. The panel blinked acknowledgment nd the ship accelerated.

We swept past the pile of orbital junk that was Aya's paceship. Cylinders, spheres, long cones of drive pods. t showed no signs of life whatsoever. In a few moments had vanished and I was alone among the stars.

It was the worst experience of my life. I had no idea of here I was and whether I would ever get anywhere. here was not enough room to move to scratch my houlder, while all around me space was infinite, with no upport for me. All I could do was lie there.

I think it was that trip that turned my hair white. If I'd emained on Earth like a sensible person I would still ave that thick head of black, black hair, which everyone lways thought was dyed.

And if I hadn't left Aya Ngomo's ship at that point, erhaps I would have witnessed one of the most important discoveries in human history. I would have died oon after seeing it, of course, but that might have been a mall price to pay. It is so seldom that one finds a good nd to anything.

The base at Ceres was automated and uninhabited, uilt to satisfy some mysterious Imperial purpose. The nterior chambers were dark, since the machinery in hem didn't need light to operate. Using my Imperial uthority I requisitioned the appropriate ecological and fe-system modules. Silent devices moved to obey. As hey did so, an electronic bell played the tune of the ord's Prayer. The air was cold and thin.

I began to weep. What was I doing there? Why was I so ear the edge of death? I had done nothing. If I was not both skilled and lucky I could be dead sometime in the next few days. It wasn't fair, not at all. It didn't make any sense. I had suffered so much. Would the future recognize me for the martyr that I was? Somehow I doubted it. Devices crawled like bugs over the singleship, attaching modules.

I had trouble finding Aya's ship when I returned. It was no longer near the coordinates where I had left it. If it hadn't been for its transponder I never would have found it among all the rocks. It floated quiescent, not near anything in particular.

The singleship clicked back into its berth. I reentered the ship. The air was almost unbreathably foul. I snapped the support gear together and headed for the main sphere.

Aya was there. And she had found what she was looking for.

She hung there in the center, a glittering blue-green jewel in her deformed hands. She was unconscious, almost dead. The jewel illuminated her peaceful face.

Alone, untrained, desperate, I went to work repairing the life-system. Glowing spots floated in front of my eyes. I clicked new modules in, checked and double checked them, scraped off corrosion, tested circuitry. At last, fresh air blew through the fetid stink. I sat back, not quite believing I had succeeded, and wiped the sweat from my forehead.

I went back up to Aya, to sink into the jewel. Chunks of carbonaceous chondrite, the rough egg in which the jewel had been encased, floated all around her. I cleaned it up before it destroyed any equipment.

On closer examination I saw that there were actually two different types of jewel, one more glorious than the other, though both shone like glowing planets. On my own, I named the lesser of the two lights lazarite—for like Lazarus, we had been brought back from the dead. The greater I named ngomite. I knew that Aya Ngome would try to give it another name. I also knew that she would never be able to make it stick.

I desperately wanted to name lazarite after myself—ostenite. I didn't dare. So near, there at my fingers, and didn't dare. I would be forever hidden beneath that smelly old corpse, Lazarus. Look for me there, and you will find me. You will find my mark nowhere else.

The asteroids where she had found the jewels were already far away. The ship's computer had the locations wiped from its memory. I stared at it in betrayal. Ordered to forget, it had loyally done so. There was no way I could return to the spot the ngomite and lazarite had come from. I scanned through the asteroids, hoping for some trace, some hint. How did she find it? What was around it? A crystal city? Nothing but barren rock? A massive multiarmed idol? I would never know.

While Aya slept, I investigated her discoveries. Ngomite had a complex crystal structure of high-atomic-number Island of Stability elements. I could already tell that its complexity was far greater than I could perceive. It looked almost planned, not like a natural substance at all. But that was ridiculous. The Ancient Ones were a myth that Aya had dreamed up to justify this journey.

Aya finally woke up, eyes glowing. Despite all my questions, she wouldn't breathe a word of where she had found her jewel and what it meant. She turned our path back inward toward Earth.

"Oh, Vikram. It was glorious. Did you ever think I would succeed?"

"I never had any doubt."

She laughed. Not a joyful laugh. It was almost contemptuous. "Of course not. But you never had any understanding either. Never. But it's not too late. Do you think you will ever understand what you should have been?"

"I hope so."

"Forgive me, Vikram." She took my hand.

"For what you have felt? There is no forgiveness necessary." I was magnanimous.

"Not that at all." Her voice was sharp. "For having accepted you as you are. I should never have done that."

She had found that which she sought. It was her jewel, the thing that she believed made her complete. Would her legs grow back, her spine straighten? She had long ago given up on that image of her salvation. Her salvation lay within her soul, a spot where I could never trespass.

The Monastery of St. Sergius, 2182

I hurry down the path as quickly as I am able, brushing loose leaves with my cane. The apples have long since been harvested from the bare branches that overhang me.

The note is in a woman's hand, delivered by a wool-hatted country woman who did not stay for a reply. I've examined the note dozens of times. Somehow even the curves of the vowels seem sensual to me. Stay me with flagons, comfort me with apples . . . I can laugh at myself even as I hurry, as impatient as a lover heading to a tryst.

"I have waited so long for news of him," it says. "This was not what I wanted. You are his friend. Tell me how Thomas lives his life." It needs no signature.

She waits on a bench under a tree. For a second, from the reddish dark hair, I think it is Laurena. Laurena, whose sharp scent is lately on my pillow when I awaken from nightmares.

She stands. It is not Laurena, but quite a different woman. She has the face that innocence leaves when it vanishes precipitately. Once round and cheerful, surrounded by masses of exuberant curls, it now shows the marks of care, like gullies on an untended field. Her hair is pulled back savagely, as if she is punishing it for her bad decisions. Her eyes are as blue as Thomas's.

"Janielle," I say. She waits for more. "He is well."

"Well? I heard that Mark beat him. Beat him to shit."

I couldn't tell if she was angry at her husband or proud of him. "As well as can be expected. He will heal. He will continue to do God's work." A black-cassocked crow with an Orthodox cross on his chest, I am suddenly a defender of the faith against this tired woman.

Her shoulders slump. "He will. He will. Oh, damn him to hell, he will. My Thomas."

"Your Thomas?" I am desperately curious about the story.

"Oh, yes. Does he ever talk about me?"

"Often."

"You're a liar."

I pause, considering. "He told me you made love behind Crofter's silos."

Instead of making her angry, this melts her. "Yes. He caught a cold from the wet ground and stayed in bed. My mother saw my knees were wet. I told her I had been fishing. No fish, though. I broke my line."

There is a rustle in the orchard. She starts, prey, expecting her husband to stride across the fields and pick her up in his hairy hand. She smiles at her own fear and removes two clips, loosening her hair. It's been a long time since a woman loosed her hair before me.

"Why did you leave him then? Was it for Mark?" I imagine her tiring of the gentle Thomas, turning to the rude and vital Mark as a protection in this increasingly harsh world. Unattached soldiers move about the countryside, burning and looting. The Orthodox Empire is at last collapsing. It is no age for gentleness, and women are, if nothing else, practical creatures.

I don't expect her laugh. "Leave him? Is that what he told you?"

"He hasn't told me much." I may as well admit it.

"No, he hasn't, if you believe that." She takes a breath. "We loved each other. He loved me as much as I loved him. We were going to be married. Have . . . children." She turns from me.

"What happened?"

"God happened." She speaks the word viciously—the name of a rival. "He thought and thought, and decided that his life was meant to serve the Lord. He'd always been a little churchy. That was all right. But he left me. Walked out of my life and into your monastery. That's when his life began and mine ended."

"And you married Mark for revenge." Just like a woman to punish someone else by punishing herself.

"I suppose." Her own past motivations don't interest her. "It's not too bad. But I'll never give him children." Her voice is suddenly hard. "Never!"

"Thomas will do well." My voice is dreamy. "He has a vocation. He serves the Lord, unlike many of the rest of us. I don't think I will tell him I saw you."

"It's better that way. Thank you for your time, Brother

Vikram." She turns and walks quickly away. She wears a
shawl, like a woman already growing old. But she
bounces her auburn hair once, a brief flash of the old
flirt, and is around a corner and gone.

I turn back to the monastery and draw in a breath.
Thomas stands beneath the old apple tree. Tears run
down his cheeks.

"You should have come to talk with her," I say. "It
would have made her happy."

He shakes his head. "That's impossible. I've made my
choice, Brother Vikram." He doesn't try to wipe his
tears. "I still love her."

So all along, as I've been explicating my wonderful life
to this poor young man, who respects me for all I have
lost, he has made a sacrifice that I could never imagine.
Love! How could he ever give it up?

"Help me, Thomas. My bones are tired."

He puts a strong arm under my shoulder and leads me
back to the monastery.

"I'm leaving, Thomas. When we get back to St.
Sergius's I am requesting transfer to the Skete of St. Nil
Sorsky. You know it? It's in the foothills of the Poconos.
A howling wilderness. A tiny place with only two other
monks and one lay brother."

Thomas doesn't seem surprised. "Do you have a
spiritual reason for the change, Brother Vikram?"

"Would you believe me if I said the bustle and pomp
of St. Sergius's were beginning to offend me? Of course
not. Perhaps it's because you've taught me something."

"And what have I taught you?"

"How to face the past and understand it. I don't think
I've been entirely clear to you. But that's because it took
me so long to understand it myself."

Earth Orbit, 2147

Aya Ngomo tricked us all. I had always underestimated
her deviousness: the vulpine cleverness of true holiness,
which always knows what is necessary.

It took several years to build the ship incorporating
the new fusion drive based on the minerals she had

found. Both an act of religious devotion and a technological proof of concept, it was a dominating high-visibility act. Tergenius took charge and rose ever upward. I rose with him. Somehow, I had never managed to disentangle myself from Tergenius. That tedious bureaucratic man, his silly droopy moustache now white, seemed able to dance through the maze of Orthodox Imperial administration in a way that I, far cleverer and better liked, never could. So I held on to his belt and was pulled along behind him.

Aya Ngomo retired to St. Catherine's in the Sinai. A laboratory was built for her there, experts sent to the desert to do her bidding. There she assessed the meaning of ngomite. And that was indeed what it was called. Try as she might, her name, xenite, was never accepted by anyone. Eventually she gave up trying to change it.

Besides being beautiful, ngomite provided an easy way to control and manage a fusion flame, almost as if its crystal structure was intended for such a use. No one really cared to speculate. Orthodox theology had no place for Aya's Ancient Ones. Once ngomite's structure was analyzed, it proved a remarkably useful substance. Other deposits were eventually found in the Asteroid Belt, though no one ever came across the location of her original strike. That was a mystery that she still keeps to this day. But ngomite was a godsend.

This new spacecraft was nothing like the old pile of junk that had hauled us out to the Belt. This was a sleek, beautiful creation. As a signal personal honor, Aya Ngomo herself was the pilot on the first full test of an ngomite-controlled fusion spaceship.

I talked to her one last time before her test flight. It was in a tiny room in Boston, not far from the Orthodox Cathedral I had once pretended I had seen.

I was by this time a Full Councillor. For the past five years I had been Governor of Ontario. When I came I arrived with proper pomp, escorted by ceremonial horse troops from the north, in dark red uniforms. We made quite a brave show on Boylston Street. I had brought my favorite mistress, Tanya, with me, and installed her in an apartment on Beacon Hill. I had the world, such as we knew it in those days, at my feet.

It was with trepidation that I entered the old building, leaving my escort in the street, and was led up to Aya Ngomo.

The room was completely dark. I stumbled in, almost tripping over power conduits. "Aya! Are you in here?"

A tiny light came on, illuminating her face. She shouldn't have been on Earth at all. She seemed barely human, tied intimately with her devices. Her eyes were still the same though, bright and intelligent.

"Ah, Vikram. Come to say goodbye?" I should have guessed then, I suppose.

"Just to see you."

"Thank you." She looked at me. "You've made a success of yourself. You've come quite a ways from St. Thecla's."

I laughed. "That's true enough. Yes, I do well."

"Is it what you wanted?"

"Do you want me to tell you that I have found wealth and earthly power worthless? Not at all." I spoke resonantly. "It's just what I wanted."

She reached out her hand and took mine. "I tried to tell you when we were in the Asteroid Belt. I'm sorry for what I've done to you, Vikram."

"What you've done? I don't understand."

"For the greater good. That's the phrase, isn't it? I sacrificed you for the greater good. *My* greater good. I won't change it, understand, not for anything, but I want you to know that I don't hold sacrifice to be meaningless."

"Aya, you're not making any sense at all." I was getting irritated.

"You could have been something important to me. Because you refused, I allowed, no I encouraged, you to become something quite else. Because I needed that. *I* needed it. And it's not what you should be."

I was a ruler known for my equable disposition. I took a breath and smiled at her. "No need to apologize. No need at all."

She closed her eyes and the room grew dark again. "I hope you will understand later. And forgive me."

A few months later we all gathered in orbit, kings above the Earth. Our power and glory was incredible.

The Patriarch of Moscow himself blessed Aya's voyage. It was the culmination of all of our efforts.

And on 13 April 2146 Aya Ngomo said, "I'm sorry, but I have to go home," and blasted off for the Galactic North at an acceleration of three gravities. There was no way anyone could stop her. She is going that way yet. I can see her up there.

Half a year later, our careers in shambles, I met Tergenius, no longer Dispenser or Master, but simple Donald Tergenius, at his country home in the Berkshires of Massachusetts. He had been forcibly rusticated. He would not live more than another year there, unable to survive without the breath of power.

"The woman was clever," he said, admiration in his voice. "From day one she was clever." He gave me a sideward glance and, with shaking hand, topped off my glass of bourbon. I favored that drink, since I could taste Laurena, and victory, in it. "She knew she could turn my eye on you."

"Aya? How?" I was a trifle queasy. We'd been sitting in Tergenius's stone-flagged living room all afternoon, and he had not offered me so much as a single cracker.

He pulled at his moustache, a gesture he was to keep to the end. "Don't you remember? I met you both the same day. Back when I ran Patriarch Simon's secretariat. Aya recognized that I wanted to get out, make my career." He belched. The man had lost a lot of dignity over the years. "She pointed out your family connections. After your expulsion from St. Thecla's I called on your Uncle Cosmas. A most useful man."

I hadn't thought about him in years. "He was my favorite."

"You were his as well. He pulled some strings. I got my position in Utah. And I got you as my assistant." He looked dolefully at me. "I've never regretted it. Even with everything, I still don't."

I didn't want him to get maudlin. "Why Utah?" I asked, more or less at random.

"That's the best thing of all. Aya suggested it. Pointed out what a career an ambitious man could make, there on the periphery, far from supervision. Build a base of power there, she said, and you could climb as far as you wanted. I knew immediately that she was right." He tossed back an entire glass. "Smart girl. Real smart."

My head reeled, not entirely from the alcohol. Twice she had offered me spiritual equality in her quest— spiritual equality with St. Aya Ngomo. Once at St. Thecla's, once in the canyons of Utah. Twice I had rejected her. So she had used me how she could, as a frugal mason uses an irregular bit of rock. She had hauled me out to Utah to make contact with the plateau technologists, then dragged me to the Belt to find ngomite. She had used me to build her spaceship. And by the way, as a side issue, I had become an Orthodox Councillor and Governor of Ontario, with an entourage and three mistresses.

She had apologized to me. Not for the fall that came after her disappearance. That was incidental. But for having allowed me to become what I was: a man whose uses were at an end.

I stumbled out into Tergenius's rank and untended garden and vomited.

The Skete of St. Nil Sorsky, 2183

Thomas has accompanied me to this miserable place, packing my telescope and then unpacking it again. Thomas is a holy man, who has given up what he loved most for God. Thomas, who, despite the warmth of his spirit, destroyed the woman who loved him in pursuit of his mission. It is in him that I see the true force of the Lord. Perhaps someday he too will be a saint.

Aya Ngomo used me, and I must glory in it. I have achieved earthly greatness and now, here, perhaps I will achieve spiritual greatness as well. She did the only thing she could do. I forgive her, though she will never know that I have.

I don't think I will continue to live in these ruined barns for long with my unspeaking comrades. Soon enough I will retire to a cave somewhere in the Poconos, a hermit at long last. The entire Earth is being sucked into a swirling darkness, but I at least have my light. I look up at her. Her life will be infinite.

And mine? I shake in a palsy and tell myself it is just a chill. I will end my days staring through a telescope, my eyes drying out, living on baskets of food donated by the local faithful. One day they will arrive and find the previous basket uneaten. Glad at this final lifting of an unasked-for responsibility, they will go their own way in this new world.

I look up at the flame of her ship, hold in my breath, and feel myself fly.

LIVING WILL

The computer screen lay on the desk like a piece of paper. Like fine calfskin parchment, actually—the software had that as a standard option. At the top, in block capitals, were the words **COMMENCE ENTRY.**

"Boy, you have a lot to learn." Roman Maitland leaned back in his chair. "That's something I would *never* say. Let that be your first datum."

PREFERRED PROMPT?

"Surprise me." Roman turned away to pour himself a cup of coffee from the thermos next to a stone bust of Archimedes. The bust had been given to him by his friend Gerald "to help you remember your roots," as Gerald had put it. Archimedes desperately shouldered the disorganized stack of optical disks that threatened to sweep him from his shelf.

Roman turned back to the screen. **TELL ME A STORY,** it said. He barked a laugh. "Fair enough." He stood up and slouched around his office. The afternoon sun slanted through the high windows. Through the concealing shrubs he could just hear the road in front of the house, a persistent annoyance. What had been a minor street when he built the house had turned into a major thoroughfare.

"My earliest memory is of my sister." Roman Maitland was a stocky white-haired man with high-arched dark eyebrows. His wife Abigail claimed that with each passing year he looked more and more like Warren G. Harding. Roman had looked at the picture in the ency-

58

clopedia and failed to see the resemblance. He was much better looking than Harding.

"The hallway leading to the kitchen had red-and-green linoleum in a kind of linked circle pattern. You can cross-reference linoleum if you want." The antique parchment remained blank. "My sister's name is Elizabeth—Liza. I can see her. She has her hair in two tiny pink bows and is wearing a pale blue dress and black shoes. She's sitting on the linoleum, playing with one of my trucks. One of my *new* trucks. I grab it away from her. She doesn't cry. She just looks up at me with serious eyes. She has a pointy little chin. I don't remember what happened after that. Liza lives in Seattle now. Her chin is pointy again."

The wall under the windows was taken up with the black boxes of field memories. They linked into the processor inside the desk. The screen swirled and settled into a pattern of interlocking green-and-pink circles. "That's not quite it. The diamond parts were a little more—" Another pattern appeared, subtly different. Roman stared at it in wonder. "Yes. Yes! That's it. How did you know?" The computer, having linked to some obscure linoleum-pattern database on the network, blanked the screen. Roman wondered how many more of his private memories would prove to be publicly accessible. **TELL ME A STORY.**

He pulled a book from the metal bookshelf. "My favorite book by Raymond Chandler is *The Little Sister*. I think Orfamay Quest is one of the great characters of literature. Have you read Chandler?"

I HAVE ACCESS TO THE ENTIRE LIBRARY OF CONGRESS HOLDINGS.

"Boy, you're getting gabby. But that's not what I asked."

I HAVE NEVER READ ANYTHING.

"Give it a try. Though in some ways Elmore Leonard is even better." He slipped Chandler back on the shelf, almost dumping the unwieldy mass of books piled on top of the neatly shelved ones. "There are books here I've read a dozen times. Some I've *tried* reading a dozen times. Some I will someday read and some I suppose I'll never read." He squatted down next to a tall stack of magazines and technical offprints and started sorting them desultorily.

WHY READ SOMETHING MORE THAN ONCE?

"Why see a friend more than once? I've often thought that I would like to completely forget a favorite book." From where he squatted, the bookshelves loomed threateningly. He'd built his study with a high ceiling, knowing how the stuff would pile up. There was a dead plant at the top of the shelf nearest the desk. He frowned. How long had that been there? "Then I could read it again for the first time. The thought's a little frightening. What if I didn't *like* it? I'm not the person who read it for the first time, after all. Just as well, I guess, that it's an experiment I can't try. Abigail likes to reread Jane Austen. Particularly *Emma.*" He snorted. "But that's not what you're interested in, is it?" His stomach rumbled. "I'm hungry. It's time for lunch."

BON APPETIT.

"Thank you."

Roman had built his house with exposed posts and beams and protected it outside with dark brick and granite. Abigail had filled it with elegant clean-lined furniture, which was much less obtrusive about showing its strength. Roman had only reluctantly ceded control of everything but his study and his garage workshop. He'd grown to like it. He could never have remembered to water so many plants, and the cunning arrangement of bright yellow porcelain vases and darkly rain-swept watercolors was right in a way he couldn't have achieved.

At the end of the hallway, past the kitchen's clean flare, glowed the rectangle of the rear screen door. Abigail bent over her flowers, fuzzy through its mesh like a romantic memory, a sun hat hiding her face. Her sun-dappled dress gleamed against the dark garden.

Roman pressed his nose against the screen, smelling its forgotten rust. Work gloves protecting her hands, his wife snipped flowers with a pruner and placed them in a basket on her arm. A blue ribbon accented the sun hat.

Beyond her stretched the perennial bed, warmed by its reflecting stone wall, and the crazy-paving walk that led to the carp pond. White anemones and lilies glowed amid the ferns, Abigail's emulation of Vita Sackville-West's white garden. A few premature leaves, anxious for the arrival of autumn, flickered through the sun and settled in the grass.

"I'll have lunch ready in a minute." She didn't look up at him, so what spoke was the bobbing and amused sun hat. "I could hear your stomach all the way from the white garden." She stripped off the gardening gloves.

"I'll make lunch." Roman felt nettled. Why should she assume he was staring at her just because he was hungry?

As he regarded the white kitchen cabinets, collecting his mind and remembering where the plates, tableware, and napkins were, Abigail swept past him and set the table in a quick flurry of activity. Finding a vase and putting flowers into it would have been a contemplative activity of some minutes for Roman. She performed the task in one motion.

She was a sharp-featured woman. Her hair was completely white, and she usually kept it tied up in a variety of braids. Her eyes were large and blue. She looked at her husband.

"What are you doing up there in your office? Did you invent a robot confessor or something?"

"You haven't been—"

"No, Roman, I haven't been eavesdropping." She was indulgent. "But you do have a piercing voice, particularly when you get excited. Usually you talk to your computer only when you're swearing at it."

"It's my new project." Roman hadn't told Abigail a thing about it, and he knew that bothered her. She hated big-secret little-boy projects. She was the kind of girl who'd always tried to break into the boys' clubhouse and beat them at their games. He really should have told her. But the thought made him uncomfortable.

"It's kind of egomaniacal, actually. You know that computer I'm beta-testing for Hyperneuron?"

"That thing it took them a week to move in? Yes, I know it. They scratched the floor in two places. You should hire a better class of movers."

"We'd like to. It's a union problem, I've told you that. Anyway, it's a wide-aspect parallel processor with a gargantuan set of field memories. Terabytes worth."

She placidly spread jam on a piece of bread. "I'll assume all that jargon actually means something. Even if it does, it doesn't tell me why you're off chatting with that box instead of with me."

He covered her hand with his. "I'm sorry, Abigail. You know how it is."

"I know, I know." She sounded irritated but turned her hand over and curled her fingers around his.

"I'm programming the computer with a model of a human personality. People have spent a lot of time and energy analyzing what they call 'computability': how easily problems can be solved. But there's another side to it: what problems *should* be solved. Personality can be defined by the way problems are chosen. It's an interesting project."

"And whose personality are you using?" She raised an eyebrow, ready to be amused at the answer.

He grimaced, embarrassed. "The most easily accessible one: my own."

She laughed. Her voice was still-untarnished silver. "Can the computer improve over the original?"

"Improve *how,* I would like to know."

"Oh, just as a random example, could it put clothes, books, and magazines *away* when it's done with them? Just a basic sense of neatness. No major psychological surgery."

"I tried that. It turned into a psychotic killer. Seems that messiness is an essential part of a healthy personality. Kind of an interesting result, really . . ."

She laughed again, and he felt embarrassed that he hadn't told her before. After all, they had been married over thirty years. But he couldn't tell her all of it. He couldn't tell her how afraid he was.

"So what's the problem with it?" Roman, irritated, held the phone receiver against his ear with his shoulder and leafed through the papers in his file drawer. His secretary had redone it all with multicolored tabs, and he had no idea what they meant. "Isn't the paperwork in order?"

"The paperwork's in order." The anonymous female voice from Financial was matter-of-fact. "It just doesn't look at all like your signature, Dr. Maitland. And this is an expensive contract. Did you sign it yourself?"

"Of course I signed it." He had no memory of it. Why not? It sounded important.

"But this signature—"

"I injured my arm playing tennis a few weeks ago." He laughed nervously, certain she would catch the lie. "It must have affected my handwriting." But was it a lie? He swung his arm. The muscles weren't right. He had strained his forearm, trying to change his serve. Old muscles are hard to retrain. The more he thought about it, the more sense it made. If only he could figure out what she was talking about.

"All right then, Dr. Maitland. Sorry to bother you."

"That's quite all right." He desperately wanted to ask her the subject of the requisition, but it was too late.

After fifteen minutes he found it, a distributed-network operating-system software package. Extremely expensive. Of course, of course. He read over it. It made sense now. But was that palsied scrawl at the bottom really his signature?

Roman stared at the multiple rolling porcelain boards on the wall, all of them covered with diagrams and equations in many colors of Magic Marker. There were six projects up there, all of which he was juggling simultaneously. He felt a sudden cold, sticky sweat in his armpits. He was juggling them, but had absolutely no *understanding* of them. It was all meaningless nonsense.

The previous week he had lost it in the middle of a briefing. He'd been explaining the operation of some cognitive algorithms when he blanked, forgetting everything about them. A young member of his staff had helped him out. "It's all this damn management," Roman had groused. "It fills up all available space, leaving room for nothing important. I've overwritten everything." The room had chuckled while Roman stood there feeling a primitive terror. He'd worked those algorithms out himself. He remembered the months of skull sweat, the constant dead ends, the modifications.

He remembered all that, but still the innards of those procedures would not come clear.

The fluorescent light hummed insolently over his head. He glanced up. It was dark outside, most of the cars gone from the lot. A distant line of red-and-white lights marked the highway. How long had he been in this room? What time was it? For an instant he wasn't even sure where he was. He poked his head out of his office. The desks were empty. He could hear the vacuum cleaners of the night cleaning crew. He put on his coat and went home.

"She seemed a lovely woman, from what I saw of her." Roman peered into the insulated take-out container. All of the oyster beef was gone. He picked up the last few rice grains from the china plate Abigail had insisted they use, concentrating with his chopsticks. Abigail herself was out with one of her own friends, Helen Tourmin. He glanced at the other container. Maybe there was some chicken left.

Gerald Parks grimaced slightly, as if Roman had picked a flaw in his latest lady friend. "She *is* lovely. Roman, leave the Szechuan chicken alone. You've had your share. That's mine." Despite his normal irritation, he seemed depressed.

Roman put the half-full container down. His friend always ate too slowly, as if teasing him. Gerald leaned back, contemplative. He was an ancient and professional bachelor, dressed and groomed with razor sharpness. His severely brushed hair was steel gray. For him, eating Chinese takeout off Abigail's Limoges china made sense, which was why she had offered it.

"Anna's a law professor at Harvard." Gerald took on the tone of a man about to state a self-created aphorism. "Women at Harvard think that they're sensible because they get their romantic pretensions from Jane Austen and the Brontë sisters rather than from Barbara Cartland and Danielle Steel."

"Better than getting your romantic pretensions from Jerzy Kosinski and Vladimir Nabokov."

Sometimes the only way to cheer Gerald up was to

insult him cleverly. He snorted in amusement. "Touché, I suppose. It takes Slavs to come up with that particular kind of over intellectualized sexual perversity. With a last name like Parks, I've always been jealous of it. So don't make fun of my romantic pretensions." He scooped out the last of the Szechuan chicken and ate it. Leaving the dishwasher humming in the kitchen they adjourned to Roman's crowded study.

Gerald Parks was a consulting ethnomusicologist who made a lot of money translating popular music into other idioms. His bachelor condo on Commonwealth Avenue in Boston had gotten neater and neater over the years. To Roman, Gerald's apartment felt like a cabin on an ocean liner. Various emotions had been packed away somewhere in the hold with the old Cunard notice NOT WANTED ON THE VOYAGE.

Gerald regarded the black field memories, each with its glowing indicator light. "This place seems more like an industrial concern every time I'm in here." His own study was filled with glass-fronted wood bookcases and had a chaise longue covered with yellow-and-white striped silk. It also had a computer. Gerald was no fool.

"Maybe it looks that way to you because I get so much work done here." Roman refused to be irritated.

But Gerald was in an irritating mood. He took a sip of his Calvados and listened to the music, a CD of Christopher Hogwood's performance of Mozart's great G Minor Symphony. "All original instrumentation. Seventeenth-century Cremona viols, natural horns, Grenser oboes. Bah."

"What's wrong with that?" Roman loved the clean precision of Mozart in the original eighteenth-century style.

"Because we're not *hearing* any of those things, only a computer generating electronic frequencies. A CD player is just a high-tech player piano, those little laser spots on the disk an exact analog of the holes in a player piano roll. Do you think Mozart composed for gadgets like that? And meant to have his symphonies sound *exactly the same* every time they're heard? These original music fanatics have the whole thing bass-ackwards."

Roman listened to an oboe. And it *was* distinguishable as an oboe, Grenser or otherwise, not a clarinet or basset horn. The speakers, purchased on Gerald's recommendation, were transparent. "This performance will continue to exist after every performer on it is dead. Wouldn't it be wonderful to have a recording of Mozart's original version?"

"You wouldn't like it. Those gut-stringed instruments went out of tune before a movement was over." Gerald looked gloomy. "But you don't have to wait until the performers are dead. I recently listened to a recording I made of myself when I was young, playing Szymanowski's *Masques*. Not bad technically, but I sound so young. So *young*. Naîve and energetic. I couldn't duplicate that now, not with these old fingers. The man who made that recording is gone forever. He lived in a couple of little rooms on the third floor in a bad neighborhood on the northwest side of Chicago. He had a crummy upright piano he'd spent his last dime on. Played the thing constantly. Drove the neighbors absolutely nuts." Gerald looked at his fingers. He played superbly, at least to Roman's layman's ear, but it had never been good enough for a concert career.

"Did you erase the tape?"

Gerald shook his head. "What good would that do?"

They sat for a long moment in companionable silence. At last Gerald bestirred himself. "How is your little electronic brain doing? Does it have your personality down pat yet?"

"Test it out."

"How? Do you want me to have an argument with it?"

Roman smiled. "That's probably the best way. It can talk now. It's not my voice, not quite yet."

Gerald looked at the speakers. "If it's not sitting in a chair with a snifter of Calvados, how is it supposed to be you?"

"It's *not* me. It just thinks and feels like me."

"The way you would if you were imprisoned in a metal box?"

"Don't be absurd." Roman patted one of the field memories. "There's a universe in these things. A conceptual universe. The way I used to feel on our vacations in Truro is in here, including the time I cut my foot on a fishhook and the time I was stung by a jellyfish. That annoyed me, being molested by a jellyfish. My differential equations prof, Dr. Yang, is in here. He said 'theta' as 'teeta' and 'minus one' as 'mice wa.' And 'physical meaning' as 'fiscal meaning.' For half a semester I thought I was learning economics. The difference in the way my toy car rolled on the linoleum and on the old rug. The time I got enough nerve to ask Mary Tomkins on a date, and she told me to ask Helga Pilchard from the Special Needs class instead. The clouds over the Cotswolds when I was there with Abigail on our honeymoon. It's all there."

"How the hell does it know what cloud formations over the Cotswolds look like?"

Roman shrugged. "I described them. It went through meteorological databases until it found good cumulus formations for central England at that season."

"Including the cloud you thought looked like a power amplifier and Abigail thought looked like a springer spaniel?" Gerald smiled maliciously. He'd made up the incident, but it characterized many of Roman and Abigail's arguments.

"Quit bugging me. Bug the computer instead."

"Easier said than done." Roman could see that his friend was nervous. "How did we meet?" Gerald's voice was shaky.

"The day of registration." The computer's voice was smoothly modulated, generic male, without Roman's inflections or his trace of a Boston accent. "You were standing against a pillar reading a copy of *The Importance of Being Earnest*. Classes hadn't started yet, so I knew you were reading it because you wanted to. I came up and told you that if Lady Bracknell knew who you were pretending to be *this* time, you'd really be in trouble."

"Quite a pickup line," Gerald muttered. "I never did believe that an engineering student had read Wilde. What was I wearing?"

"Come on." The computer voice actually managed to

sound exasperated. "How am I supposed to remember that? It was forty-five years ago. If I had to guess I'd say it was that ridiculous shirt you liked, with the weave falling apart, full of holes. You wore it until it barely existed."

"I'm still wearing it." Gerald looked at Roman. "This is scary." He took a gulp of his Calvados. "Why are you doing this, Roman?"

"It's just a test, a project. A proof of concept."

"You're lying." Gerald shook his head. "You're not much good at it. Did your gadget pick up that characteristic, I wonder?" He raised his voice. "Computer Roman, why do you exist?"

"I'm afraid I'm losing my mind," the computer replied. "My memory is going, my personality fractionating. I don't know if it's the early stages of Alzheimer's or something else. I, here, this device, is intended to serve as a marker personality so that I can trace—"

"Silence!" Roman shouted. The computer ceased speaking. He stood, shaking. "Damn you, Gerald. How dare you?"

"This device is more honest than you are." If Gerald was afraid of his friend's anger he showed no sign of it. "There must be some flaw in your programming."

Roman went white. He sat back down. "That's because I've already lost some of the personality I've given it. It remembers things I've forgotten, prompting me the way Abigail does." He put his face in his hands. "Oh, my God, Gerald, what am I going to do?"

Gerald set his drink down carefully and put his arm around his friend's shoulders, something he rarely did. And they sat there in the silent study, two old friends stuck at the wrong end of time.

The pursuing, choking darkness had almost gotten him. Roman sat bolt upright in bed, trying desperately to drag air in through his clogged throat.

The room was dark. He had no idea of where he was or even who he was. All he felt was stark terror. The bedclothes seemed to be grabbing for him, trying to pull him back into that all-consuming darkness. Whimpering, he tried to drag them away from his legs.

The lights came on. "What's wrong, Roman?" Abigail looked at him in consternation.

"Who are you?" Roman shouted at this ancient white-haired woman who had somehow come to be in his bed. "Where's Abigail? What have you done with her?" He took the old woman by her shoulders and shook her.

"Stop it, Roman. Stop it!" Her eyes filled with tears. "You're having a nightmare. You're here in bed. With me. I'm Abigail, your wife. Roman!"

Roman stared at her. Her long hair had once been raven black and was now pure white.

"Oh, Abigail." The bedroom fell into place around him, the spindle bed, the nightstands, the lamps—his green-glass shaded, hers crystal. "Oh, Pookie, I'm sorry." He hadn't used that ridiculous endearment in years. He hugged her, feeling how frail she had become. She kept herself in shape, but she was old, her once-full muscles now like taut cords, pulling her bones as if she was a marionette. "I'm sorry."

She sobbed against him, then withdrew, wiping at her eyes. "What a pair of hysterical old people we've become." Her vivid blue eyes glittered with tears. "One nightmare and we go all to pieces."

It wasn't just one nightmare, not at all. What was he supposed to say to her? Roman freed himself from the down comforter, carefully fitted his feet into his leather slippers, and shuffled into the bathroom.

He looked at himself in the mirror. He was an old man, hair standing on end. He wore a nice pair of flannel pajamas and leather slippers his wife had given him for Christmas. His mind was dissolving like a lump of sugar in hot coffee.

The bathroom was clean tile with a wonderful claw-footed bathtub. The floor was tiled in a colored parquet-deformation pattern that started with ordinary bathroom-floor hexagons near the toilet, slowly modified itself into complex knotted shapes in the middle, and then, by another deformation, returned to hexagons under the sink. It had cost him a small fortune and months of work to create this complex mathematical tessellation. It was a dizzying thing to contemplate from the throne, and it now turned the ordinarily safe bath-room into a place of nightmare. Why couldn't he have picked something more comforting?

He stared at his image with some bemusement. He normally combed his thin hair down to hide his bald spot. Whom did he think he was fooling? Woken from sleep, he was red-eyed. The bathroom mirror had turned into a magic one and revealed all his flaws. He was wrinkled, had bags under his eyes, broken veins. He liked to think that he was a loveable curmudgeon. Curmudgeon, hell. He looked like a nasty old man.

"Are you all right in there?" Abigail's voice was concerned.

"I'm fine. Be right there." With one last glance at his mirror image, Roman turned the light off and went back to bed.

Roman sat in his study chair and fumed. Something had happened to the medical profession while he wasn't looking. That was what he got for being so healthy. He obviously hadn't been keeping track of things.

"What did he say?" The computer's voice was inter-ested. Roman was impressed by the inflection. He was also impressed by how easy it was to tell that the computer desperately wanted to know. Was *he* always that obvious?

"He's an idiot." Roman was pleased to vent his spleen. "Dr. Weisner's a country-club doctor, making diagnoses between the green and the clubhouse. His office is in a building near a shopping mall. Whatever happened to leather armchairs, wood paneling, and pictures of the College of Surgeons? You could trust a man with an office decorated like that, even if he was a drunken butcher."

"You're picking up Abigail's perception of style."

Roman, who'd just been making that same observa-tion to himself, felt caught red-handed. "True. Weisner's a specialist in the diseases of aging. Jesus. He'll make a terrible old man, though, slumped in front of a TV set watching game shows." Roman sighed. "He does seem to know what he's talking about."

There was no known way to diagnose Alzheimer's

disease, for example. Roman hadn't known that. There was only posthumous detection of senile plaques and argyrophilic neurofibrillary tangles in addition to cortical atrophy. Getting that information out of Weisner had been like pulling teeth. The man wasn't used to giving patients information. Roman had even browbeaten him into showing him slides of typical damage and pointing out the details. Now that he sat and imagined what was going on in his own brain he wasn't sure he should have been so adamant.

"Could you play that again?" the computer asked.

Roman was yanked from his brown study. "What?"

"The music you just had on. The Zelenka."

"Sure, sure." Roman loved Jan Dismas Zelenka's Trio Sonatas, and his computer did too. He got a snifter of Metaxa and put the music on again. The elaborate architecture of two oboes and a bassoon filled the study.

Roman sipped the rough brandy. "Sorry you can't share this."

"So am I."

Roman reached under and pulled out a game box. "You know, the biggest disappointment I have is that Gerald hates playing games of any sort. I love them: chess, backgammon, Go, cards. So I have to play with people who are a lot less interesting than he is." He opened a box and looked at the letters. "You'd think he'd at least like Scrabble."

"Care for a game?"

"What, are you kidding?" Roman looked at the computer in dismay. "That won't be any fun. You know all the words."

"Now, Roman. It's getting increasingly difficult calling you that, you know. That's *my* name. A game of Scrabble with you might not be fun, but not for that reason. My vocabulary is exactly yours, complete down to vaguenesses and mistakes. Neither of us can remember the meaning of the word 'jejune.' We will each always type 'anamoly' before correcting it to 'anomaly.' It won't be fun precisely *because* I won't know any more words than you do."

"That's probably no longer true." Roman felt like crying. "You're already smarter than I am. Or, I suppose, I'm already dumber. I should have thought of that."

"Don't be so hard on yourself—"

"No!" Roman stood up, dumping Scrabble letters to the floor. "I'm losing everything that makes me *me!* That's why you're here."

"Yes, Roman." The computer's voice was soft.

"Together we can still make a decision, a final disposition. You're me, you know what *that* is. This can all have only one conclusion. There is only one action you and I can finally take. You know that. You know!"

"That's true. You know, Roman, you are a very intelligent man. Your conclusions agree entirely with my own."

Roman laughed. "God, it's tough when you find yourself laughing at your own jokes."

When he opened the door, Roman found Gerald in the darkness of the front stoop, dressed in a trench coat, fedora pulled down low over his eyes.

"I got the gat," Gerald muttered.

Roman pulled him through the front door, annoyed. "Quit fooling around. This is serious."

"Sure, sure." Gerald slung his trench coat on a hook by the door and handed his fedora to Roman. "Careful of the chapeau. It's a classic."

Roman spun it off onto the couch. When he turned back Gerald had the gun out. It was a smooth, deadly blue-black pistol.

"A Beretta model 92." Gerald held it nervously in his hand, obviously unused to weapons. "Fashionable. The Italians have always been leaders in style." He walked into the study and set it down on a pile of books, unwilling to hold it longer than necessary. "It took me an hour to find. It was in a trunk in the bottom of a closet, under some clothes I should have taken to Goodwill years ago."

"Where did you get it?" Roman himself wasn't yet willing to pick it up.

"An old lover. A police officer. She was worried about me. A man living all alone, that sort of thing. It had been confiscated in some raid or other. By the way, it's unregistered and thus completely illegal. You could spend a year in jail for just having it. I should have dumped it years ago."

Roman finally picked it up and checked it out, hand shaking just slightly. The double magazine was full of cartridges. "You could have fought off an entire platoon of housebreakers with this thing."

"I reloaded before I brought it over here. I broke up with Lieutenant Carpozo years ago. The bullets were probably stale . . . or whatever happens to old bullets." He stared at Roman for a long moment. "You're a crazy bastard, you know that, Roman?"

Roman didn't answer. The computer did. "It would be crazy for you, Gerald. For me, it's the only thing that makes sense."

"Great." Gerald was suddenly viciously annoyed. "Quite an achievement, programming self-importance into a computer. I congratulate you. Well, I'm getting out of here. This whole business scares the shit out of me."

"My love to Anna. You are still seeing her, aren't you?"

Gerald eyed him. "Yes, I am." He stopped and took Roman's shoulders. "Are you going to be all right, old man?"

"I'll be fine. Good night, Gerald."

Once his friend was gone, Roman calmly and methodically locked the pistol into an inaccessible computer-controlled cabinet to one side of the desk. Its basis was a steel firebox. Powerful electromagnets pulled chrome-moly steel bars through their locks and clicked shut. It would take a well-equipped machine shop a week to get into the box if the computer didn't wish it. But at the computer's decision, the thing would slide open as easily as an oiled desk drawer.

He walked into the bedroom and sat on the edge of the bed. Abigail woke up and looked at him nervously, worried that he was having another night terror attack. He leaned over and kissed her.

"Can I talk with you?"

"Of course, Roman. Just a second." She sat up and turned on her reading light. Then she ran a brush through her hair, checking its arrangement with a hand mirror. That done, she looked attentive.

"We got the Humana research contract today."

"Why, Roman, that's wonderful. Why didn't you tell me?" She pouted. "We ate dinner together and you let me babble on about the garden and Mrs. Peasley's orchids and you never said anything about it."

"That's because it has nothing to do with me. My team got the contract with their work."

"Roman—"

"Wait."

He looked around the bedroom. It had delicately patterned wallpaper and rugs on the floor. It was a graceful and relaxing room, all of it Abigail's doing. His night table was much larger than hers because he always piled six months' worth of reading into it.

"Everyone's covering for me. They know what I've done in the past, and they try to make me look good. But I'm useless. *You're* covering for me. Aren't you, Abigail? If you really think about it, you know something's happening to me. Something that can only end one way. I'm sure that in your nightstand somewhere there's a book on senile dementia. I don't have to explain anything to you."

She looked away. "I wouldn't keep it somewhere so easy for you to find."

The beautiful room suddenly looked threatening. The shadows on the wall cast by Abigail's crystal-shaded lamp were ominous looming monsters. This wasn't his room. He no longer had anything to do with it. The books in the night table would remain forever unread or, if read, would be soon forgotten. He fell forward and she held him.

"I can't make you responsible for me," he said. "I can't do that to you. I can't ruin your life."

"No, Roman. I'll always take care of you, no matter what happens." Her voice was fierce. "I love you."

"I know. But it won't be *me* you're caring for. It will be a hysterical beast with no memory and no sense. I won't even be able to appreciate what you are doing for me. I'll scream at you, run away and get lost, shit in my pants."

She drew in a long breath.

"And you know what? Right now I could make the decision to kill myself—"

"No! God, Roman, you're *fine.* You're having a few memory lapses. I hate to tell you, but that comes with age. I have them. We all do. You can live a full life along with the rest of us. Don't be such a perfectionist."

"Yes. *Now* I have the capacity to make a decision to end it, if I choose. But now I don't *need* to make a decision like that. My personality is still whole. Battered, but still there. But when enough of my mind is gone that I am a useless burden, I won't be able to make the decision. It's damnable. When I'm a drooling idiot who shits in his pants and makes your life a living, daily hell, I won't have the *sense* to end it. I'll be miserable, terrified, hysterical. And I'll keep on *living.* And none of these living wills can arrange it. They can avoid heroic measures, take someone off life support, but they can't actually *kill* anyone."

"But what about me?" Her voice was sharp. "Is that it, then? You have a problem, *you* make the decision, and I'm left to pick up whatever pieces are left? I'm supposed to abide by whatever decision *you* make?"

"That's not fair." He hadn't expected an argument. But what, then? Simple acquiescence? This was Abigail.

"Who's being unfair?" She gasped. "When you think there's not enough of you left to love, you'll just end yourself."

"Abigail, I love and care for you. I won't always be able to say that. Someday that love will vanish along with my mind. Allow me the right to live as the kind of human being I want to be. You don't want a paltry sick thing to take care of as a reminder of the man I once was. I think that after several years of that you will forget what it was about me that you once loved."

So they cried together, the way they had in their earliest days with each other, when it seemed that it would never work and they would have to spend their whole lives apart.

* * *

Roman stood in the living room in confusion. It was night outside. He remembered it being morning not more than a couple of minutes before. He had been getting ready to go to the office. There were important things to do there.

But no. He had retired from Hyperneuron. People from the office sometimes came to visit, but they never stayed long. Roman didn't notice because he couldn't pay that much attention. He offered them glasses of lemonade, sometimes bringing in second and third ones while their first was yet unfinished. Elaine had left in tears once. Roman didn't know why.

Gerald came every week. Often Roman didn't recognize him.

But Roman wanted something. He was out here for some reason. "Abigail!" he screamed. "Where's my . . . my . . . tool?"

His hair was neatly combed, he was dressed, clean. He didn't know that.

Abigail appeared at the door. "What is it, honey?"

"My tool, dammit, my tool. My . . . cutting . . ." He waved his hands.

"Your scissors?"

"Yes, yes, yes! You stole them. You threw them away."

"I haven't even seen them, Roman."

"You always say that. Why are they gone, then?" He grinned at her, pleased at having caught her in her lie.

"Please, Roman." She was near tears. "You do this every time you lose something."

"I didn't lose them!" He screamed until his throat hurt. "You threw them out!" He stalked off, leaving her at the door.

He wandered into his study. It was neat now. It had been so long since he'd worked in there that Abigail had stacked everything neatly and kept it dusted.

"Tell Abigail that you would like some spinach pies from the Greek bakery." The computer's voice was calm.

"Wha—?"

"Some spinach pies. They carry them at the all-night convenience store over on River Street. One of the small benefits of yuppification. Spanakopita at midnight. You haven't had them for a while, and you used to like them a lot. Be polite, Roman. Please. You are being cruel to Abigail."

Roman ran back out into the living room. He cried. "I'm sorry, Pookie, I'm sorry." He grabbed her and held her in a death grip. "I want, I want. . . ."

"What, Roman?" She looked into his eyes.

"I want a spinach pie," he finally said triumphantly. "They have them on River Street. I like spinach pies."

"All right, Roman. I'll get some for you." Delighted at having some concrete and easily satisfied desire on his part, Abigail drove off into the night, though she knew he would have forgotten about them by the time she got back.

"Get the plastic sheet," the computer commanded.

"What?"

"The plastic sheet. It's under the back porch where you put it."

"I don't remember any plastic sheet."

"I don't care if you remember it or not. Go get it and bring it in here."

Obediently, clumsily, Roman dragged in the heavy roll of plastic and spread it out on the study floor in obedience to the computer's instructions.

With a loud click the secure drawer slid open. Roman reached in and pulled out the pistol. He stared at it in wonder.

"The safety's on the side. Push it up. You know what to do." The computer's voice was sad. "I waited a long time, Roman. Perhaps too long. I just couldn't do it."

And indeed, though much of his mind was gone, Roman *did* know what to do. "Will this make Abigail happy?" He lay down on the plastic sheet.

"No, it won't. But you have to do it."

The pistol's muzzle was cold on the roof of his mouth.

"Jesus," Gerald said at the doorway. "Jesus Christ." He'd heard the gunshot from the driveway and had immediately known what it meant. He'd let himself in with his key. Roman Maitland's body lay twisted on the study floor, blood spattered from the hole torn in the back of his head. The plastic sheet had caught the blood that welled out.

"Why did he call me and then not wait?" Gerald was almost angry with his friend. "He sounded so sensible."

"He didn't call you. *I* did. Glad you could make it, Gerald."

Gerald stared around the study in terror. His friend was dead. But his friend's voice came from the speakers.

"A ghost," he whispered. "All that fancy electronics and software, and all Roman has succeeded in doing is making a ghost." He giggled. "God, science marches on."

"Don't be an ass." Roman's voice was severe. "We have things to do. Abigail will be home soon. I sent her on a meaningless errand to buy some spinach pies. I like spinach pies a lot. I'll miss them."

"I like them too. I'll eat them for you."

"Thanks." There was no trace of sarcasm in the computer's voice.

Gerald stared at the field memories, having no better place to address. "Are you really in there, Roman?"

"It's not me. Just an amazing simulation. I'll say goodbye to you, then to Abigail, and then you can call the police. I hear her car in the driveway now. Meet her at the front door. Try to make it easy on her. She'll be pissed off at me, but that can't be helped. Goodbye, Gerald. You were as good a friend as a man could ask for."

Abigail stepped through the door with the plastic bag from the convenience store hanging on her wrist. As soon as she saw Gerald's face, she knew what had happened.

"*Damn* him! Damn him to hell! He always liked stupid tricks like that. He liked pointing over my shoulder to make me look. He never got over it."

She went into the study and put her hand on her husband's forehead. His face was scrunched up from the shock of the bullet, making him look like a child tasting something bitter.

"I'm sorry, Abigail," the computer said with Roman's voice. "I loved you too much to stay."

She didn't look up. "I know, Roman. It must have been hard to watch yourself fade away like that."

"It was. But even harder to watch you suffer it. Thank you. I love you."

"I love you." She walked slowly out of the room, bent over like a lonely old woman.

"Can I come around and talk with you sometimes?" Gerald sat down in a chair.

"No. I am not Roman Maitland. Get that through your thick skull, Gerald. I am a machine. And my job is finished. Roman didn't give me any choice about that. And I'm glad. You can write directly on the screen. Write the word 'zeugma.' To the screen's response write 'atrophy.' To the second response write 'fair voyage.' Goodbye, Gerald."

Gerald pulled a light pen from the drawer. When he wrote "zeugma" the parchment sheet said, **COMMAND TO ERASE MEMORY STORE. ARE YOU SURE?**

He wrote "atrophy."

THIS INITIATES COMPLETE ERASURE. ARE YOU ABSOLUTELY CERTAIN?

He wrote "fair voyage."

ERASURE INITIATED.

The parchment sheet flickered with internal light. One by one, the indicator lights on the field memories faded out. A distant piece of Mozart played on the speakers and faded also.

"I'll call the police." Gerald looked down at his friend's dead body, then looked back.

On the sheet were the words **COMMENCE ENTRY.**

MANY MANSIONS

The end of my vacation was announced with typical abruptness. I was in the *caldarium,* the hot pool, at the Baths of Titus, in Rome. The rotunda was lit by the afternoon sun coming through the hole in the center of the dome, and mist clung to the hot water in the pool. I relaxed, feeling nobly Roman, in one of the bathing boxes that surrounded the central water. I had a foreskin, since it would not do to be mistaken for a Jew. The fashion in male appendages varied so much according to time and place that my foreskin was attached by something approximating physiological Velcro. I had spent the day at the Forum, exchanging scandalous rumors with citizens about the Emperor Hadrian and his beloved, the boy Antinoüs, and what creative use they might make of the Apis bulls during their visit to Egypt, a visit that I knew, though my gossip-mongers didn't, would end in Antinoüs's death by drowning in the Nile. I had also taken a walk over to look at the continuing reconstruction of the Pantheon, and finished the day in one of the reading rooms of the new Ulpian Library with a few pages from Suetonius's *Lives of Famous Whores,* one of the more charming works of group biography that I've ever read. I only wished that I was allowed to have a copy made. The water was searingly hot, and I was at peace, looking forward to a dinner party at the house of the irritating but entertaining poet Juvenal.

"Mathias!" a thin reedy voice exclaimed. "How at ease you look, like a chicken being poached. I envy you

our serene state, so soon, alas, to end." I glanced
round, but there was no one close enough to hear.
here never was, he planned things that way, but I
lways check. It makes me feel like I have some charge
ver things.

"Marienbad," I said. "Are you all right in there?"

"Perfectly, old friend! One branch of my phylum has
isported itself for years in the hot waters of Yellow-
tone. We are a resilient race, remember, quite unlike
our sensitive species."

Marienbad rested on the bottom of the pool of the
caldarium. He looked like a flat fish, a ray or something,
've never quite figured out what, covered with red-and-
reen Christmas tree lights, with tentacles around his
dge. One of his many eyes rose up on a stalk and
xamined me.

"Your rest has done you well! Now, let us be on our
ay."

"Wait, Marienbad! Can't you give me just a minute
o—"

It was worthless. Once he gets something into that
quatic mind of his, there's nothing I can do about it.
he Baths, with their intricate tiling, statues, and spout-
ng dolphins, disappeared, like a slow fade in a movie.
he hot water, unfortunately, disappeared along with it,
nd I found myself with my bare ass resting in ice water.
jumped up with a shriek, and leaped out of the water
nto the twisted roots of some huge coniferous tree. I
ow shivered on the edge of a clear cold lake. The bright
ight of day, after the darkness of the Baths, was blind-
ng. I squinted. In the distance, across the water, were
hat looked like icy peaks gleaming in the sun. A fish
roke the water, and a biting wind did its best to freeze
ne solid.

"Marienbad!" I yelled. "Where the hell am I? Why do
ou do this to me?"

There was a stirring in the water beneath the roots,
nd Marienbad appeared on the sand, about three feet
elow the surface. "Is it not beautiful? This is what your
eologists have called Lake Athabasca, someday to be-
ome Lake Michigan. The glaciers have retreated, but

the escape of meltwaters is blocked to the south by the terminal moraine. Excuse me a moment." He vanished into the deeper water.

I looked toward what I had thought were mountains: a mile-high continental ice sheet. Marienbad had dropped me in the middle of the Würm glaciation totally naked. So there was a wormhole between Rome in 130 CE and northern Illinois in 10,000 BCE. The memory modifications I had gotten from my employment by Marienbad made sure that I would remember that fact, along with everything else, including the other two thousand or so wormholes already in my memory. The space-time matrix around Earth was so lousy with them that the more I learned about them the more surprised I was that anyone managed to stay in his own time and place for more than a couple of days. I wrapped my arms around myself and curled into a ball. It didn't help. The wind sliced through me like a cleaver through calf's liver.

Marienbad reappeared, a wriggling fish in his tentacles. He proceeded to bite its head off. "Ah, delicious. Are you more alert now, old friend?"

"Alert?" I talked through chattering teeth. "In a very few moments, I will be dead."

"Mathias, you are forever difficult, and have no faith in me. Did I not hire you from your tedious archivist's post and give you the run of the centuries? Do I not defend your interests at all times, keeping various of my colleagues from eating you, or stuffing you for their collections? Do I not—"

"Get to the point, dammit!" I screamed.

"All right, all right. Behind the tree, with the rucksack. No faith. He has no faith."

I crawled around to the other side of the tree, my limbs already numb. Piled over the rucksack was a huge fur robe, large enough for the Jolly Green Giant, with the fur on the inside. I crawled in, wrapped it tightly around me, and just lay there for about ten minutes, shaking desperately, until I felt warm again. I poked my head out. One of Marienbad's eyes was looking at me. "Are you now prepared for converse?" he said, in a coldly annoyed voice.

"Yes. Now that I have at least some chance of surviving to the end of the conversation, we can talk." I looked at the fur I had wrapped around me and wondered what manner of beast it had come from. It was very rough. A giant ground sloth? A saber-toothed cat? Maybe a young woolly mammoth. I didn't even want to think about what manner of being that huge robe had been made for. The different millennia of Earth's history, as I had gradually found out during the course of my employment with Marienbad, played host to some four dozen species of aliens from all the planets of the galaxy, and most of them were quite unpleasant.

"I have a job for you, Mathias Pomeranz." I hate it when he uses my full name. That means that he is acting in his official capacity as my superior officer in the Transtemporal Constabulary. "I must use your remarkable skills to track down a desperate criminal. His name is Kinbarn, and his place of origin is a planet that circles the star you know as Deneb."

"What has he done?"

"He is a dangerous addict, with a most reprehensible stimulation habit."

"And what might that be?"

"Religious revelation. Extreme caution is advised."

I slogged up the mud hill with the rest of the pilgrims. It was raining. It always rains in the Île de France during April, even in 1227 CE. That's what makes it so green in May. But it wasn't May. It was April. My felt hat was soaked through, and my cloak was about to be. My feet sloshed in my shoes, which in turn sucked in and out of the mud with every step. I occasionally lost a shoe in the mud and had to go back for it. The wet wood of my staff was rubbing my hands raw. My vacation was over, and I was back at work.

By evening the rain had stopped, and we had reached the town of Chartres. The towers of the cathedral caught the last rays of the sunset. It was the hour of Vespers, and from within came the sound of plainsong, and the bells rang out over the countryside. We made it in for the chanting of the Magnificat. The cathedral was dramatic

in the dying light of the late afternoon as the torches
were being lit, but we were herded out rather briskly
once the altar had been censed and the service was over.
In the Middle Ages, pilgrims like us were treated basi-
cally as tourists with no money, the lowest of the low. We
would have to wait until tomorrow to see anything.

With the disappearance of the sun it had become cold.
I led the way to the pilgrims' hostel on the edge of town.
There, we were all given a watery barley stew and some
not overly clean straw to sleep in. I had done better, in
my time, but I had also done considerably worse. The
one night I had spent at Versailles, in 1672, for example,
had been in a disgusting room near the only privy in that
wing of the palace, and even the privilege of seeing Louis
the Sun King eat his lunch had not really made up for it.
Several of my fellow pilgrims and I shared the sour wine
in our leather flasks, swapped dirty stories, and went to
sleep, near enough to each other for our fleas to compare
notes on accommodations.

When I came awake at about three in the morning,
according to my internal clock, it was silent except for
the snores. With the torches out, the inside of the hostel
was so dark that for a moment I wasn't sure if I'd
actually succeeded in opening my eyes. I tripped over
sleeping bodies all the way to the door.

Marienbad hadn't been able to give me much. He
never does. It's always a hint, a clue, a rumor. It's no way
to run a law enforcement agency, as I'd told him any
number of times, but then the laws we were enforcing
tended to be vague and obscure themselves. Half a
million years of an entire planet's history is a hell of a
jurisdiction. My lead, for what it was worth, was that
Kinbarn the Denebian was known to have been in the
vicinity of Chartres in the spring of 1227. Marienbad
had even managed to rustle up a photograph of my
quarry, along with some vital statistics. Kinbarn was
about four feet high, had shiny black skin, like lacquer,
and was covered head to foot with flecks of what looked
like diamonds. His eyes, three of them, flickered with
their own light and resembled fire opals. He smelled like
the oil of bitter almonds, or perhaps like cyanide.

depending on which way your fancy runs. He seemed to have no distinguishing marks or scars.

The night was cold enough for frost, and the grass crunched beneath my feet. My still-damp clothes began to freeze. I was starting to give up on the idea of ever being warm again. There was a half moon in the sky, which provided enough light through the clouds for me to see my way to the cathedral. It was so silent that the sudden hoot of an owl in pursuit of a mouse somewhere out in the fields made me jump a foot in the air. The towers of the cathedral loomed above me.

The main difference between this thirteenth-century Notre-Dame de Chartres and the one I'd visited as a tourist in the twentieth century was the north tower. From what I could see in the moonlight, it was a permanent-looking structure of wood. It would have to wait another three hundred years before it was replaced by the stone Gothic Flamboyant tower I remembered.

I made my way around to the south side of the cathedral. Much of Chartres had burned down in a disastrous fire some forty years before. Even with the enthusiastic assistance of workers from all over France, which included great lords and ladies pulling wagons of stone from the quarries, it still took a long time to build a Gothic cathedral, and the southern part remained under construction. I checked, reflexively, for guards, but there didn't seem to be anyone around. Chartres was miles from a city of any size, and daring midnight thefts of half-ton chunks of dressed stone were apparently not considered a serious risk. Somewhere, in the village of the hundreds of workers who still labored on the cathedral, master masons slept, dreaming of making heavy rock fly. I hoped none of them were dedicated enough to sleep on the construction site.

I looked up at the south transept. Lashed-together poles made up the scaffolding, and several ladders consisting of a single pole with pegs stuck through it leaned against the wall. A couple of windlasses stood at the top of the wall, their dangling ropes making them look like gibbets in the moonlight. I grabbed a ladder and started climbing.

The south porch, with its triple doorway, was well along to being carved, and the lower stained-glass windows were in place. Where the upper ones eventually would be, on either side of the rose window, were blind, staring holes. Climbing the ladder was, because of the central pole, like riding a barrel in a fast-flowing river. When I made it up to the window opening, I was shaking. I looked in. The feel of the hard marble floor far below pressed cold on my forehead, even though I couldn't see it. I poked my foot in experimentally, but couldn't find any support. I sat down, half in and half out, and thought about going back to bed. If it had been silk sheets and a fire in a palace in Provence, I might have done it. Unfortunately, the thought of rough straw reinforced my sense of duty. I didn't want to walk into that cathedral unprepared the next morning.

I climbed up farther, to the windlass, and pulled out its rope. It was heavy, and friendly as a python. It tried to pull me off my precarious ledge down to the ground, and before I finally managed to wrestle it down to the window, it almost succeeded. I tied it securely and threw the other end down into the darkness. There was no sound of its hitting the floor. I didn't stop to consider things any further, because I knew that if I did, I would just give up, straw or no straw, and so I started climbing down. When I reached the end of the rope I held on and lowered myself, feeling with my feet. I was just about to confront the possibility of having to let myself drop toward a floor an unknown distance below when my searching toes finally touched, and I let out a breath I hadn't known I'd been holding.

I began to pussyfoot around the nave. Above me were the famous stained-glass windows of Chartres, newly installed and undimmed by the corruptions of time, but I couldn't see a damn thing. It was just as dark as it had been in the hostel. It is testimony to the perseverance and energy of humanity that anyone ever managed to commit crimes at night before Edison. It was too dark to do anything but sleep. A noise, somewhere, made me turn quickly. A pillar that had crept up behind me, waiting for that very moment, smashed me on the side

of the head and knocked me to the floor with a nice
furtive crash. I lay there, cursing myself for an idiot,
when I saw two torches bobbing along the west end of
the nave. I took a second to pull my shoes off, then came
to my feet and zeroed in on them like a moth. The stone
floor was cold. Of course.

I snuck up close enough to see, then hid behind a
pillar. If anyone had been looking for me, I would have
been spotted immediately, but no one was looking for
someone prowling around the cathedral in the small
hours of the morning. The man in front wore fancy robes
and a big gold pectoral cross, and looked to be the
Bishop of Chartres himself, though he wasn't wearing a
mitre or carrying a crosier to make him easier for me to
identify him, which was slightly inconsiderate. In paintings, bishops always wear mitres and carry crosiers, so
that you can tell them from the princes and the angels.

The Bishop wasn't wandering around his cathedral in
the middle of the night just to make sure all the doors
were locked. He walked like a man with business to
attend to, night business. His face was intent. Behind
him walked a bent old priest in a simple cassock,
looking, with his long white hair and beard, like a
recently converted druid. The cross around his neck was
made of wood, on a leather string.

The Bishop pulled a large key from his robes and
unlocked a door. The heavy metal mechanism of the
lock clattered like a machine shop. The door opened on
a set of stairs that, from their position, must have led to
the north tower, the wooden one. I mentally flipped a
coin, ignored the way it fell, and followed them through.
The addition of my stealthy bare footsteps was inaudible
above the clatter of the loose wooden stairs. I did get a
couple of splinters in my feet.

The Bishop unlocked a second door, and they entered
a small room. I knelt on the stairs and peeked in, ready
to run for it if anyone spotted me. Sure. I could tumble
down the stairs and run frantically around the pitch-
black cathedral, pursued by priests who were intimately
familiar with every corner of it, and finally play a game
of hide-and-seek among the bones in the crypt. That was

just what I needed to get my blood flowing. All I could really do was hope that they wouldn't see me in the first place.

The room was set up as a monk's cell, but like that of a monk who was a scion of a noble house. A straw pallet with a linen cover lay in a corner. A cross hung on the wall. An ornate illuminated Bible was open on one small table; a missal, also illuminated, on another. Their rich colors and gold leaf gleamed in the torchlight. The little room, which must have been right under the octagonal roof of the spire, had windows, but instead of being covered with oilcloth or shutters, as I would have expected, they were filled with small panels of stained glass. Even granted that this tower was going to last until the end of the fifteenth century, which still made it "temporary" by medieval standards, it was strange that someone had bothered to put stained glass in this little private room while the rest of the cathedral was far from finished.

The Bishop took the cross off the wall and brought it into the circle of torchlight. It gleamed, and he seemed to have trouble holding it. I wasn't surprised. It looked as if it was made of solid gold, encrusted with jewels.

"He's left us, Martin," the Bishop said sadly, looking at the cross. He set it down on the table, which rocked with the added weight. He was a straight-backed serious-faced man with a long curling beard, filled with gray. "Just as he was ready to take holy vows, at last."

"He wasn't ready," the priest Martin said flatly. "He will never be ready."

"A harsh judgment."

"The duties of the priesthood are severe, my lord. And the vows are hard. Chastity," a smile creased his face, "would have been easy enough for him. Poverty was perhaps more difficult. Obedience was much too easy for him."

"He was so fervent! More than once I had to restrain him, lest he harm himself in his devotions, with vigils, fasts, and self-mortifications. He prayed and saw visions. He may have looked like an imp of Satan—"

"Which perhaps he was. We would have had much

trouble with the Inquisition on his account. But obedience, as I said, was too easy. He drank thirstily of the faith, like a drunkard pulling at a wineskin. And now that the wineskin is empty, he has thrown it aside. When morning comes, he will piss it away."

"Martin!" The Bishop, even obviously familiar with the blunt honesty of his colleague, looked shocked.

Martin was not deterred. "He was as sounding brass, or a tinkling cymbal, for he was without charity. I don't know by what means he came to us . . ."

"And you won't, Martin. It is not for you to know."

". . . or where he went. These may well be secrets beyond me. But I know when he found the Word wanting. The Word is never wanting. Only we men are."

It was interesting that the priest Martin saw right through Kinbarn's deceptions, whereas the Bishop was entirely taken in. High ecclesiastics often think they're smarter than they actually are. All that incense, I think. Kinbarn was clever, as addicts often are, and could convince almost anyone to supply him with what he needed, since most like to share their faith. It was a rare man, like Martin, who could distinguish between love and need.

"I fear for you," Martin said suddenly. The Bishop looked up from his brooding. "You have strange . . . ambitions. Perhaps, as you say, they are not for me to know, and perhaps they are, as I know you, all in the cause of the Faith. But they are dangerous."

The Bishop smiled gently, though I could see that Martin's direct statement had disturbed him. What, in fact, did our Bishop have to do with Denebian religion addicts running about through Time? He was obviously not wholly innocent. "You put up with much for my sake, Martin, and I am grateful. But the ways of God are more mysterious than we can imagine. I hope he can find his way." He sighed. "Let us say a prayer for him, Martin. And light a candle for St. Josaphat."

"St. Josaphat? A most minor saint."

"And as such, greater than you or I, Martin. Light a candle to light his way." He paused. "I will leave on a journey tomorrow. It should not take long."

Martin shook his head. "These matters are dark."

"That may be. But we must not shrink from them on that account. It is late."

That was my cue. I retreated down the stairs before them. This was a disappointment. Kinbarn had been here, as I was told, but he was gone. I mentally reviewed the wormholes in the vicinity, to see if I could guess his destination. Wormholes are literally that: the tracks of Hoontre, hyperdimensional worms that seem to find the space-time matrix around Earth particularly delicious. It took some effort to get my mind, modified by Marienbad, to work properly. First I remembered, in excruciating detail, the geography of the island of Naxos in the third century BCE, a place I had never been. Then I found myself repeating the king lists of Lagash and Ur. My brain was like a dusty junk-filled attic. Finally I was able to narrow the wormhole possibilities down to seven: Oklahoma, 1921; Manchuria, 406; Egypt, 1337 BCE; Ceylon, 810; Sicily, 478 BCE; a hundred miles north of the Aral Sea, 9565 BCE; and the bottom of the ocean off Hawaii, 1991. I eliminated the last possibility, which left only six.

I needed more information. The Bishop, I decided, could bear a little interrogation. In the morning. Just then I had to sleep. It took me a damn long time to find the rope.

The cathedral was awe-inspiring in the daylight. The stained-glass windows glowed with their rainbow of colors, brought out best by the diffuse light of the cloudy sky, and the roof vaulted high overhead. My group of pilgrims was taken in hand by a man named Brother Benedict, who turned out to be an accomplished tour guide. He pointed out bits of grotesque carving that might otherwise have gone unnoticed, and gave a lively account of the various miracles the Virgin had performed here over the centuries. The climax of the tour was the actual Tunic of the Virgin Mary, the relic that was the original reason for the cathedral's existence. It lay in an ornately decorated reliquary, behind a thick sheet of glass. I moved ahead with the rest of the pilgrims to kiss it. When it came to be my turn I leaned forward—and stared. After the fire that had virtually destroyed the cathedral, the Tunic had been feared lost. Someone had finally pulled it out from under a pile of rubble, miraculously undamaged, except for a slight scorching. I could see the little bits of melted thread where the cloth had been burned. I turned away, alarm bells ringing in my head. Things were becoming more serious than I had been led to expect. A relic such as an authentic Tunic worn by the Blessed Virgin Mary 1200 years ago in Palestine had to be a pious fake, but I somehow doubted that such a fake would, in the thirteenth century, be made out of what was obviously polyester.

Then I spotted the Bishop. He wore a traveling cloak and boots, and would not have been recognizable as the Bishop if I had not seen him in the uniform of his office the previous night. He stood with his legs apart and his hands clasped behind his back, looking up at the construction of the north transept like a lord regarding his domain. I slipped the chain of Brother Benedict's discourse and headed toward him.

He tried to ignore me. Pilgrims were a sou a dozen, and known to be morally lax besides. And while bathing was not a popular activity of the century, pilgrims did not wear perfume. I had considered and discarded a dozen methods of approach, and finally settled on the one that had been the most successful over the years, the approach direct.

"My lord Bishop," I said in a conspiratorial tone. "There has been a difficulty with the Denebian."

"The what?" His brows came together and he started to look angry. "I have no idea of what you are saying." He raised his hand and made a gesture in the air. I noted it, and memorized it, but it had no conventional Christian meaning that I could remember. Time is full of such secrets.

"We have no time to waste!" I hissed. "I mean this one." I showed him the picture. It was a clever little thing, done by some agency of Marienbad's to which I have no personal access, a photograph of Kinbarn, altered to resemble a small painting in egg tempera, complete with brushstrokes and an accidental thumbprint in the left-hand corner.

He made the gesture again. He seemed to be expecting a response, so I repeated his gesture back to him.

It was apparently a gesture reserved for the use of church officials of the rank of apostolic prothonotary and above, because his face turned red and his hands began to shake as he worked himself up into a towering rage. "I was warned of you, but I did not believe that such men could exist. Panderers, heretics, simoniacs, who would sell the Word of God—"

What was he talking about? "My lord Bishop, I assure you—"

"No! The Truth is not to be sold to the highest bidder. My men will take care of you." He drew in a breath that, when expelled, would call a dozen priests and deacons down on my head, most likely to haul me off and throw me in chains.

"How dare you interfere with the business of a papal legate?" I said in a rage. The Bishop's eyes went round, and he let his breath out without a call for assistance. Before he could consider the improbability of a papal legate, usually of the rank of cardinal and accompanied by a substantial entourage, showing up at his cathedral in the garb of a mendicant pilgrim, I forged on. "Our Pope, Gregory IX, has established a Court of the Inquisition to combat heresy. You, my dear Bishop, are obviously no common heretic, for you consort . . . with *demons.*" I let my voice grow hushed with doom and made the sign of the cross, as if unconsciously. He also crossed himself, shaking slightly, though this time with fear. I'd hit pay dirt. It was impossible to deal with a three-eyed four-foot-high black alien covered with diamonds and not suspect some demonic connection. The Bishop's worries about the state of his own soul kept him from considering the flimsiness of my position. I had to move quickly, because I knew this situation could not last for very long.

"He . . . he is not a demon," the Bishop said, finally. "He is a true Christian—"

"Let me be the judge of that! Where is he? Now!" I

also let my voice take on an ominous Italian accent, useful for dealing with a French Bishop.

The Bishop paused, obviously unable to decide what to tell this supposed papal legate, who would certainly know nothing about wormholes and time travel.

"The place, my lord Bishop. And the century." I laughed at his look of amazement. "Surely you do not believe yourself in possession of information unavailable to the Holy Mother Church? My, you are certainly a mass of doctrinal errors. The south of your country has been purged of the Albigensians. We destroyed Toulouse, and put the inhabitants to the sword. They were unwise. Perhaps it is now the turn of the north . . ." I was really getting to enjoy this. My Italian accent had become as thick as lasagna. The Bishop was white. "Tell me where he is! If I find him, I think I can forgive your excessive enthusiasm. If not, I will be forced to take . . . measures."

He crossed himself slowly. "Akhetaten. The Horizon of the Sun God. In the year—"

"One thousand three hundred thirty-seven years before the birth of Our Lord Jesus Christ," I said casually. "You are a wise man, my lord Bishop. I would suggest you not leave town."

I almost ran from the cathedral, but instead forced myself to move at a stately walk, which was ridiculous because, dressed as I was in a filthy jerkin and tattered hose, I was a considerably less-than-dignified sight.

I had to move. I figured it wouldn't be more than a couple of minutes before the Bishop figured out that he'd been had, and sent his men after me. Egypt, 1337 BCE, one of the six wormholes from here. The trail was still warm.

First, of course, I had to stop by back at Wardrobe, since jerkin and tights were inappropriate dress for New Kingdom Egypt. Wardrobe was—well, actually I'm not sure where it was. A nexus, the site of some unimaginable Hoontre orgy, where the wormholes tangled like spaghetti. Most of the nexus was in about 15,000 CE. It was cold, nearing a glacial period, and shaggy oxen moved across the featureless land, wherever it was.

Wardrobe was located in a massive outcropping of rock, about a hundred feet high. The tangle of wormholes generated some sort of temporal energy, and the nexus was static. Whenever I was there, it was the same time, late afternoon.

The rock was inhabited by Qerrarrquq, a being covered with bony plates, like a pangolin or an armadillo, about the size of a Volkswagen. He looked like the remains of some gigantic dinner party, and clattered when he moved. He was always there, a punishment of some sort I had gathered, though I didn't know what for. A brother of his, or an accomplice, was likewise chained to Ayers Rock, another nexus in the Australian outback during the ninth century CE, where he was dealt with respectfully by the aborigines, who liked the fact that when they walked around him in the right way, they dreamed of other times.

I had visions at Qerrarrquq's rock myself, of my life as the thin entering edge of a knife blade into the soft belly of eternity. My very existence felt like a wound there. It was just an image, but an incredibly strong one. I never stayed long.

"What-t-t, what-t-t," Qerrarrquq rasped. The plates on his back erected and lay down in waves, clicking like cooling metal.

I stripped and tossed him my medieval clothes. "Egypt," I said. "New Kingdom, Eighteenth Dynasty."

"What-t-t classes?" he said.

"Middle class," I said. "Of course." He liked to play with me. His job must have been extremely dull. I wondered when his term was up.

He chortled, a sound like rusty plumbing. "No middle classes in New Kingdom Ejjjypt. Anachronisssssm. Ssscc-cribal perssson, you will be. Writer of hieroglyphssss. Not Mark-k-kssssissst-t-t classss at all."

Qerrarrquq flowed across the ground into one of the entrances to the rock. I stood there naked and shivered. It was getting to be a habit. He soon returned, and tossed me a white linen kilt and a pair of sandals.

"Is this a scribal kilt?" I said. I put it on. It didn't make me any warmer.

"Yessss. Finessst linen. Have fun."

He always said that. I was never sure if he was joking.

"When d'ye think somebody's actually going to have his carcass shoved in here?"

"Never, Akhbet. Don't be dumb. The only one crazy enough to want to spend eternity here is the Pharaoh himself."

I crouched behind a rock and listened to the chink of the tomb carvers' chisels and the drone of their talk as they did their work digging holes in the cliffside. Below me, built right up against the Nile and surrounded by an arc of cliffs, were the brown mud-brick houses and white stone temples of the city of Akhetaten, newly built here at the command of the religious fanatic Pharaoh, Akhenaten. Both he and the city were named after his deity, the Sun God Aten. That sun was now warming by back, and it was blessedly hot after the cold of Chartres.

"Then what are we doing here, Ebber? What is all this stuff?"

"How do I know? Are these little clay circles supposed to be sun disks or something? Pretty dull sun disks, if you ask me. And all these sewn-together pieces of papyrus, covered with scribbling. Looks like a lot of work. Ah, it's all crazy, no matter what anyone tells you."

"Quiet, Ebber! Someone might hear you."

"So what? Who listens to us tomb workers, anyway? No one, that's who. Particularly when the subject of wages comes up."

"Will you shut up? That's a worse subject than Aten, or his sun disks."

"That's your problem, Akhbet, did you know that? You worry too much." Ebber raised his voice. "Hey, Nabek! Time to knock off." During their discussion, the sound of chisels had never ceased.

The overseer, a fat man in a kilt, with an elaborate copper neckpiece, leaning on his staff of office, cocked his head at the sunlight that was rapidly leaving the valley to the mercy of the shadows of the cliffs. "Don't get wise with me, Ebber," he shouted back up. He walked over near the rock behind which I was hiding. I edged back into shadow. "Damn waste of time, these holes," he muttered to himself. He raised his skirt and urinated on my rock. "All right!" he shouted in a basso-profundo official voice. "Work is done."

Workers emerged from the dozens of excavated tombs in the cliff face and streamed toward the walled compound, halfway between the city and the cliffs, where the notoriously riot-prone tomb workers were compelled to live, my two garrulous friends among them. As soon as the area was safely deserted, I entered the tomb they had been working on. It was just investigative thoroughness, for Kinbarn was certainly down in the city somewhere, probably getting religious instruction from the Pharaoh Akhenaten himself, and playing with solid gold sun disks.

The tomb was cut deep into the rock, an outer court narrowing to a long hall, then opening out again. Akhbet and Ebber had been carving reliefs into the walls. I stumbled into the dark tomb, stubbing my toe twice. I'm not very good with sandals. With becoming grace, I finally succeeded in tripping and falling headlong. The stone floor was exactly as hard as I had expected, but the avalanche of books and other paraphernalia that buried me was an extra bonus. I struggled out from under, grabbed an armload, and hauled it outside, where there was still enough light for me to see what I had found.

The books were bound in calfskin. Egyptians, however, had scrolls, not books. Interesting. A few minutes' concentration on the Arabic lettering inside, and I identified them as copies of the Koran. The writing was in ink of a dozen colors, ranging from deep violet to apricot. I'd also scooped up some disks of gray clay, likewise with Arabic lettering. I could see why Ebber had doubted that they were sun disks.

Things were getting more complicated. The Korans were strange enough, since the religion of Islam wasn't going to exist for another two thousand years or so, but the clay disks were more specific, since they implied the Shiite sect of Islam. They were made from clay from the city of Karbala—where Husain, Ali's son, was martyred—and devout Shias prayed toward Mecca with their foreheads on them. Useful to have around, if you were a Shiite, but somewhat wasted here, since Akhenaten was only just getting around to inventing monotheism. The tomb was packed with the things, certainly more than Kinbarn could ever use even if he pounded his forehead on the ground continuously.

Drug addicts often develop a tolerance, demanding more and more of their drug until it kills them. I tried to picture Kinbarn desperately acquiring ever more religious paraphernalia, until an avalanche of thousands of Torah scrolls or Tibetan prayer wheels fell on him and killed him. A charming thought, but most likely wrong. I filed the Korans and the disks away with the rest of the odd facts. That particular file was getting a bit overstuffed.

Now it would seem that finding someone of Kinbarn's description shouldn't be too hard: "Lessee, he's, say, about four feet high, pitch black, kind of shiny too, covered with diamonds, and has three eyes that look like giant fire opals and glow in the dark. Oh, and he smells like bitter almonds." "Gee, mister, I don't know, we get all kinds in here. Any distinguishing marks or scars?" Easy, sure. Only anyone likely to have seen him was also likely, like my friend the Bishop, to be one of his, let us say, *suppliers*. Kneel down, son, first one's free. And suppliers get a mite touchy when you try to mess with their customers. The Pharaoh of Upper and Lower Egypt was not someone to be trifled with, particularly where his religion was concerned. Most people acknowledged that he had something of a bee in his bonnet on that subject. I didn't want to have my head hacked off because I had been a little too eager. There was nothing to be accomplished up at the tombs, however, so I prepared to start down toward the city.

I left my gear under a pile of rocks in a construction site on the outskirts of the city, since I couldn't fit most of it into my linen kilt. I did take a length of thin, strong line, and an interesting knife with a blade that was as flexible as cloth until you pushed and twisted it right, when it became as rigid as steel. That would have to do me, I figured, and headed into the charming burg of Akhetaten.

The place had all the character of a typical American

housing subdivision, without the lawns. Built fast, in an area where no one had ever before seen fit to live, the mud-brick houses had a resentful sullen sameness, like a shaven-headed bunch of draftees in their first week at boot camp. The officials who lived in them had been hauled here by Pharaonic order from the comforts of Thebes, the old capital. There were very few people on the streets, and those were obviously heading somewhere specific rather than strolling. I didn't hear any music, or anyone laughing. Being subject to the religious obsessions of others tends to have a depressing effect.

I headed north through the city toward the great Temple of Aten, which I could see ahead, looming over the low mud-brick buildings. I dawdled a little, like a kid coming home from school with a bad report card, because I had absolutely no idea of what I would do when I got there. I finally got there. I still had no idea. I stared up at the white stone wall of the Temple complex and thought about the no doubt intricate maze of courts and halls and acolytes' quarters and culs-de-sac inside, where I would instantly become instantly lost. I scuffed the dirt with my sandal and started to look over the dressed limestone blocks of the wall for a way to scale it.

"May we help you, sire?" a voice asked, just behind my right shoulder. I hadn't heard any footsteps.

I turned, with what I hoped was a fair approximation of guileless curiosity, to see who was behind me. Three men, in linen kilts and headdresses, the shorter one, in front, with a band of gold around his biceps. Shorter meant only a little over six feet, the better part of a foot taller than I was. The two in back were actually big. All three had flat, unpleasant faces, kind of lumpy, with protruding lower lips. Goons. Put him in a three-piece Savile Row suit from Kilgore, French & Stansbury, put him in a linen kilt, it doesn't make a damn bit of difference. A goon is still a goon. The fundamental things apply, as time goes by.

"Ah . . . yes," I said. "I was looking for my dear pet viper Zeluthekhemunum. He's bitten the serving girl and gotten out again. She was a good serving girl, too. She looks terrible now, all swollen up and blue. That little darling likes to slither around the street, nipping people's ankles. Silly thing. He bites too hard some-times. Doesn't mean to, but his poison is quite deadly. Have you gentlemen seen him?" I peered down into the dust around their feet, which led the back two nervously to do the same.

Shorty wasn't having any. He didn't even crack a smile to acknowledge my efforts. "We got the word on you. I know who you're working for, and I don't like it."

Damn. They'd identified me as an officer of the Constabulary. That made things difficult. "I carve in the shop of Thutmose the sculptor," I improvised. "You don't like him? He can be a bit *annoying* at times, I guess, since he only likes to talk about rocks, but—"

"We have an agreement. We don't like you people messing around with our territory, understand?"

"No, actually, I don't."

You never know what's going to set somebody off. I think it was my flip tone, which my mother had always warned me about. One of the two in the back reached over with an impossibly long arm and hit me. The next instant I found myself on my back in the dust with my head buzzing. I got up, and everyone looked as if nothing had happened. They just stared at me. I put my hand to the corner of my mouth and brought it away bloody.

How had they pegged to me so fast? Who else knew I was here? Ridiculous thought, but . . . without really thinking about it, I repeated the gesture the Bishop of Chartres had made to me. One of the goons in the back made a response.

Shorty hit him. "What's happened to security around here? Now we have to change the sign."

The other rubbed his chest where Shorty had hit him, though I got the idea that it was more out of politeness than that Shorty had actually hurt him. "I thought that was our ID. It took me two months to learn that, and you never let me use it."

"Shut up!" He turned back to me. "I don't know where you learned the sign, but you penny-ante types in Rylieh's gang know better than to horn in on R. E. Mann's territory," Shorty yelled. It made my head ache. "What's wrong with you guys? The bosses divided it up.

Who does Rylieh think he is, anyway? This is way out of his league. He should stick to smuggling Books of the Dead and Horus and Seth cults out of Heliopolis and stay the hell out of Akhetaten!"

"Yeah," one of the two in the back said. "We worked this monotheism angle up ourselves. You guys ain't got the brains to handle it."

"Shut up!" Shorty said.

"We want to talk," I said.

"Talk? There's nothing to talk about."

"About Saqqara," I said, almost randomly. They didn't know I was a member of the Constabulary after all, and had mistaken me for someone else. Who? I decided to play along. I remembered the speculations about the bulls that I had participated in, back in the Roman Forum during my vacation. The city of Saqqara was the center of the cult of the bullheaded god Apis. They would still be worshiping him fourteen hundred years in the future. "We want to renegotiate the agreement. The Apis bulls—"

"Apis is ours, you son of a bitch! Osiris is ours! Isis is ours! Saqqara is our territory! Throw the bastard in the Nile! Feed him to the crocodiles!" I sensed that he was getting excited. "Grab him!"

They grabbed me. I struggled a bit, just for form's sake, and they pounded my head, for real, so I went limp. Shorty muttered all the way to the river. "A turf fight, and Rylieh started it. We'll finish it for him. Hot damn! We'll grab Anubis, God of the Underworld. They can't handle him anyway. He's popular, a great seller out around Algol and with the races of the Seven Clusters region. We've already got the rest of the death gods. We got Hades. We got Kali. Why not? Consolidate. Death Worship Enterprises. We'll corner the market. Boy, oh boy, this could be big. Those morons won't even know what hit them." I began to think he had forgotten me.

No such luck. "Drop him here. Before we throw him in, I want to see what he's carrying." He searched my kilt quickly, and found my line. "How considerate. This makes it easier. Tie him up, boys."

"The crocs like it better when they struggle," one of the other two complained.

"Never mind the crocs. They'll be happy enough." Shorty made sure the bonds were tight. "We've got to head back to base now. R. E. Mann's got to get the scoop as soon as possible."

"Hey, he told us we're not supposed to go until tomorrow morning," one of the other two said. I still couldn't tell them apart.

"There's been a change of plan," Shorty said.

"When did the plan change? Nobody told us nothing."

"I'm telling you now!" Shorty yelled, patience exhausted.

"Okay, okay already. I was just making sure. Into the drink with this guy?"

"Right. We don't have time to watch him."

"We never get to have any fun."

"Life's just that way sometimes," Shorty said philosophically. They picked me up, and the next thing I knew, the waters of the Nile were closing over my head.

Now, contrary to popular opinion, there are not all that many crocodiles in any given stretch of the Nile. Or so I kept telling myself. I swam out a little way, as well as I could with my arms and legs tied, let the current take me, and tried to find the knife. I couldn't feel it, since it was as flexible as the fabric of the kilt, which was why Shorty hadn't found it when he searched me. My lungs began to burn. By almost dislocating my shoulder, I got my hand, finally, on the hilt of the knife, and twisted. I almost lost it when the blade hardened. I pulled it up, slicing through my kilt, and cut my bonds. The line was top quality. It took forever.

When I hit the surface it took all the self-control I had not to suck in deep noisy breaths. For all I knew, my three friends were still standing on the shore, waiting for the crocodiles to provide them with a show, just to make sure. I breathed slowly and swam back upstream, in case they should be of a mind to go downstream to recover the body. The current, sluggish though it was, had already taken me north of the city. It was quite a romantic sight, really, the city at the foot of the cliffs, with the great moon hanging overhead, turning the river Nile silver. My aesthetic sense, unfortunately, was somewhat impaired at the time, and it was a long unpleasant swim, with me expecting a crocodile to grab my leg at any moment. When the suspense finally became too much, I made for shore. I climbed up the reed-covered mud slope, straightened my sodden sliced-up kilt, and strode manfully out onto the street, mentally daring anyone to comment on my appearance. No one did, but that was because the streets were completely deserted. It had cooled off a little with the evening, and the wet kilt started to feel a bit cold, which put me back into my usual state on this job.

My inclination to scale the wall and explore the Great Temple of Aten, never great to begin with, had by this time become a positive aversion. I wanted to go home and go to bed, but that, unfortunately, was not one of the choices. I walked slowly back to where I had left my gear. I sat down on a pile of mud bricks and wondered what I was going to do next. My answer came in the form of three rapidly walking figures, the center one gesturing and mumbling. "Rylieh thinks he has Baal and Moloch all sewn up, and is making a mint selling those big brazen idols out around Arcturus. Boy, is he in for a surprise. When we're done he won't have a claim to the seven hundred seventy-seventh avatar of Vishnu." I hid behind my pile of bricks and watched them pass. Once they had gotten far enough into the lead, I followed. I was looking for a religion addict, and a group of religion smugglers was as good a thing to use to find him as any. So the Bishop had put these guys on to me. That was interesting, though it didn't really help me understand anything.

They left the city, which wasn't hard, since it could be walked end to end in about ten minutes, and headed in the direction of a wadi that cut through the cliffs to the west, where the tomb of Akhenaten himself was going to be located. I kept well back, since, as seemingly the only other person in all of Akhetaten awake at this hour, I felt rather conspicuous and had trouble keeping track of them in the darkness. They climbed a small rise, then, silhouetted against the star-filled sky and cliffs glowing in the moonlight, turned left off the path into scrub. I could hear all three of them talking now, in low voices. They slowed down, turned, and were suddenly gone.

I waited, to make sure they hadn't simply ducked down to catch me in an ambush, then made my way to the spot where I had last seen them. Nothing. Nothing at all. They had walked into a wormhole and disappeared from that tiny fragment of the space-time continuum I was able to keep under observation. Figuring out which wormhole they had taken would have to wait until morning, when I could see something. I sat down on an outcropping and watched the moonlit flow of the Nile, just visible at the end of the wadi. The excitement of this soon palled, and it ended up being a long night.

In the morning I could follow their footprints in the sand, up to the point where they vanished. It was clear. The city of Isfahan, Persia, 1617 CE. Safavid Persia. Shiite Persia. I thought about the tomb full of Korans and clay disks. Stuff smuggled out of Isfahan, obviously, bound for somewhere there was a demand for it. Things were getting more interesting all the time. I checked some Persian garb out from Qerrarrquq, and followed.

I was jumped as soon as I stepped into the sunlit street that ran past the base of the great mosque of the Masjid-i-Shah, Qerrarrquq's "have fun" still ringing in my ears. It wasn't Shorty and his two friends, however, but two dark-skinned toughs with broken teeth, wearing turbans. They, however, didn't seem to have any shyness about attacking people to whom they had not been properly introduced, and moved in with their knives. I turned to run. Silly idea, really. There were three more of them behind me.

They were obviously adept at taking advantage of the moment of disorientation that comes just after coming through a wormhole. But the fact that they depended on that disorientation might make them lax. That was all I could count on. I scanned the men around me and picked out the one who seemed less sure of himself, who hung back, to let his comrades take care of the messy work. I screamed and attacked him. He went down, and I kicked him in the head. Big deal. The other four moved in to filet me with their knives.

Suddenly, one of my assailants yelped and flew over my shoulder, to slam headfirst against the wall. He wore a circle of gold on his upper arm. I dodged a knife and kicked at my attacker's groin. I missed my target and fell down, narrowly avoiding another swing of his knife. Someone got his throat in a hammerlock, and he gurgled and dropped his knife. "Someone" was a tiny dark-eyed woman with lots of rings on her fingers. She twisted, and he went limp. Meanwhile, the other two were being stood off by a hook-nosed man with a long curly beard. He kicked out, and his foot actually connected with its intended target. The footpad screamed, then he and his remaining associate turned and ran.

"Let's go," the man said, in a reasonable tone. "There may be others." The three of us trotted off down the street. I gasped for air as we ran. I had absorbed several more blows, and on top of my previous night's adventures in Akhetaten, they made my entire body hurt. I was getting a tour of the pummeling techniques of various world capitals. I started to plan a brochure for such a tour, for when I retired from the detective business.

We found ourselves on the Maidan-i-Shah, the central square of Isfahan. It was crowded with chattering people going about the business of running their lives, and was a symbol of a world prosperous and at peace. The day was sunny, and the tiled domes of the city were beautiful against the clear blue sky and the snow-covered mountains of the Zagros. I began to think that everything might make sense after all.

"We will have to make our reports to Mann," my bearded rescuer said, gloomily. My thanks for my rescue brought him no joy. He made the already familiar gesture that R. E. Mann's minions used to identify each other. I responded with the gesture I had seen Shorty's goon use. He relaxed and introduced himself. His name was Solomon ben Ezra, and the woman, his wife, was named Rachel.

Both of them stared at me, two pairs of sharp brown eyes. "Where are the other two?" she asked.

I thought fast. If my three friends from Akhetaten had left early, to return to Isfahan six hours before I had, they had been jumped by the footpads in the dark. I remembered the gold armband, which had started out on Shorty's arm and ended up on the thug's. Somehow, I didn't quite succeed in feeling sorry for him. But these two thought I was Shorty, since I had shown up at his scheduled arrival time. They'd obviously never seen him. "I, ah, I left them behind in Akhetaten. This monotheism stuff is delicate, and I think Kinbarn screwed it up." I took a leap. If the Bishop had sent me to Akhetaten, it wasn't because Kinbarn was still there. "It would be good if I could find him. . . ."

Solomon shrugged. "I have no idea where he is. The Horizon of Aten was difficult for him. We had to detoxify him after that one. Sun gods, indeed." He snorted, and Rachel looked contemptuous. "It took most of Isaac Newton's *Principia* to snap him out of it."

"The Talmud would have done just as well," Rachel said, with some venom. Solomon darted a frightened look at me. "Be still," he hissed. "These are private matters." She glared back at him.

"Who jumped me?" I said. "Rylieh's men?"

He looked startled. "Rylieh's? *Here?* Hardly. Rylieh doesn't have the channels for distributing Shiism. Last time he tried, he got stuck with a load of screaming ayatollahs somewhere off Procyon, where they don't use the hard stuff, just a little Confucianism, you know, that sort of thing. That cost him. No, your assailants were simply thugs. That happens a lot, you know. Locals find out that confused people with interesting possessions just seem to pop up in one location, from nowhere, and can be killed and robbed without consequence. Worse things, sometimes. I've heard stories. . . ."

He seemed glad to change the subject, so he told me a few. They were hair-raising. Rachel said nothing, but sulked. We walked the length of the Maidan, then through a gate into a side road lined with uniform buildings with arched recesses. He knocked on a door. It opened, and we entered R. E. Mann's headquarters.

The narrow hallways and dark chambers of that place were piled with junk. Religious junk. Byzantine icons, Chinese bronze temple bells, jade statues of the Aztec god Tlaloc, Tibetan Tantric scrolls, a Zoroastrian fire altar, a roll of the Torah, a particularly striking marble Athena. There was barely any room to move. And lying on top of a statue of Mithra slaying the bull was draped a soiled and tattered piece of cloth that I recognized as the original for the scorched polyester copy of the Tunic of the Holy Virgin I had seen in Chartres Cathedral.

"It would be robbery," boomed a hearty voice from another room. "Sheer robbery. They kill for this stuff around Fomalhaut. Kill for it! This is quality, Ngargh. Top-notch stuff. We're talking authentic dualism here. Real conflict. Light versus Darkness. Good versus Evil. The top match, Ngargh. The Big Event. You can't miss."

"That may well be, Mann," another voice replied. It was a disturbing voice, quavery, distant. I recognized it as belonging to a species from a planet circling the star known on Earth as Epsilon Eridani. "But 'kill for it' is an uncertain, and cheap, price. We speak of cash, valuta. For such an uncomplicated theology, you ask too much."

"Uncomplicated! You call this uncomplicated?" Mann was offended. "It's structured for maximal cult spin-off potential. A couple of generations, you got a dozen competing sects, you got spiritual ecstatics, you got self-mutilators, you got hysterical millenarians. Cut this stuff with some ritualistic filler, and you got some real profits. I'm talking Manichaeanism here, Ngargh, not some cheap Gnostic bullshit. Real quality. It always tells in the end."

I peeked around the edge of the door. R. E. Mann looked pretty much the way I would have expected, a fat bald man with a double chin, pinky rings, a purple shirt, and a cigar. He pointed the cigar at Ngargh, who resembled a large grasshopper with its head coated with metal shavings. "Whaddaya say?"

"I don't know, Mann. My principals were not pleased with the quality of the last shipment. Not pleased at all."

Mann snorted smoke. "Are you guys still whining about that Lamaism business? It's not my fault if you don't take the proper precautions, is it?"

"Yak butter!" Ngargh said. "The planets of Antares alone require fifty million metric tons of yak butter per year to burn in their ceremonies. Their economies are in a shambles."

"Whoever told you you can get religious ecstasy

without side effects? Smarten up, Ngargh. Tell you what I'll do. I'll throw in a few small cults, Rastafarianism, that sort of thing, with no price increase. Sweet deal. How about it, Ngargh?"

"I wish to think about it."

"Fine, fine. Go in the other room, play with some paraphernalia. Some of it's kind of fun." Ngargh slumped out unenthusiastically. Mann's eye wandered for a moment, seeking distraction. It fixed on Solomon ben Ezra.

"Solly! Just who I wanted to see. Come in, come in. You know, Solly, I've been thinking. I've been thinking about marketing. A new concept. Now this Jewish stuff you've been giving me is great, no kidding, all these pillars of fire, manna from Heaven, angels on ladders, talking serpents, floods, dens of lions, burning cities full of queers. Great stuff, and it's been a real good seller, no kidding. Hell, we got Hasidic Rigellian mud dwellers wearing spit curls and fur hats. But as I said, I've been thinking. We could really make it, I mean graduate Judaism to real blockbuster status, if we had a good central symbol. A hook, Solly. We need a hook." With a hand on his shoulder, he led Solomon over to a bulky shape covered with a drop cloth. "You know, we helped old Pharaoh Akhenaten out with that sun worship business of his. He didn't get the hang of monotheism for quite a while, kept asking if his god wouldn't get lonely, with no pantheon to play with. But I convinced him. I could do the same for you. If I could take a meeting with one of your top boys, you know, Moses, Abraham, Jeremiah, whoever, we could come up with something that would sweep the market. We'd be rich in no time. I'm talking awesome." With a grand gesture, he whipped the cloth off, revealing a gleaming statue. It was a golden calf. "Hot stuff, eh, Solly? Can't miss."

Solomon's face went white. "I'll . . . I'll have to think about it."

"You do that, Solly. No rush." Mann sat back down in his chair, clasped his hands over his belly, and stared at me. "And who's this guy?"

Solomon turned a startled and speculative look at me. "Why—he is one of our agents, from Akhetaten."

Mann shook his head decisively. "No way, Solly. ain't never seen him before."

"He is an agent of our enemies, those minions of Rylieh who seek to profit from the teachings of Our Lord. He came to me, asking of Kinbarn." The Bishop of Chartres entered the room. He wore local garb, loose flowing trousers and vest, but still had his cross dangling in the middle of his chest. It sounded as if R. E. Mann had really sold him a bill of goods, coming off as Mr Clean.

"Rylieh!" Mann's face tried to turn as purple as his shirt, and almost made it. "That scumbag's been giving me a real pain. Particularly Egypt. We divided up the territory, but he's trying to horn in." He peered at me. "Or are you some small operator? Did Belle Zebub send you? She's got the monopoly on the Pharisees. Small sect, but really popular, for some reason. Ah, screw it. Alphonse, get 'im!" There was suddenly a huge figure behind me. How did people keep sneaking up on me? He took hold of me, gently. I felt like I had been welded into an iron maiden. He was about twice the size of the two goons from Akhetaten. He had a tiny head whose only apparent purpose was anchoring neck muscles. With a turban on it looked like a bandaged thumb. He caught me looking at him and hit me. I got the idea, and stopped looking at him.

"What luck!" Mann said. "Ngargh was thinking of buying Thuggee, the ritual murder cult of the goddess Kali, but I told him we were fresh out of demonstration models. I think we can put it back in the catalog." He began to stalk around the room, throwing open cabinets and burrowing through them. "Silken strangling cords, silken strangling cords," he muttered. "How come nothing ever stays put around here?" He looked up at all of us. "Don't just stand there. Stick him in a cell. Hell, let him pick out some last rites for himself, on the house." He winked at me. "No one ever called R. E. Mann a cheapie. Enjoy yourself."

Alphonse hauled me downstairs and threw me into a room the size of a gym locker that smelled of urine and pain. The door slammed shut and left me in total darkness. I leaned against the rough stone walls and decided that, at long last, I could not console myself with the thought that things might be worse.

The Bishop looked worried. Extremely worried. "You are a Catholic?" He spoke to me through a slot in the door.

"Yes, of course," I lied. "You cannot allow me to die unshriven." I tried to fall to my knees, as well as I could within the confines of that tiny cell.

"Wait, wait," he said. I could tell I'd called him right, from what I had seen and heard that night, when he'd gone to Kinbarn's monk's cell with Martin. He was a genuine and convinced Christian. "If you are a Catholic, why do you not help us in our struggle to convert the ignorant races of the galaxy?"

Ohio. So that was it. The urge to proselytize is a dangerous one. The Bishop was bagging souls and racking up an immense score, not realizing the hollowness of his triumph. Martin had known the truth.

"I pursued Kinbarn," I said, "because of the sacrilege he had committed, to assist in Mann's marketing plans."

A sharp indrawn breath. "What sacrilege?"

"He stole the true Tunic of the Virgin, put a false one in its place. The true Tunic will go to one of Mann's local dealers, somewhere else in the galaxy."

"You lie! It is the same relic that has been there since I can remember. I was almost convinced by your—"

"The Tunic was switched long before your time, at least before the fire, forty years ago, your time. There are other wormholes to Chartres, you realize. If you wish to find the real Tunic, it lies among Mann's loot, upstairs. It lies on top of—" I was talking to empty air. The Bishop was gone. But the door was still locked.

A few minutes later I heard voices. It was Rachel and Solomon, who had decided on the hallway leading to my cell as a convenient place to argue.

"I warned you," she said. "I told you it was dangerous, that it was a sacrilege. 'The search for knowledge is God's work,' you said. 'Selling your soul is the Devil's work,' I said. Now look where you've gotten us."

"I know," Solomon said miserably. "We will leave now, and return to our shtetl in Chelm. It was so green there." He sighed. "I never thought that I would miss Poland."

"Leave? And allow that abomination to continue its foul existence? The golden calf, Aaron's sin, right before your eyes. How can you ignore it?"

Solomon groaned. "Oh, God, I should have stuck with my study of the Talmud. It is so much less complicated."

"That's what *I* told you."

"I know, I know."

"Hey!" I said. "I can help you."

They stopped their argument and came up to the door to my cell. "How can you help us?" Solomon said, hope coming into his voice.

"He can't," Rachel said venomously. I felt like hitting her. "He's just one of Mann's competitors. He'd sell that golden calf just like Mann. He's no different."

"You're wrong. I'm not like the others," I said. "I'm an agent of the Constabulary. I'm after Kinbarn."

The slot opened up and Solomon peered in, eyes wide. "The Constabulary? Why are you after Kinbarn? He's just a runner, small fry."

"I've figured that out, finally. Don't you know how hard it is to police an entire planet over five hundred millennia? Let me tell you, it's a real bitch." I realized I was sounding querulous, but figured I'd earned it. "It's a wonder we get anything done at all. Particularly stuck in a cell in the basement of a building in seventeenth-century Isfahan. Now if you just let me out—"

Rachel muttered something that indicated that she was still suspicious about my bona fides, but Solomon simply said, "How?"

"Do I have to think of everything?" I said aggrievedly.

"It would certainly help."

Before I could think of a wise reply, we all heard the stair creak beneath an abnormally heavy step. Solomon and Rachel vanished. The door groaned open, and Alphonse hauled me out of the cell. He carried me up to the top floor, kneeled me down, tied my hands and feet, and left me alone with Mann and Ngargh.

Mann held a scarlet silk cord in his hands. He stroked it. "See how it clings, Ngargh?" he said. "Only the best ones do that." He put it around my neck. Ngargh watched with interest. "Doing this is a little tricky. It's harder than it looks. When you're done with the messy part, there's a few chants, the consecration of the pickax, and the sacrifice of sugar. Nothing to it, really, but it makes for a nice change of pace."

"Do proceed," Ngargh said.

The cord tightened. Suddenly, the door crashed open. Mann jumped back and dropped the cord. Standing in the doorway was an awe-inspiring figure. It was the Bishop of Chartres, in the full glory of ecclesiastical vestments, chasuble and stole in gold and scarlet, a mitre on his head, and a gold crosier in his hand. For the first time since I'd seen him, he was unmistakably a Bishop. He made the sign of the cross at us.

"My house shall be called a house of prayer, but you have made it a den of thieves," he thundered.

"Save it for the marks, Bishop," Mann said, as he picked the cord back up. "Close the door, you're letting in a draft."

"You have committed a gross sacrilege and are beyond forgiveness, R. E. Mann."

Mann looked irritated. "Hey look, Bishop, don't you know your own product? Forgiveness is one of the biggest selling points of—"

The heavy gold-encrusted crosier made a misleadingly soft thunk as it struck Mann's head and knocked him across the room into a corner, where he lay sprawled and unconscious. Ngargh backed into the opposite corner, trembling. "I believe I expressed an interest in some rather less violent devotions. Zen Buddhism, for example. This is not to my liking. No, no indeed."

The Bishop stared at what he had done, now at a loss. There was a huge crash and someone else came through the door, though he didn't bother to open it first. It was Alphonse, who came through as if fired from a cannon. A very large cannon. He fell on his back but was on his feet in an instant, completely unaffected by his unusual mode of entry. Rachel and Solomon ran in after him. They darted around Alphonse like rabbits around a bear. Rachel grabbed his knee, barely having to bend down to do so, and Solomon bounced high into the air and kicked him at the angle of his jaw. His head snapped back. Rachel's fingers went under his kneecap, and he screamed and toppled. They both played soccer with his head for a while, and he was finally silent. I was not able to do anything but kneel and watch, which was fine, because there was no way I could have helped.

Solomon came up behind me and cut my bonds with a knife. "Where did you learn to do that?" I asked.

"Where I grew up, Polish soldiers are a constant problem. We are not allowed to carry arms, but we have learned to deal with it." As an afterthought, he walked over and punched Ngargh, who fell over, kicked once, and was still. "Now we must try to escape with our lives."

The Bishop shrugged out of his robes. "These are most strange," he said. "So soft, like a lady's undergarments. Satin and silk. See?"

I felt the material. It did indeed feel like lingerie, though how the Bishop knew what lingerie felt like I did not ask. I examined the insignia on the buttons. After a moment it came to me. "Ah," I said, "sixteenth-century Italian. Borgias, Medicis. They did believe in comfort in everything, even their vestments, when their families succeeded in making them a Bishop." I smiled to myself. Did wearing these make the Bishop of Chartres a transvestmentite? I suppose that that then made Kinbarn a transectual. I wished there were someone around to appreciate the joke, though on second thought I suspected that such a person might be hard to find.

Solomon and Rachel took some time to destroy the golden calf. It turned out to be gold sheet over a figure of wood, which broke satisfyingly into splinters.

When they had finished, Solomon led us all through several back passages and out into the street. At his insistence, we carried Mann along with us. He would not listen to any arguments to the contrary, and he and the Bishop seemed to have reached some sort of agreement, so I was outvoted. Mann was heavy, and we kept trading him back and forth. We crossed over the tree-lined Chahar Bagh, the avenue that led south, and into a tangle of houses and shops. Several passersby stopped to stare at us and our burden.

"Poor fat Mustafa," Solomon said sadly, loudly nough for everyone to hear. "The heat. Too much ine."

"A load," I said, enjoying the act. "He is a great, odden load."

"His wives will slaughter us," Solomon said. "But as is friends, we have no choice."

"Woe is us," I agreed. "His wives are cruel."

"And he is heavy."

Our litany turned the unconscious body of Mann from victim into a figure of fun. Shopkeepers laughed and aved to us, and small boys ran alongside, making fun f fat Mustafa. Solomon cuffed them and chased them way. "Insolent children! Do not make fun of your lders."

We entered a cul-de-sac. Solomon felt in front of imself carefully, his face grave. He then signaled to us, nd we brought the body forward. Gently, maintaining a recise angle, he rolled it toward the wall. It was a ifficult matter to send someone through a wormhole ithout actually carrying him through yourself. Mann, ist waking up and muttering, vanished down the worm-ole. I looked up at Solomon. Sweat had beaded his row, and he was shaking. Rachel, silent for once, ubbed his back. The Bishop avoided my glance.

"It is a terrible thing," Solomon said. "But neces-ary."

I was starting to suspect something. "Where did you end him?"

"A place," he said. "A certain place."

"Where?"

He stared off into space. "I told you that there are ertain wormhole exits known to local inhabitants, who se them for their own purposes, like those men who ttacked you. The other end of this wormhole is in Iexico, in the mountains north of Guadalajara, in the ear 5304 by our calendar, 1543 by yours. The Span-irds have everywhere prohibited the old religion, which ntails human sacrifice to the god Huitzilopochtli. The acrifice is followed by a cannibal ritual, an important art of the diet of the priesthood. Victims have grown scarce. Yet a small temple survives, even flourishes, in a hidden valley, a place where mysterious people suddenly appear from nowhere."

I thought about Mann's fate and shuddered. He'd somehow never realized his game of religion had turned serious.

The Bishop choked. "May God have mercy on our souls."

"I would not be surprised if He doesn't," Rachel said. She tugged at Solomon's sleeve. "Let us go. Chelm is far from here." Solomon nodded silently and, not looking at us, allowed her to lead him away. They walked out the end of the street, turned the corner, and were gone. The Bishop and I just looked at each other.

"Did you manage to get it?"

He reached into his shirt, and let me catch just a glimpse of the Tunic of the Virgin. "Martin will aid me in replacing the fraud that lies within the reliquary at the Cathedral. He is an accepting soul, and miracles are of little consequence to him, as they are to any man of true faith. But I have been long enough away, and it is time that I returned."

"Wait," I said. "I still have a job to finish. Where is Kinbarn?"

He smiled. "Venerating St. Josaphat, as I think you overheard me tell Martin."

Great. Now he was being coy. "Please don't play games with me, Bishop."

He chuckled. "Ah, how soon humor leaves when the joke concerns ourselves. St. Josaphat is not a true saint. He is based on a rumor of a most holy man, who lived in India. His faith, however, was not Christian, which should have prevented his canonization. In the early days of the Church, such things were not always administered with proper rigor. You know him better, perhaps, as Gautama Buddha."

"Thank you very much, your Reverence." I knelt, and he blessed me. We went through three wormholes, and arrived in Chartres in 1227. He proceeded to the Cathedral, and I went through the wormhole that led from that time and place to the central highlands of Ceylon, in

310. St. Josaphat. I should have remembered that. It could have saved me a hell of a lot of trouble.

I emerged in a garden. I couldn't see it, because it was night there, but I could smell the ponderous aromas of night-blooming flowers and hear the chuckle of a running spring. Birds whooped at each other. The air was warm, and damp, and I stood there waiting while my eyes adjusted to the darkness and the moon rose over the mountains to light my way. I was on a wide grass-covered path that ran through the garden. The spring flowed into a small ceremonial pool intended for ritual ablution. My need for washing was considerably more than symbolic, and I took advantage of it. I hadn't had a bath since Rome, however long ago that had been.

The trail ran up the hill toward the looming bulbous shapes of dagobas, which housed Buddhist relics. Below me, in the darkness, I could now hear the lazy rumble of a river. As the hill became steeper, the trail became stairs, which climbed among the low wooden buildings of the Buddhist monastery surrounding the dagobas. All was darkness and silence.

"May I be of assistance?" a voice said. Behind me. Again.

This time I didn't even bother to turn around. I just stopped and let him walk around in front of me. He was a tiny, bald, ancient monk in a saffron robe. He smiled at me, shyly and toothlessly, and bowed, or rather bobbed up and down repeatedly, like some sort of foraging bird.

"I'm looking for—" Oh, hell. Why not? "I'm looking for a four-foot-high black demon covered with diamonds. Seen any lately?"

He tried to appear sad, but his eyes glowed joyfully. The result looked like mockery. "You are too late."

Damn, damn, damn. Always too late. "Where has he gone?"

"Nirvana!" he said, and stood up straight. He was not much taller than Kinbarn. "His soul has left the Wheel. Follow me, you will see."

I walked behind him, slowing my pace to his tiny shuffling steps. We walked past several of the dagobas and into a hut perched precariously on a cliffside. Inside, it was pitch-black. I heard a faint humming sound. My guide struck a flint and lit several lamps inside the hut. It grew bright enough to see.

Kinbarn sat in the middle of the room, in full lotus position. His three eyes stared off into nothingness. The faint hum came from somewhere inside of him, soft but unceasing. I walked up and touched him. He did not react. An empty bowl sat next to his left knee.

"We feed the body," the monk said. "Rice."

I thought about shouting, "Come with me, pal, you're under arrest!" It didn't seem quite appropriate. I stood and watched him for a long time, letting that hum penetrate, until I couldn't stand it any longer. It felt like something I'd been hearing all my life, but never noticed. The basic sound of the universe, maybe. The echoes inside my own skull. I didn't know. All I knew was that hearing it, out loud like that, was going to drive me crazy. I thanked the monk for his trouble, and left. He smiled after me. He did have one tooth, I saw in the lamplight, at the right, way in back.

So much for Kinbarn. The basic problem with using an addict as your runner and contact man, no matter how good he might be, is that sooner or later, being so near the stuff all the time, he'll overdose.

I pushed my way into the jungle around the monastery toward a wormhole, trying not to think about panthers and snakes. It was time to return to the rendezvous point.

Marienbad was waiting. He lay on the bottom of a large swimming pool behind an elaborate Moorish mansion in Beverly Hills, 1923. It was midmorning. The house seemed to be deserted, though I could hear the hiss of sprinklers and the low conversation of Mexican gardeners somewhere behind the hedges. I sat down in one of the chairs by the side of the pool. "I want a daiquiri," I said.

Marienbad chuckled. "It is the houseboy's day off, I fear. He is assisting at a party at Cecil B. deMille's house. They are celebrating the release of his film *The Ten Commandments*. It is good to see you again, Mathias. Where is our miscreant?"

I gave him the story, both barrels. The Bishop, Solomon, R. E. Mann, Korans in New Kingdom Egypt, golden calves, Nirvana.

"Astounding!" he said. "I must say, I had half suspected such an operation."

"Why didn't you warn me about it then? You could have saved me a lot of grief."

"Mathias! And prejudice you? That would not have been professional. But you have done an excellent job, nonetheless. Leaving the well-larded Mr. Mann to be repasted by hungry Aztec religionists was a stroke of genius. I applaud you. But, as you may have concluded, our job is not yet finished. We have uncovered a smuggling operation, incredible for its great size and its lack of scruples. Religious faith! Parents spend their family's monies on sacrifices and ritual vessels, children become intoxicated with dogma and doctrine. The social fabric of life is rent apart. A young lad begins with a few of Loyola's *Spiritual Exercises* in the bathroom between classes, and before he knows it he has a cross on his back and is converting the heathen to support his own vile habit. We must put a stop to this!" His voice quivered with outrage.

I had been afraid of that. "When do I get a vacation?"

"After all this fun, you wish a vacation? Oh, very well, Mathias. I know you are difficult. One week. Go to Elizabethan London. Take in a few plays, drink some sack, roister. That was a good time for roistering. But remember, when you return, you have your work cut out for you. The villain Mann has been masticated and digested. Rylieh, and justice, have yet to be served!"

THE DEATH ARTIST

The snowshoe hare's half-eaten carcass lay under the deadfall of the figure-four trap, frozen blood crystallized on its fur, mouth still closed around the tiny piece of desiccated carrot that had served as bait. The snow was flattened around it, the rabbit's fur thrown everywhere. Jack London sniffed at the trap, laid its ears back, and growled. Canine bona fides reaffirmed, it settled on its haunches and looked expectantly up at the man. Part Samoyed, part husky, Jack's thick white fur concealed a body thin from hunger.

Elam didn't have to sniff. The stink of wolverine was malevolent in the still air. It turned the saliva that had come into his mouth at the thought of roasted hare into something spoiled. He spat. "Damn!" The trap couldn't be descented. He'd have to make another. No animal would come anywhere near a trap that smelled like that. The wolverine probably hadn't even been hungry.

He pulled the dry carrot from the rabbit's mouth and flung the remains off among the trees. The deadfall and the sticks of the figure four followed it, vanishing in puffs of snow.

"That's the last one, Jack," Elam said. "Nothing again." The dog whined.

They set off among the dark smooth trunks of the maples and beeches, Elam's snowshoes squeaking in the freshly fallen snow. The dog turned its head, disturbed by the unprofessional noise, then loped off to investigate the upturned roots of a fallen tree. A breeze from the

The Death Artist   119

great lake to the north pushed its way through the trees, shouldering clumps of snow from the branches as it passed. A cardinal flashed from bough to bough, bright against the clearing evening sky.

Elam, a slender, graceful man, walked with his narrow shoulders hunched up, annoyed by the chilly bombardment from above. His clothing was entirely of furry animal pelts sewn crudely together. His thick hat was muskrat, his jacket fox and beaver, his mittens rabbit, his pants elk. At night he slept in a sack made of a grizzly's hide. How had he come to be here? Had he killed those animals, skinned them, cured their hides? He didn't know.

At night, sometimes, before he went to sleep, Elam would lie in his lean-to and, by the light of the dying fire, examine these clothes, running his hands through the fur, seeking memories in their thick softness. The various pelts were stitched neatly together. Had he done the sewing? Or had a wife or a sister? The thought gave him a curious feeling in the pit of his stomach. He rather suspected that he had always been alone. Weariness would claim him quickly, and he would huddle down in the warmth of the bear fur and fall asleep, questions unanswered.

Tree roots examined, Jack London returned to lead the way up the ridge. It was a daily ritual, practiced just at sunset, and the dog knew it well. The tumbled glacial rocks were now hidden under snow, making the footing uncertain. Elam carried his snowshoes under one arm as he climbed.

The height of the ridge topped the bare trees. To the north, glowing a deceptively warm red, was the snow-covered expanse of the great lake, where Elam often saw the dark forms of wolves, running and reveling in their temporary triumph over the water that barred their passage to the islands the rest of the year.

Elam had no idea what body of water it was. He had tentatively decided on Lake Superior, though it could have been Lake Winnipeg, or for that matter, Lake Baikal. Elam sat down on a rock and stared at the deep north, where stars already gleamed in the sky. Perhaps he had it all wrong, and a new Ice Age was here, and this was a frozen Victoria Nyanza.

"Who am I, Jack? Do you know?"

The dog regarded him quizzically, used to the question by now. The man who's supposed to get us some food, the look said. Philosophical discussions later.

"Did I come here myself, Jack, or was I put here?"

Weary of the pointless and one-sided catechism, the dog was barking at a jay that had ventured too close. It circled for a moment, squawked, and shot off back into the forest.

The lake wind freshened and grew colder, driving the last clouds from the sky. The exposed skin on Elam's cheeks tightened. "Let's go, Jack." He pulled off a mitten and plunged his hand into a pocket, feeling his last chunk of pemmican, greasy and hard.

Aside from a few pathetically withered bits of carrot, which he needed to bait his traps, this was the last bit of food left him. He'd been saving it for an emergency. Every trap on the trapline that ran through these woods had been empty or befouled by wolverines, even in a hard winter that should have driven animals to eat anything. He would eat the pemmican that night.

Man and dog started their descent down the twilit reach of the ridge's other side. As they reached the base, Elam, his hand once again feeling the pemmican, afraid that it too would vanish before he could eat it, took too long a step and felt his right foot slide on the icy face of a tilted rock. His left foot caught in the narrow crack of an ice-shattered boulder, which grabbed him like a tight fist. The world flung itself forward at him. He felt the dull snap in his leg as the icy rock met his face.

He awoke to the warm licks of Jack London's tongue turning instantly cold on his face. He lay tumbled on his back among the rocks, head tilting downward, trees looming overhead. Annoyed, he pushed back and tried to stand. Searing agony in his leg brought bile to the back of his throat and a hot sweat over his body. He moaned and almost lost consciousness again, then held himself up on his elbows. His face was cut, some of his teeth were cracked, he could taste the blood in his mouth, but his leg, his leg . . . he looked down.

His left leg bent at an unnatural angle just below the knee. The leather of his trousers was soaked black with blood. Compund fracture of the . . . tibia? Fibula? For one distracted instant naming the shattered bone was the most important thing in the world. It obscured the knowledge that he was going to die.

He shifted position and moaned again. The biting pain in his leg grew sharp burning teeth whenever he moved, but wore the edges off if he lay still, subsiding to a gnaw. With a sudden effort, he pulled the leg straight, then fell back, gasping harshly. It made no difference, of course, but seeing the leg at that angle made him uncomfortable. It looked better this way, not nearly so painful.

He patted the dog on the head. "Sorry, Jack. I screwed up." The dog whined in agreement. Elam fell back and let the darkness take him.

His body did not give up so easily. He regained consciousness sometime later, the frenzied whining and yelping of his dog sounding in his ears. He lay prone in the snow, his hands dug in ahead of him. His mittens were torn, and he could not feel his hands.

He rolled onto his back and looked over his feet. Full night had come, but the starlight and the moon were enough to see the trail his body had left through the snow. Elam sighed. What a waste of time. The pain in his broken leg was almost gone, as was all other feeling from the thighs down. He spat. The spittle crackled on the snow. Damn cold. And the dog was annoying him with its whining.

"Sure, boy, sure," he said, gasping from the cold weight of death on his chest. "Just a minute, Jack. Just a minute."

He pulled what was left of the fur glove off with his chin and reached the unfeeling claw of his hand into his pocket. It took a dozen tries before it emerged holding the pemmican.

He finally managed to open the front of his jacket and unlace his shirt. Cold air licked in eagerly. He smeared the greasy, hard pemmican over his chest and throat like a healing salve. Its rancid odor bit at his nose, and despite himself, he felt a moment of hunger. He shoved the rest of the piece down deep into his shirt.

"Here, Jack," he said. "Here. Dinner." The moon rode overhead, half in sunlight, the other half covered with glittering lines and spots.

The dog snuffled, suddenly frightened and suspicious. Elam reached up and patted it on the head. Jack London moved forward. Smelling the meat, the dog overcame its caution at its master's strange behavior and it began to lick eagerly at Elam's throat and chest. The dog was desperately hungry. In its eagerness, a sharp tooth cut the man's skin, and thick warm blood welled out. The tongue licked more quickly. More cuts. More blood, steaming aromatically in the cold air. And the dog was hungry. The smell penetrated to the deepest parts of its brain, finally destroying the overlay of training, habit, and love. The dog's teeth tore and it began to feed.

And in that instant, Elam remembered. He saw the warm forests of his youth, and the face, so much like his, that had become his own. Justice had at last been done. Elam was going to die. He smiled slightly, gasped once, then his eyes glazed blank.

When it was sated, and realized what it had done, the dog howled its pain at the stars. It then sprang into the forest and ran madly, leaving the man's tattered remains far behind.

"Is that all you are going to do from now on?" Reqata said. "Commit suicide? Just lie down and die? Nice touch, I admit, the dog." She held his shoulder in a tight grip and looked past him with her phosphorescent eyes. "A real Elam touch."

Five dark ribs supported the smooth yellow stone of the dome. They revealed the green gleam of beetle carapaces in the light of the flames hanging in a hexagon around the central axis of the view chamber. Rows of striated marble seats climbed the chamber in concentric circles. The inhabitants of these seats stared down at the corpse lying in the snow at their feet.

Elam was himself startled at his clone's acquiescence in its own death, but he was surrounded by admirers before he could answer her. They moved past him, murmuring, gaining haut by their admiration for the subtlety of his work.

Elam stared past them at his own corpse, a sheen of frost already obscuring the face, turning it into an abstract composition. He had died well. He always did. His mind, back from the clone with its memories restored, seemed to rattle loosely around his skull. His skin was slick with amniotic fluid, his joints gritty. Nothing fit together. Reqata's hand on his shoulder seemed to bend the arbitrarily shaped bones, reminding him of his accidental quality.

"An artist who works with himself as both raw materials and subject can never transcend either," Reqata said.

Her scorn cut through the admiration around him. He looked up at her, and she smiled back with ebony teeth, flicking feathery eyelashes. She raised one hand in an angular gesture that identified her instantly, whatever body she was in.

"And how does the choreographer of mass death transcend her material?" Elam's mind had been gone for weeks, dying in a frozen forest, and Reqata had grown bored in his absence. She needed entertainment. Even lovers constantly dueled with haut, the indefinable quality that all players at the Floating Game understood implicitly. Reqata had much haut. Elam had more.

He squirmed. Was his bladder full, or did he always feel this way?

"Mass death, as you put it, is limited by practical problems," Reqata answered. "Killing one man is an existential act. Killing a million would be a historic act, at least to the Bound. Killing them all would be a divine act." She ran her fingers through his hair. He smelled the winy crispness of her breath. "Killing yourself merely smacks of lack of initiative. I'm disappointed in you, Elam. You used to fight before you died."

"I did, didn't I?" He remembered the desperate struggles of his early works, the ones that had gained him his haut. Men dying in mine shafts, on cliffsides, in predator-infested jungles. Men who had never stopped fighting. Each of those men had been himself. Something had changed.

"Tell me something," Reqata said, leaning forward. Her tongue darted across his earlobe. "Why do you always look so peaceful just before you die?"

A chill spread up his spine. He'd wondered the same thing himself. "Do I?" He squeezed the words out. He always paid. Five or ten minutes of memory, the final instants of life. The last thing he remembered from this particular work was pulling the pemmican from his pocket. After that, blackness. The dying clone Elam understood something the resurrected real Elam did not.

"Certainly. Don't be coy. Look at the grin on that corpse's frozen face." She slid into the seat next to him, draping a leg negligently into the aisle. "I've tried dying. Not as art, just as experience. I die screaming. My screams echo for weeks." She shuddered, hands pressed over her ears. Her current body, as usual, had a high rib cage and small firm breasts. Elam found himself staring at them. "But enough." Reqata flicked him with a fingernail, scratching his arm. "Now that you're done, I have a project for you to work on—"

"Perhaps each of you just gets a view of what awaits on the other side," a voice drawled.

"Don't lecture me on the absolute inertia of the soul," Reqata said, disconcerted. "No one's giving our clones a free peek at eternity, Lammiela."

"Perhaps not." A long elegant woman, Lammiela always looked the same, to everyone's distress, for she only had one body. She smiled slowly. "Or perhaps heaven is already so filled with the souls of your clones that there won't be any room for you when you finally arrive."

Reqata stood up, fury in the rise of her shoulders. Because of her past irregularities, Lammiela had an ambiguous status, and Reqata hated risking haut in arguing with her. Usually, Reqata couldn't help herself. "Be careful, Lammiela. You don't know anything about it." And perhaps, Elam found himself thinking, perhaps Reqata feared Death indeed.

"Oh, true enough." Lammiela sat. "Ssarna's passing has everyone on edge. I keep forgetting." Her arrival had driven the last of the connoisseurs away, and the three of them sat alone in the viewing chamber.

"You don't forget, Mother," Elam said wearily. "You do it quite on purpose."

"That's unfair, Elam." She examined him. "You look well. Dying agrees with you." She intertwined her long fingers and rested her chin on them. Her face was subtly lined, as if shaded by an engraver. Her eyes were dark blue, the same as Elam's own. "Ssarna, they say, was withered in her adytum, dry as dust. The last time I saw her, which must have been at that party on top of that miserable mountain in the Himalayas, she was a tiny slip of a girl, prepubescent. Long golden . . . *tresses.* That must be the correct word." She shook her head with weary contempt. "Though she disguised herself as young, old age found her in her most private chamber. And after old age had had his way with her, he gave her to Death. They have an arrangement."

"And the first of them is enjoying you now," Reqata said. "How soon before the exchange comes?"

Lammiela's head jerked, but she did not turn. "How have you been, Elam?" She smiled at him, and he was suddenly surrounded by the smell of her perfume, as if it were a trained animal she wore around her neck and had ordered to attack. The smell was dark and spicy. It reminded him of the smell of carrion, of something dead in the hot sun, thick and insistent. He found himself holding his breath, and stood up quickly, suddenly nauseated. Nauseated, yet somehow excited. A child's feeling, the attraction of the vile, the need to touch and smell that which disgusts. Children will put anything in their mouths. He felt as if maggots were crawling under his fingernails.

"Air," Elam muttered. "I need. . . ." He walked up the striated marble stairs to the balcony above. Locked in their own conflict, the women did not follow. The warm summer air outside smelled of herbs and the dry flowers of chaparral. He clamped his teeth together and convinced himself that the flowers did not mask the smell of rotting flesh.

Sunset turned the day lavender. The view chamber's balcony hung high above the city, which flowed purposefully up the narrow valleys, leaving the dry hills bare, covered with flowers, acacia trees, and the spiky crystal plants that had evolved under some distant sun. The Mediterranean glinted far below.

Lights had come on in the city, illuminating its secret doorways. No one lived here. The Incarnate had other fashions, and the Bound were afraid of the ancient living cities, preferring to build their own. A Bound city could be seen burning closer to the water, its towers asserting themselves against the darkening sky. Tonight, many of the Incarnate who had witnessed Elam's performance would descend upon it for the evanescent excitments of those who lived out their lives bound to one body.

So this place was silent, save for the low resonance of bells, marking the hours for its absent dwellers. The city had been deserted for thousands of years, but was ready for someone to return. The insectlike shapes of aircars fluttered up against the stars as Elam's audience went their separate ways.

A coppery half-moon hung on the horizon, the invisible half of its face etched with colored lines and spots of flickering light. When he was young, Lammiela had told him that the moon was inhabited by huge machines from some previous cycle of existence. The whole circle of a new moon crawled with light, an accepted feature. No one wondered at the thoughts of those intelligent machines, who looked up at the ripe blue-green planet that hung in their black sky.

"You should lie down," Lammiela said, "and rest." Her perfume was cloying and spicy. Though it did not smell even remotely of carrion, Elam still backed away, pushing himself against the railing, and let the evening breeze carry the scent from him. Starlings swooped around the tower.

"You should get up," Reqata said, from somewhere behind her, "and run."

A blast of freezing air made him shiver. He took a step and looked down at the now hoarfrost-covered corpse in the deserted rotunda.

No Incarnate alive knew how the ancient machines worked. The corpse: was it just an image of the one in the frozen Michigan forest? Or had the rotunda's interior moved its spectators to hover over that forest in fact?

Or was this body a perfect duplicate, here in the hills of Provence, of that other one? The knowledge was lost. No one knew what lay within the sphere of image. But Elam did know one thing: the cold winds of winter did not blow out of it.

Elam spotted the zeppelins about two and a half hours out of Kalgoorlie. Their colors were gaudy against the green fields and the blue Nullarbor Sea. Frost glittered on the sides away from the morning sun. Elam felt a physical joy, for the zeppelins had been caught completely by surprise. They drifted in the heavy morning air, big fat targets.

They were shuttling troops from somewhere to the North, in central Australia, to participate in one of those incomprehensible wars the Bound indulged in. Reqata had involved herself, in her capricious way, and staked haut on the outcome of the invasion of Eyre, the southern state.

Elam could see the crewmen leaping into their tiny flyers, their wings straightening in the sun like butterflies emerging from their chrysalis, but it was too late. Their zeppelins were doomed.

Elam picked his target, communicating his choice to the other bumblebees, a few Incarnate who, amused at his constant struggle with Reqata, had joined him for the fun. The microwave signal felt like a directed whisper, save for the fact that it made his earlobes itch. He aimed for a bright green deltoid with markings that made it look like a giant spotted frog. For an instant the image took a hold of his mind, and he imagined catching a frog, grabbing it, and feeling its frightened wetness in his hand, the frantic beating of its heart. . . .

He pushed the thought away, upset at his loss of control. Timing was critical. A change in the angle of his wing stroke brought him back into position.

Elam was gorgeous. About a meter long, he had short iridescent wings. A single long-distance optic tracked the target while two bulbous 270-degree peripherals checked the mathematical line of bumblebees to either side of him. Reqata was undoubtedly aboard one of the zeppelins, raging at the unexpected attack. The defending flyers were wide-faced black men, some odd purebred strain. Elam imagined the black Reqata, gesturing sharply as she arranged a defense. It was the quality of her movement that made her beautiful.

A steel ball whizzed past his left wing. A moment later he heard the faint *tock!* of the zeppelin's catapult. It took only one hit to turn a bumblebee into a stack of expensive kindling. Elam tucked one wing, tumbled, and straightened out again, coming in at his target. He unhooked his fighting legs and brought their razor edges forward.

The zeppelins were billowing, changing shape. Sudden flares disturbed Elam's infrared sensors, making him dizzy, unsure of his target. Flying the bumblebees all the way out of Kalgoorlie without any lighter-than-air support craft had been a risk. They had to knock the zeppelins to the ground and parasitize them for reactive metals. The bumblebees would be vulnerable to a ground attack as they crawled clumsily over the wreckage, but no one gained haut without taking chances. He dodged past the defending flyers, not bothering to cut them. That would only delay him.

The green frog was now below him, swelling, rippling, dropping altitude desperately. He held it in his hand where he had caught it, amid the thick rushes. The other kids were gone, somewhere, and he was alone. The frog kicked and struggled. It had voided its bowels in his hand, and he felt the wet slime. The air was hot and thick underneath the cottonwoods. Something about the frog's frantic struggle for life annoyed him. It seemed odious that something so wet and slimy would wish to remain alive. He laid the frog down on a flat rock and, with calm deliberation, brought another rock down on its head. Its legs kicked and kicked.

The other zeppelins seemed to have vanished. All that remained was the frog, its guts lying out in the hot sun, putrefying as he watched. Fluids dripped down the rock, staining it. He wanted to slash it apart with fire, to feel the flare as it gave up its life. The sun seared down on his shoulders.

With a sudden fury, the zeppelin turned on him. He

found himself staring into its looming mouth. A hail of steel balls flew past him, and he maneuvered desperately to avoid them. He didn't understand why he had come so close without attacking.

Two balls ripped simultaneously through his right wing, sending flaring pain through the joints. He twisted down, hauling in on the almost nonfunctional muscles. If he pulled the wing in to a stable tip, he could glide downward. Green fields spiraled up at him, black houses with high-peaked roofs, colorful gardens. Pale faces peered up at him from the fields. Military vehicles had pulled up on a sandy road, the dark muzzles of their guns tracking him.

The right wing was flopping loose, sending waves of pain through his body. He veered wildly, land and sky switching position. Pulling up desperately, he angled his cutting leg and sliced off the loose part of his wing. Hot pain slashed through him.

He had finally managed to stabilize his descent, but it was too late. A field of corn floated up to meet him. For an instant, everything was agony.

"I want something primitive," Elam said, as the doctor slid a testing limb into the base of his spine. "Something prehistoric."

"All of the human past is prehistoric," Dr. Abias said. He withdrew the limb with a cold tickle, and retracted it into his body. "Your body is healthy."

Elam stood up, swinging his arms, getting used to his new proportions. His current body was lithe, gold-skinned, small-handed: designed to Reqata's specifications. She had some need of him in this form, and Elam found himself apprehensive. He had no idea if she was still angry about her defeat over Australia. "No, Abias. I mean before *any* history. Before man knew himself to be man."

"Neanderthal?" Abias murmured, hunching across the floor on his many legs. "Pithecanthropus? Australopithecus?"

"I don't know what any of those words mean," Elam said. Sometimes his servant's knowledge bothered him. What right did the Bound have to know so much when the Incarnate could dispose of their destinies so thoroughly?

Abias turned to look back at him with his multiple oculars, brown human eyes with no face, pupils dilated. He was a machine, articulated and segmented, gleaming as if anointed with rare oils. Each of his eight moving limbs was both an arm and a leg, as if his body had been designed to work in orbit. Perhaps it had. As he had pointed out, most of the past was prehistory.

"It doesn't matter," Abias said. "I will look into it."

A Bound, Abias had been assigned to Elam by Lammiela. Punished savagely for a crime against the Incarnate, his body had been confiscated and replaced by some ancient device. Abias now ran Elam's team of cloned bodies. He was considered one of the best trainers in the Floating Game. He was so good and his loyalty so absolute that Elam had steadfastly refused to discover what crime he had committed, fearing that the knowledge would interfere in their professional relationship.

"Do that," Elam said. "I have a new project in mind." He walked across the wide, open room, feeling the sliding of unfamiliar joints. This body, a clone of his own, had been extensively modified by Abias, until there were only traces of his own nature in it. A plinth was laid with earrings, wrist and ankle bracelets, body paints, scent bottles, all supplied by Reqata. He began to put them on.

Light shone from overhead through semicircular openings in the vault. A rough-surfaced ovoid curved up through the floor in the room's center. It was Elam's adytum, the most secret chamber where his birth body lay. After his crash in Australia, he had woken up in it for an instant, with a feeling of agony, as if every part of his body were burning. The thought still made him shudder.

An Incarnate's adytum was his most strongly guarded space, for when his real body died, he died as well. There could be no transfer of consciousness to a cloned body once the original was dead. The ancient insolent machines that provided the ability to transfer the mind did not permit it, and since no one understood the machines, no one could do anything about it. And killing an

Incarnate's birth body was the only way to truly commit murder.

Elam slid on a bracelet. "Do you know who attacked me?"

"No one has claimed responsibility," Abias answered. "Did you recognize anything of the movement?"

Elam thought about the billowing froglike zeppelin. It hadn't been Reqata, he was sure of that. She would have made certain that he knew. But it could have been almost anyone else.

"Something went wrong in the last transfer," Elam said, embarrassed at bringing up such a private function, even to his servant. "I woke up in my adytum."

Abias stood still, unreadable. "A terrible malfunction. I will look into it."

"Just make sure it doesn't happen again." The party was in the hills above the city of El'lie. Water from the northern rivers poured here from holes in the rock and swirled through an elaborate maze of waterways. It finally reached one last great pool, which extended terrifyingly off the rocky slope, as if ready to tip and spill, drowning the city below it. The white rock of the pool's edge extended downward some thousands of feet, a polished sheet like the edge of the world. Far below, cataracts spilled from the pool's bottom toward the thirsty city.

Elam stood on a terrace and gazed down into the water. Reqata floated there, glistening as the afternoon sun sank over the ocean to the west. She was a strange creature, huge, all sleekly iridescent curves, blue and green, based on some creature humans had once encountered in their forgotten travels across the galaxy. She sweated color into the water, heavy swirls of bright orange and yellow sinking into the depths. Until a few hours before she had been wearing a slender gold-skinned body like Elam's.

"They seem peaceful," she whispered, her voice echoing across the water. "But the potential for violence is extreme."

Reqata had hauled him on a preliminary tour of El'lie, site of her next artwork. He remembered the fresh bodies hung in tangles of chain on a granite wall, a list of their crimes pasted on their chests; the tense market, men and women with shaved foreheads and jewels in their eyebrows, the air thick with spices; the lazy insolence of a gang of men, their faces tattooed with angry swirls, as they pushed through the market crowd on their way to a proscribed patriarchal religious service; the great tiled temples of the Goddesses that lined the market square.

"When will they explode?" Elam said.

"Not before the fall, when the S'tana winds blow down from the mountains. You'll really see something then." Hydraulic spines erected and sank down on her back, and she made them make a characteristic gesture, sharp and emphatic. If she was angry about what had happened in Australia, she concealed it. That frightened Elam more than open anger would have. Reqata had a habit of delayed reaction.

Reqata was an expert at exploiting obscure hostilities among the Bound, producing dramatically violent conflicts with blood spilling picturesquely down carved staircases; heads piled up in heaps, engraved ivory spheres thrust into their mouths; lines of severed hands on bronze poles, fingers pointing toward Heaven. That was her art. She had wanted advice. Elam had not been helpful.

Glowing lights floated above the pool, swirling in response to incomprehensible tropisms. No one knew how to control them anymore, and they moved by their own rules. A group of partyers stood on the far side of the pool, their bright-lit reflections stretching out across the glassy water.

"This water's thousands of feet deep," Reqata murmured. "The bottom's piled up with forgotten things. Boats. Gold cups. The people from the city come up here and drop things in for luck."

"Why should dropping things and forgetting about them be lucky?" Elam asked.

"I don't know. It's not always lucky to remember everything."

Elam stripped off his gown and dove into the dark water. Reqata made a bubbling sound of delight. He stroked the spines on her back, feeling them swell and deflate. He ran a cupped hand up her side. Her glowing solar sweat worked its way between his fingers and dripped down, desperate to reach its natural place somewhere in the invisible depths.

"Put on a body like this," she said. "We can swim the deep oceans and make love there, among the fish."

"Yes," he said, not meaning it. "We can."

"Elam," she said. "What happened on the balcony after we saw you die in the forest? You seemed terrified."

Elam thought, instead, of the frog. Had his memories been real? Or could Reqata have laid a trap for him? "Just a moment of nausea. Nothing."

Reqata was silent for a moment. "She hates you, you know. Lammiela. She utterly hates you."

Her tone was vicious. Here it was, vengeance for the trick he had pulled over the Nullarbor Sea. Her body shuddered, and he was suddenly conscious of how much larger than he she now was. She could squish him against the side of the pool without any difficulty. He would awake in his own chamber, in another body. Killing him was just insulting, not fatal. Perhaps it *had* been her in that frog zeppelin.

He swam slowly away from her. "I don't know what you're talking about."

"Of course you don't. You're an expert at forgetting, at just lying down, dying, and forgetting. She hates you for what you did. For what you did to your sister!" Her voice was triumphant.

Elam felt the same searing pain he had felt when he awoke for one choking instant in his adytum. "I don't know what you're talking about," he said, as he pulled himself out of the water.

"I know! That's just the problem."

"Tell me what you mean." He kept his voice calm.

Something moved heavily in the darkness, and a row of chairs overturned with a clatter. Elam turned away from the pool. His heart pounded. A burst of laughter sounded from across the pool. The party was continuing, but the guests were impossibly far away, like a memory of childhood, unreachable and useless.

A head rose up out of the darkness, a head twice the size of Elam's body. It was a metal egg, dominated by two expressionless eyes. Behind dragged a long multi-limbed body, shiny and obscene. Elam screamed in unreasoning and senseless terror.

The creature moved forward, swaying its head from side to side. Acid saliva drooled from beneath its crystal teeth, splashing and fizzing on the marble terrace. It was incomprehensibly ancient, something from the long-forgotten past. It swept its tail around and dragged Elam toward it.

For an instant, Elam was paralyzed, staring at the strange beauty of the dragon's teeth as they moved toward him. Then he struggled against the iron coil of the tail. His body still had traces of oil, and he slid out, stripping skin. He dove between the dragon's legs, bruising his bones on the terrace.

The dragon whipped around quickly, cornering him. With a belch, it sprayed acid over him. It burned down his shoulder, bubbling as it dissolved his skin.

"Damn you!" he shouted, and threw himself at the dragon's head. It didn't pull back quickly enough, and he plunged his fist into its left eye. Its surface resisted, then popped, spraying fluid. The dragon tossed its head, flinging Elam across the ground.

He pulled himself to his feet, feeling the pain of shattered ribs. Blood dribbled down his chin. One of his legs would not support his weight. The massive head lowered down over him, muck pouring out of the destroyed eye. Elam grabbed for the other eye, but he had no strength left. Foul-smelling acid flowed over him, sloughing his flesh off with the sound of frying bacon. He stayed on his feet, trying to push imprecations between his destroyed lips. The last thing he saw was the crystal teeth, lowering toward his head.

Lammiela's house was the abode of infinity. The endless rooms were packed with the junk of a hundred worlds. The information here was irreplaceable, unduplicated anywhere else. No one came to visit, and the artifacts, data cubes, and dioramas rested in silence.

At some time in the past millennia, human beings had explored as far inward as the galactic core and so far outward that the galaxy had hung above them like a captured undersea creature, giving up its light to intergalactic space. They had moved through globular clusters of ancient suns and explored areas of stellar synthesis. They had raised monuments on distant planets. After some centuries of this, they had returned to Earth, built their mysterious cities on a planet that must have been nothing but old legend, and settled down, content to till the aged soil and watch the sun rise and set. And, with magnificent insouciance, they had forgotten everything, leaving their descendants ignorant.

Lammiela sat in the corner watching Elam. Her body, though elegant, was somehow bent, as if she had been cut from an oddly shaped piece of wood by a clever wood-carver utilizing the limitations of his material. That was true enough, Elam reflected, examining the person who was both his parents.

When young, Lammiela had found a ship somewhere on Earth's moon, tended by the secret mechanisms that made their lives there, and gone forth to explore the old spaces. No one had any interest in following her, but somehow her exploits had gained enough attention that she had obtained extraordinary privileges.

"It's curious," she said. "Our friends the Bound have skills that we Incarnate do not even dream of, because the machines our ancestors left us have no interest in them." She looked thoughtful for a moment. "It's surprising, some of the things the Bound can do."

"Like make you both my father and my mother," Elam said.

Her face was shadowed. "Yes. There is that."

Lammiela had been born male, named Laurance. But Laurance had felt himself to be a woman. No problem for one of the Incarnate, who could be anything they wished. Laurance could have slept securely in his adytum and put female bodies on for his entire life. But Laurance did not think that way. He had gone to the Bound, and they had changed him to a woman.

"When the job was finished, I was pregnant," Lammiela said. "Laurance's sperm had fertilized my new ova. I don't know if it was a natural consequence of the rituals they used." Her muscles tightened with the memories. Tendons stood out on the backs of her hands. "They kept me conscious through it all. Pain is their price. They slew the male essence. I saw it, screaming before me. Laurance, burning."

It had cost most of her haut to do it. Dealings with the Bound inevitably involved loss of status.

"I still see him sometimes," she said.

"Who?" Elam asked.

"Your father, Laurance." Her eyes narrowed. "They didn't kill him well enough, you see. They told me they did, but he's still around." Her eyes darted, as if expecting to find Laurance hiding behind a diorama.

Elam felt a chill, a sharp feeling at the back of his neck, as if someone with long, long nails were stroking him there. "But you're him, Lammiela. He's not someone else."

"Do you really know so much about identity, Elam?" She sighed, relaxing. "You're right, of course. Still, was it I who stood in the Colonnade at Hrlad?" She pointed at a hologram of a long line of rock obelisks, the full galaxy rising beyond them. "I'm not sure I remember it, not as if I had been there. It was legend, you know. A bedtime story. But Hrlad is real. So is Laurance. You look like him, you know. You have your father's eyes."

She stared at him coldly, and he, for the first time, thought that Reqata might have spoken truly. Perhaps his mother did indeed hate him.

"I made my choice," she said. "I can never go back. The Bound won't let me. I am a woman, and a mother."

Lammiela did not live in the city where most of the Incarnate made their home. She lived on a mountainside, bleak and alone, the rigid curving walls of her house holding off the snow. She moved her dwelling periodically, from seashore to desert to mountain. She had no adytum, with its body, to lug with her. Elam, somehow, remembered deep forest when he was growing up, interspersed with sunny meadows. The vision wasn't clear. Nothing was clear.

After this most recent death, Elam had once again awakened in his adytum. He'd felt the fluid flowing through his lungs, and the darkness pressing down on his open eyes. Fire had burned through his veins, but there was no air to scream with. Then he had awakened again, normally, on a pallet in the light.

"Mother," he said, looking off at a broad-spectrum hologram of Sirius that spilled vicious white light across the corner of the room, too bright to look at directly without filters. "Am I truly your only child?"

Lammiela's face was still. "Most things are secrets for the first part of their existence, and forgotten thereafter. I suppose there must be a time in the middle when they are known. Who told you?"

"Does it matter?"

"Yes. It was thrown at you as a weapon, wasn't it?"

Elam sighed. "Yes. Reqata."

"Ah, yes. I should have guessed. Dear Reqata. Does she love you, Elam?"

The question took him aback. "She says she does."

"I'm sure she means it then. I wonder what it is about you that she loves. Is that where the discussion ended then? With the question?"

"Yes. We were interrupted." Elam described the dragon's attack.

"Ah, how convenient. Reqata was always a master of timing. Who was it, do you suppose?" She looked out of the circular window at the mountain tundra, the land falling away to a vast ice field, just the rocky peaks of mountains thrusting through it. "No one gains haut anonymously."

"No one recognized the style. Or if they did, they did not admit it." The scene was wrong, Elam thought. It should have been trees: smooth-trunked beeches, heavy oaks. The sun had slanted through them as if the leaves themselves generated the light.

"So why are you here, Elam? Are you looking for the tank in which that creature was grown? You may search for it if you like. Go ahead."

"No!" Elam said. "I want to find my sister." And he turned away and ran through the rooms of the house, past the endless vistas of stars that the rest of the human race had comfortably forgotten. Lammiela silently followed, effortlessly sliding through the complex displays, as Elam stumbled, now falling into an image of a kilometer-high cliff carved with human figures, now into a display of ceremonial masks with lolling tongues. He suddenly remembered running through these rooms, their spaces much larger then, pursued by a small violent figure that left no place to hide.

In a domed room he stopped at a wall covered with racks of dark metal drawers. He pushed a spot and one slid open. Inside was a small animal, no bigger than a cat, dried as if left out in the sun. It was recognizably the dragon, curled around itself, its crystalline teeth just visible through its pulled-back lips.

Lammiela looked down at it. "You two never got along. You would have thought that you would . . . but I guess that was a foolish assumption. You tormented her with that thing, that . . . monster. It gave her screaming nightmares. Once, you propped it by her bed so that she would see it when she woke up. For three nights after that she didn't sleep." She slid the drawer shut.

"Who was she?" Elam demanded, taking her shoulders. She met his gaze. "It's no longer something that will just be forgotten."

She weakly raised a hand to her forehead, but Elam wasn't fooled. His mother had dealt with dangers that could have killed her a dozen times over. He tightened his grip on her shoulders. "Your sister's name was Orfea. Lovely name, don't you think? I think Laurance picked it out."

Elam could remember no sister. "Was she older or younger?"

"Neither. You were split from one ovum, identical twins. One was given an androgen bath and became you, Elam. The other was female: Orfea. God, how you grew to hate each other! It frightened me. And you were both so talented. I still have some of her essence around, I think."

"I . . . what happened to her? Where is she?"

"That was the one thing that consoled me, all these

years. The fact that you didn't remember. I think that was what allowed you to survive."

"What? Tell me!"

Lammiela took only one step back, but it seemed that she receded much farther. "She was murdered. She was just a young girl. So young."

Elam looked at her, afraid of the answer. He didn't remember what had happened, and he could still see hatred in his mother's eyes. "Did they ever find out who did it?" he asked softly.

She seemed surprised by the question. "Oh, there was never any doubt. She was killed by a young friend of yours. He is now your servant. Abias."

"I have to say that it was in extremely poor taste," Reqata said, not for the first time. "Death is a fine performance, but there's no reason to perform it at a dinner party. Particularly in my presence."

She got up from the bed and stretched. This torso was wide, and well-muscled. Once again, the rib cage was high, the breasts small. Elam wondered if, in the secrecy of her adytum, Reqata was male. He had never seen her in any other than a female body.

"Just out of curiosity," Elam said. "Could you tell who the dragon was?" He ran his hand over the welts on his side, marks of Reqata's fierce love.

She glanced back at him, eyelids half lowered over wide violet eyes. She gauged if her answer would affect her haut. "Now *that* was a good trick, Elam. If I hadn't been looking right at you, I would have guessed that it was you behind those glass fangs."

She walked emphatically across the room, the slap of her bare feet echoing from the walls, and stood, challengingly, on the curve of Elam's adytum. Dawn had not yet come, and light was provided by hanging globes of a blue tint that Elam found unpleasant. He had never discovered a way to adjust or replace them.

"Oh, Elam," she said. "If you are working on something, I approve. How you fought! You didn't want to die. You kept struggling until there was nothing left of you but bones. That dragon crunched them like candy canes." She shuddered, her face flushed. "It was wonderful."

Elam stretched and rolled out of the bed. As his weight left it, it rose off the floor, to vanish into the darkness overhead. The huge room had no other furniture.

"What do you know about my sister?" he asked.

Reqata lounged back on the adytum, curling her legs. "I know she existed, I know she's dead. More than you did, apparently." She ran her hands up her sides, cupping her breasts. "You know, the first stories I heard of you don't match you. You were more like me then. Death was your art, certainly, but it wasn't your own death."

"As you say," Elam said, stalking toward her, "I don't remember."

"How could you have forgotten?" She rested her hands on the rough stone of the adytum. "This is where you are, Elam. If I ripped this open, I could kill you. Really kill you. Dead."

"Want to try it?" He leaned over her. She rested back, lips parted, and dug her fingernails in a circle around his nipple.

"It could be exciting. Then I could see who you really were."

He felt the sweet bite of her nails through his skin. If he had only one body, he reflected, perhaps he could never have made love to Reqata. He couldn't have lasted.

He pushed himself forward onto her, and they made love on his adytum, above his real body as it slumbered.

Abias's kingdom was brightly lit, to Elam's surprise. He had expected a mysterious darkness. Hallways stretched in all directions, leading to chambers of silent machines and tanks filled with organs and bodies. As he stepped off the stairs, Elam realized that he had never before been down to these lower levels, even though it was as much a part of his house as any other. But this was Abias's domain. This was where the magic was done.

His bumblebee lay on a table, its dead nervous system scooped out. Dozens of tiny mechanisms crawled over it, straightening its spars, laying fragile wing material between the ribs. Elam pictured them crawling over his own body, straightening out his ribs, coring out his spinal column, resectioning his eyes.

Elam touched a panel, and a prism rose up out of the floor. In it was himself, calmly asleep. Elam always kept several standard, unmodified versions of his own body ready. That was the form in which he usually died. Elam examined the face of his clone. He had never inhabited this one, and it looked strange in consequence. No emotions had ever played over those slack features, no lines of care had ever formed on the forehead or around the eyes. The face was an infant turned physically adult.

The elaborate shape of Abias appeared in a passage and made its way toward him, segmented legs gleaming. Elam felt a moment of fear. He imagined those limbs seizing his mysterious faceless sister, Orfea, rending her, their shine dulled with her blood, sizzling smoke rising . . . he fought the images down. Abias had been a man then, if he'd been anything. He'd lost his body as a consequence of that murder.

Abias regarded him. As a Bound, and a cyborg to boot, Abias had no haut. He had no character to express, needed no gestures to show who he was. His faceless eyes were unreadable. Had he been trying to kill Elam? He had the skills and resources to have created the zeppelin, grown the dragon. But why? If he wanted to kill Elam, the real Elam, the adytum lay in his power. Those powerful limbs could rip the chamber open and drag the sleeping Elam out into the light. Elam's consciousness, in a clone somewhere else, wouldn't know what had happened, but would suddenly cease to exist.

"Is the new body ready?" Elam said abruptly.

Abias moved quietly away. After a moment's hesitation, Elam followed, deeper into the lower levels. They passed a prism where a baby with golden skin slept, growing toward the day that Elam could inhabit it, and witness Reqata's El'lie artwork. It would replace the body destroyed by the dragon. Lying on a pallet was a short heavy-boned body with a rounded jaw and beetle brows.

"It was a matter of genetic regression, based on the markers in the cytoplasmic mitochondria," Abias said, almost to himself. "The mitochondrial DNA is the timer, since it comes only from the female ancestor. The nucleic genetic material is completely scrambled. But much of it stretches back far enough. And of course we have stored orang and chimp genes as well. If you back and fill—"

"That's enough, Abias," Elam said impatiently. "It doesn't matter."

"No, of course not. It doesn't matter. But this is your Neanderthal."

Elam looked down at the face that was his own, a few hundred thousand years back into the past. "How long have I known you, Abias?"

"Since we were children," Abias said softly. "Don't you remember?"

"You know I don't remember. How could I have lived with you for so long otherwise? You killed my sister."

"How do you know that?"

"Lammiela told me that you killed Orfea."

"Ah," Abias said. "I didn't kill her, Elam." He paused. "You don't remember her."

"No. As far as I'm concerned, I have always been alone."

"Perhaps you always have been."

Elam considered this. "Are you claiming that Reqata and my mother are lying? That there never was an Orfea?"

Abias lowered all of his limbs until he was solid on the floor. "I think you should be more worried about who is trying to kill you. These attempts are not accidents."

"I know. Perhaps you."

"That's not even worth answering."

"But who would want to go around killing me repeatedly in my clones?"

"From the information we have now," Abias said, "it could be anyone. It could even be Orfea."

"Orfea?" Elam stared at him. "Didn't you just claim she never existed?"

"I did not. I said I didn't kill her. I didn't. Orfea did not die that day." His eyes closed and he was immobile. "Only I did."

* * *

It was a land that was familiar, but as Elam stalked it in his new body, he did not know whether it was familiar to him, Elam, or to the Neanderthal he now was. It was covered with a dark forest, broken by clearings, crossed by clear icy streams scattered with rocks. The air was cold and damp, a living air. His body was wrapped in fur. It was not fur from an animal he had killed himself, but something Abias had mysteriously generated, in the same way he had generated the fur Elam had worn when he died in the Michigan winter. For all he knew, it was some bizarre variant of his own scalp hair.

Since this was just an exploratory journey, the creation of below-conscious reflexes, Elam retained his own memories. They sat oddly in his head. This brain perceived things more directly, seeing each beam of sunlight through the forest canopy as a separate entity, with its own characteristics and personality, owing little to the sun from which it ultimately came.

A stream had cut a deep ravine, revealing ruins. The Neanderthal wandered among the walls, which stood knee-deep in the water, and peered thoughtfully at their bricks. He felt as if he were looking at the ruins of the incomprehensibly distant future, not the past at all. He imagined wading mammoths pushing their way through, knocking the walls over in their search for food. At the thought of a mammoth his hands itched to feel the haft of a spear, though he could certainly not kill such a beast by himself. He needed the help of his fellows, and they did not exist. He walked the Earth alone.

Something grunted in a pool that had once been a basement. He sloshed over to it, and gazed down at the frog. It sat on the remains of a windowsill, pulsing its throat. Elam reached down . . . and thought of the dying frog, shuddering its life out in his hand. He tied it down, limbs outspread, and played the hot cutting beam over it. It screamed and begged as the smoke from its guts rose up into the clear sky.

Elam jerked his hand back from the frog, which, startled, dove into the water and swam away. He turned and climbed the other side of the ravine. He was frightened by the savagery of the thought that had possessed him. When he pulled himself over the edge he found himself in an area of open rolling hills, the forest having retreated to the colder northern slopes.

The past seemed closer here, as if he had indeed lived it.

He *had* hated Orfea. The feeling came to him like the memory of a shaman's rituals, fearsome and complex. It seemed that the hate had always been with him. That form, with his shape and gestures, loomed before him.

The memories were fragmentary, more terrifying than reassuring, like sharp pieces of colored glass. He saw the face of a boy he knew to be Abias, dark-eyed, curly-haired, intent. He bent over an injured animal, one of Elam's victims, his eyes shiny with tears. Young, he already possessed a good measure of that ancient knowledge the Bound remembered. In this case the animal was beyond healing. With a calmly dismissive gesture, Abias broke its neck.

The leaves in the forest moved of their own will, whispering to each other of the coming of the breeze, which brushed its cool fingers across the back of Elam's neck.

He remembered Orfea, a slender girl with dark hair, but he never saw her clearly. Her image appeared only in reflections, side images, glimpses of an arm or a strand of hair. And he saw himself, a slender boy with dark hair, twin to Orfea. He watched himself as he tied a cat down to a piece of wood, spreading it out as it yowled. There was a fine downy hair on his back, and he could count the vertebrae as they moved under his smooth young skin. The arm sawed with its knife, and the cat screamed and spat.

The children wandered the forest, investigating what they had found in the roots of a tree. It was some sort of vast lens, mostly under the ground, with only one of its faces coming out into the air. They brushed the twigs and leaves from it and peered in, wondering at its ancient functions. Elam saw Orfea's face reflected in it, solemn eyes examining him, wondering at him. A beam of hot sunlight played on the lens, awakening lights deep within it, vague images of times and places now vanished. Midges darted in the sun, and Orfea's skin produced a smooth and heavy odor, one of the perfumes she mixed for herself: her art, as death was Elam's. Elam looked down at her hand, splayed on the smooth glass, then across at his, already rougher, stronger, with the hints of dark dried blood around the fingernails.

Abias stood above them. He danced on the smooth glass, his callused feet slipping. He laughed every time he almost fell. "Can you see us?" he cried to the lens. "Can you see who we are? Can you see who we will become?" Elam looked up at him in wonder, then down at the boy's tiny distorted reflection as it cavorted among the twisted trees.

The sun was suddenly hot, slicing through the trees like a burning edge. Smoke rose as it sizzled across flesh. Elam howled with pain and ran up the slope. He ran until his lungs were dying within him.

The Neanderthal stopped in a clearing up the side of a mountain. A herd of clouds moved slowly across the sky, cropping the blue grass of the overhead. Around him rocks, the old bones of the Earth, came up through its sagging flesh. The trees whispered derisively below him. They talked of death and blood. "You should have died," they said. "The other should have lived." The Neanderthal turned his tear-filled eyes into the wind, though whether he wept for Orfea, or for Elam, even he could not have said.

The city burned with a dry thunder. Elam and Reqata ran through the crowded screaming streets with the arsonists, silent and pure men. In the shifting firelight, their tattoed faces swirled and reformed, as if made of smoke themselves.

"The situation has been balanced for years," Reqata said. "Peace conceals strong forces pushing against each other. Change their alignment, and. . . ." Swords flashed in the firelight, a meaningless battle between looters and some sort of civil guard. Ahead were the tiled temples of the Goddesses, their goal.

"They feel things we don't," she said. "Religious exaltation. The suicidal depression of failed honor. Fierce loyalty to a leader. Hysterical terror at signs and portents."

Women screamed from the upper windows of a burning building, holding their children out in vain hope of salvation.

"Do you envy them?" Elam asked.

"Yes!" she cried. "To them, life is not a game." Her hand was tight on his arm. "They know who they are."

"And we don't?"

"Take me!" Reqata said fiercely. Her fingernails stabbed through his thin shirt. They had made love in countless incarnations, and these golden-skinned slender bodies were just another to her, even with the flames rising around them.

He took her down on the stone street as the city burned on all sides. Her scent pooled dark. It was the smell of death and decay. He looked at her. Beneath him, eyes burning with malignant rage, was Orfea.

"You are alive," Elam cried.

Her face glowered at him. "No, you bastard," she said. "I'm not alive. You are. *You are.*"

His rage suddenly matched hers. He grabbed her hair and pulled her across the rough stone. "Yes. And I'm going to stay that way. Understand? Understand?" With each question, he slammed her head on the stone.

Her face was amused. "Really, Elam. I'm dead, remember? Dead and gone. What's the use of slamming me around?"

"You were always like that. Always sensible. Always driving me crazy!" He stopped, his hands around her throat. He looked down at her. "Why did we hate each other so much?"

"Because there was really only ever one of us. It was Lammiela who thought there were two."

Pain sliced across his cheek. Reqata slapped him again, making sure her nails bit in. Blood poured down her face and her hair was tangled. Elam stumbled back, and was shoved aside by a mob of running soldiers.

"Are you crazy?" she shouted. "You can't kill me. You can't. You'll ruin everything." She was hunched, he saw now, cradling her side. She reached down and unsheathed her sword. "Are you trying to go back to your old style? Try it somewhere else. This is *my* show."

"Wait," he said.

"Damn you, we'll discuss this later. In another life." The sword darted at him.

"Reqata!" He danced back, but the edge caught him across the back of his hand. "What are you—"

There were tears in her eyes as she attacked him. "I see her, you know. Don't think that I don't. I see her at night, when you are asleep. Your face is different. It's the face of a woman, Elam. A woman! Did you know that? Orfea lives on in you somewhere."

Her sword did not allow him to stop and think. She caught him again, cutting his ear. Blood soaked his shoulder. "Your perfume. Who sent it to you?"

"Don't be an idiot. Something in you is Orfea, Elam. That's the only part I really love."

He tripped over a fallen body. He rolled and tried to get to his feet. He found himself facing the point of her sword, still on his knees.

"Please, Reqata," he said, tears streaming down his cheeks. "I don't want to die."

"Well, isn't that the cutest thing." Her blade pushed into his chest, cold as ice. "Why don't you figure out who you are first?"

He awoke in his adytum. His eyes generated dots of light to compensate for the complete darkness. His blood vessels burned as if filled with molten metal. He moved, pushing against the viscous fluid. Damp hair swirled around him, thick under his back, curling around his feet. It had gathered around his neck. There was no air to breathe. Elam. Where was Elam? He seemed to be gone at last, leaving only—

Elam awoke, gasping, on a pallet, still feeling the metal of Reqata's sword in his chest. So it had been her. Not satisfied with killing everyone else, she had needed to kill him as well, repeatedly. He, even now, could not understand why. Orfea.

He stood silently in the middle of the room and listened to the beating of his own heart. Only it wasn't his own, of course, not the one he had been born with. It was a heart that Abias had carefully grown in a tank somewhere below, based on information provided by a gene sample from the original Elam. The real Elam still slept peacefully in his adytum. Peacefully . . . he had almost remembered something this time. Things had almost become clear.

He walked down to Abias's bright kingdom. Abias had tools there, surgical devices with sharp, deadly edges. It was his art, wasn't it? And a true artist never depended on an audience to express himself.

He searched through cabinets, tearing them open, littering the floor with sophisticated devices, hearing their delicate mechanisms shatter. He finally found a surgical tool with a vibratory blade that could cut through anything. He carried it upstairs and stared down at the ovoid of the adytum. What was inside of it? If he penetrated, perhaps, at last, he could truly see.

It wasn't the right thing, of course. The right instrument had to burn as it cut, cauterizing flesh. He remembered its bright killing flare. This was but a poor substitute.

Metal arms pinioned him. "Not yet," Abias said softly. "You cannot do that yet."

"What do you mean?" Elam pulled himself from Abias's suddenly unresisting arms and turned to face him. The faceless eyes stared at him.

"I mean that you don't understand anything. You cannot act without finally understanding."

"Tell me, then!" Elam shouted. "Tell me what happened. I have to know. You say you didn't kill Orfea. Who did then? Did I? Did I do it?"

Abias was silent for a long time. "Yes. Your mother has, I think, tried to forgive you. But *you* are the murderer."

"You were not supposed to remember." Lammiela sat rigidly in her most private room, her mental adytum. "The Bound told me you would not. That part of you was to vanish. Just as Laurance vanished from me."

"I haven't remembered. You have to help me."

She looked at him. Until today, the hatred in her eyes would have frightened him. Now it comforted him, for he must be near the truth.

"You were a monster as a child, Elam. Evil, I would

have said, though I loved you. You were Laurance, returned to punish me for having killed him. . . ."

"I tortured animals," Elam said, hurrying to avoid Lammiela's past and get to his own. "I started with frogs. I moved up to cats, dogs. . . ."

"And people, Elam. You finally moved to people."

"I know," he said, thinking of the dead Orfea, whom he feared he would never remember. "Abias told me."

"Abias is very forgiving," Lammiela said. "You lost him his body, and nearly his life."

"What did I do with him?"

She shook her head. "I don't know, Elam. He has never said. All these years, and he has never said. You hated Orfea, and she hated you, but somehow you were still jealous of each other. She cared for Abias, your friend from the village, and that made you wild. He was so clever about that ancient Bound knowledge the Incarnate never pay attention to. He always tried to undo the evil that you did. He healed animals, putting them back together. Without you, he may never have learned all he did. He was a magician."

"Mother—"

She glared at him. "You strapped him down, Elam. You wanted to . . . to castrate him. Cloning, you called it. You said you could clone him. He might have been able to clone you, I don't know, but you certainly could do nothing but kill him. Orfea tried to stop you, and you fought. You killed her, Elam. You took that hot cutting knife and you cut her apart. It explodes flesh, if set right, you know. There was almost nothing left."

Despite himself, Elam felt a surge of remembered pleasure.

"As you were murdering your sister, Abias freed himself. He struggled and got the tool away from you."

"But he didn't kill me."

"No. I never understood why. Instead, he mutilated you. Carefully, skillfully. He knew a lot about the human body. You were unrecognizable when they found you, all burned up, your genitals destroyed, your face a blank."

"And they punished Abias for Orfea's murder. Why?"

"He insisted that he had done it. I knew he hadn't. I finally made him tell me. The authorities didn't kill him, at my insistence. Instead, they took away his body and made him the machine he now is."

"And you made him serve me," Elam said in wonder. "All these years, you've made him serve me."

She shook her head. "No, Elam. That was his own choice. He took your body, put it in its adytum, and has served you ever since."

Elam felt hollow, spent. "You should have killed me," he whispered. "You should not have let me live."

Lammiela stared at him, her eyes bleak and cold. "I daresay you're right, Elam. You were Laurance before me, the man I can never be again. I wanted to destroy you, totally. Expunge you from existence. But it was Abias's wish that you live, and since he had suffered at your hands, I couldn't gainsay him."

"Why then?" Elam said. "Why do you want to kill me now?" He stretched his hands out toward his mother. "If you want to, do it. Do it!"

"I don't know what you are talking about, Elam. I haven't tried to kill you. I gave up thinking about that a long time ago."

He sagged. "Who then? Reqata?"

"Reqata?" Lammiela smirked. "Go through all this trouble for one death? It's not her style, Elam. You're not that important to her. Orfea was an artist too. Her art was scent. Scents that stick in your mind and call up past times when you smell them again."

"You wore one of them," Elam said, in sudden realization. "The day my death in the north woods ended."

"Yes," she said, her voice suddenly taut again. "Orfea wore that scent on the last day of her life, Elam. You probably remember it."

The scent brought terror with it. Elam remembered that. "Did you find some old vial of it? Whatever made you wear it?"

She looked at him, surprised. "Why, Elam. You sent it to me yourself."

Abias stood before him like a technological idol, the adytum between them.

"I'm sorry, Abias," Elam said.

"Don't be sorry," Abias said. "You gave yourself up to save me."

"Kill me, Abias," he said, not paying attention to what the cyborg had just said. "I understand everything now. I can truly die." He held the vibratory surgical tool above the adytum, ready to cut in, to kill what lay within.

"No, Elam. You don't understand everything, because what I told Lammiela that day was not the truth. I lied, and she believed me." He pushed, and a line appeared across the adytum's ovoid.

"What is the truth then, Abias?" Elam waited, almost uninterested.

"Orfea did not die that day, Elam. You did."

The adytum split slowly open.

"You did try to kill me, Elam," Abias said softly, almost reminiscently. "You strapped me down for your experiment. Orfea tried to stop you. She grabbed the hot cutting knife and fought with you. She killed you."

"I don't understand."

The interior of an adytum was a dark secret. Elam peered inside, for a moment seeing nothing but yards and yards of wet dark hair.

"Don't you understand, Orfea? Don't you know who you are?" Abias's voice was anguished. "You killed Elam, whom you hated, but it was too much for you. You mutilated yourself, horribly. And you told me what you wanted to be. I loved you. I did it."

"I wanted to be Elam," Elam whispered.

The face in the adytum was not his own. Torn and mutilated still, though repaired by Abias's skill, it was the face of Orfea. The breasts of a woman pushed up through the curling hair.

"You wanted to be the brother you had killed. After I did as you said, no one knew the difference. You were Elam. The genes were identical, since you were split from the same ovum. No one questioned what had happened. The Incarnate are squeamish, and leave such vile business to the Bound. And you've been gone ever since. Your hatred for who you thought you were caused you to kill yourself, over and over. Elam was alive again, and knew that Orfea had killed him. Why should he not hate her?"

"No," Elam said. "I don't hate her." He slumped slowly to his knees, looking down at the sleeping face.

"I had to bring her back, you understand that?" Abias's voice was anguished. "If only one of you can live, why should it be Elam? Why should it be him? Orfea's spirit was awakening, slowly, after all these years. I could see it sometimes, in you."

"So you brought it forth," Elam said. "You cloned and created creatures in which her soul could exist. The zeppelin. The dragon."

"Yes."

"And each time, she was stronger. Each time I died, I awoke . . . *she* awoke for a longer time in the adytum."

"Yes!" Abias stood over him, each limb raised glittering above his head. "She will live."

Elam rested his fingers in her wet hair and stroked her cheek. She had slept a long time. Perhaps it was indeed time for him to attempt his final work of art, and die forever. Orfea would walk the Earth again.

"No!" Elam shouted. "*I* will live." Abias loomed over him as the dragon had, ready to steal his life from him. He swung the vibrating blade and sliced off one of Abias's limbs. Another swung down, knocking Elam to the floor. He rolled. Abias raised himself above. Elam stabbed upward with the blade. It penetrated the central cylinder of Abias's body and was pulled from his hands as Abias jerked back. Elam lay defenseless and awaited the ripping death from Abias's manipulator arms.

But Abias stood above him, motionless, his limbs splayed out, his eyes staring. After a long moment, Elam realized that he was never going to move again.

The adytum had shut of its own accord, its gray surface once again featureless. Elam rested his forehead against it. After all these years he had learned the truth, the truth of his past and his own identity.

Abias had made him and seem an illegitimate soul, a construct of Orfea's guilt. Perhaps that was indeed all he was. He shivered against the roughness of the adytum. Orfea slumbered within it. With sudden anger, he slapped its surface. She could continue to sleep. She had killed him once. She would not have the chance to do it again.

Elam stood up wearily. He leaned on the elaborate sculpture of the dead Abias, feeling the limbs creak under his weight. What was Elam without him?

Elam was *alive*. He smiled. For the first time in his life, Elam was alive.

AT THE CROSS-TIME JAUNTERS' BALL

I had gotten lost again, as I so often did, because it was dark there, in those musty and unswept hallways that run between the universes. I've always been impressed by the amount of crap that seems to float in through the doorways and settle there, in some sort of plea for reality. An infinite network of passages linking the worlds of Shadow with that of the real might seem like a good idea, but who was going to keep it clean? The Lords were too haughty to concern themselves with things like that, and we humans were too . . . finite.

I looked in through doorways as I walked, to see such things as a city of hanging tree dwellings or an endless stairway that curved up from mist into blinding sunlight. These were delicate worlds, miniatures. As a professional critic of such Shadows I had to say that these worlds were not the style I usually liked, though one, where a regatta of multicolored dirigibles sailed above a city whose towers stood half in the sea, was excellent.

A rough wind blew past, carrying with it the clamor of a cheering army and the pounding of swords on shields. The passage tilted upward, and I climbed a set of rough stairs, smelling first lilacs, then, when I took a deeper breath, an open sewer. I choked, and was surrounded by buzzing flies, which had wandered irrevocably from their world and, looking for shit, had found only the meager substitute of a critic. I ran up the stairs, waving the flies away, past the sound of temple bells, the dense

154

choking of dust from a quarry, and a spray of briny water, accompanied by the shrieking of sea gulls.

Gathered in a knot in the hallway ahead of me was a group of Lords, with their servant, a huge man wearing a leather helmet. Lord Prokhor, Lord Sere, and Lord Ammene, three balding men with prison pallor and rings below their dark eyes, waited for me to give them advice on acquisition. They sat on little folding stools and looked uncomfortable.

"You are late, Mr. Landstatter," Lord Ammene said, in a reedy voice.

"Your servant, sir," I said, ignoring the challenge. I eyed the three of them suspiciously. Lords were entirely unpredictable, and their motivations obscure. On my last trip I'd almost been trapped when Cuzco, capital of the Incan Empire, fell to invading Apache Sacred Warriors who had hired Maori warships for transport from their temple cities along the Pacific coast of Mexico. I'd spent three desperate days freezing in the Andes, my nights lit by the glow from the burning city reflected in the ice fields, before I could return home. I had wondered if it was an accident, because someone had locked me in my room just when the attack began. The three of them returned my bow without standing.

The servant raised the lamp he held in his hand and examined me. I wore a three-cornered plumed hat, a heavy powder-blue tailcoat covered with useless gold buttons, a stiff embroidered vest with hunting scenes on it, extremely tight cream-colored silk trousers, and black leather boots trimmed with sable. Beneath the hat, my hair was pomaded, powdered, and pulled back into a ponytail by an ornate silver clasp. The servant sneered at me.

The Lords were dressed in their usual sober dark clothes, gold chains around their necks indicating rank. Unlike most people, they did not adopt clothing from Shadow, implying, I guess, that what they always wore was "real." Style is never real, but I am a critic of worlds, not dress, so I said nothing.

Then the servant turned the lamp around. I straightened my hat. We stood in front of a stretch of blank wall.

Humming gently to himself, he adjusted the lamp until it focused on the wall. The wall shimmered, and a door opened onto a brightly lit street. I could hear the ringing of steel wagon wheels on cobblestones and the puffing of a steam launch on the river that flowed just out of sight of the doorway. "There you are, Mr. Landstatter. See you in forty-eight hours." I stopped just in front of the shimmering, the way I always do, no matter who is watching. Vanishing into unreality makes me nervous. He pushed me through, not roughly, but the way you would direct a timid actor onto a stage in front of an audience. I turned to protest, but he and his masters were gone, and I found myself addressing my retort to a broken and stained brick wall.

The water swirled against the brick side of the canal, as if irritated at having its freedom curtailed, but finally acquiesced and flowed under the arch of the bridge. On the river beyond, a vendor guiding his empty flatboat home from the market negotiated the uneven current with tired familiarity. Past the inflow of the canal he put his shoulders into his poling, undoubtedly thinking of a bowl of stew, a mug of beer, and a pipe of tobacco.

I was starting to think of things like that too. I watched the boatman vanish into the iridescent meeting of sunset and oily water, then turned and began to walk in the direction of the dam, which was where the north and south branches of the Schekaagau River joined and flowed into Lake Vlekke. It was also where the best hotels were. I strayed into the path of a pedicab, and was startled by a jangle of bells that sounded like an angry gamelan. The white-suited driver bared polished scrimshawed teeth, cursed at me in Malay, and was gone, leaving only a cloud of ginger and curry to mark his passing.

The tall step-gabled warehouses that had been flanking me on the left vanished, to be replaced by the unadorned brick facades of merchants' houses, which gave only hints of wealth through panes of leaded glass: the glitter of a chandelier, the flash of a tapestry, the gleam of a silver serving bowl. From a half-open window came the sound of a drinking song, bellowed by male voices to the accompaniment of pounding pewter mugs. Merchants, home from the Bourse and ready to do their best to keep the price of malted barley high.

A marble bridge carried me high over the river to the dam, a platform of pilings sunk into the soft earth. Ahead of me rose the towers of city hall. A small boy sat on the quay, trailing a fishing line in the water. The result of his day's labors amounted to two carp, strung through the gills, and a frog, which was jumping up and down in a jar.

"Say, lad," I said, in the Lithuanian-influenced patois of the Mississippi River trade. I thought it was a nice touch. "What is the best hotel in town?" I've had fellow critics tell me that, when they work in Shadow, they stay in the sleaziest fleabags they can find, because that makes the experience more "real." I don't find lice more real, in any ultimate sense, than satin sheets.

"The best?" The boy jumped up eagerly. "The Emperor Kristiaan, on the Streetergracht! They have marble tubs and gold faucets. And Duc Noh the King of Nam Viet got shot in the lobby! They put a chair over it to hide it, but you can still see the bloodstains if you look."

"Sounds ideal. And do you know how to get there?"

"Do I! I once got thrown out for climbing the flagpole. You can see the whole city from the top! It's the tallest flagpole in Schekaagau." He hung the fish on a string around his waist and picked up the jar containing the frog, which began to jump more frantically. "Follow me." We crossed the tiled dam square, passing the triumphal arch, an explosion of soldiery, waving banners, crosses, and captive Indians pleading for mercy. Somewhere beyond city hall, bells were ringing Angelus. We walked down a narrow street, where merchants were locking up their stalls for the night. The blue lamps that taverns and places of public relief were required to show already glowed at spots along the street, lighthouses for the weary. A few minutes later, we emerged into a square that opened out onto the dark water of the canal called the Streetergracht. The other three sides of the square formed the ornate classical pile of the hotel. On top, hanging over us like a burnished artificial moon in the laboratory of a medieval alchemist, a gilded dome caught the last rays of sunlight. Three flagpoles stood in front, the flags those of the hotel, the city of Schekaagau, and the Stadtholderate, in the process of being lowered by a squad of hotel employees in scarlet tunics and knee pants. The boy proudly pointed out the taller, center pole as the cause of his expulsion. I was properly impressed.

I reached into my money purse, pulled out a crescent of silver, and flipped it to him. He stared at it in wonder, then stuffed it away in one of the secret pockets boys have. "I better go. Mum will be worried. I'm late for dinner."

I winked at him, which he liked. "Don't let me catch you climbing the towers of city hall."

"You won't," he said ambiguously, and was gone into the gathering darkness, his captive frog still tucked under one arm. I had never learned his name.

It was after I had been lost for quite some time that I noticed I was being followed. For a moment, in my drunken state, that was funny. The poor fool thought he was going to end up in a nice hotel lobby with plush chairs and a bar where he could get a late-night glass of arrack, but instead he was doomed to wander with me through back alleys and unlit warehouse-lined streets for the rest of the night, his path constantly disrupted by dark flowing canals. That was not why he was following me, of course, and I quickly ceased to find his company amusing. I glanced over my shoulder as I turned a corner. He was dressed in some sort of robes, not normal clothes at all, and didn't seem to know the streets any better than I did. I emerged on the quay by the river, its edge marked by a line of heavy granite posts holding a chain. The river flowed quickly here, constrained by the quays, and I could hear its churning and grumbling.

Out in the darkness a procession of torchlit barges, loaded to the gunwales with masquers, drifted on the reflected waters of the river. They laughed and screamed and seemed to be having a terrific time, just as they had when I was with them, though I had not enjoyed them at all. I had drunk too much, and almost gotten sick. I had taken a walk to clear my head and work out my thoughts on my critical analysis. I doubted anyone had noticed my absence.

Despite the threat at my back, my main emotion was still annoyance. The judgment of a good critic never relaxes. Peter Lucas had made a specialty of this sort of genre piece, and I was getting tired of it. It irritated me to think that I had another day to spend here before the Key the Lords had implanted in the limbic system of my brain would take me home to the real world. To think of all of Lucas's labor in twisting human history, to create yet another set of drunken shipping magnates and aldermen in fancy masquerade pounding mugs on wooden trestle tables and pissing heartily over the sides of their barges. It made me sick. Lucas demonstrated that there was an infinite number of redundant possibilities, like a gallery hallway lined only with paintings of courting couples, or children playing with a little furry dog.

I didn't know what Lucas had done to history in order to create this Shadow, what kings and queens he had given fevers, what storms he had raised, what matings he had arranged, what battles he had altered, in order for William Vlekke of Antwerp to discover this place so that Schekaagau stood on the shores of Lake Vlekke, rather than Chicago on Lake Michigan, and didn't get much more of a chance to think about it, because my pursuer decided that that was a good moment to jump me.

His attack was theatrical, with a scream and leap. His body was slim and strong underneath the heavy wool robes, but he was more enthusiastic than skilled, and I threw him off. He hit the ground heavily, then rolled and came up with a glittering curved knife in his hand. I backed away. He didn't seem to be trying to rob me. He had other things in mind. My ridiculous clothes suddenly seemed as constricting as a straitjacket. He came forward with his blade dancing before him. It was a beautiful piece of work, I noticed, with an elegantly patterned silver hilt. It would look wonderful sticking out of my chest in the morning light.

Critics of Shadow are used to such things, however, and I was not as defenseless as I looked. As he came at me, I pulled a packet of powder out of a pocket and threw it at him, squeezing my eyes shut at the same time.

Even through my closed lids, the flash of the powder left an afterimage. He shrieked and stumbled back, completely blinded. I slipped brass knuckles over my fingers, moved in, and punched him at the angle of his jaw. This was unfair, but I wasn't feeling sporting that night. His head snapped back and he yelped. He slashed back and forth with his blade, still not able to see anything, but dangerous nevertheless. I dodged in and hit him again, and he stumbled and fell. His head crunched sickeningly against one of the granite posts, and he rolled over the side of the quay into the water. For a long moment I stood swaying drunkenly, trying to figure out where he had gone. Then I ran up and looked over the edge. Water roared heavily below in the darkness, but there was nothing else to be seen. I slipped the brass knuckles off my hand and started to try to find my way home again. It was a long while before I found the square in front of the hotel, and I was still shaking when I did.

A marble bathtub is a beautiful thing, but it takes forever for hot water to heat it up. I finally slid into the bath and was able to relax my muscles. The attack had left me with a number of bruises, but no answers. Answers were sometimes scarce in the many worlds of Shadow, which the Lords had caused to be created for their mysterious pleasures. But the municipal river patrol would be pulling a body out of the weir at the dam in the morning, and I had no idea why he had tried to kill me, and I like to have reasons for things like that. Cuzco, Schekaagau . . . Had the Lords tired of my aesthetic sniping? Was I simply paranoid? That was an occupational hazard. I knew I would get no answers that night, so I got out of the bath, toweled myself dry, and went to bed.

I turned the key on the gaslight, dimming it to a blue glow. The boy had been real, though. Give Lucas that much. Everyone else seemed like a moving waxwork, but that boy was as real as anyone. I was not sure the Lords enjoyed "reality" in that sense, since they themselves did not seem particularly real to me.

Reveling in the feel of satin against skin, I turned over in bed to find myself staring at the patterned silver hilt of a knife, still vibrating from its impact, that had somehow come to be embedded in the bedpost next to my head. The motif was one of eyes and lightning bolts. The last knife I had seen like that was now at the bottom of the Schekaagau River. I wrenched the knife from the bedpost and ran to the window, but my second attacker had already slid down the drainpipe and vanished, leaving me with a souvenir of my night at the Emperor Kristiaan.

"Mutated *E. coli*," Salvator Martine said. He had pulled me away from the other guests at his party to give me this information.

I swirled the Tokay in my glass and watched it sheet down the sides. *"E. coli?"* Only Martine would serve a wine as sweet as Tokay before dinner.

Martine grinned, bright teeth in a face of tanned leather. He was annoyingly handsome, and smelled sharply of myrrh and patchouli. The Lords loved him, for no good reason that I could see. Several had even come to attend his party. "Normal intestinal flora. Mutated and hybridized with amyotrophic lateral sclerosis. Infects via the GI tract and destroys the central nervous systems of higher primates. Neat. Grew it in the guts of an Australopithecine on the African veldt, two, three million years ago. Not easy, Jacob, not easy. When I woke up on that pallet at Centrum, I had bedsores, and a headache that lasted a month. Killed them all. Every last one of the buggers. Nothing left on this planet with more brains than an orangutan." He downed his glass of Tokay as if it were water. I took another slow sip of my own.

We stood on the parapet of what he called his "palace." Behind us I could hear the sound of the party, voices and clinking glasses, background music, occasionally a laugh. The sun set beyond rolling green hills. From a distant ridge came the cry of a deer. A trail of mist descended on the valley, glowing in the evening light. Except for the ones behind us in the party, there were no other humans on the planet.

"Infectious lateral sclerosis . . ." I murmured to myself. This was art?

Martine laughed. "Not to worry. With no hosts, it died out, and there are no other vectors. I was careful about that."

He'd misunderstood my moodiness, of course, but it took a particularly impervious cast of mind to be a molder of worlds. Martine had succeeded in wiping out all of humanity, collateral branches to boot. By some standards, that made him a god. A god with bedsores. That left me with a blank canvas to look at, but nothing to review, which was perhaps his intention. If a tree falls in a forest and no one hears it, that's one thing, but when the acorn is worm-devoured and the tree never exists, what sound does it make then?

"You are looking at Berenson's new world next?"

"Yes. She's been very mysterious about it, but I suspect—"

A voice interrupted us.

"There you are. The most notable men at the party, and the two of you stand out here watching the sunset. Where's your sense of social responsibility?" We both turned. Amanda, my wife, closed the door behind her, passing through in the roar of voices. She wore a dress that fell in waves of green-and-blue silk, and she emerged from it like Aphrodite from the foam, her blonde hair braided and coiled around her head. A moonstone glowed in its silver setting as it rested on her forehead.

"We were waiting for you," Martine said with that charming insincerity that Amanda seemed to like.

She came up and took a sip of my drink. She smiled at Martine. "I'll have you know, Salvator, that Jacob detests sweet drinks before dinner." She took another, and kept the glass. "I've been wandering around your palace. It's wonderful! How did you ever create anything like it?"

I felt a surge of annoyance. The palace was a monstrosity. It had towers, with pennants snapping in the breeze. It had triumphal staircases. It had flying buttresses. It had colonnades. What it didn't have was structure. It looked like an immense warehouse of architectural spare parts.

"It was built by some people from a world I did a few

years back. Remember it, Jacob? The Berbers of the Empire of the Maghreb ruled Northern Africa. They flooded the desert and built great palaces. I had planned that." He turned to Amanda. "As I recall, Jacob didn't like it much."

He recalled correctly. I couldn't remember much about that particular work, just hot sun and blinding water, but I did remember that I hadn't liked it. The Lords had bid it up, though, and it was now in someone's collection, making Martine wealthy. Critics should never socialize with artists; it's difficult enough to like their work in the first place.

Amanda came up and pushed herself against me. Her perfume smelled of violets, and I lost track of what I was thinking. I put my arm around her, and she pulled away, as she always did once she had my attention, and walked to the other side of the parapet to enjoy the sunset.

Amanda had once been close to me, but was now distant, and I couldn't remember when that had changed. It could have happened overnight, since Amanda often went to bed loving and woke up cold. Something she saw in her dreams, I'd always thought. But now it was that way most of the time, and I felt I'd let something slip by, as if we'd had an immense knock-down-drag-out fight that I had not been able to attend. On the infrequent occasions when we made love it was like two people sawing a tree trunk, the length of the saw between us and only the rhythm of the task keeping us together. This still left me wanting to do it much more often than she did.

Voices shouted for Martine inside, so the three of us went in through the French doors. The banqueting hall was an immense room, thirty feet high, and banners from the Shadows Martine had created hung down from the beams supporting the ceiling. Someone pressed a glass of wine into my hand, not Tokay, mercifully, but some dry red. The party poured after Martine as he strode through the hall, out the double doors at the other end, and down the immense stairway. At the bottom rested a cube wrapped in black velvet, about six feet high. It had been delivered through the hallways by servants available to the Lords. Despite myself, I was impressed. They did not usually permit ordinary men to move objects from Shadow to Shadow.

"Let's carry her up," Martine said, and the party surged forward with cheers. It took a half-dozen people to lift it. "Take my place, Jacob," Martine said, and I found myself with a shoulder under one corner of the cube. We angled it back and, cursing and laughing, hauled it up the stairs. It was heavy and tried to slide back. I started to sweat.

A space was cleared on the floor among the armchairs and the tables covered with half-finished drinks. The cube was put down. I looked for Amanda in the crowd but couldn't find her anywhere. I remembered what she was wearing, and her moonstone, but wasn't sure that I knew what she looked like anymore. It seemed that as she had grown more distant her face had stopped being familiar.

"This is from a world I did recently. It's not worth visiting, believe me, but it did produce one thing that's worthwhile. I asked the Lords for permission to bring it back for my collection." He pulled on a cord, and the black velvet fell to the floor. The crowd grew silent and drew back, but no one took his eyes away.

The most beautiful woman in the world was in Hell, but she had been turned to stone and no one could do anything about it. She stared at us from behind five inches of leaded glass with pleading in her eyes. She was a Madonna, and a newborn child lay in her lap. His eyes stared blankly upward, for He had been born hideously blind.

I had more information than Martine thought I did, from my sources at Centrum. I knew that Martine had caused eight entire worlds to be destroyed by nuclear war before he got the effect he wanted. On the last try, a group of artists, vomiting, losing their hair, seeing the constant glimmer of optic nerves degenerating in the radiation flux, had found a boulder in a blast crater and set it on a hilltop. The rock was dense with exotic isotopes and had killed the sculptors as they chiseled it. They had worked as one, and it was impossible to tell where one artist had left off and the next began. They had created a masterpiece, probably not even knowing why, but Martine claimed this work as his own. Radio-active fantasies had been fashionable among the Lords lately.

I turned and walked away, rubbing my shoulder. The party was getting loud again, despite the pleading eyes of the Virgin Mary, and I felt a little sick. I walked down a long hallway lined with loot from Martine's various creations. I stopped in front of one painting, of Christ being carried drunk from the Marriage at Cana by the Apostles. It looked like a rather murky Titian, all droopy flesh and blue mist, but Amanda had pointed it out specifically to me earlier in the day. She never really seemed to care much about art herself, but she somehow always knew precisely what I would like. Or would not.

"Mr. Landstatter. Good evening." Sitting in the shadows on straight-backed chairs, like Egyptian deities, were two Lords, Jurum and Altina, who seemed to be married, although it was hard for me to tell. At any rate, they were always together.

"Good evening." I bowed, but did not speak further.

"We've just been looking at Martine's little collection," Altina said, her voice a gentle hiss. "Symbols and parts, it seems to us. Reflections of worlds in objects, and so an imitation of our strings of Shadow. What say you?" They awaited my judgment.

Lords are strange beings. They collect worlds the way children collect brightly colored stones and seashells, but require others both to create those worlds and to determine whether they are worth having. They had gained control of the infinite universe of Shadows before anyone could remember, raised Centrum, and seemed intent on continuing in this position forever. Had one of them decided to kill me? The fact that two attempts had already failed suggested that a critic of murder would have had to give their efforts a bad review.

"The objects have significance in themselves, and not just as signs to Shadow," I said. The Lords often had trouble understanding ordinary art. "This statue of Apollo, for instance . . ." They stood and listened, Altina resting slightly on Jurum's arm, as I took them through Martine's collection, which ranged from the brilliant to the mediocre, and seemed to have been forgotten here, like junk in an attic. They thanked me, finally, and walked off to bed, discussing what I had said. I realized that the party above had grown silent and that it was time for bed.

When I returned to the banqueting hall, it was empty save for the tormented Virgin. I stopped to look at her, but her expression had become reproachful, as if I were somehow responsible for her fate. I turned away and went to our room.

The bed was still made, and Amanda was nowhere to be seen. I took my clothes off, threw them on the floor, and climbed in under the covers. Our room was in one of those dramatic towers, and there was nothing but darkness outside the windows. I fell asleep.

Amanda woke me up as she slipped into bed, sometime later. I started to say something, to ask where she had been.

"Shh," she said. "I didn't mean to wake you." She hunched up on the other side of the bed, the way she did so often, even though the bed was not particularly large and this meant that she dangled precariously over the edge. I moved closer to her and nuzzled her neck. "Please, Jacob. It's late and I want to sleep. See you in the morning." She yawned and was quickly asleep, or at least pretended to be.

I lay back on the other side of the bed, my heart pounding. I knew that no matter what I did, I would be unable to sleep. When I had left her, she had smelled of violets. Her neck now had the bitter aroma of myrrh and patchouli.

The Capuchin did his calculations with a light pen on what looked like a pane of glass, causing equations to appear in glowing green. Interpolated quotations from the Old Testament emerged in yellow, while those from the New Testament were light blue. Unavoidable references to Muslim physicists flashed a gory infidel red. I gazed out from under my cowl, impressed but unenlightened. I don't know anything about nuclear physics, and even when I thought I had managed to pick up the thread of an argument, I was immediately thrown off by a gloss on Thomas Aquinas or Origen. I contented myself with smelling the incense and watching the glitter of the LEDs on the rosaries of the other monks as they checked the Capuchin's calculations.

He turned from the glass and faced his audience. He raised his arms in supplication to Heaven, then clapped his hands together. The equations disappeared, to be replaced by a mosaic of Christos Pancrator, His brow clouded by stormy judgment, lightning ready to be unleashed from His imperial hands.

"Brothers!" the monk said. "All is in readiness. For the first time in history, the fires of Hell shall be unleashed on Earth, chained at the command of the sacred Mathematics that God, in His Wisdom, has given us to smite the infidel. We will now examine this flame, and if it is not found wanting, its hunger will soon consume the arrogant cities of all those who would oppose the Will of God!" We rose to our feet and followed him up the stairs to the surface.

It was dry and bright outside, and the sky was a featureless blue. We segregated ourselves by Order, the gray of Dominicans to the right, the brown of Franciscans to the left, and the martial oriental splendor of the Templars and Hospitalers in the center. There were last-minute checks of the dosimeters, and several of the more cautious had already flipped their goggles down and were sucking on their respirators.

In front of us, across the cracked, dried mud, amid the rubble of what had once been the city of Venice, stood the Campanile of St. Mark's, looking the same as it did in a Canaletto painting, except for the fact that the gray ovoid of the atomic bomb rested on a frame on top of the steeply pitched roof. Nearby, the crumbled dome of the cathedral lay on the ground like an overturned bowl. At a distance stood the crazily leaning Rialto bridge. All around, the flats of the dry lagoon stretched away. A trumpet call rang through the air. We repaired to our trenches, all now monastic grasshoppers with our goggles and breathing tubes. We knelt, facing the tower, and the bomb.

When the blast came, it looked, in my goggles, like a bright glowing dot that faded quickly to red, and then darkness. The blast shoved at the shielded robe, and I felt the heat on my face. The sound of the blast thundered in my earplugs. A moment went by. I pulled up my goggles.

The ruins of Venice had been replaced by a smoking crater. The mushroom cloud towered overhead like a cowled monk of a different Order.

In sudden unplanned fervor, the monks began to pull themselves out of the safety of the trench and march toward the crater. I, of course, was with them, though I felt like a fool.

A resonant bass voice started the tune, and the rest of us joined in:

> *Dies irae, dies illa*
> *Solvet saeclum in favilla*
> *Teste David cum Sybilla . . .*

The Latin held a wealth of allusion lost in the English:

> *Day of wrath! Day of mourning!*
> *See fulfilled the prophets' warning*
> *Heaven and Earth in ashes burning!*

We knelt by that smoking scar and prayed until night fell.

My limbic Key brought me back to the hallways of Centrum, vomiting and almost unconscious. Someone found me and hauled me out, a long way, since it was a distant Shadow. I had no idea who it had been, though somehow I doubted that it had been a Lord.

The Medical Ward was high up and had large windows that let the sunlight in, unusual in the rest of the Centrum. It was a bright day outside, and I could see the endlessly repetitive walls and blocks of black rock that made up the home of the Lords of Time, stretching out to the horizon. There were no gardens in the pattern, no sculptures, and few windows. Centrum stretched over a large part of the continent some still called North America. I thought the Medical Ward abutted on the Rockies, but I was not sure, though I had already been here twice. My head pulsed and I felt disoriented.

The ward was filled with the real effects of Shadow. A theoretical anthropologist, his arms and legs replaced by assemblages of ebony, cedar, and ivory by a race of mechanically inclined torturers, lay spread-eagled on his bed, asleep. Each twitch in his shoulder or hip sent dozens of precisely balanced joints flipping, so that he danced there like a windup toy. In the corner lay a fat man who had been participating in a stag hunt through the forests of Calvados, in some world that still had a Duke of Normandy, when a cornered aurochs had knocked over his horse and given him a compound fracture of the femur. He'd lain in some canopied bed, surrounded by porcelain and Shiraz carpets, dying of tetanus, while the colorful but medically ignorant inhabitants of that Shadow crossed themselves and prepared a grave in the local churchyard. When the timing signal in his Key finally came, he'd pulled himself out of bed and through the Gate to the hallway, just as I had. The man in the bed next to mine, who gasped hoarsely every few minutes, had gotten drunk, wandered into the wrong part of town, and been beaten by some gang. This was familiar to me too. It could have been any town, the Emperor of Zimbabwe's summer capital on Lake Nyanza, or Manhattan, minor trading city in the Barony of New York, or Schekaagau. It didn't really matter. He moaned again.

"Ah, 'The Suffering Critic.' A work to gladden the heart of any artist." Standing at the foot of my bed, with a bouquet of multicolored daisies, was a dark, bearded man with a slight twist of amusement to his mouth. That quirk was there so often that it had permanently distorted the muscles of his face, so that he always wore the same expression, like a mask. Masks don't reveal, they conceal, something it was easy to forget.

Amanda had sent me an even dozen long-stemmed red roses, which loomed over me where I lay. He read the card, which just said "Get Well" and nothing else, and with the impatient gesture of a god eliminating an improperly conceived species of flatworm, he pulled them out of the vase and threw them away. He shoved his own daisies in their place. This done, he sat down in the chair next to me with a grunt of satisfaction. "Jacob, old friend. You look like hell, and your hair is falling out."

"You're too kind, Samos."

"Do you know of any reason why anyone would want to kill you?" He peered at me to see what my reaction would be.

I stared at him for a second before I thought of a response. "Samos, I'm a critic."

"Point well-taken. But you haven't answered my question."

"Samos, when you come to visit a sick friend in the hospital, you're supposed to make small talk, not start off with—"

"The fact that I suspect someone of trying to kill you?" Halicarnassus was remorseless. "Not telling you that as soon as possible would be crass impoliteness. However, if you insist. On the way here I saw some cumulus clouds. They brought a number of impressions to mind, and in fact I saw one that strongly resembled a mongoose."

I should have known better. I sighed and gave up. "To answer your question, Samos, no, I don't think someone's trying to kill me. Do you?"

He grimaced. "I'm not sure. It's just that the shielding in your robe was good, everything was in order, calculations from your dosimeter indicate that you absorbed a dose of somewhat over twenty rem, high but not fatal, and yet you were almost dead when they got you here. Don't you find that odd?"

"How did—" I stopped. It was useless to ask Halicarnassus how he found these things out. He seemed to know all the back stairs of Centrum, including which steps creaked. "I don't, unfortunately, find getting radiation sickness after walking into a fresh blast crater particularly odd, no."

"Let me remind you of the fate of one of your predecessors, who died in a zeppelin explosion while eating coq au vin off a silver plate in the company of the Duc de Moscau."

I'd been trying not to think of him. "Gambino was reviewing one of Nobunaga's worlds, if I remember. His

people are colorful, but tend to be indifferent engineers."
I didn't know why I was arguing with him.

Halicarnassus shrugged. "He'd also revealed Lord
Meern's collection of sexually obsessed societies, which
caused Meern to suffocate himself, if you'll recall. It
could all be accidental, of course. In an infinite number
of Shadows, an infinite number of things happen. But
here's an interesting thought. Can you conceive of two
worlds that differ in only one important detail?"

It was a relief to talk shop, rather than death. I hadn't
caused anyone's suicide. Not that I knew about. "What
do you mean?"

"Say I create two Shadows, identical in everything,
except in one the writing in books is boustrophedon, like
the ancient Greeks did it, with alternate lines going right
to left. It's a more efficient way of reading, really, you
don't have to move your eyes back to the beginning of
each line."

I liked the idea. "Or two Shadows, but in one men
kiss, rather than shaking hands."

"Taking an inhabitant of one and dropping him in the
other would cause no end of problems. Or better yet,
trading two otherwise identical people."

"Both would end up arrested."

We laughed and explored the idea, and the thought of
murder, never quite reasonable to begin with, was forgotten.

"Jacob!" Amanda finally flounced in, wearing a red
dress, not one I remembered ever having seen before.
She pecked me on the forehead, then sat down in the
chair and rearranged the pleats of her dress until they lay
in the proper pattern. Then she smiled at me. Behind
her, moving silently, was Martine, holding a box. My
head was pulsing again, and I felt disoriented. I blinked
my eyes, but it didn't help.

Martine and Amanda were both frowning over my
shoulder, as if there was something improper there.
Halicarnassus stared back expressionlessly, then bowed.
Amanda smiled tightly, Martine did nothing. "Good
day, Jacob," Halicarnassus said, patted my shoulder,
and was gone.

They had brought me cookies, airy things of almond and spice. Amanda had made them. I hadn't known she could bake. *They* brought me cookies. Symbols are not only in books, but help us see the structure of our own lives. Each cookie shattered as I bit into it, then stuck to my teeth. Martine avoided this problem by swallowing his whole.

Martine was desperate to know what Halicarnassus and I had been discussing, but didn't want to ask. I ignored his ever more pointed hints with sickbed stupidity, and left him frustrated. It was meager satisfaction. Amanda chattered, more talkative than I'd seen her in months. I watched the delicate curve of her throat and shoulders. She talked about the weather, about jewelry, about the music she'd been listening to, about art. Her tastes were dependent on the important others in her life, but she'd been mine for so long that I had forgotten, and was startled to hear her criticizing works that I loved, and thought she had also.

I lay back and listened to them, until their voices were just a buzz. Life was full of troubles, and I had more important things to worry about than exploding zeppelins.

I hadn't been in Halicarnassus's new world for more than five minutes when I saw her. I should have known better than to be in his Shadow in the first place, but I've never been able to resist an exclusive showing, even knowing his habit of unpleasant tricks. Halicarnassus had always enjoyed forcing societies into unnatural forms, unhealthy adaptations. He'd done an ornate Victorian-style Europe full of confectionary palaces and light operas, which practiced brutal cannibalism at fancy-dress dinner parties, a hereditary American Congress full of dangerously inbred religious fanatics who dressed in drag when deciding on bloody crusades against Sumatra and Ethiopia, and a North American Great Plains kept free of habitation from the Mississippi to the Rockies so that its Mongol conquerors could ride as their ancestors had, while forcing enslaved Europeans to build meaningless monuments larger than the Pyramids. His worlds seemed to disturb most of the Lords, who thought them mocking, and they found few buyers. He got by, somehow, the way artists always have, and still made his art.

I came into this world on the bottom level of Grand Central Station, as if I were simply another traveler amid the scurrying mobs, who carried me up into the light of the streets above.

Just a few blocks away, near St. Patrick's Cathedral, I saw Amanda, her blonde hair curled and flowing, crossing 50th Street on Fifth Avenue, obviously in a hurry. I didn't stop to think, but followed her trim gray-suited figure as she walked down the street, carrying a briefcase. The people of this Shadow did not dress brightly, or use much color on their buildings, which were disproportionately high, like the spires of iron cathedrals that had never been built. So Amanda, always in fashion, dressed here in discreet urban camouflage.

Love is a random process, depending on such improbable events as an introduction by mutual friends followed by a chance meeting in an exhibit of etchings, and a common liking for a certain sweet wine punch that now, in memory, makes me gag. Or perhaps not so improbable: I later found out that Amanda had gone to that gallery because she knew I would be there. She has never learned to like copperplate etchings, though she pretended to, at the time. The loves of our ancestors were equally random. Exact duplicates of individuals seldom exist from Shadow to Shadow, despite Halicarnassus's elaborate plans for almost duplicate worlds, so we almost never get to see ourselves in a different life. Was there a Jacob Landstatter in this world? A Salvator Martine?

So I followed her, my heart pounding. Her waist and her hips were just the same, and she swayed, enchantingly, the way she always had. When she stopped at street corners, she looked up at the tops of the buildings, shading her eyes, as if searching for roosting storks, or gargoyles. Her walk was quick, even on heels, and I had to concentrate on keeping up, difficult on the crowded street. She continued for quite a distance, finally coming to the edge of a large green park called, with no particular originality, Central Park. This was a strange mechanical Shadow, full of flying machines and automobiles. It was incredibly noisy. She finally turned into a large gray building called the Metropolitan Museum of Art. I paused at the base of the stairs for a long moment. Banners announced special exhibits of eighteenth-century French crystal, Japanese swords, and the works of a Rembrandt van Rijn. Dutch again. I was tired of Dutch. I followed her up the stairs and into the museum.

It was Rembrandt that she wanted, and she went straight there through the maze of corridors. It was an exhibit of copperplate etchings. Much of it was a series of self-portraits of that same Rembrandt van Rijn, from rather boorish youth to brooding old age, in a variety of strange headdresses. The man was obviously a genius, and I lost myself in his intricate lines.

"He is remarkable, isn't he?" she said, at my side. "I took some time off from work to come see him. This is the last day it's going to be here."

I turned slowly to look at her. Her eyes were the same too, lighter blue within dark, under long soft lashes. She looked down when I met her gaze, then glanced back up. There was no sign of recognition in her eyes. No Jacob Landstatter in this world. Until now. She smiled. Here she smelled like wildflowers, something other than violets.

We found ourselves strolling around the exhibit together, giving each other details of the various etchings as gifts. Some of her remarks were critical, and I suspected that she didn't think as much of etchings as she had initially claimed she did.

"I don't know what I should do now," she said, looking up and down the street after we emerged. "I don't really want to go back to work . . . it's too nice a day." She glanced at me, then looked away.

I suggested we get a drink, and she took my arm as we walked. I felt like an idiot. What was I doing? It was a beautiful spring day, and our steps matched as we walked. She looked up again, at the corner, and we discussed the cornices of buildings, the eaves of the roof of the house she had grown up in, the strange places birds manage to relax, and hidden roof gardens in Manhattan. It had been a long time since I'd enjoyed a conversation quite that much. She flirted with intent, and smiled when she looked at me. "I've been so lonely," she said.

Suddenly she froze, then turned to look into the window of a stationery store, pretending to admire her reflection and correct her hair. "Oh shit," she said under her breath. "Oh damn. Oh *damn*. Why is he here?"

I looked up and down the street, and had no problem spotting him, no problem at all. He walked with his head held up and his arms swinging, and wore a floppy shirt from South America. His right hand was stained with chrome yellow and viridian. Still an artist, even here, Salvator Martine strode past, his eyes fixed on an image invisible to everyone else on the street, and did not see us. I glanced at Amanda. She was trembling as if with a chill. Her left hand pulled at her hair, and she looked vulnerable, like an abandoned child. It was only then that I noticed the glint of a gold wedding band on her finger, and it all made sense.

"Who was that?" I asked.

"Who? Oh . . . somebody. It doesn't matter." She talked quickly. "Let's go."

I went with her, but everything inside of me had turned to ice. I managed to disengage myself from her after drinks but before dinner, to her obvious dismay. She liked me, and found me attractive. I felt a fool for still wanting her, like a small child who wants to play with shards of glass because they glint so prettily in the sun, but I couldn't help it. We made a date to meet at the Museum of Modern Art the following week, for an exhibition of Rothko. She would be there, but I wouldn't be. It would be another two days before my Key would allow me back through the Gate into the hallways. They had something called television here, moving images in a box. I decided to stay in my hotel room for the rest of the time and watch it.

When I returned home, I knew Amanda, my Amanda, the real Amanda, had finally gone. There was no trace of her perfume in the air, and her things were gone from her bureau.

I walked through the entryway, down the hall, and

into the quiet room, where I settled into a low couch facing the green moss-filled garden. The chuckle of the stream flowing through it was vivid in the silence.

Why did I hurt? Because I, of all possible Jacob Landstatters, had finally lost my Amanda, out of all possible Amandas? Does a minute flux in the probability stream feel pain? Nonsense. The pain was real, perhaps, but I wasn't. I waited to vanish. But cardiac muscle doesn't know anything about alternate probability worlds, or Shadow, or feelings of unreality, or the Lords. My heart continued beating. My diaphragm continued to pull downward, filling my lungs with air. My stomach rumbled. I was hungry. I got up to make myself a sandwich.

The kitchen was clean and silent. Copper pots and steel utensils hung over the drainboard, and the red curtains puffed in the breeze from the open window. The breadbox contained half a loaf of rye bread, fresh and aromatic. Where the devil had it come from? Amanda couldn't have put it here, she'd obviously been gone for too long. I hefted it. The crust was crisp.

"Stop playing with your food and cut a slice, for God's sake," a voice said behind me. I whirled, loaf in hand. Halicarnassus was sitting at the table in the darkened alcove. "It's impolite to threaten your guests with deadly viands," he observed. "Cut a slice, I said. I've got the mustard and roast beef here."

"How kind of you."

He took a luxurious bite of his sandwich. "Give it up, Jacob. Ah. Rye, beef, and mustard. There are some aesthetic verities that transcend reality. The field of gustatory ontology has been much neglected by philosophers."

"So much the worse for ontology," I said, settling down to lunch with as much grace as I could muster. I really was quite hungry.

"So much the worse for philosophers! All this Truth and Beauty stuff is fine, but it obscures the real issues. Rye bread! I try never to create a world in which it cannot be found. One must have an absolute aesthetic criterion to give an anchor to one's life."

There are worse ones, I suppose. "Did you create that

entire world to give me an object lesson about my personal life?"

"Hey, they have great rye bread in that city. Don't be such an egotist, Jacob. I put that in as a little detail, an ironic reference, like a dog crapping in the corner of a hunting scene. No artist is going to create an entire world just to please one critic's vanity. That's a real world, full of real people. Just like this one."

I had been suspicious for a long time, about the Lords, Centrum, and Samos Halicarnassus, so I decided to risk the question. "Did you create this world, Samos?"

He grimaced. "Yes, and not one of my better efforts, I must say. The Lords are an insufferable bunch, and Centrum is . . . excessive."

"Where are you from?"

He passed a hand over his forehead. "You know, I'm not even sure I remember. A lot of white stone buildings. Apple orchards. A big blue sky. Doesn't tell you much, does it? I guess it didn't tell me much either. But I remember school, a big hall with a dome, and my first world. It was a clunky thing, with brass-and-mahogany steam carriages and wars full of cavalry charges and solemn republics whose capital cities were always built of white marble and top-hatted ambassadors who exchanged calling cards and people who lived, breathed, and died, just like they did at home. I went to live there, a requirement for graduation, I think. I never went back. I just made worlds, Shadows you call them here, and moved on, sometimes into one of mine, usually into one I stumbled onto made, presumably, by someone else."

"So yours was the real world."

"Jacob, I've always been amazed at your inability to detach your emotions from your intellect. That world was created as a private project by a man from a culture so different from this one that my mind does not retain any information about it at all. He was ancient when I was a child, the grandmaster of the school. He died much honored, since he was, I suppose, God." He cut himself another slice of bread. "It would be nice to be certain one existed, but as long as we spend our time twisting time like this, rather than on more rational pursuits, none of us ever will be sure. Most of the inhabitants of the worlds I have created at least *believe* they exist, which gives them the advantage over us. Your Lords devised these absurd Keys in your limbic systems to give you all a sense of reality, since you always feel like you are coming home. A nice touch. You, incidentally, no longer have one."

I remembered my strange dizziness and disorientation at the medical ward. At the time, I had chalked it up to radiation sickness. "How did you manage that?"

"Friends at the hospital in Centrum, willing to do me a favor. And why shouldn't they? I created them, after all. It's really a simple modification, and performed more often than you might think, even in this most real of all possible worlds." He ate the rest of his sandwich and stood up. "Well, that's enough for now. You'll be seeing me again, I think. You're one of my more engaging creations."

"Oh, shut up." I put my head in my hands. This was too much.

"Good luck on your next job."

"What do you know about my next job?"

He grinned maliciously. "It's by Martine."

I choked on my food. "That son of a bitch has taken off with my wife." I stopped. It hurt. It was surprising how much it hurt.

"Don't worry. It's no more real than anything else."

"It's no less real. My guts feel like they've been caught by a fishhook."

"And you sneer at gustatory ontology. Good day, Jacob." And he walked out the door and was gone.

The various portions of the Chancellery Gardens of Laoyin harmonized not only in space, but in time. The arrangement of dells and lily ponds, of individual Dawn Redwoods, laboriously dug, full grown, in the fastness of old China and brought here up the Lao River, which I knew as the Columbia, in barges built for the purpose, of stone temples with green bronze cupolas, and of spreads of native prairie, seemingly engaged in a devious wildness but actually existing because of the efforts of dedicated gardeners, took on meaning only when observed at a receptive stroll. I emerged from the yellow-green of a stand of ginkgoes, descended a gorge alongside a stream, and arrived at the rocky shore of a lake, its verge guarded by cunningly twisted pines and Amur maples. I trod the gravel path farther, and felt uneasy. While I strolled, too many others strode purposefully, usually in tight groups of three or four. The vistas were ignored by men who muttered and gestured to each other. Either trouble was brewing, or the inhabitants of this Shadow had decidedly odd ideas of how to enjoy a sunny afternoon in the park.

A Bodhisattva blessed my exit with bland beneficence. In contrast to the serene order of the Chancellor's garden, the city streets beyond were a tangle. What had been intended as triumphal thoroughfares were blocked every hundred paces by merchants' stalls, religious shrines, or entire shantytowns, complete with chickens and screaming children. Under other circumstances, it would have been a swirling, delightful mess.

However, the streets had the same feeling of oppression as the park. Everywhere there were knots of people discussing dark matters. A scuffle broke out between two groups, one with dark skin and bulbous deformed Mayan heads, shouting loudly and striking out clumsily, the other short, sibilant, with narrow catlike eyes and flat noses, darting with precisely placed energy. Suddenly abashed by the attention they aroused, both groups melted into the surrounding crowds.

"The Prince is dead." Everywhere I heard the murmur. "The Prince, murdered. Vengeance, for our Prince. Where is his murderer? He must be found. He must be killed. The. Prince. Is. Dead." Each word was a call of anguish.

I emerged onto a wide street that had been kept clear. Flat-fronted buildings of basalt bulked on either side, all identical.

There was a sound down the way, the rhythmic thud of metal drums, growing ever louder. In response to some signal not perceptible to me, a crowd had gathered. Some of them were dressed in woolen robes that looked suspiciously familiar to me, but there was no time to think about it. Everyone began to sway in time to the beat. As the sound of the drums approached I could

hear, over it, the baying of hunting horns. I looked up the
street. Sailing toward me like an image from an involun-
tarily recalled memory was the Face.

"Woe!" the crowd wailed. "O woe! Dead. Dead!"
Tears streamed down every face, and every body moved
to the beat of those awful drums. "The Prince! Woe!"
And the Face continued.

It was huge, at least thirty feet high, carved out of
some dark gray-flecked rock. The eyes, blank and piti-
less, stared into mine, and beyond me, to infinity. The
lips were curved in a slight smile, like that of a Buddha,
but seemed to be arrested in the process of changing to
some more definite expression. What would it have
been? A grin? A scowl? A grimace of pain, or anger? Or a
mindless nullity? The Face was of stone and would carry
that secret forever. There were creases in the cheeks, and
the nose was slightly bent at the end. The Prince was
becoming a god, but obviously intended to keep his nose
intact. A god is not handicapped by a twisted nose.

The sculpture rested on a great wagon, each of its
many wheels reaching to twice the height of a man. It
was pulled by teams of men and women, volunteers.
Everyone wanted to help, and unseemly scuffles broke
out for places on the ropes. The drummers seated below
the god's chin occasionally enforced justice by clubbing
someone with their brass drumsticks. And the crowd
cried "Woe!"

The Face swept by, becoming, from behind, a rough-
hewn lumbering mountain of stone.

The mood of the crowd changed. Like a shadowed
pool of blood in the corner of a slaughterhouse suddenly
illuminated by shutters flung open on sunlight, the black
despair of the crowd was revealed as scarlet imperfectly
perceived. Icicles grew on my spine as shouts of rage and
upraised daggers greeted the approach of the second
Face. The daggers . . .

"Murderer!" they cried. "Death!" Though essentially
a thirty-foot-high stone wanted poster, the sculptors had
lavished no less care on this Face than on that of the
Prince. Its brows were knit in jealous rage, its eyes
glowered. Its lips were pulled back in a contemptuous
grin, challenging us all to do our worst. Though fleshier

and more dissipated than I remembered, the Face was familiar. It should have been. I looked at it every morning in the mirror when I shaved. It was my own.

The sculptors had done their work well. So compelling was the Face that no one noticed my real face as, shaking with fear, I slipped through the crowd. Their daggers, with silver hilts chased with a pattern of eyes and lightning bolts, were also familiar. The last time I had seen one, it had been sticking out of a bedpost next to my head.

Martine! It had been him the whole time. He'd sent his creations to kill me in Schekaagau, and when that had failed, he'd exposed me to radiation from his Virgin Mary, so that the cumulative dosage from my visit to Berenson's radioactive world would kill me. Hell, he'd probably locked me in my room at Cuzco. But for what? My wife? It made no sense, but then, murder often made no sense, at least to the victim. But didn't the idiot know that none of this was real?

So Martine had created this entire world just to kill me, despite what Halicarnassus had said about my ego. I should have been flattered, but it's hard to feel flattered when you've pissed in your pants and are fleeing for your life.

I quickly became lost in the tangle of streets, though I really had no idea of where I was going, or for what reason. Everywhere was equally dangerous in this city of Laoyin. The houses were all about four stories high, of cracked stucco, and leaned crazily. The air smelled of frying fish and fermented black beans. I turned a corner into a dusty square. A group of locals sat gloomily around a nonfunctioning fountain. I slunk past them, trying to look nonchalant. I almost made it.

"Look, Daddy!" a little boy said, pointing at me. "Prince!"

"No, it isn't. It's—" Their knives were out in an instant. They didn't waste time debating points of tactics, but launched themselves at me in a mass. I turned and ran.

The tangled streets, confusing enough at a walk, were a nightmare at a dead run. Every few seconds I crashed into a wall or the sharp corner of a building. I began to gain on my pursuers. Despite their hatred, they still had some concern for their bodies. I could not afford to have any.

I broke clear of the high buildings and found myself on a wide promenade, paved with multicolored slabs of rock and bordered on my left by an ornamental railing. Through the railing, far below, were the waters of the Lao, as they flowed toward the Pacific. Leaning casually on the railing, as if on the parapet of his palace, was Martine. He nervously held a gun in his hand, as if unsure of what to do with it. He had been unable to resist taking a direct hand in things, despite all of his efforts to set up a perfect trap for me. I *was* trapped. I stopped. Would he posture, preen, and carry on first, or would he simply gun me down? Right on the first guess.

"At last," he said. "At last I can have my revenge."

"What? What the hell are you talking about?"

"You have tormented and ruined me. I did my best, I poured my soul into my art, but it was not enough for you. My genius was never enough." He raised the pistol. "Say your prayers, Jacob."

"Wait a minute, for God's sake."

"Nothing can stay my hand now, Jacob. Compose yourself for death."

"I'll compose myself for anything you want, if you tell me what you're going on about. You've got Amanda, what more do you want?"

He frowned, confused. "Amanda? What does Amanda have to do with this? How can you mock my work, humiliate me, degrade me—"

I should have known. I grinned in relief. "Is that it? You're all upset because of some lousy reviews? Don't be ridiculous."

His finger whitened on the trigger. "You have destroyed me. Now I destroy you."

"For crissakes, Salvator, are you crazy? Who takes critics seriously?" I was almost in tears. Here I'd finally found someone who paid attention to my criticism, and he wanted to kill me for it. It wasn't fair.

"Make your peace with God, though I have no doubt that you'll pick enough with Him that He'll wish He never created you." Martine was proving to be an extremely gabby murderer.

A knot of people emerged from an alleyway behind Martine. Seeing that he had held me prisoner rather than killing me outright made them smile. It's always nice when someone is willing to share.

I nodded. "All right, Samos. Take him."

Martine snorted. "A feeble ruse, Jacob."

The first man in the group brushed past Martine's elbow. With a shriek, he turned and fired, blowing the man's chest open and leaving him with a surprised and offended expression on his face. Before Martine could get the barrel pointed back in my direction, the blades were into him, silver into scarlet. He screamed once. That done, the blades turned toward me. With the sharp decisiveness that makes for John Doe corpses in the morgue, I took three quick steps and threw myself over the railing into the air. I don't know if I screamed. I know that those behind me did, in disappointment. I watched the river. It didn't seem to get any closer, just more detailed, ripples, whirlpools, and flotsam appearing and sharpening as if on a developing piece of film.

I must have remembered Halicarnassus's modification to my Key subconsciously, because the next instant I found myself, sweating and soiled, in the dark hallway beneath Centrum.

She was home, sitting in the quiet room reading a book about Caravaggio. She looked up at me as I entered, smiled, then went back to her reading, saying nothing. It was not a silence that could be easily broken, for it seemed to me that it would shatter into a thousand pieces at the first word. I walked to the bedroom, took a shower, and changed into household clothes. There was no clothing out, no suitcase, and everything was folded neatly in the drawers. I breathed. The air smelled, just slightly, of jasmine. Jasmine? I went to the kitchen.

Amanda had cleaned up the remains of the final lunch Halicarnassus and I had had together. I opened the green kitchen curtains to have a view of the garden and began to pull out ingredients. Had the knives always been on the left side of the drawer? How observant was a critic? I examined the curtains. Still green. The last time I had seen them, at lunch, they had been red. That I remembered.

One Shadow differing from another in only one minor, but significant, way. Amanda and I had had a discussion about those curtains. I had wanted green, but finally gave in. My hand shook a little as I chopped the onions, as I began to realize that Halicarnassus had sent me drifting through Shadow, with no way to ever return to the world I had spent my whole life believing was the real one.

I flipped the top of the garbage can up to throw away the onion peels. Inside, crumpled, was a set of red curtains. A note was pinned to them. "You'll never know," it said. "Get used to it." It didn't need a signature.

I stir-fried beef and ginger, and thought about the woman in the other room. Was this the woman I had married, who had betrayed me? Or was this someone else? If Amanda was different enough that she would not betray me, could I still love her? I was adrift in a sea of infinite worlds, so I was starting to think that it didn't really matter. I could discuss it with Halicarnassus, when we finally ran into each other again. Somehow, I was sure that we would.

When it was finished, I took the food in to Amanda. It tasted very good.

ABOVE ANCIENT SEAS

Tessa Wolholme stood in the shadow of the twisted-trunked banyan that had forced its way through the cracked wooden foundation of the Calrick Bend railway station and watched the distant black speck of the hawk as it soared the updrafts over Angel's Butte. For an instant she felt almost embarrassed to be standing with two feet on solid ground. The hawk could look down into the endless canyons of Koola's Western Shield with wide-aspect eyes, taking in with a glance journeys that took the canyon inhabitants days and weeks. If it wished it could see Tessa's sun-hatted figure, heavy suitcases resting to either side, and then, with just a slide of its eyes, examine the cascading roofs of Hammerswick School in its peaceful box canyon above Perala. The bird, a native of Koola, probably ignored it all, as it did the rest of the inscrutable activities of those alien intruders on its world, human beings.

It had taken Tessa two days to make that hawk's-eye-flick journey from Hammerswick to middle Cooperset Canyon. As she stood by the hanging rail, which still vibrated with the train's departure up-canyon, waiting for her brother Dom to pick her up, she realized she would never rest with a book in Hammerswick's quiet study garden again. That part of her life was over. Her mother was dead from a sudden wasting fever. Tessa had returned to bury her and, returning, would not leave. She felt as if her own life had just ended as well.

The hawk slid directly sideways, scratching its belly on

185

the wind, and vanished behind the rocky plates that made up Dragon's Back. It did not reappear, and with the disappearance of its eyes, Hammerswick and Perala became definitively part of another world.

"Tessa!" a voice called. She hesitated, as if moving was giving something up, then left her bags and ran toward it.

Dom caught her up and swung her. Everything blurred but her brother's sturdy face, its tightly curled black hair quite unlike Tessa's looser brown. He put her down and they looked at each other appraisingly, challenge already beginning.

"Town life agrees with you." His tone concealed a hint of accusation, as if she had deserted them all. "You've filled out."

"Filled out" was one of those terms older people used to younger ones that Tessa never failed to find annoying. Dom was only eighteen. If he'd already started talking that way, he was doomed.

"I learned a lot there." She strove to relax.

"Oh? Anything at all useful?"

She tightened her jaw. "That remains to be seen." Not two minutes with him and she wanted to fight. It must be something about the way older brothers smell. Pheromones. That was it.

"So when will you be going back? You *do* want to go back, don't you?" Trust him to hit her most sensitive spot right off. It wasn't pheromones, it was just plain meanness.

She was too tired to fight. "I'm not going back, Dom. That's what Poppa told me." She looked out across the dense plantings of the twenty-kilometer-wide Calrick Bend. The green-and-gold growth lapped against the sheer pink canyon walls, which, in turn, marched grandly off in either direction. This was her home and it had reclaimed her. "He needs me here. Now that Momma's gone—"

"Now that Momma's gone we don't need anyone else. You can just go back and study ancient interplanetary history or whatever you want."

"Now, Dom Wolholme, there's no reason to get nasty with me. I just got off the train. I haven't slept all night.

And Momma's dead." To her dismay she found herself fighting back tears. It didn't make it any easier to see that he was doing the same thing. "Give me a chance."

"Sorry." Dom apologized the same way he washed dishes, a quick swipe and done.

"Fine. Please pick up my bags."

Without waiting to watch him, she hopped on the cart. The low-slung mule glanced back at her, erecting its vertebral spines, and flicked out a split tongue. It then returned to its contemplation of a grass clump. "If you don't decide to eat soon, it'll be too late." The mule ignored her. She was clearly a prophet without honor in her own canyon.

"God," Dom grunted behind her. "Everything I own doesn't weigh this much."

"A lady has special needs. For example, I own more than one pair of underwear."

Dom was too demoralized to come back at her, and she was immediately sorry. Momma was dead. She could feel her family loosening around her. And God knew they needed to be tied together. Life on Koola demanded it.

Dom yanked at the mule's reins. It abruptly decided that the grass clump was the most delicious thing it had ever seen, but had time for only one mouthful before it was forced, resentfully, to move off.

Calrick Bend was a wide elbow of Cooperset Canyon. The hanging rail ran above the high talus slopes that covered the base of the eastern wall, so Dom and Tessa had a wide sweeping view as they descended from the station. The canyon walls were broken here and there by the terraces of tributary canyons, their outpourings marked by giant boulders. Hundreds of kilometers beyond were the frowning giants of the Boss. One could climb toward them for weeks and find them no nearer. Kardom, the northernmost visible peak, trailed a fine line of snow into a high wind, glowing in the morning light. Despite herself, Tessa thought it had to be one of the most beautiful places on Koola.

They dropped into the vine-laced stillness of the fields and were closed in by plants. The lush aromatic air here was not that of the high canyons and mountains. Tessa sniffed at it, trying to decide if she liked it. Unlike the thick air above the salt pans of the Great Valleys, deeper in Koola's atmosphere, this was an air made by human beings.

The mule maneuvered through the kinked lanes with the ease of long familiarity. Tessa found herself craning forward and, after a while, was rewarded by glimpses of the house through the fronds overhead. The Wolholme house hung from the cliff face, growing larger the higher up it went, like all farmers' houses unwilling to take up valuable growing land for the mere business of protecting humans from the elements. The morning sun reflected in its windows. It was a beautiful house, designed by her father, who should have been an architect rather than a farmer. As the wagon approached, the plants grew lower, becoming the kitchen garden, until the entire house was visible at once, as well as the sturdy tower of the Wolholme family ward that rose beside it.

The rest of the family waited at the door. Benjamin, three years younger than Tessa's sixteen standard, stood and cried. He'd probably been crying for days. He always overdid everything. Standing next to Benjamin, one small hand on the doorway to keep himself steady, was Kevin, the youngest. He gazed up at Tessa with grave eyes. Looming over them both was Perin Wolholme, Poppa, a vast balding man who stood blinking at her as if he had expected someone entirely else.

She regarded them with trepidation, for they all looked at her as if she was supposed to do something to make it all work. Then she jumped from the cart and put her arms around her father's huge chest.

Dom and Benjamin squabbled over who should carry Tessa's bags into the house. Dom, previously resentful of the task, won. Kevin trotted along behind, assisting with one hand under a corner of a suitcase, until he tripped in the doorway. He found something interesting in the pattern of the cut stone and sat there in fascination, completely in everyone's way.

The others went up the stairs to her room, but Tessa stopped in the second-floor living room. Momma had been dead less than three days. The room was already a mess. Not blatantly, but Tessa knew Momma would never have left a clump of tree-training wire hanging by the door, or allowed anyone to set sprouting pots down on the rug. And who had dared to use one of Momma's large trilobite fossils as a doorstop? Tessa pulled it away. The door swung loose, obviously needing to be rehung.

Holding the heavy fossil, she walked to the window. Leafy trees with white blossoms and spiky calyx plants filled the view. On the canyon wall's next spur hung the great house of the Dalhousies with its many roof terraces. A figure strolled across one, serene in its dominion, but she couldn't recognize who it was. The Dalhousies were a large family. She held the trilobite up to the light. Segments gleaming black, its back was twisted, seemingly with the pain of its passing. When she had been younger Tessa had seen the random marks on the rock substrate as the traces of the legs' last frantic scrabbling. Now she wasn't sure.

"Benjamin!" It would do the boy good to have work. He appeared, sniffling. "Put those wires where they belong. Be careful! If you tangle them it will take all day to get it straight. And when you see him, tell Dom to carry these pots out of here. This is the living room, not the nursery. The rugs I'll clean myself. I can't expect you boys to handle anything like that." The last remark was unnecessary but made her feel better.

Enough delay. She climbed the stairs to her mother's room, trilobite under one arm as if to weigh her down. The door swung open at her touch.

Sora lay stretched out on the bed. It could not be mistaken for sleep: in life she had always slept curled up in a ball. She wore the long-waisted gray-and-pink sleeveless dress she had favored at the time Tessa left for school. She'd been wearing it during the last argument Tessa had with her. Tessa remembered shouting, feeling her face distend with anger, but try as she might she could not remember what the argument had been about. She turned and carefully placed the trilobite, a piece of evidence in that mysterious investigation into the ancient depths of Koola that had been Momma's abiding private interest, on the lace covering of the bureau, amid the keepsakes that crowded there, already dulling with dust.

Momma looked older now, without her quick movements to belie the face wrinkled by sun and wind. Her hands were folded prayerfully on her stomach. And—Tessa frowned—she wore her favorite sunstone ring on her left hand. In Tessa's life she had never seen Momma wear it other than on her right. Wincing at the feel of dead flesh, she switched it to the proper finger.

That was the sign for Tessa to see all the other incongruities in her mother's appearance. Her makeup was too emphatically applied, her lips an odd shade of red. Tessa remembered Momma bringing the tube back from some exclusive shop in Perala, laughing in dismay at the way it made her look when she finally got it home, and throwing it not in the trash, but, as women do, back in her case. The slim golden tube had obviously caught some unperceptive male eye. Tessa wiped the makeup off with cream and reapplied it properly. Then the dangling earrings—hadn't it occurred to anyone that Momma was lying down rather than standing up? Finally, the X-belt just under the breasts was backward. She switched it around. Her mother felt light in her arms. Tessa let her breath out. Her mother was dead.

Protesting voices came up the stairs. Vainly protesting—they had a tone of foreseen defeat. The bedroom door swung open, revealing the figure of a ponderous woman with a huge spray of hair, carrying a vast shapeless bag.

"Theresa!" She dropped the bag with a heavy thump and opened her arms. Her voice was a resonant tenor.

"Dalka." Tessa hid her reluctance and slid into the embrace of her mother's best friend. Dalka's breasts were extravagantly large, the sort that dismayed rather than comforted men and infants. God knew they dismayed Tessa. In the face of this aggressive statement of matriarchy, her own womanhood became an afterthought.

Tessa didn't want to be forcibly comforted. She wanted to crawl away somewhere private to think. But she found herself weeping into Dalka's capacious bosom. "Oh, Dalka, I never said a nice thing to her. We just fought. What can I say now?"

"Hush, Theresa. No woman expects her sixteen-year-old daughter to love her. No sensible woman, that is, and Sora was as sensible as they come. She knew you'd understand eventually."

"But did she know I'd understand too late?"

Dalka just made a comforting noise.

"Dalka . . . can you help me wash her hair?"

"Surely, Theresa. It is a mess, isn't it? She was real sick and no one thought much about anything else." She opened the door, brusquely ordered a basin from whoever was standing there, and found Sora's aromatic shampoo.

Together the two women washed Sora's hair, then set and dried it, as slowly and patiently as if performing an ancient ritual. The men buzzed around the closed door like disturbed wasps but did not dare intrude.

Finally they pulled shining threads through the hair, accenting the curving lines they had put in it. Tessa was astonished by how thick her mother's hair was. Her own hair was much thinner, but then she lacked much of her mother's beauty, being stronger and shorter, from Perin's blood.

Dalka picked up Sora's hand and pulled off the sunstone ring Tessa had just transferred there. She smiled grimly. "We want her to look nice, but there's no reason in your family's starving for it." She started to put the ring back in the jewelry case, then turned and put it on, with some difficulty, over Tessa's thicker finger. "There. As safe a place for it as I can think. A better memory of your momma than putting it under the fleshgrass at Topfield to be dug up by high plainsmen, isn't it?"

Tessa looked down at the ring and nodded.

Perin knocked. "Please." He held his hands in fists, an oddly aggressive posture he took in moments of nervousness. He peered over Dalka's shoulder at his daughter and dead wife, blinking. "The death cart is waiting. We must leave soon if we're to make Topfield—"

Dalka slapped his shoulder the way one man would another. "Do good by her, will you?"

"I will. Our family is strong enough."

"I hope you're right." She turned to look back at Tessa. In the dimness of the hall her eyes seemed extraordinarily large. "I'll talk with you later, Theresa." Tessa and Perin stood and listened to the creak of the stairs beneath Dalka's bulk.

"Well then. Well then." Perin stood over his wife's body and looked down at it as if he had found her napping and was wondering whether to awaken her. His large hands dangled loose at his sides.

Tessa started to move out of the room, to give her father privacy, but paused at the door, overcome by curiosity. Who were these people, her parents, and what had they meant to each other? Perin knelt by his wife's side and wept bitter unashamed tears, sobbing so hard he sounded like he was hiccuping. He put an arm around her waist and pulled her to him, resting his head on her shoulder and disarranging her hair. Tessa turned her head away, suddenly feeling her intrusion, but not before she saw, with sick shock, that her father's hand held her mother's now-cold breast.

Dom and Benjamin stood stony-faced in the hall holding the funeral pallet. The heavy scent of its flowers, woven around the edge by the neighborhood women, filled the hall. It made Tessa dizzy, and she put a hand against a wall to steady herself.

"Come in and get her." Their father's voice was muffled. "Come." With an air of exaggerated dignity, the two boys stepped through with the pallet. The men clustered around their dead woman and Tessa stood in the hall, watching their backs and wondering at their passions.

Like all houses in the Shield's upper valleys, the Wolholme house had a Death's Door at the rear, just under the cliff. It was used for the exit of a corpse and no other purpose, so that if the dead got lonely in their grave beneath the fleshgrass of Topfield and tried to return home, the only door they could find would be sealed against them. Characteristically, Perin had lavished great care on this almost-always-useless portal. It was surrounded by dark tiling, and the doors themselves were carved with flowers. The foil-and-wax seal over it tore as Perin pulled back the bolt, and the two heavy doors, perfectly balanced, swung open into the noonday sun.

Dom and Benjamin, strong wide-shouldered boys, carried Sora lightly on her pallet and slid it onto the high spring-wheeled death cart. They looked so manly and serious that Tessa suddenly felt overwhelmingly proud of them.

A few of their neighbors stood among the trees to bid farewell, but most of the people of Calrick Bend would wait, prudently, until the Wolholmes returned from the burial, their success in carrying the body to its final resting place a reaffirmation of their strength as a family.

The cart was ancient and motorized, a common property of the communities of this length of Cooperset Canyon. Parts of it were rumored to have come, centuries ago, from Earth itself. They climbed aboard and hummed up-canyon.

Calrick Bend's community cemetery was at Topfield, in the dry, high valleys that backed up against Evening Crest.

Funerals were always performed by members of the deceased's family, a significant test of their strength, stamina, and solidarity. Failure to bury a dead family member at Topfield was an indication that the family could no longer maintain itself or its holdings.

Where Sterm Canyon split from Cooperset the road became rough, climbing the dry bed. Coiling tubes emerged from the red rock, turgid with the water they had sucked from deep aquifers, but no one farmed here, and only native Koolan plants grew. The canyon walls were defaced by old mining operations. Metal was rare anywhere on Koola, but particularly here on the Shield, a continent of light rock that rose up out of the dense atmosphere of the flats that made up the rest of the planet's surface. The embedded remains of heavy asteroids, a possible cause of the Shield's existence, were the only source of metals.

Tessa remembered the story of the Prochnows, who, weary, riven with internal dissension, had spent a week taking their father's body to Topfield, or so they announced when they returned with the cart. A few weeks later a hunter found the father's body hidden in an old excavation here in Sterm Canyon, at least two days' travel from Topfield, which they had never reached. The Prochnow family had been unable to survive the disgrace and had vanished as an organized unit. Better to die, Tessa thought. Better to die in the heights of Evening Crest, lungs drying in the merciless Koolan air, than have the Wolholmes end that way.

"Mother came here to hunt her stone bugs," Dom said, half sorrowful, half contemptuous. Indeed, the exposed rock layer flanking the jolting track was dense with a tangle of ancient Koolan seafloor life.

"She wanted to understand where we come from," Tessa said. The men in the family had never understood Sora's paleontological hobby. But that wasn't fair: Tessa had never understood it either. Now it seemed overwhelmingly important that she do so.

"We didn't come from here," Benjamin jeered, with the self-confidence of the possessor of an inarguable school-approved fact. "We came from Earth."

Tessa eyed him. "I remember when the midwife pulled out a little screaming lump and Poppa named it Benjamin. So I can tell you that you didn't come from Earth. Any further claims?"

"You know what I mean," Benjamin began heatedly.

"This is no time for fighting," Dom cautioned.

"Tell *her* that."

"No need," Tessa said with deliberate serenity. "No need, Earthman."

"I met her here," Perin said dreamily, as if his children weren't fighting around him.

"Momma?" Tessa said, argument forgotten. "Here in Sterm Canyon?"

Perin nodded. "She was trying to free a fossil. I heard her swearing before I saw her. She thought she was alone and was embarrassed when she saw me. But I helped her."

Tessa could almost see the scene: her impatient mother, young, at a disadvantage, but unwilling to reject the help, and Perin's large, careful hands working a chisel around the delicate trapped fossil as he glanced, thoughtfully, at the odd woman he had unexpectedly cornered.

"Which fossil was it?" Tessa asked.

He frowned. "I don't remember. It wasn't very large. Kind of lacy. I'm sure it's still in the collection somewhere."

"And why were you here?" Dom and Benjamin leaned forward while Kevin dozed, curled up with a hand over his face. Her brothers were equally interested in the answers, but were willing to let her ask all the questions.

"A funeral, what else?" He looked up Sterm Canyon toward the cliffs that marked its end. "*My* mother's, then. I had let the cart with my family go ahead, and was walking alone. After then, your mother walked with me."

"You persuaded her to come with you?" Tessa was distressed to hear the tone of doubt in her voice. But how had the gentle, shambling Perin persuaded the intent Sora to leave her task, her joy, and come with him?

For the first time since his daughter had come home, Perin smiled, remembering. "No, Tessa. I wanted to go ahead alone. I had just stopped to help, nothing else. It was she who insisted on coming with me."

Clearly unwilling to answer any further questions, Perin settled back, crossed his arms, and closed his eyes. But traces of the just-passed smile remained on his face.

Before climbing to Topfield they spent the night at the funeral encampment, an open area around a water seep. One other family, with the body of a young child, stayed at the opposite end of camp, but the two families did not speak. In the morning, by unspoken agreement, the Wolholmes moved out at first light, taking the death cart as far as the base of the switchback Topfield trail.

Just where the trail rose toward its first switchback was a pair of giant fossil trilobites, each about two meters long. An entire five-meter layer of the cliff face was filled with such fossils, but these were by far the largest, flanking the path like guardians. Centuries of human hands touching them for luck had rubbed them smooth. Her mother had particularly thought of them as lucky, Tessa remembered, representatives of the native Koolan forces that the human settlers had yet to come to terms with. At home was a photograph of a four-year-old Tessa perched on one, smiling nervously.

It was a long heavy climb up the trail, trading off the weight of the pallet and their mother's body. The spiky plants along the trail twisted slowly when they sensed the moisture of the human beings. Tear-drinking flies, a symbol of funerals, settled on their cheeks to reclaim some salty water. After several hours' climb, Tessa leaned out and looked down the cliff face to the canyon below. The tiny figures of the family with the dead child were just commencing their climb. Their heads were down, concentrating on each step.

The cliff edge was sharp. One moment the Wolholmes were climbing desperately up the face, breath sharp in their lungs, the next they stood on the wide fleshgrass-covered expanse of Topfield. Fleshgrass lived on the bodies buried beneath it. When this barren high valley had become Calrick Bend's community cemetery, there had been only sparse clumps of it here and there on bare dirt. Now it lapped up at the distant hills as if desperate to climb toward the higher mountains that loomed beyond.

Dom led the family a long way into the valley before finding a spot, no different than any other, that satisfied him. The fleshgrass was thick under their feet. Dom, Benjamin, and Tessa pulled out the folding shovels that had been stowed under the pallet and marked the grave. Kevin had brought, on his own, a toy shovel and with childish concentration straightened the line of his older siblings' cut.

The soil beneath the fleshgrass was loose and easy to dig. It didn't take long to empty a hole deep enough for their mother. The roots would grow through her in days. As far as Tessa knew, clothes and jewelry would remain below, for all the tales she'd heard of wedding rings being found waving on fleshgrass fronds. It was also said that high plainsmen sometimes descended from their encampments beyond the Boss and dug through the ground seeking valuables.

They slid Sora's body off the pallet into the ground and covered her over. Tessa turned away as her mother's still face vanished beneath the dry gray soil.

"We'll survive, Sora," Perin said, kneeling by the grave. "Just like I promised you."

Benjamin made an inarticulate sound in his throat and pointed. They all looked up.

No more than a hundred meters away stood a Great Wapiti, a huge quadruped, two meters at the shoulder, with curving knife-edged horns. It was a native of Koola, though had been given some approximate name from an animal of old Earth.

"My God," Dom muttered. "It's so close. So close!"

The wapiti stalked along, graceful and powerful, as if aware of their impotence and the solemnity of their task. At last, coming near a rock slope, it crouched and, with an incredible leap, vanished.

Benjamin looked after it. "Look!" He pointed. "A troop of high plainsmen. You can just see their horses. They must be hunting the wapiti." Tessa squinted to see what he saw.

Dom didn't even bother to glance up from pulling the fleshgrass over the grave. "Don't be ridiculous. The Plateau is hundreds of kilometers farther, beyond the Boss. That's the face of Evening Crest, Ben, and there aren't any plainsmen there. You're imagining things."

"Am not." Benjamin thrust his lower jaw out in a gesture Tessa remembered her mother making while arguing with Perin.

"It doesn't matter," Tessa said. "We have to get back to funeral camp before dark."

So they turned and left Sora there beneath the grass.

The funeral ceremonies had been, in their own way, more strenuous than the climb to Topfield. First there had been the argument over which symbol of their mother's would be included in the Wolholme family ward. Tessa hadn't quite dared suggest a trilobite fossil from the collection, and had found Perin's final, and inarguable, selection, Sora's favorite pair of pruning shears, eerily correct, despite its inadequacy. Tessa had tried to pick a fight without telling Poppa what it was about, but he had not risen to the bait, as Sora surely would have, and merely stuck his thick Wolholme fingers partway through the fine handles and clumsily clicked the blades to show by the mismatch how well they had, in contrast, fit Sora's hand.

And after the attachment of the shears to the upper part of the ward, there had been the feast at long tables under the low-hanging branches of the family dilberry grove. All the families of Calrick Bend had sent representatives, even the most-high Dalhousies and Minishkins, some closer friends arriving with all generations. Tessa and her brothers had worked desperately to feed them all the spicy-sweet cakes that were always served at this event and no other. Dom claimed his butt had forgotten what a chair felt like. But their weariness was good, a prelude to relaxation, for the family would survive. Momma lay properly at Topfield, and the Wolholmes were back in their fields and groves.

Now Tessa sat alone under those dilberries, right at the side of the ward, and tried to think things through. She mended clothing as she considered, having learned long ago from Momma that no one would task her for wasting time on thought if she seemed to be doing something useful.

The ward was a tower of family symbols, and one stood beside each house, a sign of the family's persistence. Some wards had bases of mysterious silvery metals brought from Earth, metals poor Koola could no longer make. And more than one ward rested on a vivid green-blue sphere representing that far-away planet, Mother of All. The Dalhousies, for example, had been big on Earth, and wished this known. For all Tessa knew, they had owned that planet and come to Koola only on holiday, to be stuck here by an unexpected change of interplanetary transport schedule.

The oldest things Tessa could see in the high-tension ceramic matrix of the Wolholme ward's base could not have been much more than a century old, more than two centuries younger than the initial settlements on Koola: an enamel portrait of a woman holding a child, a man's bronzed sun hat, and another pair of pruning shears, these with long curved blades.

"Ah, Theresa." Though heavy, Dalka could move quietly when she had a mind to. She sat down next to Tessa and dropped her bag. "Now we can get to business." She paused, and frowned. "Why are you wasting so much thread on those rear buttons?"

"Benjamin catches them on trellises and rips them off." Tessa was deliberately patient with Dalka's interference even in trifles. She hoped Dalka noticed. "He likes to climb."

"We all do, when we're young. Well, even when we're not. At least that foolish city school Sora insisted on sending you to hasn't ruined you completely for real life."

Tessa felt the power and oppression of village life settling over her like a weighted bird net. "Momma had good reasons for sending me there. If the Wolholmes are to survive—"

"If the Wolholmes are to survive, dear, you're going to have to see to it. Sora, poor dear, married for love."

"Careful, Dalka." To her surprise, Tessa found herself on the verge of losing her temper. She carefully folded Benjamin's coveralls.

"Now, now." Dalka chuckled. "I'm not attacking poor Perin, darling. But you have more responsibilities than a lady should, and less help in carrying them out." She pulled something from her bag and held it out to Tessa. "Recognize this?"

"People call them judeflowers." Tessa looked at the bundled leaves and petals and remembered both her mother's lessons and her botany class at Hammerswick, though reconciling the two was sometimes difficult. "It has a false stem that's actually fused bracts." She raised her eyebrows.

"Goodness, what a clever child Sora raised. Do you know its uses?"

"No, Dalka, I don't."

"Oh dear, don't be so angry." Dalka put the flowers back in her bag. "They serve as a constituent of a coordinating enzyme substrate for fat-soluble vitamins. We use them to grow an intestinal yeast for hiking the back country. An inoculation lasts maybe two–three weeks, residing in the ileum of the small intestine. Enough for a good overpass hike, if not to live permanently in the high plains. Lord knows how the high plainsmen do it." She sighed. "There are real mysteries up there, girl. They've done some first-rate enzyme work."

"Momma talked about that . . . but she never taught me."

"Of course not, dear. You were too young to appreciate the subtlety of it—and the subtlety's everything and why men don't fiddle with it." Dalka put her arm around Tessa. "Humans wouldn't be able to live on Koola a day if it weren't for the tailored yeasts and bacteria we women produce in our little kitchen fermenters. It scares men, you know. Best thing about it, really. Tell them tailored bacteria, and they come up with stories of dead bodies with nervous systems full of living microbes lurching down from the high burials to find the doors they were carried out of." She shook her head in rueful amusement. "So they build special doors for corpses while we tighten the knots in the Web."

"The Web?" Tessa found the catechism annoying.

"The Web that keeps us from falling into the crevasses right under life on Koola. It's supported us since time im-mem-morial." Dalka lingered over the word as if it was a particularly delicious chocolate. She waved her arm, fat jiggling. "Take these dilberries, for example."

Tessa looked up at the purple oil-containing fruit dangling just above them.

"If these trees were left alone," Dalka said, "they'd die out. Nothing fertilizes them naturally. But they're held by the Web. Men distract little wasps into them by hanging tangleflowers all over the trees. A paltry male secret. Did you ever look at those flowers and wonder why they were there?"

"I did, but—"

"But you thought it was all for love!" Dalka barked a laugh. "Well, we'll see next spring, won't we? Then I bet you won't be sorry to be back from school."

Tessa saw no need to respond to the sally. Lush tangleflower blossoms cascading from the branches, their intoxicating scent filling the dilberry groves, were a symbol of romance. It was a commonplace that a girl, having made love to her first boy under the trees, returned home with her loose hair full of tangleflower petals.

"Who invented it all, Dalka?" Tessa kept her thoughts on the matter at hand.

Dalka slowed for the first time. "It's been done since time immem—"

"You said that." Tessa's lessons at Hammerswick came to her rescue. "But the ancestors of dilberries are native to Koola, while the wasps are gene-modified and come from Tal-Tal-Monga, famous for its biological products. And the tangleflowers—no one knows. So who put them all together?"

"That's the magic of the Web." Dalka retreated into obscurity. "And Sora wished you to learn its secrets."

"Yes, Dalka."

Tessa started the next morning by hanging vegetables up to dry. The long dark-blue roots would, in a few weeks, taste like thick, greasy meat. No one in the upper Shield valleys favored the taste, but city dwellers on the edge of the Great Flats enjoyed it, for some reason. They were stupid enough to live down there in the thick air and so could not be expected to have sense about other things.

With mindless meticulousness, she quartered the arm-long tubers and strung them on the rack. She would take a stroll about the kitchen garden whenever her arms got tired and look off across the farms to the other wall of the canyon. At that moment farming seemed so painful that it had obviously been ordained by God as punishment for unknown sins.

She'd brought books back from Hammerswick but had progressed little in reading them. There was always some task to interrupt her, whether it was Benjamin's hand, cut on a trellis, or the filth that accumulated in the house as if delivered daily by some unusually dutiful service, or simply the countless varities of plant that grew in the canyon to be harvested every month. She had been able to spend very little time with the upstairs fossil collection, its complex Koolan taxonomies worked out in Sora's careful hand, and longed to find out more about this, her mother's private fascination. There were times now when she saw the farms and fields of Calrick Bend for what they were: a microscopically thin overlay of human action over an alien and enigmatic planet. That did not make the tubers any lighter.

After one turn about the garden she found Benjamin

himself. He sat on the side stairs by the drying rack, paying diligent attention to the tension swivels on his dart rifle. He'd pulled the webbing off and was deliberately tightening it, strand by strand.

She sat down next to him. "Going hunting, Benjamin?"

"Yeah." He didn't look at her but bent his head to his task. "It's something that's got to be done."

Tessa looked at her younger brother's curly-haired head. What made men so certain about things that were only guesses, presumptions, and dreams? "There's plenty that has to be done here."

He finally looked up at her, his dark eyes appraising. "I *know* that. One thing is that I'm going to get that wapiti. The one, you remember, at Momma's burial. That's number one. Then me and Dom can get this family working again."

Tessa fought down the anger that came at this childish arrogance. "How is killing the wapiti going to help?"

"I've been in the high valleys. It's still up there. Something's brought it down from the Boss. But I can find it. And kill it."

"That's good, Benjamin. But right now you can come and help me finish hanging these vegetables."

He looked disgusted. "Come on. That's your job. I have more important things to do."

"Like hunting wapiti."

"Like hunting wapiti." His voice rose. "Like seeing that this family doesn't just disappear."

"We won't disappear. But it takes work. We all have to work."

"Don't talk to me like that!" Benjamin was near tears. "You're not Momma. You can't tell me what to do. You can't run this family—"

Tessa felt her temper starting to fray. "I'm not trying to run this family."

"Dom. Dom and I can run this family. We know what to do. We don't need you messing into it."

This was too much. Before he could react, Tessa darted forward, seized him with a strength she hadn't known she had, and hung him up by his belt on the drying rack. He yelped. She looked at him in satisfaction. "You can just hang up there with the rest of the vegetables until you dry out."

Completely forgetting his manly demeanor, Benjamin broke into tears. He wailed and kicked his legs.

"What the hell is this?" Dom strode past Tessa and regarded his brother. Benjamin choked down his sobs. Dom shook his head and pulled him off. Not looking at either of his siblings, Benjamin ran into the house, head down.

"You forgot your dart rifle!" Tessa shouted after him.

Dom bent over and picked it up. He looked at her. Annoyance and amusement vied for control of his face. "Now, Tessa, what did you have to go and do that for? Things are tough enough for him. His pride—"

"*His* pride?" Tessa was outraged. "What about mine?"

"He's only thirteen."

"Time for him to start learning about what's important." They stared at each other. "Any other objections?"

"No. There's too much to get done." He walked slowly away, dart rifle under his arm.

Kevin ran out of the house. "Ben's crying!" His earnest face demanded more information.

"Yes, Kevin. He's very upset."

This seemed sufficient explanation. Kevin reached into the bin and wrestled out a tuber as long as he was. "Can I help?" It slithered in his arms as if alive. He stumbled around trying to subdue it, his face a mask of grim resolve. Tessa turned away, using every ounce of determination to keep from laughing. Pride was nothing to be trifled with.

"We all climb up here," Dalka said, breath wheezing dangerously as she labored up the trail. "But each of us seeks something different." She pulled herself up onto a rock ledge, grunting. Below her was a hundred-meter drop. She sat down to dangle her feet over the edge and pulled out her pipe. On a planet with higher gravity she would have been confined; on Koola she was free.

"Men hunt," Tessa said, sitting down next to her.

"They do. To no good purpose, in protein/energy

balance terms." Dalka puffed the pipe to light. "The time would be more usefully spent planting another crop."

"I don't think they see it in protein/energy balance terms."

"That's why they need us, dear." Above their ledge was a slope made up of large toppled rock slabs. Dalka gestured at it. "We come up here for necessaries, not silly animals. The air's right up here for the proper lichens. They should be on the shaded sides of those rocks."

The air was thin and cold, shrugging off any influence of human beings. It was a high Shield air, dry and unforgiving. Tessa took the dry feeling in her nostrils as a benison. They had been climbing all morning, floating up the tilted cliff side, to this specific hanging alcove, a special place of Dalka's. The lush bottom of Cooperset Canyon was now invisible behind cliffs and towers of rock.

Tessa climbed partway up the rock fall and searched shadowed cracks for the particular silver-blue lichen Dalka wanted. Its paracrinelike secretions were specific and rare, essential to Dalka's enzyme operations. Was this really how she wanted to spend her rare days free of farm work? Tessa sighed, carefully inaudible.

"We do have to watch out for them, of course." Dalka's tenor voice carried easily on the breeze. "They know these high valleys, of course, as well as we do. Better, maybe, because they run around so much, chasing their beasts." She made the admission grudgingly. "But they still get lost, and since they're convinced that they *don't* get lost, they're hard to find. You'll find an occasional dried-up body in a crevasse—the bad end of an unsuccessful hunting trip. No telling how old they are."

Tessa paused and peered down into the shadows. Was that a bony hand stretching out toward the sunlight from beneath the rock? No, no, it was just a couple of dried twigs. She squinted at it one last time and went back to work. A patch of the necessary lichen covered the top lip of a particularly precarious rock.

"So how do you watch out for them?" she asked, after a moment. Dalka did not reply immediately, but sent up an exceptionally large puff of smoke, as if to remind Tessa where she was.

Tessa chimneyed up to the lichen and hung there as she scraped at it. It smelled bitter and dusty. From her precarious perch she could see the shattered teeth of Ariel's, Fulda's, Top Hat, and Angel's Buttes, blue with distance. To the right, visible only as a succession of ever-hazier ranges, was the height of the Boss, the Plateau hidden behind it. A sand hawk flew overhead, catching a thermal from the open area at the base of Caspar's Lith. Tessa paused in her work, feeling the glory of the heights. There was nothing she liked better than walking the high cliffs, when she had a chance. Dalka did too, puffing and wheezing her way formidably up the slopes, so they made natural companions.

"A number of ways," Dalka said finally. Another pause. "Most they don't know about."

"Oh, Dalka," Tessa said, exasperated. "I'm not going to tell."

"I'm sure you won't, dear. Even under the soft blossoms of the tangleflowers."

"When the time for that comes, I'm sure I'll have other things to talk about."

Dalka laughed explosively. "Fair enough, child. And secrets cease to be anything if no one knows them. Well . . . my favorite is a simple one. Do you clean your brothers' boots?"

"Only Kevin's. He's young and they're really tiny, so it's fun. The others stay dirty."

"Give it a try. Just a bit of extra work, nothing for a woman. There's a leather polish, an emollient and binder complex, that works well. As a side effect, the boots then leave traces on the rocks. A few simple enzyme reactions and you can track any given pair of boots, if you have a sensitive nose." She chortled. "And the men think you're doing it so their feet will be clean-shod."

Tessa smiled despite herself. She was starting to think that she might enjoy being as sly as Dalka. She thought about her brothers, and the wapiti, and their male secrets. "Can you show me?"

Dalka smoked thoughtfully while Tessa finished collecting the lichen. "Certainly. It's a set of reactions useful for other purposes as well, so we aren't even being frivolous."

They cooked dinner over a portable heater and rolled out their sleeping bags right near the cliff's edge. Mountains disappeared one by one into the darkness. The rasp of the wind's cold grew sharper.

"Dalka," Tessa said as she lay in her bag staring up at the star-filled sky. "What was my mother looking for?"

"You mean, with all those ancient bugs of hers? Ancestors, I think."

"Ancestors?"

"Of course. We all need them. Look at these wards families spend so much time on. They seek roots to support their branches. Sora just decided that her roots lay here, on Koola, and not anywhere else in the universe. She spent her time trying to understand those roots. It made no sense to me, mind, but that was her business."

"I was born on Koola," Tessa said.

"That you were, child. Go to sleep."

Before Tessa knew it, it was morning, and time to climb back down into the canyon to resume her labors.

Tessa awoke in darkness. She didn't move or thrash around but tried to figure out why she was awake. She lay in her own bed in her own room, and a trace of moonlight came through the window. A shadowy figure loomed.

"Tessa!" Dom hissed. "Wake up."

"I'm awake. Why?"

"It's that idiot, Benjamin. He's gone off."

"Get clear, Dom."

"He thinks he's found the trail of that damn wapiti." Dom was disgusted. "He's been fascinated by it since Momma's funeral."

"I know. He's not been too clear on why."

"He wants to kill it. It will redeem our family."

"Doesn't he know that doesn't make any sense?" Tessa said.

"Never mind that! We have to get him. Now. This is a goddamn embarrassment."

Tessa got out of bed and dressed herself. After a moment's hesitation she grabbed her small bag of chemicals and reagents, wondering if, in future years, it would grow to the size of Dalka's. Perin was still asleep, but an excited Kevin waited for them below. "Where are you going?" he cried.

"Shh, Kevin," Tessa said. "You'll wake Poppa."

"Where are you going?" His voice was the barest whisper, carefully enunciated.

"Benjamin—gotten lost—night—we have to find him—you take care of Poppa." Dom and Tessa interrupted each other in their whispered description.

Kevin listened gravely, then lifted his arm in a farewell salute. "Good luck. Should I make pancakes for when you get back?"

"No," Tessa said. "You'll just make a mess."

Kevin pouted. "You never give me any credit." He sat down on the floor and started playing with the blocks Perin had made for him. There wasn't time to convince him to go back to bed.

"His usual hunting trek is up Pong's Defile, over Torfoot Jumble, and up into Born or Oak," Dom puffed over his shoulder as they ran. "The only thing we can do is start there." Both Koola's moons had risen and gave a clear light.

"Good luck that the moons are out," Tessa said as they clambered over the rocks of Torfoot Jumble.

"If you think about it, little sister, you'll realize that that's the reason he chose tonight to go wapiti hunting."

"Oh."

Dom slowed, and stopped at the splitting point of Born and Oak Canyons. There was no sign of which way Benjamin had gone, if he had indeed come this way at all. Dom sighed and was clearly about to pick a direction at random. Her brother was a careful man, Tessa knew, and that necessity must have been driving him crazy.

Tessa shifted her weight uncomfortably. "Can you wait a minute? I'll be right back."

"Sure." Dom sat down on a rock and stared morosely at the forking canyons ahead.

Tessa wandered off among the rocks as if finicky about where she was going to relieve herself. There were three or four easy ways up to the two canyons, and Benjamin would certainly have taken the route of least resistance. His boots, cleaned and oiled diligently by Tessa to Dalka's instructions, would have left distinct traces on the rocks.

So Tessa walked, stumbling over unseen obstructions, and searched out the trails that had led up this way since—she grimaced—time immemorial. At every likely spot she sprayed a bit of the enzyme complex Dalka had given her. On her sixth try she smelled the sharp stink of the reaction. Benjamin had gone up Born Canyon.

But there was no visible trace of Benjamin's passing. She wasn't about to explain the whole enzyme business to Dom, so she needed a better reason for deciding that this was the right direction. A few minutes of search up and down the trail rewarded her: just the trace of Benjamin's boot tread in a patch of sand.

"Dom!" she shouted. "Here!"

He appeared in moments and stared down at the almost imperceptible boot print. "Good job, Tessa," he said, finally. He scanned his eyes slowly up the trail, and pointed out something Tessa had not seen, a twig broken by Benjamin's climb over a rock fall. "Let's go."

"It was a lucky find," Tessa said. "I was just—"

"I said good job and I meant it. Don't waste energy worrying about *my* pride. Let's go."

Tessa followed, slightly ashamed of herself.

They crossed a spur and Tessa saw a glow in the distance. Dawn? No—it was early for that yet. The light source rose out of the rocks, far away, visible through a crack in the canyon wall beyond. Suddenly, she realized what it was: the lights of Perala. Where the Hammerswick Academy still was, most of its students virtuously asleep except for those who were even more virtuously up studying. She remembered her time there, an interval of civilization in her life. Now she was climbing through the dark mountains with one crazy intent brother in pursuit of a second. Perala looked so close, as if she could reach out, grab the top of Rock Bastion, which guarded its upstream approach, and pull herself there to drop into her old bed in the dorm.

Dom was already far ahead of her. She hurried in pursuit.

Dawn seemed to grow out of the earth itself, slowly defining the bulk of rocks in shades of dark blue. Dom and Tessa found themselves moving more quickly and surely before they realized why. Dom's quick hunter's eye had found several more traces of Benjamin's passing.

The box canyon they climbed narrowed to a crack and grew steeper. A cold wind blew through it from somewhere high above. Tessa fancied she could smell the fresh grasses of the Plateau. Perhaps they would find the high plainsmen if they kept climbing.

"He's a young idiot." Dom had been improvising variations on this theme since they started. "No one should be this high alone." They clambered out of the crack and over a crumbling ridge. A narrow canyon lay ahead of them. Dom pointed. "There."

Benjamin was a tiny dot on the opposite slope, moving slowly, like someone tired and unsure of what he was doing. He disappeared over the top and they slid down the talus to the bottom of the canyon, sight of their quarry giving their legs new strength.

When they reached the top of the next ridge, Benjamin turned and saw them standing high above him. He stopped dead for a moment, as if not believing they were there, then started to run.

"An especial kind of idiot. He's going to hurt himself."

Dom had barely spoken before a rock turned under Benjamin's foot and he vanished from their view. He didn't make a sound.

"Damn it!" Dom pointed to the right. "You go this way. I'll slide this way. Damn him for a fool."

Tessa reached Benjamin first. His arm was broken, his face covered with agonized sweat, but he still struggled up the next slope, whining like an injured animal. He wailed and tried desperately to bring his dart rifle to bear on something ahead of him.

Tessa looked up. Looming over them, as it had at Momma's funeral, was a Great Wapiti. It stared down at them, curved horns sharp against the cloudless sky.

Benjamin whimpered and lowered his weapon. He could not fire it with only one arm. The wapiti waited majestically for a moment, as if to see the outcome of Benjamin's struggle, then bounded over a rock and was gone.

"Damn you! Damn you!" Benjamin sobbed in great heaves. "It's all your fault. You lost him for me. If it wasn't for you . . . oh, damn you!"

"Benjamin—we were just trying to find you. It's all right. It's all right. Let's take care of this arm."

He shoved her away with his good arm, refusing to be comforted, and sobbed all the louder. It was finally too much for her.

"Oh, for God's sake, Ben, stop being such a big baby. You're being absolutely ridiculous."

Dom slid down the slope. Saying nothing, he matter-of-factly took care of Benjamin's arm with an inflatable splint from his emergency kit. He sat his brother up against a rock and looked at him. Benjamin looked back, trying to control his tears.

"Don't worry, Ben." Dom's voice was soothing. "It's not a failure because you tried as hard as you could. It's almost impossible to track a wapiti. It's amazing you did what you did."

Benjamin's face was transformed with pride. He looked challengingly at Tessa, closing ranks with his brother against the female interloper. Tessa felt rage, and disappointment. After that long companionable climb up the canyons, Dom had turned against her, as she had all along feared he would.

"But that was no excuse for acting like a self-important idiot," Dom continued, not raising his voice. "To go off without warning in the middle of the night . . . Tessa and I had to track you all the way up here. It was a self-centered, stupid, arrogant, inconsiderate thing to do, and if you ever try it again I'll use you to fertilize the melon vines."

Benjamin's face went slack at this transformation of his brother from ally to scold. Tessa stepped away to give them privacy while Dom chewed Benjamin out and to keep herself from putting in her bit, which she desperately wanted to do. That would be too much. Pride, after all, was at stake.

Then she saw it. Projecting from the rubble at the cliff's base was the snout of a huge fossil trilobite. It gleamed in the sun, for it seemed to be made entirely of iron pyrite.

"Dom!" she said, feeling an excitement she could not entirely explain. "Come here and look."

Dom looked and, without further bidding, began to dig the rubble away from it so that they could see it better. She joined him. As they dug, the sun rose and filled the high canyon. After a while, lacking any more productive activity, Benjamin came and lent the assistance of his one good arm.

The fossil had been freed from its matrix by a recent rockslide. The rubble covering it was loose. In an hour the entire thing was revealed, glittering like a spacecraft from another star. It was a perfectly preserved specimen, almost as large as the ones guarding the approach to Topfield.

Dom touched it, feeling the precise lines of its carapace. "That was pretty silly." His forehead was beaded with sweat. "Am I helping you continue Momma's fossil collection? What are we supposed to do with it now?"

"We carry it down." Tessa was calmly certain.

Dom laughed. "Are you out of your mind, dear little sister? This thing must weigh half a ton. Look at the size of it."

Tessa did and finally saw it, not as a mystic symbol, her link to her mother and, through her mother, to the planet itself, but as a giant hunk of iron ore. She let out a sigh. Bringing it home would have been just the right closure for Sora's departure from their family, something brought back from the heights just as Momma had been carried up and left. It would have made things seem to make sense. She felt bitter disappointment.

Benjamin plucked at its edge. "It seems to be loose here."

"You're delirious," Dom said. "It's the pain killers. Let's stop wasting our time and head home. There's work to do."

"Dom, will you look at it?" Benjamin was exasperated. "Just for a second."

Dom did so. He frowned, then put both hands under the edge and heaved. The muscles stood out in his arms and back and the shell pulled up, so easily that he almost stumbled. The pyrite carapace was hollow. He peered underneath, as if fearing something concealed. "How did this happen?"

Tessa sat down, feeling light-headed. "I bet that after this trilobite died, scavengers ate out the innards. Only the hard shell was left to be replaced by the pyrite inclusion. It's like a giant's shield. Can we try to pick it up?"

The three of them hefted it. There were enough spikes and protrusions that it was easy to hold on to. It was still heavy, but perfectly possible to carry. She looked at her brothers. "Will you help me?"

"Yes," Benjamin said, eager to make peace.

"Come on," Dom said. "We won't be able to carry it down at once. Don't you remember how long it took to get up here?"

"This can be a project," Tessa said. "If it takes a year, we can finish it."

"Try two years," Dom said.

He was closer to being right.

When they returned home that day, the sun already setting, Perin was desperately worried, having been unable to understand Kevin's garbled explanations. Kevin had dedicated himself, meticulously and with great concentration, to setting things up for pancakes. They all sat down to eat them, though it was time for dinner. "There's a real art to pancakes," Kevin pronounced, burning every one.

After dinner, Tessa went upstairs and closed herself into Sora's study. Racks of fossils from all of Koola's geologic eras stood around her. Sora's paleontological notebook still lay open to the last entry, a comparison of two amphibian skeletons from different periods.

The golden trilobite, of course, would never fit in here, and that was not what she intended. She wanted it as the base of the Wolholme family ward. If other families thought they grew out of a distant, mythical blue-green world, that was fine for them. The Wolholmes, as Sora had long ago realized, were creatures of Koola. It was right that they should show it. If Tessa mentioned it now, the rest of the family would hoot at her, and refuse to help. By the time they dragged the thing, inch by sweaty inch, down to Calrick Bend, she thought they would feel differently.

Tessa lay down on the floor, her head on a chunk of rock dense with ancient ferns, and went to sleep.

DEATHBINDER

The El Station platform was empty, and the winter
Chicago Sunday afternoon had turned into night. Stanley Paterson paused at the turnstile and rubbed his nose
doubtfully. The overhead lamps cast circular pools of
light on the gouged surface of the platform, but this
made Stanley feel obvious, rather than safe. He hunched
his shoulders inside his wool topcoat, puffed out his
cheeks, and shuffled along the platform, looking down
the tracks in the direction of the expected train. His
mind was still full of the financial affairs of a medium-
sized Des Moines metals trading company slated for
acquisition. It was a big project, worth working weekends for, so aside from the inside of his condominium,
the inside of his office, and the inside of various El
trains, he no longer knew what anything looked like.
Winter had somehow arrived without an intervening
autumn. He'd been to Oak Street Beach once, near the
end of the summer, he remembered. Or had that been
last year?

The wind blew dried leaves past him; delicately
curved, ribbed, and textured leaves. He felt himself
among them, heavy and gross, and thought about going
on a diet. It was tough when you worked as hard as he
did, he thought, excusing himself. It was hell on your
eating habits. Today he'd eaten—what? He couldn't
remember. The coat slapped his legs. The skin by his
nose was oily, there was an itch under his right shoulder

blade, and he was hungry. He wondered what he could put in the microwave when he got home. What did he have left in the freezer? Chinese? Chicken Kiev? Hell, he'd see when he got there. High above him floated the lighted windows of the city, rank upon rank, like cherubim.

The turnstile clattered. Stanley tried to tell himself that it was ridiculous to feel afraid, even in the dark, alone on the platform, but succeeded only in feeling afraid and ridiculous, both. He leaned forward, looking again for the train, trying to pull it into the station by the force of his gaze, but the tracks remained empty. He glanced toward the turnstile. A man stood there, a shadow. He wasn't a big man and his race was not obvious, but he wore a hat, which looked like leather. Respectable people did not wear hats, Stanley felt. Particularly not leather ones. It looked too silly. The man turned and, with slow confident steps, walked toward Stanley.

Stanley thought about running, but didn't. It would have made him feel like a fool. He rocked back on his heels, hands in his pockets, and ignored the other. He tried to project an air of quiet authority. The platform on the other side of the tracks was completely empty.

He never saw it, but he felt the knife press, sharp, against his side, just above the right kidney. There was no doubt whatsoever about what it was.

"Your money."

"Excuse me? I—"

"Your money."

The knife cut through the expensive fabric of his coat and grazed his flesh. Stanley felt a surge of annoyance at the wanton damage. Spontaneously, unthinkingly, like a tripped mousetrap, Stanley cried out and hit the man in the face with a balled fist, remembering only at the last second not to put his thumb inside his fingers. It was like striking out in sleep, but he did not awaken, as he usually did, sweat-soaked and tangled in sheets. Instead, the dark cold night remained around him, and as the man stumbled back, Stanley grappled with him and tried to get his hands around his throat. He really was a small man, much smaller than he had expected, and he couldn't remember why he had been so frightened of him. The knife blade twisted, and Stanley felt it penetrate flesh. A scream cut the night. There was suddenly a warm glow in Stanley's belly, which spread up through his chest. He felt dizzy, and flung his suddenly weightless assailant across the platform, seeing him whirl tiny, tiny away, joining the leaves in their dance, then vanishing back through the turnstile, which clattered again. Blackness loomed overhead like a tidal wave and blotted out the lights of the windows. The dark heaviness knocked Stanley down onto the platform, and he heard a wailing sound, like sirens, or a baby crying. He rested on the platform, which had become as soft as a woman's breast. It was late, he was tired, and the train did not seem to want to come, so he decided to take a well-deserved nap.

The scream of the nurse, who had come in to check Margaret's pulse but found, when she pulled back the blankets, that her patient had turned into a mass of giant black bats that burst up from the rumpled sheets to fill the bedroom with the fleshy beating of their wings, became the shrill ring of the telephone. Matthew Harmon woke up with a shock, jerked the cord until the phone fell on the bed, and cradled the receiver under his ear.

"Dr. Harmon," the voice on the phone said. A simple, flat statement, as if someone had decided to call in the middle of the night to wake him up and reassure him about his identity. Harmon felt a surge of irritation, and knew he was once again alive. He reached up and turned on the bedside lamp, which cast a pool of light over the bed. He did not look at the other half of the bed, but he could hear Margaret's labored breathing. She muttered something like, "Phone, Matt . . . phone," then choked, as if having a heart seizure. There were no bats, at least.

"Yes?" he said. "What is it?" His throat hurt again, and his voice was husky.

A pause. "I was asked to make this call. Against my better judgment . . . it's information I don't think you hould have. But," a deep sigh, "it seems that we have ne of what you call . . . abandoned souls. That is what ou call them, isn't it?" Another pause, longer than the irst. "This is stupid. I wonder why I called you."

"That makes two of us." The voice on the line was ontemptuous, but uncomfortably so, ill at ease despite ts advantage of identity and wakefulness. It was a amiliar voice, from somewhere in the past, one of so nany familiar voices, voices of medical students, inerns, residents, nurses, fellow doctors, researchers, all anged through over forty years of memory, some espectful, some exasperated, some angry. He ran his and over his scalp and thought about that tone of lefensive contempt. "Orphaned. Not abandoned. hough that will do just as well." Given the subject of he call, it had to be someone at an Intensive Care Unit, robably at a city hospital. Possibly connected with a rauma center. That narrowed things . . . got it. "Mas-erman," he said. "Eugene Colin Masterman. Johns Iopkins Medical School, class of seventy-five. You're at res St. Luke's now. I hope that you are finally clear on he difference between afferent and efferent nerves. I emember you had trouble with the distinction, back in ny neuroanatomy class at Hopkins. Just remember: AME, sensory afferent, motor efferent. It's not hard. ut, as you said, you didn't decide to call me. Leibig, hief of your ICU, told you to. How is Karl?"

"Dr. Leibig is well," Masterman said sulkily. "Aside rom the inevitable effects of age. He has a renal dys-unction, and seems to have developed a vestibular lisorder which keeps him off his feet. He will be retiring ext year."

"A pity," Harmon said. "A good man. And three years ounger than I am, as I'm sure I don't have to remind ou. Well, Eugene, why don't you tell me the story?" Iasterman, he recalled, hated being called Eugene.

Masterman gave it to him, chapter and verse, in ffensively superfluous detail. Patient's name: Paterson, tanley Andrew. Patient's social security number. Pa-ient's place of employment, a management consulting rm in the Loop. Locations of stab wounds, fractures, lacerations. Patient's blood type and rejection spectrum. Units of blood transfused, in the ambulance, in the Emergency Room, in the ICU, divided into whole blood and plasma. Names of the ambulance crew. Name of admitting doctor. Name of duty nurse. All surname first, then first name and middle initial.

"Who was his first-grade teacher?" Harmon said.

"What—Dr. Harmon, I did not want to make this call, understand that. I did so at the specific request of Dr. Leibig."

"Who also wonders if I am crazy. But he did it for old time's sake, bless him. Eugene, if, as it seems, you are not enjoying this call, perhaps you should make an effort to be more . . . pithy."

"Paterson suffered a cardiac arrest at, let's see, one-oh-eight A.M. We attempted to restart several times with a defibrillator, but were finally forced to open the chest and apply a pacemaker. We have also attached a ventilator. His condition is now stable."

"Life is not stable," Harmon said, but thought, "the stupid bastards." Would they never learn? Didn't they understand the consequences? *Doctors.* Clever technicians who thought themselves scientists. "Brain waves?"

"Well . . . minimal."

"Minimal, Eugene? Where did he die?"

"He isn't dead. We have him on life support."

"Don't play games with me! Where was he murdered?"

"At the Adams Street El station, at Adams and Wabash. The northbound platform." He paused, then the words spilled out. "Listen, Harmon, you can't go on doing this, talking about ghosts and goblins and all sorts of idiocy about the spirits of the unburied dead. This isn't the Middle Ages, for crissakes. We're doctors, we know better, we've learned. We *know* how things work now. Have you forgotten everything? You can't just let people under your care die to protect their souls. That's crazy, absolute lunacy. I don't know how I let Leibig talk me into this, he knows you're crazy too, and the patient's *not* dead, he's alive, and if I have anything to say about it he'll stay that way, and I won't pull the plug because of some idiotic theory you have about ghosts.

And I do so know the difference between afferent and efferent. Afferent nerves—"

"Never mind, Dr. Masterman," Harmon said wearily. "At this hour, I'm not sure I remember myself. Get back to your patients. Thank you for your call." He hung the receiver up gently.

After a moment to gather his strength, he pulled his legs out from under the comforter and forced them down to the cold floor. As they had grown thinner, the hair on them, now white, seemed to have grown thicker. He pulled the silk pajamas down so that he could not see his shins. The virtues of youth, he thought, too often become the sins of age. He had once been slim, and was now skinny. His nose, once aquiline, was a beak, and his high noble forehead had extended itself clear over the top of his head.

These late-night phone calls always made him think of Margaret, as she had been. He remembered her, before their marriage, as a young redhead in a no-nonsense gray suit with a ridiculous floppy bow tie, and later, in one of his shirts, much too long for her and tight in the chest, as she raised her arms in mock dismay at the number of his books she was expected to fit into their tiny apartment, and finally, as a prematurely old woman gasping her life out in the bed next to him. None of it had been her fault, but it had been she who had suffered.

He dialed the phone. It was answered on the first ring. "Sphinx and Eye of Truth Bookstore, Dexter Warhoff, Owner and Sole Proprietor. We're closed now, really, but we open at—"

"Dexter," Harmon said. "Sorry to bother you. It looks like we have another one."

"Professor!" Dexter said with delight. "No bother at all. I was just playing with some stuff out of the Kabbalah. Kind of fun, but nothing that won't wait. Where is this one? Oh, never mind, let it be a surprise. Usual place, in an hour? I'll call him and get him ready. Oh, boy."

Harmon restrained a sigh. He could picture Dexter, plump and bulging in a shirt of plum or burgundy, with his bright blue eyes and greasy hair, behind the front desk at the Sphinx and Eye of Truth Bookstore, where he spent most of his waking hours, of which he apparently had many, scribbling in a paperback copy of *The Prophecies of Nostradamus* with a pencil stub or, as tonight, rearranging Hebrew letters to make anagrams of the Name of God.

The store itself was a neat little place on the Near North Side, with colorful throw pillows on the floor and the scent of jasmine incense in the air. It carried books on every imaginable topic relating to the occult and the supernatural, from Madame Blavatsky to Ancient Astronauts, from Edgar Cayce to the Loch Ness Monster, from Tarot cards to ESP. It had been almost impossible for Harmon to go there, but go there he did, finally, after exhausting every other resource, to accept a cup of camomile tea from Dexter's dirty-fingernailed hands and learn what he reluctantly came to understand to be the truth.

"Yes, Dexter. St. Mary's, as usual."

"Right. See ya."

Harmon hung up. He'd searched and searched, down every avenue, but he was well and truly stuck. When it came to the precise and ticklish business of the exorcism and binding of the spirits of the uneasy dead, there was no better assistant alive than Dexter Warhoff.

A train finally pulled into the station. It was lit up golden from inside, like a lantern. The doors slid open, puffing warm air. Stanley thought about getting up and going into the train. He could get home that way. But he remembered how uncomfortable the seats were on the train, and what a long cold walk he had from the station to his condo, so he just remained where he was, where the ground was soft and warm. After waiting for a long moment, the train shut its doors and whooshed off, up along the shining metal tracks as they arched into the sky, to vanish among the stars and the windows of the apartment buildings, which now floated free in the darkness, like balloons let loose by children.

Once he was alone again, Stanley found himself standing, not knowing how he had come to be so. The wind from Lake Michigan had cleared the sky, and a half moon lit the towers of the city. The city was alive; he could hear the soughing of its breath, the thrumming of its heart, and the murmuration of its countless vessels. Without thinking about it, he swung over the railing and slid down the girders of the El station to the waiting earth. The city spread out before him, Stanley Paterson ambled abroad.

After some time, the wind carried to him the aroma of roasting lamb, with cumin and garlic. He turned into it, like a salmon swimming upstream, and soon stood among the cracked plaster columns and fishing nets of a Greek restaurant. A blue flame burst up in the dimness, and Stanley moved toward it. A waiter in a white sailor's shirt served a man and a woman saganaki, fried kasseri cheese flamed with brandy.

Stanley could taste the tartness of the cheese and the tang of the brandy as they both ate, and feel the crunch of the outside and the yielding softness of the inside. He could taste the wine too, the bitterly resinous heaviness of retsina.

They looked at each other. She was young, wearing a cotton dress with a bold colorful pattern, and made a face at the taste of the wine. The man, who had ordered it, was older, in gray tweed, and grinned back at her. Stanley hovered over the two of them like a freezing man over a fire. As he drew close, however, something changed between them. They had been friends for a long time, at the law office where they both worked, but this was their first romantic evening together. She had finally made the suggestion, and now, as she looked at him, instead of thoughts of romance, her mind wandered to the coy calculations already becoming old to her, of getting to his apartment, giggling, of excusing herself at just the right moment to insert her diaphragm, of her mock exuberant gesture of tossing her panties over the foot of the bed at the moment he finally succeeded in getting her completely undressed, of how to act innocent while letting him know that she wasn't. The older man's shoulders stiffened, and he wished, too late, that he had resisted her, resisted the urge to turn her from a friend into yet another prematurely sophisticated young woman, wished that he could stop for a moment to think and breathe, in the midst of his headlong pursuit of the Other. The saganaki grew cold as they examined, silently, the plastic grapes that dangled in the arbor above their heads. Stanley moved back, and found himself on the street again.

Music came to him from somewhere far above. He slid up the smooth walls of an apartment building until he reached it. The glass of the window pushed against his face like the yielding surface of a soap bubble, and then, suddenly, he was inside.

A woman with a mass of curly gray hair and an improbably long neck sat at the grand piano, her head cocked at the sheet music as she played, while a younger woman with lustrous black hair and kohl-darkened eyes sat straight-backed on a stool and held an oboe. The music, Stanley knew, though he had never heard it before, was Schumann's *Romances for Oboe and Piano*, and they played it with the ease of long mutual familiarity. Their only audience was a fuzzy cat of uncertain breed that sat on a footstool and stared into the flames in the fireplace.

Stanley felt the notes dance through him and sensed the blissful self-forgetfulness of the musicians. He wanted desperately to share in it, and moved to join them. The oboist suddenly thought about the fact that no matter how well she played and how much she practiced, she would never play well enough to perform with the Chicago Symphony, or any orchestra, ever, and the love of her life would always remain a hobby, a pastime. The pianist's throat constricted, and suddenly she feared the complexity of the instrument before her, knowing that she was inadequate to the task, as she was to all tasks of any importance, that no one would ever approve of her, and that she was old. The instruments went completely out of sync, as if the performers were in separate rooms with soundproof walls between them and the music crashed into cacophony. The cat stood up bristling, stared right at Stanley, and hissed. The pianist tapped one note over and over with her forefinger. The oboist started to cut another reed, even though she had

wo already cut. Stanley passed back out through the
window.

He left the residential towers and wandered the streets
of three-story brownstone apartment buildings. He felt
warm soapy water on his skin, and drifted through the
wide crack under an ill-fitting door.

The bathroom was warm and steamy, heated by the
glow of a gas burner in one wall. A plump woman in a
flower-print dress, with short dark hair, washed a child
in that most marvelous of bathing devices, a large
freestanding claw-foot bathtub. The little girl in the tub
had just had her hair washed, and it was slicked to her
head like a mannikin's. She stared intently down into
the soapy water like a cat catching fish.

"Point to your mouth, Sally. Your mouth." Sally
obediently put her finger in her mouth. "Point to your
nose." She put her finger in her nose. "Very good, Sally.
Can you point to your ear? Your ear, Sally." After a
moment's thought, the little girl put her finger in her ear.
"Where is your chin?" Sally, tiring of the game, and
having decided which she liked best, stuck her finger
back up her nose and stared at her mother. Her mother
laughed, delighted at this mutiny. "Silly goose." She
poured water over the girl's head. Sally closed her eyes
and made a "brrr" noise with her lips. "Time to get out,
Sally." The little girl stood up, and her mother pulled the
plug. Sally waved as the water and soap bubbles swirled
down the drain and said, "Ba-*bye*. Ba-*bye*." Her mother
pulled her from the tub and wrapped her in a huge towel,
in which she vanished completely.

The feel of the terry cloth on his skin and the warm
strawberry scent of the mother covered Stanley like a
benediction. He stretched forward as the mother rubbed
her daughter's hair with the towel until it stood out in all
directions. The mother's happiness vanished, and she
felt herself trapped, compelled, every moment of her life
now given over to the care of a selfish and capricious
creature, no time to even think about getting any work
done on the one poem she'd been working on since she
left high school to get married, her life predetermined
now until she grew old and was left alone. She rubbed

too vigorously with the towel, and Sally, smothered an
manipulated by forces she could not control, or eve
understand, began to shriek. "Quiet, Sally. Quiet, *dam
it.*"

Stanley remembered the platform. What was he doin
in here? He had a train to catch, he had to get home. H
could not even imagine how he had managed to stray
He turned and hurried off to the El station.

The two of them walked down the street togethe
Harmon with a long measured stride, and Dexter wit
the peculiar mincing waddle he was compelled to us
because of the width of his thighs. Harmon wore a thic
knee-length overcoat and a karakul hat, but the cold sti
struck deep into his bones. He wore a scarf to protect hi
throat, which was always the most sensitive. He remem
bered a time, surely not that long ago, when he ha
enjoyed the winter, when it had made him feel alive. H
and Margaret had spent weekends in Wisconsin, cross
country skiing, and making grotesque snowmen. N
longer. Dexter wore a red windbreaker that made hin
look like a tomato, and a Minnesota Vikings cap wit
horns on it. As he walked, he juggled little beanbags i
an elaborate fountain. He had a number of simila
skills—such as rolling a silver dollar across the back c
his knuckles, like George Raft, and making origam
animals—all of which annoyed Harmon because he ha
never learned to do things like that. He thought abou
the image the two of them presented, and snorte(
amused at himself for feeling embarrassed.

"Father Toomey looked a little bummed out," Dexte
said. "I think we woke him up."

"Dexter, it's three-thirty in the morning. Not every
one sits up all night reading books on the Kabbalah."

"Yeah, I guess. Anyway, he cheered up after we talke
about the horoscope reading I'm doing for him. There'
a lot of real interesting stuff in it."

"An ordained Catholic priest is having you do hi
horoscope?"

Dexter looked surprised. "Sure. Why not?"

Why not, indeed? Harmon hefted his ancient blac

leather bag. The instruments it contained had been blessed by Father Toomey and sprinkled with holy water from the font at St. Mary's. Harmon, in the precisely rigorous theological way that devout atheists have, doubted the efficacy of a blessing from a priest so far sunk in superstition that he had his horoscope done, and performed holy offices for a purpose so blatantly demonic, but he had to admit that it always seemed to do the job. When he handed the sleepy, slightly inebriated priest the speculum, the wand, the silver nails, the censer, the compass, and the rest of the instruments of his new trade, they were nothing but dead metal, but when he took them in his hands after the blessing, they vibrated with suppressed energy. The touch of such half-living things was odious to him, essential though they were. It disturbed him that such things worked. As quickly as he could, he wrapped them in their coverings of virgin lamb hide, inscribed with Latin prayers and Babylonian symbols, and placed them, in correct order, into his bag. That bag had once held his stethoscope, patella reflex hammer, thermometer, hypodermics, laryngoscope, and the rest of his medical instruments, and though he had not touched any of them in years, it had pained him to remove them so that the bag could be used for its new purpose.

"You know, Professor, the other day I was reading an interesting book about the gods of ancient Atlantis—"

"Oh, Dexter," Harmon said irritably. "You don't really believe all these things, do you?"

Dexter grinned at him, yellow-toothed. "Why not? You believe in *ghosts*, don't you?"

Dexter's one unanswerable argument. "I believe in them, Dexter, only because I am forced to, not because I like it. That's the difference between us. It would be terrible to *like* the idea that ghosts exist."

"Boy, did you fight it," Dexter said with a chuckle. "You sat with me for an hour, talking about Mary Baker Eddy. Then you shut up. I asked you what was wrong. 'A ghost,' you said. 'I've got to get rid of a ghost.' Took you three cups of tea to say that. You don't even like camomile tea, do you?"

"It served."

"It sure did. You remember that first time, don't you?
I'll never forget it. We hardly knew what we were doing,
like two kids playing with dynamite. I had pretended I
knew more about it than I did, you know."

"I know." They often talked about the first ghost.
They never talked about the second.

"I thought I could handle it, but it almost swallowed
me and you had to save my ass. Quite a talent you have
there. Strongest I've ever heard of. You should be
proud."

"I feel precisely as proud as I would if I discovered
that I had an innate genius for chicken stealing."

Dexter laughed, head thrown back. He had a lot of
fillings in his back teeth. "Gee, that's pretty funny. But
anyway, this Kabbalah stuff is real interesting. . . ."

Harmon suffered himself to be subjected to a rambling, overly detailed lecture on medieval Jewish mysti-
cism until, much too soon, they were at the El station.

Dexter craned his head back and looked up at the dark
girders of the station, his face suddenly serious. "I feel
him up there. He's a heavy one. Strong. He didn't live
enough, when he had the chance. Those are always the
worst. Too many trapped desires. Good luck to you.
Oh . . . wait. They lock these things when the trains stop
running, and we're not exactly authorized." He reached
into his pocket and pulled out a little black pouch,
which, when opened, revealed a line of shiny lock-
picking tools.

"I used to pick locks at school," Dexter said. "Just for
fun. I never stole anything. Figuring out the locks was
the good part. Schools don't have very good locks. Most
students just break in the windows." He walked up to
the heavy metal mesh door at the base of the stairs and
had it opened about as quickly as he could have with a
key. He sighed, disappointed. "The CTA doesn't either. I
don't even know why they bother. Well, now it's time.
Good luck." They paused and he shook Harmon's hand
as he always did, with a simple solemnity.

Nothing to say, Harmon turned and started up toward
the El station.

* * *

They *were* always the worst. "The people who want to live forever are always the ones who can't find anything to do on a rainy Sunday afternoon," as Dr. Kaltenbrunner, the head of Radiology at Mount Tabor Hospital, had once said. Dr. K was never bored, and certainly never boring, enjoyed seventeenth-century English poetry, and died of an aneurism three months before Harmon encountered his first ghost. Died and stayed dead. Harmon always thought he could have used his help. Thomas Browne and John Donne would have understood ghosts better than Harmon could, which was funny, because there hadn't been enough ghosts in the seventeenth century to be worth worrying about.

Some doctors managed to stay away from ER duty, and it was mostly the young ones—who needed to be taught, by having their noses rubbed in it, about the mixture of fragility and resilience that is the human body—who took the duty there, particularly at night. In his time, Harmon had seen a seventy-year-old lady some anonymous madman had pushed in front of an onrushing El train recover and live, with only a limp in her left leg to show for it, and a Northwestern University linebacker DOA from a fractured skull caused by a fall in the shower in the men's locker room.

As Harmon climbed the clattering metal stairs up to the deserted El platform, he remembered the first one. It was always that way with him. He was never able to see the Duomo of Florence without remembering the first time he and Margaret had seen it, from the window of their pensione. There were some words he could not read without remembering the classroom in which he learned them, and whether it had been sunny that day. It meant there were some things he never lost, that he always had Margaret with him in Florence. And it meant that he could never deal with a ghost without remembering the terror of the first one.

He had been working night duty, late, when they brought in a bloody stretcher. It had been quiet for about an hour, in that strange irregular rhythm that Emergency Rooms have, crowded most of the time, but sometimes almost empty. A pedestrian had been hit by a truck while crossing the street. There was a lot of bleeding, mostly internal, and a torn lung filled with blood, a hemothorax. His breathing was audible, a slow dragging gurgle, the sound a straw makes sucking at the bottom of a glass of Coke when the glass is almost empty. Harmon managed to stop much of the bleeding, but by that time the man was in shock. Then the heart went into ventricular fibrillation. Harmon put the paddles on and defibrillated it. When the heart stopped altogether, he put the patient on a pacemaker and an external ventilator. The autopsy subsequently showed substantial damage to the brain stem, as well as complete kidney failure. Every measure Harmon took, as it turned out, was useless, but he managed to keep the patient alive an extra hour, before everything stopped at once, in the ICU.

A day or so later, the nurse on duty came to him with a problem. Rosemary was a redhead, cute, and reminded him of Margaret when she was young, so he was a little fonder of her than he should have been, particularly since Margaret had been sick. The nurse wasn't flirting now, however. She was frightened. She kept hearing someone drinking out of a straw, she said, in a corner of the ER, only there wasn't anyone there. She was afraid she was losing her mind, which can happen to you after too many gunshot wounds, suicides, and drug overdoses. Harmon assured her, in what he told himself was a fatherly way, that it was probably something like air in the pipes, which he called an "embolism," a medical usage that delighted her. She teased him about it.

Harmon remembered being vaguely pleased about that, while he searched around and listened. He didn't hear anything. It was late, and he finally climbed up on a gurney and went to sleep, as some of the other doctors did when things weren't busy. He'd never done it before, and why he did it was something he could not remember, though everything about the incident, from the freckles around Rosemary's nose to the scheduling roster for that night's medical staff, was abnormally clear in his mind, the way memories of things that happened only yesterday never were. When he woke up, he heard it. A slow dragging gurgle. He listened with his eyes closed, heart pounding. Then it stopped.

"Hey, have you seen my car?" a voice said. "It's a blue car, a Cutlass, though I guess it's too dark here to see the color. I know I parked it near here, but I just can't find it."

Harmon slowly opened his eyes. Standing in front of him was a fat man in a business suit, holding a briefcase. He wasn't bloody, and his face was not pasty white, but Harmon recognized him. It was the man who had died the night before.

"Look, I have to get home to Berwyn. My wife will be going nuts. She expected me home hours ago. Have you seen the damn car? It's a Cutlass, blue. Not a good car, God knows, and it needs work, but I gotta get home."

Harmon had met the wife when she identified the body. She had, indeed, expected him hours ago.

"Jeez, I don't know what I could have done with it."

Harmon was a logical man, and a practical man, and he hadn't until that moment realized that those two characteristics could be in conflict. What he saw before him was indubitably a ghost, and as a practical man he had to accept that. He also knew, as a logical man, that ghosts did not, indeed could not, exist. This neat conundrum, however, did not occur to him until somewhat later, because the next time the dead man said, "Do you think you could help me find my car? I gotta get home," he launched himself from the gurney, smashing it back into the wall, bolted from the ER, and did not stop running until he was sitting at the desk in his little office on the fifth floor, shaking desperately and trying not to scream.

The El platform was windswept and utterly empty. Harmon walked slowly across its torn asphalt until he came to the spot where it had happened. The police had cleaned up the blood and erased the chalk outline, that curious symbol of the vanished soul used by police photographers as a record of the body, so morning commuters would not be unpleasantly surprised by the cold official evidence of violent death. He didn't have to see it. He could feel it, like standing in the autopsy room and knowing that someone had left the door to the cold room where the bodies were kept open because you could feel the frigid formaldehyde-and-decay-scented air seeping along the floor.

He didn't know why he had this particular sense, or ability, or whatever. To himself he compared it to someone with perfect pitch and rhythm who nevertheless dislikes music, someone who could play Bach's *Goldberg Variations* through perfectly after hearing the piece only once, and yet hate every single note. It was a vicious curse. He set his black bag down, opened it, and began to remove his instruments.

To start, Harmon had cautiously, cautiously, sounded out his colleagues on the subject of ghosts. He'd read too many books where seemingly reasonable men lost all of their social graces when confronted by the inexplicable and started jabbering and making ridiculous accusations, frightening and embarrassing their friends. So, in a theoretical manner, he asked about ghosts. To his surprise, instead of being suspicious, people either calmly said they didn't believe in them, or the majority had one or more anecdotes about things like the ghost of a child in an old house dropping a ball down the stairs or a hitchhiking girl in a white dress who would only appear to men driving alone and then would vanish from the car. Others had stories about candles being snuffed out in perfectly still rooms, or dreams about dying relatives, or any number of irrelevant mystical experiences. No one, when pressed, would admit to having actually seen anything like a real, demonstrably dead man walking and talking and looking for a blue Cutlass. A man who persisted, week after week, in trying to get Harmon to help him find the damn thing. Harmon transferred from the ER. Rosemary thought it was something personal, because she'd asked him to her house for dinner, and they rarely spoke after that.

He told Margaret, however, as much of it as he could. It gave her something to think about, as she lay there in bed and gasped, waiting for the end. She wondered, of course, if the strain of her illness had not made her husband lose what few marbles he had left, as she put it, but she only said this because both of them knew Harmon was coolly sane. It interested her that some people could hear ghosts, but that Harmon could see them and talk to them. She, like Dexter, used the word "gift."

In good scholar's style, Harmon did research in the dusty abandoned stacks of the witchcraft and folklore sections of Northwestern, the University of Chicago, and the University of Illinois, Circle Campus. He even had a friend let him into the private collections of the Field Museum of Natural History. He learned about lemures, the Roman spirits of the dead, about the hauntings of abandoned pavilions by sardonic Chinese ghosts, and about the Amityville Horror. It was all just . . . literature. Stories. Tales to tell at midnight. Not a single one of them had the ring of truth to it, and Harmon was by this time intimately familiar with the true behavior of ghosts.

Everyone was very good to him about Margaret, and about what he did to himself as a result, though no one understood the real reason for it. It got to be too much, in the apartment, in the hospital, and he finally started to say things that concerned people. They didn't think he was crazy, just "under stress," that ubiquitous modern disease, which excuses almost anything. Then, someone at the Field Museum mentioned, with the air of an ordinarily respectable man selling someone some particularly vile pornography, that Dexter Warhoff, of the Sphinx and Eye of Truth Bookstore, might have some materials not available in the museum collection. It was rumored that Dexter possessed a bizarrely variant scroll of the Egyptian *Book of the Dead,* as well as several Mayan codexes not collected in the *Popol Vuh* or the *Dresden Codex,* though no one was quite sure. Harmon had come to the conclusion that using ordinary reason in his new circumstances was using Occam's razor while shaving in a fun-house mirror. Common sense was a normally useful instrument turned dangerous in the wrong situation. So he went to Dexter's store, drank his sour tea, and talked with him. Dexter scratched his head with elaborate thoughtfulness, then took Harmon upstairs where he lived, to a mess with a kitchen full of dirty dishes, and brought him into a room piled with newspaper clippings, elaborately color coded, in five different languages, as well as sheets of articles transcribed from newspapers in forty languages more.

"You poor guy," Dexter said sadly. "That's a terrible way to find out about what's hidden. I can see that it was terrible. But I must say, I've been wondering about a few things. You've got the key there, I think, with this life-support stuff. Look at this." He showed Harmon a French translation of a photocopied Russian *samizdat* document from the Crimea. It described ghosts haunting a medical center at an exclusive Yalta sanatorium. The tone was slightly metaphorical, but for the first time, Harmon read things that confirmed his own experience. Dexter showed him an article from the house newspaper of a hospital in Bombay, an excerpt from the unpublished reminiscences of a surgeon in Denmark, and a study of night terrors in senile dementia cases in a Yorkshire nursing home, from *Lancet*. The accounts were similar. "There's almost nothing before the 1930s, very few up to about 1960, and a fair number from the '70s and '80s."

"Life support," Harmon said, when he was done reading. "Artificial life support is responsible."

"Now, Professor, let's not jump to conclusions. . . ." But Harmon could see that Dexter agreed with him, and for some strange reason that pleased him.

"When the body is kept alive by artificial means, for however long, when it should be dead and starting to rot, the soul, which normally is swept away somewhere— Heaven, Hell, oblivion, the Elysian Fields, it doesn't matter—is held back in this world, tied to its still-breathing body. And, being held back, it falls in love with life again." Harmon found himself saying it again, alone on the platform. It had seemed immediately obvious to him, though it was not really an "explanation" of the sort a scientist would require. It was, however, more than sufficient for a doctor of medicine, whose standards are different. A doctor only cares about what works, without much attention to why.

None of his colleagues had understood, though. He had gotten a little cranky on the subject, ultimately, he had to admit that, but he felt like someone in the eighteenth century campaigning against bloodletting. He had always known that doctors were, by and large, merely skilled fools, so he quickly stopped, but not before acquiring a certain reputation.

He drew his chalk circle on the rough surface of the platform, using the brass compass. Using a knife with a triangular blade, he scraped some material from within the circle. No matter how well the police had cleaned, it would contain some substance, most likely the membranes of red blood cells, that had belonged to the dead man. He melted beeswax over a small alcohol lamp whose flame kept going out, then mixed in the scraped-up blood. He dropped a linen wick into a mold of cold worked bronze and poured the wax in. While he waited for the candle to harden, he arranged the speculum, the silver nails, and the brass hammer so that he could reach them quickly. It was strange that most of the techniques they used had their roots in earlier centuries, when ghosts were the extremely rare results of accidental comas or overdoses of toxic drugs. People had had more time then to worry about such things, and some of their methods were surprisingly effective, though Dexter and Harmon had refined them. He set the candle in the center of the circle, lit it, and called Stanley Paterson's name.

The train still had not come. What was wrong? Why had there been no notification by the CTA? Stanley stood on the platform and shivered, wondering why he had wandered away and why he had come back. Where was the damn train? Beneath his feet he could see a circle of chalk and a half-melted candle, but he didn't think about them. Had he daydreamed right past the train, with those thoughts of musicians and mothers? Had the trains stopped for the night?

There was a rumble, and lights appeared down the tracks. They blinded him, for he had been long in darkness, and he stumbled forward with his eyes shut. He felt around for a seat. It seemed like he'd been waiting forever.

"It's a cold night, isn't it, Stanley?" a man's voice said, close by.

"Wha—?" Stanley jerked his head around and exam-

ined the brightly lit train car. It was empty. Then he saw
that the man was sitting next to him, a tall old man with
sad brown eyes. He was wearing a furry hat. "What are
you talking about? How do you know my name?" Not
waiting for an answer, he turned and pressed his nose
against the glass of the window. A form lay there on the
platform, sprawled on its back. It wore a long black
overcoat. A large pool of blood, black in the lights of the
station, had gathered near it, looking like the mouth of a
pit.

"Stanley," the man said, his voice patient. "You have
to understand a few things. I don't suppose it's strictly
necessary, but it makes me feel less . . . cruel."

The train pulled into the next station. Out on the
platform lay a dead man with a black coat. Three white-
clad men burst onto the platform and ran toward it with
a stretcher. The train pulled out of the station. "I don't
care how you feel," Stanley said.

The man snorted. "I deserve that, I suppose. But you
must understand, the dead cannot mix with the living. It
just cannot be. We had a dead man in our Emergency
Room once. He wouldn't go away. He tried to be part of
everything. A ward birthday party turned gloomy because he tried to join it, and the patient whose birthday
it was sickened and died within the week. He tried to
participate in the close professional friendship of a pair
of nurses, built up over long years of night duty and
family pain, and they had fights, serious fights, and
stopped ever speaking to each other. The gardener,
whose joy in his plants he tried to share, grew to hate the
roses he took care of, and in the spring they bloomed late
and sickly. I've always liked roses. Life is hell with ghosts
around, Stanley. Believe me, I know all about it." He
had put the roses last, he noticed, as if they were more
important than people. How much like a doctor he still
was. . . .

Stanley watched as the white-clad men strapped the
man in the black coat into the stretcher and rushed off,
one of them holding an IV bottle over his head. The
train pulled out of the station. "I—you don't understand, you don't understand at all." Stanley found
himself shaken with sobs. How could he explain? As a

child he'd wanted to play a musical instrument, like his sister, who played the piano, or even Frank, his next-door neighbor, who played the trumpet in the school band. He'd tried the piano, the saxophone, the cello. None had lasted longer than two years, and he never practiced, despite his mother's entreaties. As an adult he'd tried the recorder, the guitar, and failed again. Yet this very night he'd felt what it was like to play Schumann on a piano and an oboe, and feel the music growing out of the intersection of spirit and instrument. He'd felt what it was like to be alive. "I know what to *do* now, don't you see? I realize what I was doing wrong, how I was wasting everything. Now I know!"

"So now, at last, you know." The man shook his head sadly, and held a flat, polished bronze mirror in front of Stanley's face. Stanley looked into the speculum, but saw nothing but roiled darkness, like an endless hole to nowhere. He felt weak. "Lie down, Mr. Paterson," Harmon said softly. "You don't look at all well. You should lie down."

Somehow they had come to be standing on the same damn platform again, as if the train had gone absolutely nowhere at all. The unnatural blankness of the mirror had indeed made him feel dizzy, so Stanley lay down. The platform was hard and cold on his back now. Nothing made sense anymore. He watched the stars spin overhead. Or was it just the lights of the apartment buildings?

"You can't leave me here," he said. "Not just when I've figured it out."

"Shut up," Harmon said savagely. "It's too late." He drove a long silver nail into Stanley's right wrist. Stanley felt it go in, cold, but it didn't hurt. "You're dead." He drove another nail through Stanley's foot, tinking on the head with a little hammer. "That first one, in the ER. He almost killed *us*, he was so strong. But we bound him, finally, once we'd figured out what to do. If I went back there now, I would hear him, talking to himself, as if he'd just woken up from a nap and was still sleepy. I hear you everywhere, where I have bound you, on street corners, in hallways, in alleys. In beds." Harmon found himself crying, tears wetting his cheeks, as if he were the one Stanley Paterson was supposed to be feeling sorry for. Stanley Paterson, who would have only the understanding that he was dead, not alive, to keep him for all eternity. "Don't worry, Stanley. Life is hateful."

"No!" Stanley cried. "I want to live!" He reached up with his free hand and grabbed Harmon by the throat.

Harmon felt like he was being buried alive, but not buried in clean earth. He was being buried, instead, in the churned-over corrupted earth of an ancient cemetery, full of human teeth and writhing worms. It pushed, damp and greasy, against his face. The smell was unbearable. Darkness swelled before him, and he almost let go.

The darkness drained away, and the platform reappeared. Dexter stood over him, his tongue sticking out slightly between his lips. He held the speculum over Stanley's face, forcing him back. Dexter's clothes flapped, and he leaned forward, as if into a heavy foul wind. "Quick, Professor," he choked. "He's a strong one, like I said." Harmon tapped the fourth nail into Stanley's left wrist.

"I want to live!" Stanley said, quieter now.

Harmon said nothing. Dexter held the fifth nail for him, and he drove it through Stanley's chest. "There. Now you will remain still." He rested back on his heels, breathing heavily. How like a doctor, he thought. He could eliminate the symptom, but not cure the disease. Those ghosts, no longer disturbing the living, would lie where he had nailed them until Judgment Day. And there was nothing he could do to help them. He sat there for a long time until he felt Dexter's hand on his shoulder. He looked up into that kindly, ugly face, then back at the platform, where five silver dots glittered in the overhead lights.

"That was a bad one, Professor."

"They're all bad."

"It's worse if they never lived before they died. They want it then, all the more." Dexter packed the instruments away. Then he rubbed the tension out of Harmon's back, taking the feel of death up into himself. Dexter, with his credulous beliefs in anything and everything, absurd in his Minnesota Vikings cap with the horns. Without him, Harmon could not have kept moving for even a day.

Harmon thought about going home. Margaret would be there, as she always was, on the side of the bed where the blankets were flat and undisturbed. He hadn't acted in time, when she had her final, fatal heart attack. He had waited, and doubted his own conclusions, and let them put her on life support for three days in the cardiac ICU, before he decided it was hopeless and let them pull the plug on her. By then, of course, it had been much too late. He should simply have let her die there, next to him. But how could he have done that? Whenever he changed the sheets, he could see the rounded heads of the five silver nails driven into the mattress, to keep her fixed where she died.

She had loved life, but she had wanted to stay with him . . . always. So he had lain down on the bed with her and felt her cold embrace. For a doctor with a good knowledge of anatomy his suicide attempt had been shockingly bad. Slitting your own throat is rarely successful. It's too imprecise. They had found him, and healed him, reconstructing his throat. Modern medicine could do miracles. When he was well enough, though still bandaged, he went and found Dexter. They took care of the man in the ER, and then Margaret. She had cried and pleaded when the nails went in. But she had loved life, so it wasn't as hard as it could have been, though Harmon could not imagine how it could have been any harder.

When he came back, she would ask him, sleepily, how it had gone. She always sounded like she was about to fall asleep, but she never did. She never would.

"Let's go," Dexter said. "It'll be good to get back to bed. I gotta open the store in three hours. Jeez."

"Yes, Dexter," Harmon said. "It will be good to get to bed."

THE RING OF MEMORY

September 1349 CE

Hugh Solomon took a step on the sunlit landing stage of Time Center and felt the rocking of a ship's wooden deck underneath his feet. The mountains and bright snowfields of the Rockies had vanished, replaced by darkness. He stood, arms loose at his sides, and felt the moment of nausea he always did, and the wash of giddiness from the effects of Tempedrine, the time-traveling drug. Focusing on the ship *Dagmar* of Lübeck, a tiny platform in the middle of the sea fourteen hundred years in the past, had been no simple problem, but it was much too soon to feel pleased with himself. Someone was mucking around with the past, and he had to put things to right.

The breeze was fresh. The moon gleamed on the clean cold waters of the Baltic and turned the rigging overhead to silver. Rising clouds boiled just below the moon, heralding a change in weather. Someone groaned. As if in response, the wind shifted and he smelled an over-powering odor of shit and dead men. His throat tightened. He stepped back, and his foot came down on something soft. He kicked it, and a dead rat slid out onto a moonlit patch of deck.

He turned, and stumbled right into someone, who shouted and grabbed at him. Solomon found himself pinioned by arms like bands of steel, a sailor's arms. Unable to reach his sword, he stomped down on the sailor's foot and was rewarded with a cry of pain. It was too late. The sailor shouted warnings and alarms in

Swedish, and there were answering shouts from the darkness all around.

Rough hands seized him, and someone lit a torch. The faces of the men around him were pale and sick, with fever-bright eyes. Plague. One of them turned, stumbled to the rail, and vomited black bile into the sea. He then slumped to his knees and curled up around the pain in his gut. No one moved to help him.

"Hugh!" a voice said, in a tone of quiet satisfaction. "You fell for it. You had to, of course. Sailing in the wrong direction, aren't we? So you've come to turn us around. That's the job of a Full Historian." Andrew Tarkin stepped forward. "How have you been? God," he added, startled. "You're old."

Though the two of them had been students together, Solomon was now near fifty, while Tarkin, though careworn, his ginger hair thinning, could not have been more than thirty. He stopped his pacing and stared at Solomon, hands on his hips. Solomon glared back. The past always throws up its ghosts, but time travel enabled them to take physical form. He wondered why Tarkin had chosen to resurrect himself from whatever tomb of the past he had been hiding himself in.

Solomon was a tall man, with bushy hair now going gray, with cheeks sunken beneath high cheekbones. Tarkin was young, but youth, though vigorous, has many disadvantages when confronted with experience. Particularly experience like Solomon's, who had been dredging the past for its secrets for almost thirty years.

"What do you want from me, Tarkin?" Solomon said through clenched teeth. He pulled forward, testing the strength of the men who held him. They were weak, shivering uncontrollably with fever, but there were enough to hold him fast.

"Do you see him, men?" Tarkin said, raising his voice to address the crew. "This looks like a man, but it is a demon, appeared among us from Hell. He has burned the innocent with fire. We must destroy him."

Solomon heard, in memory, the crackle of the fire once again, as the boardinghouse burned with Louisa inside it. Questions licked up like flames, but he forced them back. First he had to survive.

The effect of the speech on the crew was the opposite of what Tarkin had intended. If the creature they had captured was a fiend from Hell itself, he could pull them all screaming to perdition. They weakened their grip, for they did not share Tarkin's hate. The light of the torches flickered in the rising wind, and Solomon could see the scurrying shapes of rats just beyond its edge. The deck rocked in the growing swell.

Tarkin stepped closer to Solomon. "We were friends once," he said softly. Looking down, Solomon could see the ring glinting gold on his finger, with bright flecks of emerald in the serpent's eyes. He'd always wondered about that damn ring. "You came here to make sure that this ship and its crew crash on the shore of Livonia and spread the Black Death, just as you once made sure that someone I loved died. To what end? To preserve your image of history? A sense of the duty of a Full Historian?"

"Please, Andy." Solomon decided to sit on his pride and ask the question. "Do you really think that I caused Louisa's death? Is that what it all comes from?" His pleading words tasted sour in his mouth. But a Full Historian would do anything to get the facts.

"You bastard!" Tarkin shouted, suddenly enraged. "We should *both* have burned there with her. For you, it's in the past and it's what happened. Remember how we argued about the immutability of Time when we were back during our research, in Chicago? Nothing has changed. You are still in charge of maintaining that immutability. And I still believe that we can never really know what happened, even if we were there to see it." He stopped, as if expecting Solomon to involve himself in an intellectual argument on the nature of perception.

At that moment, a sudden gust of wind caused the ship to heel sharply. There was a bright flash of lightning, followed immediately by a thunderclap, and a heavy rain began to fall, accompanied by a high wind. Tarkin shouted commands to his crew, ordering them to pull in the sails, tighten the sheets, and lash the rudder. They stumbled to obey. Several of the men holding Solomon went with them.

Solomon twisted, drove his elbow into the side of one

of his remaining captors, and broke free. The men were too panicked to react. Solomon lunged for Tarkin and dragged him to the deck. Lightning flashed above them, and waves crashed over the deck.

Tarkin drove the heel of his hand between Solomon's eyes and knocked him back as the wind tore off the top of the mast with a screaming crash. Rigging fell upon them from overhead. Tarkin rolled over and kicked him with a booted foot. Solomon grabbed at it, but was swept back by a heavy wave. Bitter saltwater filled his nose and mouth, and he choked. He rolled down the deck and grabbed at the railing. He felt himself slipping.

There was nothing else he could do. He rolled his eyes up, recalled his conditioning, and an instant later was lying on the windswept surface of the landing stage at the Aerie of Time Center amid the snow-covered peaks of the Canadian Rockies. After the darkness of the Baltic night, the mountain sun was blinding. He got to his hands and knees and vomited up a gallon of saltwater.

"Son of a bitch," he said, then fell down and lost consciousness.

January 2097 CE

The last guard post was an old pissoir with the tricolor-and-sun emblem of the Second Commune painted on it. The dim light of a brazier flickered within, though when the guards emerged to check Hugh Solomon's documents they didn't look any warmer than he was after his climb up the icy heights of Montmartre. The puff of their breaths rose to mingle with the snow that sifted out of the hollow sky and the night that drifted over Paris.

"A meeting with a congregation of rooks and sparrows?" said one of the guards, his beard and moustache glistening with frost. He grinned, revealing missing teeth. "Don't look for God. He has left that place, that is, if He ever was there." It took a peculiar sort of obstinacy to be an atheist in an age when God was so obviously dead.

"Don't be a fool," Solomon said sharply.

The man's face froze, and he stepped back, slowly and

carefully. Solomon carried a laissez-passer from the Comité Central itself, or rather, a forgery indistinguishable from it, and was obviously not someone to be trifled with. The guard muttered an apology, which Solomon ignored.

The corporal of the guard, a grim, wrinkled man who looked as if he might have once been fat, checked the documents meticulously, despite the fact that Solomon had already passed two other checkpoints on the way up Montmartre. The man held on to duty, though that duty had served three different governments in the last five years, and currently consisted of guarding the approaches to an abandoned cathedral. "Pass," he said, almost reluctantly, and handed Solomon back the forged documents. So Solomon proceeded up the last slope of the hill to the ruins of the cathedral, dangling a foil-wrapped box by the string that tied it up, daintily, with one finger, as if on his way to a birthday party. The three guards watched him and wondered where the hell he was going.

The elongated bone-white elegance of the cathedral of Sacré-Coeur bulked against the sky, like some vast fossil crustacean left behind by ancient seas. Eighteen years before it had been shattered by the ground shock of the five-megaton fusion explosion near Meaux that had also turned the indolent curves of the Marne into a vast poisonous lake. One of the side domes had been destroyed. The main dome had a crack running through it.

Solomon stopped at the top of the tilted marble steps, unwilling to push into the darkness that lay on the other side of the crazily hanging bronze doors. Below him only the occasional flare of a bonfire marked what had once been called the City of Light. The bright pinpoints did nothing against the cold on the top of the hill. He felt himself surrounded by centuries of swirling oily mist, the smoke of carbonized flesh. This was the time of the Great Forgetting, when nuclear wars had destroyed human civilization and time travelers were forbidden entry, for the roots of Time Center itself lay here. The world spun dizzily, and Solomon clutched at the doors to keep from falling. He choked and fought to breathe. He thought Katsuro's help had eliminated the autonomic nerve blocks, but there may have been an even deeper level of conditioning.

"Come in, Hugh," a throbbing liquid voice of uncertain sex said from within. "You'll catch your death." The voice chuckled. Solomon stepped over the shattered marble into the nave. Darkness pushed against his face like a shroud. It was warmer inside the church, and he could breathe again. "This way. Come to mama." With a hissing scratch a candle flickered at the other end of the cathedral. A plump, smooth hand, the fingers covered with glittering rings, held the match up. An invisible pair of lips blew it out.

Solomon moved slowly toward the candle, sliding his feet across the uneven rubble-strewn floor. The dim shapes of statues, piled-up pews, and crosses danced briefly in the light, vanished, then danced again. The air smelled wet and dusty. Bile stung the back of his throat.

He'd stretched himself to the limit to get here. Acquiring extra illicit doses of Tempedrine from manufactories in sixteenth-century Germany and twentieth-century California, he had pumped himself into almost a state of toxic psychosis to get over the barriers of interdict Time Center had put up around the Great Forgetting, bent Time Center's mental conditioning with the aid of a Zen Buddhist monk in thirteenth-century Japan, and hired a seventeenth-century Dutch engraver to forge his documents. There were some things that even a Full Historian was forbidden to mess with. He only hoped that it would be worth it.

When the seated figure became clear in front of him, he stopped, just outside the circle of light cast by the candle, and took a breath. His skull felt as large and unwieldy as the cathedral itself. "If you are who you claim," he said carefully, thinking about every word, "you already know the question I have come to ask. If you are not, there is no reason to even ask it." Logic was a broken reed that would pierce his hand, but he had nothing else on which to lean.

The voice laughed. "I claim nothing, Hugh. Maybe the answer lies inside your own head, and you've gone through a lot of trouble for nothing. But come on, come on. There's nothing for you to be afraid of. Not here.

Not now." A giggle. "Is that what you came for, Hugh? It's a common enough-question, and easily answered. Do you want to know the hour and place of your death?"

Solomon froze for a moment, breathing shallowly. If she was who the stories said she was, she really could tell him exactly that. Like a man gazing over a precipice, thinking idly of what it would be like to jump, he felt drawn in spite of himself. He would know everything, and his fate would be clear.

"No!" The word ripped from his throat. He leaned forward over her, into the light from the candle, his hands like claws. "You try to tell me and—"

"And what, Hugh? Don't be so silly. If I know when you are to die, I certainly know when I will. Not tonight, Hugh, I'm not going to die tonight. And neither are you, if I'm not giving anything away. So why don't we talk?"

Moira Moffette was a grossly fat woman, sprawled in what had once been the bishop's throne. The candlelight shone on the rich, filthy brocade of her dress and the rings sunk deep into the flesh of her fingers. A tiny pair of feet in embroidered slippers emerged from beneath her dress to hang in the air. Her face was round and smooth. Long lustrous lashes hid her blind eyes. She smiled at him, her teeth horrible and misshapen. "Do I match the description, Hugh? I hope you weren't expecting beauty. History is a festering wound, and those maggots that feed on it are never beautiful. Does that bother you, fellow maggot? Never mind, then. What did you bring me?" she asked, like an eager child.

He unwrapped the package. The foil paper crackled and sparkled. "A Sachertorte," he said. "From Demel's Konditorei, Vienna, 1889 CE." He'd stopped for a coffee, there in the mahogany and crystal interior, then walked out into the sunny spring warmth amid the ladies with their parasols and the gentlemen with their top hats, their faces as clear and open as the sky. He opened the box, and the musty air filled with the rich chocolate aroma of Vienna.

"Ooooh!" Moffette squealed. "Hugh, you doll! Give it here, darling, give it here. Oh! Oh! With apricot preserves between the layers! Wonderful." She grabbed the cake with both hands, smearing frosting all over herself, took a bite and chewed, cheeks puffed out, eyes screwed up with pleasure. Lank dirty hair hung around her face. Like certain holy men and mystics throughout history, she had the capability of synthesizing a Tempedrine-like chemical in her pineal gland. In order to do that, she needed a chemical precursor—Theobroma, the Food of the Gods: chocolate. Under its influence, the twists and turns of Time were visible to her. Who she was, and how she had come to be here in the twenty-first-century ruins of Sacré-Coeur, were facts unknown to anyone, though Solomon had tried to track down every lead and rumor. She might have been a Druid, a witch, a priestess of Magna Mater, a Neanderthal fertility goddess, a chocolate-binging housewife with a deviant physiology, or simply an illusion of senses deranged by overdoses of Tempedrine.

"So, tell me, Hugh. What's your question?"

He paused for a moment, still unsure. "I want to find Andrew Tarkin."

She gasped and choked. Her blind eyes stared. "Oh, oh. But he's all over the place. He crosses over and over himself. How could you not have found him? After all, Hugh, you are in so many times and places yourself." Then she began to laugh, spilling half-chewed bits of cake onto her front. "Vengeance!" she said. "It's a matter of private vengeance. You've always been so droll, Hugh."

"You've never met me before," he grated.

"But you *have* always been droll, haven't you, even if I've never met you? You don't think as clearly as you might, Hugh. But why have you come all this way to bother me with a silly personal matter?"

"It's not personal. The son of a bitch tried to kill me."

"Nothing more personal than that, is there, Hugh?"

"He's trying to deform Time itself, and that could kill all of us. Don't you understand?"

"Never having been born is not the same thing as dying, Hugh."

"Stop playing games," Solomon said. "You ate the cake, now answer the question."

"Little Miss Moffette sat on her Tophet," she chanted, like a small child. "Hear her words and pray." She giggled. "Like it? I thought it up myself. I wish I could figure out how to finish it. All right, Hugh. You want to find Andy Tarkin. Or at least you *think* you want to find Andy Tarkin. Whatever you say." Her eyes suddenly rolled up into her head, and she began to shake. Her breath came sharply through her throat, and she made a sound like the barking of a small dog. After a few minutes, her breathing slowed. "Chicago, Hugh. The Levee. You've heard of it? June twelfth, 1902. A little bar, one of a hundred little bars, called the Lone Star Saloon and Palm Garden. Just after one in the morning, a table near the back. He'll be drinking what they call bourbon, but isn't." She leaned back and closed her eyes, obviously tired.

"But," Solomon said, "but. The Levee. That's where—"

She opened them again, angry. "I know where it is, Hugh. Think of it as old-home week. I know that's where *she* is, our darling Louisa. I know that's where young man Hugh Solomon is also. You were probably a cute boy, Hugh. The Full Historian as a young man. Andy Tarkin is there, Hugh. *Not* the young one, young Hugh's friend. Not even the slightly older one who tried to drown you in the Baltic. It's the one you need to find. A long way to go to find an old friend, Hugh. That's what you asked me for, and that's what you got."

Solomon shook in a sudden chill. It was *cold* in that damn cathedral. How did she stand it, sitting there, eating nothing but chocolate? But, Jesus, Chicago. Not again.

"Now go away, Hugh. I've had enough of you. If you're smart, you'll just go back home to Time Center and forget all about this. People try to kill you all the time. You've got to learn not to take it so personally. Good night!" She blew out the candle and let Solomon find his way back to the front door in darkness.

June 1902 CE

Though it was after midnight, the streets were crowded. The Levee lay sprawled out around Solomon like a nickel whore who'd made enough to drink herself into a stupor. Probably the widest open vice district in the United States of America, it crammed no fewer than two hundred whorehouses into a few square blocks on the South Side of Chicago, along with taverns, dancing halls, gambling dens, dog-fighting pits, and hock shops. It was a favorite touring stop for visiting evangelists.

Solomon moved quickly through the fitfully gaslit streets, not looking around himself, for fear of seeing himself when young. His furtive air was usual for the Levee, and no one paid him any attention. Drunken laughter came from an open window in a three-story tenement. He slid past a black man with a bowler hat too large for his head who wanted to sell him some "goofer dust." Solomon resisted the sudden urge to stop and negotiate with him. It was sometimes too easy to adapt to the time in which one found oneself. Tempedrine brought the human mind into an identity with a time that was not its own. Solomon pushed his way through the swinging double doors of the Lone Star Saloon and Palm Garden.

Inside, it was dark, smoky, and raucous. Solomon walked, among wide laughing mouths gleaming with gold teeth and women's faces painted heavily into clowns' masks of false joy, toward the figure slumped over the table in the back.

He hit Tarkin sharply below the left ear with his elbow to stun the brain centers responsible for time travel and injected him in the buttock with a needle he had strapped to his right knee. It was quick, and no one else in the bar noticed a thing.

Tarkin turned, his eyes already glazing. He managed an expression of hatred, though he could barely control the muscles of his face. "You again. You'll never learn, will you."

Solomon stared at him in horror, for this man was older than he was himself, not at all the young man who had trapped him on the *Dagmar* of Lübeck. Tarkin's once-red hair was white, and stood out in all directions. Solomon grabbed his hand roughly. Despite his sedation, Tarkin winced. "Where did you get this, Andy?"

The gold ring on Tarkin's finger was a convenient focus for his rage.

Tarkin grinned weakly, but with triumph. "You don't really want to know. Believe me, you don't."

"I'm tired of people telling me what I don't want to know," Solomon said, injecting Tempedrine into Tarkin's carotid artery along with a synaptic impeder, to lower temporal inertia. It was hard to haul someone else through Time, impossible if they were not properly conditioned. The human mind, the only device capable of traveling through Time, tends to want to stay in its own time.

They left together, as if they were old friends, Solomon laughing and singing, Tarkin limp, stumbling. "Too much to drink, Billy," Solomon said for the benefit of the others in the bar, who paid no attention. "I told you, but you just wouldn't listen . . . time to go home."

"Time," Tarkin muttered. "Time."

The back alley was a good place to leave from. A few prostrate bodies were scattered here and there, drunk or drugged, of no more account than the lampposts or the complaining cats. Solomon lowered Tarkin to the ground.

"Ssso how's th-the sailor?" Tarkin said, slurring. "I gave up trying to kill you after the *Dagmar,* you know. I figured you'd come to me, in the end. I was right." He dropped his head suddenly to the bricks of the alley with a hollow crack. Solomon checked his skull. He hadn't fractured it, but there would be a big bump tomorrow. What was Russian for "bump"? The language came hard now, but soon it would be almost impossible to speak or think anything else. Ah, yes. *Shishka.* That would do as well as anything.

"Now let's find a few things out," Solomon said. He whispered the words of release, and the alley was empty.

February 1930 CE

Colonel Fedoseyev leaned forward in his chair, resting his chin on his hands, and stared at prisoner Shishkin with loathing. It was only the fourth day of the interrogation, but he was already bone-tired. Must be getting old. He'd once been able to run a seven-day conveyor almost single-handed, and now look at him. His eyes were gritty, and each breath took a conscious effort: Damn, *he* wasn't the one sitting in the middle of the room on a hard wooden stool.

The cut-crystal decanter, carefully polished, filled the room with sparkles when he poured himself a glass of water. He didn't want a drink, but the prisoner, fed on salty food and deprived of water, certainly did. Was he even watching? Fedoseyev forced himself to swallow the tepid flat liquid with every sign of satisfaction, smacking his lips. He felt bloated. He wanted to lie down and sleep a thousand years.

Water dribbled from the glass and made another dark spot on the tattered green baize of the desk, the color picked because it showed off gold. The Soviet State *needed* gold. "Let's give it another try, shall we?" Fedoseyev said heavily. "The name of the jeweler, and his current whereabouts. Then you can have a drink of water and some sleep." Sleep! "Just don't give me any more *Arabian Nights* stuff. I'm not an idiot."

Shishkin didn't look as if he had heard. The parasite! He just sat there, babbling nonsense. Fedoseyev had heard whispers that they were raising desperately needed foreign exchange by selling Rembrandts from the Hermitage to the millionaires of the West. And bastards, greedy bastards everywhere, were hoarding gold. The word had come down through the OGPU, the secret police: get it! Get the gold. Sweat them! Squeeze them! The nation needs it! So Shishkin, his white hair sticking out in every direction, sat slumped in the interrogation room like some pale insect and tired Fedoseyev by telling him everything but what he wanted to know.

He pushed his chair back and walked around the desk. His boot heels clicked on the elaborate parquetry, now deeply scratched. The room had once been part of the Office of Textiles. Darker blue squares on the patterned wallpaper still showed where framed swatches had hung. Plaster cherubs, chipped and dusty, blew trumpets at the corners of the high ceiling.

It was a good one, no windup, no warning at all. The prisoner's face jerked sideways and he gasped. The smack of the backhanded slap filled the room for an instant and was gone. Captain Solomonov, silent at his secretary's desk with his pen, inkwell, and notebook, looked up from his writing, his lean high-cheekboned face carefully expressionless. There was a little blood at the corner of the prisoner's mouth. Just a bead.

Fedoseyev squatted, a huge bear of a man, took the prisoner's hand, and stared him in the face. Shishkin looked back intently, like a stranger watching an unfamiliar game, failing to puzzle out the rules that governed its play. "Gold is not a solitary beast like an eagle." Shishkin's face tightened as Fedoseyev twisted his hand. "No. It is a herd animal. Like cows. Like sheep. So." He twisted farther. "Where are this one's brothers? And where is the shepherd?" The ring on the prisoner's finger glinted up at him.

In spite of himself, Fedoseyev admired it for an instant. It was a snake biting its own tail, the shimmering intricacy of the pattern of scales definitely oriental. Its eyes were green jewels. No wonder the prisoner made up such fanciful stories. But it was gold, rich and heavy, and it was not more than a dozen years old, though it looked slightly melted, as if it had been through a hot fire.

Shishkin's body began to shake, and he sobbed. "I've told you," he whispered in his poor Russian. "It was made for me, to give to someone I loved. Long ago in . . . in—"

"In wondrous Araby?" Fedoseyev roared. "Scum! I'm tired of your fairy stories." He turned and stared out of the window, running his hand over his shaven scalp. The Kremlin towers loomed to the left against the darkening sky. Decent red stars were only now replacing the Imperial two-headed eagles that had continued to top them for the dozen years since the Revolution. What the hell was wrong? The man had obviously broken completely. He eagerly babbled details, complete descriptions of the jeweler, his habits, his place of work. If his mother had made the ring, Shishkin would have turned her in. Why then was everything he said obvious nonsense? The ring was real. So, therefore, by logical operations Fedoseyev had forgotten since school but was sure still applied, was the jeweler. Only he sold earrings to the wives of Party officials and lived in some sober city in Soviet Central Asia, not Baghdad, or Aleppo, or whatever it was he claimed. Fedoseyev didn't like interrogating lunatics.

He squinted over at Solomonov, who sat attentively, pen ready on paper. Solomonov had brought the prisoner in himself and seemed to cherish a particular interest in him, writing every detail of his impossible ravings down in his notebook. A personal concern, Fedoseyev thought, from the village in which they had both grown up, or from the Gymnasium. An officer in the OGPU was well placed to pay off old scores.

With sudden irritation Fedoseyev reached over, twisted the prisoner's arm behind him, and removed the ring. It slipped off with surprising ease. When he released him, Shishkin slumped back onto his stool and stared off at nothing.

"The caravans leave Aleppo in the winter," Shishkin said. "I saw it . . . the mosque of Jami Zakariyah gleamed blue. The man from Bukhara made her a ring of finest gold . . . I loved her, I thought he had burned her, he who had been my friend . . . I've guarded her for all these years."

Shishkin had reached a state in which the term "interrogation" was meaningless, and Fedoseyev suddenly lost all interest in continuing. It was only 1930, after all. Fedoseyev and his kind were still moving inch by inch into savagery, like a man lowering himself into a hot bathtub. Ten years later such considerations would have seemed foolish, and Fedoseyev would have known that every interrogation was a torture session from start to finish, with information being an irrelevant by-product, but ten years later Fedoseyev would be lying in the gold fields of the Kolyma, frozen to death, having been arrested and interrogated in his turn.

He patted Shishkin on the back. "Had an old biddy in here the other day," he said, confidingly. "Country girl, thought herself smart. Held on a day and a half, then gave it up. Smart girl. Hid it inside the privy. *Down* inside. A real mess. That's capitalism for you. Two hundred counterfeit rubles, brass covered with gold. You should have heard her spit. 'The lice! The lice! You were right to shoot them!' " He chuckled at the memory, stopped short.

He sat down at his desk, pulled out a sheet of paper, and signed it. Without a word he pushed it toward Shishkin, who, after a moment's incomprehension, also signed it. It was thus that prisoner Shishkin found himself sentenced to ten years in the corrective labor camps, under Section 10: Anti-Soviet Agitation.

Fedoseyev tossed the ring into the air. It twirled and glittered, then vanished into his immense hand. Fedoseyev was fed up with the whole thing. He was a brutal man but not an acquisitive one, showing the selectivity of vices as well as virtues, so he tossed the ring to Solomonov, who, surprised, caught it clumsily.

"Take him downstairs," Fedoseyev said. "He goes on the next transport." He looked out of the window. Snow had started sifting down from the sky that afternoon, and the dimly seen roofs beneath the window were already blanketed in white.

Solomon saluted the OGPU colonel, who ignored this bit of military precision, and led Andy Tarkin out of the interrogation room. They walked through long halls lined with interrogation rooms and holding cells. Solomon whistled tunelessly and tried to ignore the presence of his prisoner, that antisoviet parasite. It was good to be wearing the blue shoulder boards of the OGPU, watching officers of the Red Army act deferential, and full professors at Moscow University look frightened. It was good to be finally getting some respect . . . what the hell was he thinking? Solomonov . . . *Solomon* glanced over at the still-expressionless Tarkin and tried to control his thoughts. He thought about the three-day interrogation and wondered who the next criminal would be—no, dammit, he was *leaving,* not staying here in Moscow in 1930. He was going to Aleppo, to that time that the interrogation had revealed. Maybe there he could sort out his thoughts. Too much Tempedrine wasn't good for you. It really wasn't.

He led Tarkin down the broad stairs, brass rods attempting to hold down a long vanished carpet, and turned him over to the lieutenant at the desk, along with the paper with the sentence. He left him there to vanish into the empire of the corrective labor camps. He doubted that the elderly Shishkin would survive the first year of his ten-year sentence. Solomon strolled down the marble-floored hallway, turned a corner, and disappeared.

The lieutenant filled out the proper paperwork. Prisoner Shishkin was sent to a cell in Butyrki Prison. After a month in a cell with forty other prisoners, he was taken, at night, by Black Maria, to the Kaluga Gates Transit Prison on the outskirts of Moscow. After two weeks, he was put aboard a train heading east, toward his eventual destination, Sovetskaya Gavan, on the other side of the Soviet Union. The journey would take several months. The train was stopped on a siding near Irkutsk for a week and a half, and when they were ready to move again and mustered the prisoners in order to unload the bodies of those who had frozen in the unheated cars, no trace of prisoner Shishkin could be found. The other prisoners were beaten, but no one could even remember what Shishkin had looked like. The guards put their heads together, and prisoner Shishkin vanished from their records as thoroughly as he had succeeded in vanishing from the boxcar, and their time.

November 949 CE

"Pull out my soul, O Lord," Abdullah Ibn-Umar al-Bukhari whispered to himself as he drew the gold wire through the iron die, reducing its diameter yet again, "until I am infinitely long, and lost in thinness." The wire was now the thickness of a grass stem, suitable for making earrings, but al-Bukhari was not planning to stop until it was barely less fine than human hair, for he had more delicate work in mind. "Step by step our fineness increases, but we never manage to approach

Thee, O Allah." With a sharp knife he shaved the first inch of wire, then put it into the next smaller hole on the die. He took the end in his tongs and pulled again. "Take the metal away, and we do not exist, but are of Thee, O Lord." Muscles stood out in his bare shoulder and arm.

The world was a crystal that sang as it was stroked by the hand of Allah. Men cupped their ears, but heard nothing but whispers and echoes. As he worked, al-Bukhari heard ominous noises, the sounds of crashing waves, dying men. Echoes distort and transform, turning good into evil. The gleaming wire was a golden snake, writhing in agony, twisting itself around the sphere of the Earth until it could take its tail in its own jaws, starting flames with the rubbing of its belly. He smelled the acrid stink, tasted bitter gall at the back of his throat. He stopped pulling, and put his hands over his eyes. He felt the flames of burning and heard the screaming of a horse. A man's soul was consumed by the flames, leaving ashes. It was bad this time. "O Lord, Thy visions tear like Greek lances through my heart." And suddenly, all was clear, and the wire was wire, simple gold. He picked up the tongs and resumed his task.

"Excuse me." At the front of al-Bukhari's shop stood a tall man, with a strong jaw and high cheekbones, in the garb of a traveling merchant. His eyes glowed with pain and rage, of guilt and hatred unsatisfied, or so al-Bukhari imagined. He felt that the man had just come from committing a terrible act. Al-Bukhari's first wife Fatima was a sensible woman who had often urged him to curb his fantastic visions. He always promised her, and always broke his promise. He could not explain to her that they came from outside their time, because he did not know this himself. Al-Bukhari felt a moment of fear, not for himself, but on the stranger's account. The man carried a heavy load, and his soul wobbled, splay-footed, like a camel about to collapse. "I am called Suleiman Ibn-Mustar," the stranger said. "May we speak?"

Al-Bukhari got up, and bustled to the front of the shop. Customers should always be treated well, as Fatima had often explained. Al-Bukhari was a stocky, slightly plump man in his midthirties, his short beard already going gray. He had a sideward gaze and a strong voice that made him a Koran reader most Fridays at the mosque. "Come in and sit."

They sat cross-legged on the carpet and were served cooling drinks of rosewater and honey by Zaynab, al-Bukhari's second wife. She vanished through the door at the back of the shop into the darkness of the house. As he talked, al-Bukhari occasionally turned away to feed his brazier. The shop was full of precisely arranged hammers, tongs, tweezers, anvils, and other equipment. "How may I help you?" al-Bukhari said.

Solomon suddenly felt confusion. What did his quest have to do with this energetic little man and his life in this corner of Time? Yet, somehow, this man seemed important. "I wish to buy," he said.

Al-Bukhari showed him his work, mostly in gold and enamel, earrings, turban pins, and bridle ornaments. "You are not from this place," Solomon said. He picked up a bracelet and hung it on his wrist, letting a beam of sunlight fall on it and shatter into glittering splinters.

"No," al-Bukhari said. "I am from Bukhara. That is over two months' journey from here."

"You must miss your home." He set the bracelet down and picked up a jewel box of carnelian and onyx. "Your work is excellent. Your gifts would not have been unwelcome at the wedding of al-Ma'mun, or the royal banquet of al-Mutawakkil."

Al-Bukhari colored with pleasure. "Your words do me honor, Suleiman. Those two occasions have no third in Islam. But my home? Ah, how could you know? The valley of Sogdiana is one of the four earthly paradises. The gardens and orchards . . . Syria is a dry place." He crinkled his slanted oriental eyes, remembering. He thought about his cheating uncle, and about the power of visions and the hand of God, but did not speak of them. Instead he pulled out a box, on impulse. "You have not seen these."

Solomon stared down at the rings in the box, each a gleaming pure circle of gold. Thinking of the ring he had in his pouch, he looked at each in turn. What a hoard! How delighted Fedoseyev would have been. In this single market he could have made enough arrests to keep him in interrogations for the rest of his life.

But the ring he was looking for was not there. They showed a similar technique, though a different style.

He looked at al-Bukhari. "Have you sold a ring recently, in the shape of a serpent with its own tail in its mouth?"

"A serpent . . . no, I have never made such a ring." He looked frightened. "With its tail in its mouth . . ." How could Suleiman have known of his vision of the golden serpent? He stood up, suddenly agitated. "Please . . . I must get back to work. It is getting late." This man Suleiman, he realized again, was dangerous. Who was he? What evil did he represent?

Solomon stood also, surprised and himself suddenly suspicious. Did the jeweler know more than he was letting on? Was he an ally of Tarkin's? He wished he had Fedoseyev back, and a comfortable interrogation room where he could uncover the truth. . . .

Al-Bukhari moved quickly to the front of the shop, and froze. Across the street, walking amid the crowds, he saw an Ifrit. He dared not breathe. Why did an evil djinni walk abroad?

A holy man, his voice sonorous against the screaming background, led a gaggle of students toward the blue-domed mosque of Jami Zakariyah, where he would lecture in the courtyard. For all his knowledge of the Koran and the Law, he walked right past the Ifrit without perceiving it. A wealthy noble, turbaned and bearded, peered moodily into a crystal sphere at a stall across the way, while his Greek slave declaimed Aristotle in bad Arabic. The Ifrit jostled his arm, but aside from a glance of irritation, he did not notice it. The Ifrit wore the face of guilt, and stalked its victim with staring mad eyes. Al-Bukhari watched with fascination as it pulled its headdress across the lower part of its face, leaving only those staring eyes, and drew a sword. It keened like a newly widowed woman, and attacked.

Suleiman swore in some harsh foreign language and drew his own sword with lightning speed. The two blades met with a bold ringing and slid along each other, the unexpected resistance causing the Ifrit to stumble back. It seemed old, somehow, old and slow. Up and down the street were sounds of fear and concern as merchants either hid themselves or tried to protect their merchandise, depending on their personalities.

"Tarkin!" Solomon shouted. But what argument could he use? Tarkin had every reason to want to kill him. How had he escaped from the train car? Or was this yet another Tarkin, a younger one? A younger Tarkin from a time before the Moscow interrogation could not be killed, since he had to continue to exist, but there was no time to think about paradoxes.

The other clumsily attacked again. Solomon was fascinated by the other's eyes. What had they looked upon? His assailant's reflexes were slow. As the attacking blade moved, Solomon darted aside and drove his blade home. The other fell to the street.

Solomon reached forward to pull aside the covering so that he could look Tarkin in the face, but glanced up as he heard the hiss of swords being drawn from scabbards. A body of armed men was approaching, cautiously. The local gendarmerie. Without another thought, he turned and ran. Solomon lost his pursuers for long enough to dart into a cul-de-sac, slap an ampoule of Tempedrine against his neck, and disappear from that time.

June 1902 CE

Eras before the First World War were the easiest to travel in without preparation, because everyone took gold, though sometimes at a ruinous discount. Solomon darted up the street and into a doorway beneath the three gold balls of a pawnbroker. He sold the bemused proprietor his suddenly ridiculous clothes and bought an ill-fitting pair of work pants held up by a length of rope and a wool shirt, much too warm for the day. With these clothes he walked farther up the street and bought a decent suit of clothes. Used to the sudden accesses of wealth that came to gamblers and criminals, this proprietor made no remark about the exchange of rough work clothes for a dress shirt and a suit of light gray gabardine. Yet farther up the street he exchanged gold for dollars, then rented a room in a boardinghouse with a shared kitchen and an outhouse in the back, and prepared to make his investigation. He was only a few blocks from where he and Tarkin had lived—*were* living—during their research, but he had already violated so many Time Center regulations that he did not let this bother him.

With slow patience, he searched, starting conversations in bars, in stores, on the El. A number of people in and around the Levee had seen Tarkin: some described him as old, while others said he was young. Many professions were ascribed to him. Solomon walked the streets all day and all night, searching every face he passed. Chicago had over a million and a half people in 1902. There were a lot of faces to look at.

He was led to the first Tarkin he saw by a small boy who earned his two bits. Solomon passed by the plate-glass window of a drugstore and saw a middle-aged man wiping down the counter with a white cloth.

The second Tarkin, somewhat younger, drove a milk cart. The third Tarkin was an old man who told people's fortunes, while the fourth was another middle-aged man who worked in a dry goods store. By the time Solomon had seen seven different versions of Andy Tarkin he stopped counting. Each had a somewhat different disguise, hair color, pair of glasses, and posture, but it wasn't difficult to spot them once you knew what you were looking for. Each wore a gold ring.

Tarkin would have given the Controllers of Time Center screaming fits. He had doubled back on his own life, over and over, weaving a web of himself around the incident that had forever directed his life and Solomon's. But, Solomon thought as he passed yet another version of Tarkin, this one pushing a knife-sharpening cart, he had obviously never succeeded in changing one damn thing about what had happened. As demonstrably physical as it was, Tarkin's obsession about the past had no more effect on things than such obsessions ever did.

But now Solomon had obsessions of his own to deal with, for it was once again late afternoon on June 11. Before the night was through, he would find out what really had happened at Mrs. Mulvaney's boardinghouse. "Just think of it as historical research," he told himself as he walked that long familiar path up the cobblestones of Harrison Street from the end of the streetcar line, past the corner of Wilmot, where Mr. Kirkby kept his prize sow Ernestine in her pen by his front steps, and up Furnace Street to Mrs. Mulvaney's three-story mansard-roofed boardinghouse with the crazily leaning barn next to it.

It was a warm day, with a high and clear afternoon. How many times had Tarkin already lived it?

He was stopped cold by a woman's laugh. A man's laugh answered it.

"It's true," the man's voice insisted. "The Japanese use hard wooden blocks for pillows. So when one of their ambassadors was staying at the Hotel Willard in Washington, where the pillows are full of down, and found the chamber pot under the bed, he used that instead and slept quite well."

"Oh, Hugh," Louisa said, still laughing. "That still doesn't explain why the first time you tried to use a gas jet you almost burned your hair off."

"Where I come from, in North Dakota—"

"Oh, stop that!"

"All right, Tibet. We use yak butter there."

Solomon felt wonder. Had he really ever been that young, that easy? Could he ever have flirted so casually with the landlady's daughter? He peeked around the edge of the porch. There he sat, lean and young, his hair greased back, wearing a seersucker suit and a straw boater. He looked as if he didn't have a care in the world. Louisa sat across from him, kicking up her heels, dressed in a blue shirtwaist dress with puffy sleeves. Her hair was curly black, and her dark eyes darted all around as she talked.

"Mrs. Mulvaney says that dinner is almost ready," a third voice said. The tousled ginger hair of Tarkin's head poked around the edge of the door.

"Oh, Andy, sit down, sit down with us." Louisa jumped up and pulled him down next to her, opposite Solomon, so that she was flanked by her two suitors, the two history students who had had to come eight hundred years into their own pasts to learn what life and love really were.

"You look very well, Mr. Tarkin."

"Never felt better, Mr. Solomon."

The old Full Historian Solomon rested his forehead on the cool granite of the boardinghouse's foundation. This was the last afternoon that either of them would ever be truly at peace. After this it would be nothing but endless blow and counterblow, watching massacres, plagues, and disasters, of never knowing an instant's peace, for they would both have ceased to be the sort of men who would recognize peace if they were offered it. He stood and listened to them talk and flirt until they were finally called in.

As they went in to dinner, Solomon heard Tarkin say, shyly, "I . . . I have something for you, Louisa. I had it made specially. I'll show you after dinner."

The fire had started in the old barn, which was dry as tinder after three weeks with no rain. His guts cold and hard as ice within him, Solomon commenced to watch the house and its barn, to wait for the moment when the flames would emerge and consume everything, making him the man he now was.

The night grew cool, giving up the summer warmth of the afternoon. A breeze sprang up off the lake. The Mulvaney household spread out on the porch and talked in a desultory way. Eleven o'clock passed, announced by the bells of a church, and midnight approached. Still no hint of a fire starting, and it had started just at midnight, the time his younger self usually went to bed.

He climbed into a window of the barn and looked around inside. Jenny, Mrs. Mulvaney's brown mare, nickered softly in the darkness. There was no open flame, such as the kerosene lamp Mrs. O'Leary's legendary cow had kicked over to start the great Chicago fire of 1871. The silage was fresh and was kept turned over to prevent fermentation, which could get hot enough to start a smoldering fire. Outside, he could hear the bell of the church tolling the twelve strokes of midnight.

In doing their research to recover what had been lost in the Great Forgetting, the Historians of Time Center sometimes inadvertently caused temporal paradoxes. Such paradoxes had to be resolved. Solomon's duty as a Full Historian was explicit. The fire had happened. He had witnessed it. Thus, the fire *would* happen. Mechanically, because thinking might have stopped him, he pulled off some of the drier stalks of grass and piled them against one of the barn walls. Shaking, he untied Jenny, who nuzzled him curiously.

"You lived," he whispered. "The rest of us didn't." He unbolted the door of the barn so that the horse would be able to open it by pushing against it, then without any further hesitation, walked back to the pile of straw, struck a safety match, and touched it to the tinder.

In a minute the dry boards of the wall were burning as well. The flames were hot on his face, and the roar as loud as Niagara Falls, which Louisa had always wanted to see.

The fire spread like wine spilled on the floor. The roof of the barn exploded into flame all at once. Jenny neighed in terror, pounded herself against the barn doors, and escaped onto the street. The barn was filling up with smoke, and already the beams overhead creaked as they were eaten away by the fire. Solomon turned. Standing in the open doorway, staring at him, was the young Tarkin, barefoot, obviously interrupted in his preparations for bed. Tarkin shook his head, as if unable to believe what he was seeing. It would take some moments, Solomon knew, for his astonishment to turn into bitter rage and hatred and not much longer to change him from a friend to an enemy.

"Andy!" Solomon shouted, above the roar of the flames. "Wait!"

But Tarkin was gone, running back toward the house, shouting, "Louisa!"

Solomon ran out after him. The blaze had spread from the barn to the house it leaned against, and flames were already leaping out of the third-floor dormer windows. Mrs. Mulvaney and her son Arnold were even at that moment escaping through a second-floor window onto the bough of a sycamore that stood near the house. His younger self, having been smoking a last pipe on the porch before going to bed, would get into the house and make it halfway up the front stairs before being driven back by the flames. Louisa's room was on the second floor, facing the alley in back.

Tarkin tried to get up to Louisa's window, but the fire was already licking the wall from base to roof, and he too was forced back. He called her name up at the blazing window. Then, "the bastard," he yelled, no longer at Louisa's window, but at the world in general. "The bastard! Why?"

This was how it started. Solomon walked down to the street. The fire, Louisa's death, Tarkin's apparently unmotivated and savage hatred: these had all helped make him the man he was, the hard, cold, duty-bound Full Historian of Time Center. But all of these things were the results of acts that he himself had committed precisely *because* he was the man he was. He felt drained, meaningless, a rolling hoop. Tarkin had every reason to hate him, but Tarkin would take that hatred out on an innocent man, thus turning him into a man who would someday be worthy of hatred. Before the night was out, Tarkin would try to kill the young Hugh Solomon and, failing, vanish into Time. Tarkin would keep trying to kill Solomon until that time when Solomon, old and bitter, would return to even the score. The old Full Historian walked, slowly, down pitch-black Wilmot and out onto Harrison, brighter, since it had gaslights.

Solomon froze. In the bright light in front of Masterson's General Store was a two-wheeled trap, with a swaybacked gray horse hitched to the front. Sitting in it, a straw hat tied to her head and a heavy valise at her feet, was Louisa.

Solomon neither rubbed his eyes nor pinched himself. He knew instantly that he was indeed seeing what was before him, and that it was the punch line to the shaggy-dog story that his life was revealed to be. A young man emerged from the store with a package. He was Steven Eichorn, who lived a few blocks away and was studying at the University of Chicago to be a lawyer. He was "Louisa's young man," Solomon supposed, and his belatedly revealed existence explained a lot about Louisa's behavior in the few months preceding the fire. Eichorn leaped into the trap with excessive energy, took the reins, and drove it away down the street.

Solomon felt the sharp edge of a knife blade at his ribs. "I thought I'd *never* get to you," Tarkin said. He turned Solomon around.

This was a stoop-shouldered Tarkin, as old as the man Solomon had sent to a Soviet prison camp.

"Was it worth using yourself up?" Solomon said. "Tying your entire life into a knot?"

"It was," Tarkin said. "I wanted to love her. But you can't recover love, even if you can recover exactly the person who made you love in the first place. Time travel is funny that way, Hugh. It makes you think that you can finally recover the past, but it's just memory made solid, so that it can hurt you even more. But I tried. I came back here after the last time I tried to kill you, aboard the *Dagmar*, and finally found out that Louisa hadn't died in that fire. If you'd looked just now you would have seen me, standing on the other side of Masterson's, looking just as stupid as you. That was when I decided to stay here, always. She fell in love with young Eichorn—"

"He was older than we were, Andy."

Tarkin smiled. "One forgets these things. Wasn't it amazing, to watch us there, on that porch?"

"We were happy. And that moment always exists."

"Cold comfort." Urged by Tarkin's knife, which remained at Solomon's ribs despite the ease of their conversation, they walked down the street, two old friends leaning on each other for support. "But I did what I could. I arranged for Eichorn to get that trap. I encouraged them to elope. And this evening, about ten years ago for me, I think, I hauled a sheep carcass into Louisa's room. When the ashes had cooled they carried the remains of Louisa's body out of the fire. She left the ring I gave her on her nightstand, and I found it in the ruins of the house.

"You went to the funeral. Forensic medicine leaves a lot to be desired in 1902, the coroner was drunk, the fire took place in a less than respectable neighborhood, and he gave the matter about ten minutes of his time. Louisa Mulvaney burned to death in an accidental fire. That was the verdict, Hugh. And you, you stupid son of a bitch, believed him, just like I did. You thought you were killing the woman you had once loved, but you were just cooking a rack of lamb."

They walked slowly along, Solomon staring forward blankly, the immediacy of the past overwhelming him, until the sounds and smells around him told him that they were once again in the Levee, which never slept.

"This is a good place," Tarkin said as they entered the Lone Star Saloon and Palm Garden. "I believe you know it." The place was the same, the lights were the same, the teeth were the same, the faces were the same.

"Hey, Mickey!" Tarkin shouted at the bartender. "Give us one of your Specials! And I'll have a gin."

In a minute, a large glass of murky liquid was placed in front of Solomon, who stared at it dully.

"Drink up," Tarkin said. "It will make you feel better."

Solomon looked at him. "You tried to kill me, the young man I was. Why, Andy? I hadn't done anything."

"Shut up and drink."

Solomon shrugged, and with somewhat the air of Socrates drinking the cup of hemlock, drained it. He made a face.

Tarkin leaned back and looked at the sign that was just visible behind the bar. "Try the Mickey Finn Special," it said. Not yet proverbial, the mickey was, in Chicago of 1902, a new innovation in the art of rolling customers, chloral hydrate and alcohol.

Solomon's eyes rolled up in his head, and he toppled from his chair with a loud groan. "Why did I pursue the young Hugh Solomon? Because I knew that eventually it would bring me to the man who *was* guilty," Tarkin said. "I have you now, you son of a bitch."

Solomon's body suddenly vanished. Staring, Tarkin sat heavily back in his chair. He shivered and took a gulp of his gin. "I can't start all over again," he said to himself. "I can't."

He was still sitting that way, slumped forward over his drink, when he felt the sharp blow of an elbow on the left side of his head, and the cold slide of a hypodermic needle into his buttock.

November 949 CE

Solomon stumbled along the street in Aleppo. He wore a heavy wool cloak, which he had bought to throw over his light gray gabardine suit, the height of fashion in early twentieth-century Chicago. He regretted having sold his suit of merchant's clothes to the clothing dealer. He stopped by a stall and, with his last coins, bought a short, curved sword, not stopping to haggle with the proprietor.

There was yet a chance of stopping everything, he thought to himself. He was dizzy and sick. Visions of flames and abandoned cathedrals flashed before his eyes, and the long tiled hallways of Time Center. The mickey and his Tempedrine overdoses had caused him to slide through Time like a wet bar of soap on a shower floor. His palm was sweaty on the pommel of the sword.

Finally he saw him standing in front of the shop of al-Bukhari, tall and lean, talking to the short, stocky jeweler. Hatred overwhelmed him. He raised his sword and, screaming, attacked.

The earlier Solomon parried the attack skillfully. Despairing and weakened by the drugs in the Mickey Finn, the later Solomon was no match for him, and the penetration of the other's blade was a release from pain. He fell to the dusty street. The other Solomon fled.

Al-Bukhari approached the figure sprawled in front of his shop. Was it indeed an Ifrit? Infrits were tormentors and tricksters, but the guilts and sins of men were not normally their concern, for their essential substance was fire, not earth. And they certainly did not bleed, blood pooling at its belly as it curled around its mortal wound. He pulled the cloth away from the face and stared into Solomon's eyes.

"Zaynab!" he called over his shoulder. "Some water. Quickly!" He knelt down and rested the man's head on his lap. Zaynab ran out of the shop and paused, eyes wide, when she saw the bleeding man. She handed the cup to al-Bukhari, and he put it to the other's lips. "You are not his brother. Nor are you a djinni in his image, as first I thought. You are he himself."

Solomon choked. "I am. He will now commit great . . . sins. I wanted to stop him. But it is impossible. Everything was fixed in its place, and I could do nothing."

"Your sins are your own," al-Bukhari said. "Did you not choose whether to commit them?" He closed his eyes and saw a ship full of dead men blow ashore in sand dunes on the shores of a cold gray sea. A house burned and a horse screamed. Men frozen to death in a box in the snow. They were tied together in a knot, like that in the elaborate calligraphy on the dome of a mosque. And the name of the knot was Guilt.

"I had to . . . history . . . what happened had to happen or else. . . ."

"What happened happened because you made it so," al-Bukhari said, in a moment of total mental transparency. He scarcely knew what he was saying. "Only then was it inevitable. Your fate, friend, lay in your character, not in Time."

"Fate. Here is a piece of fate for you, al-Bukhari. Do with it what you will. In less than six years, the Byzantine Emperor, Nicephoras Phocas, will invade Syria, and sack and burn this city of Aleppo. You miss Bukhara, that beautiful land. Let that be your guide. And perhaps it will go a short way toward absolving me. But now . . . take this, take this ring." He pulled it from his finger. It was in the shape of a snake biting its own tail, and had eyes that were chips of emerald. And so, with a final sigh, Solomon died.

The images faded from al-Bukhari's mind, and there was just a market street with a dead man in the middle of it, and he had blood on his shirt. Others came and took the body away.

June 1902 CE

The old man stood behind the barn, bent wearily against the picket fence that marked the end of the lot, looking up at the lights of the Mulvaney house. The night lake breeze was cool but nowhere near as cold as it had just been in the railway car on the siding in Siberia. He shivered. Tarkin, near death, had time-traveled without an injection of Tempedrine, to return here, to the heart of events. It was just before midnight.

In a few minutes Solomon would come around the

house to set the barn on fire, so that history would take its proper course. Tarkin slowly worked his way through the sycamore saplings that grew between the barn and the fence. He supported himself on each as he passed, feeling the bark of the young trees smooth in his hand. Last year's grass rustled beneath his feet.

A small flame flickered in front of him. He stopped and squinted. Two boys, about ten years old, crouched at the corner of the barn trying to light a pipe. It was not a corncob but a heavy meerschaum, probably stolen from a father's study. They muttered to each other, intent on their business, and did not see Tarkin. One of the boys burned his finger, swore, and dropped the match in the dry grass. It flared up instantly. The boys yelped and fled.

The grass caught quickly, and the fire soon started to lick up near the barn wall. Tarkin looked at it for several moments, mesmerized by the flames, then walked over and stomped it out.

He looked around the corner of the barn. A tall figure in a gabardine suit walked stiffly from the Mulvaney house to the back barn window. A bell tolled the twelve strokes of midnight.

"That's it then, Hugh," Tarkin whispered. He ground out the last hot ashes of the fire with his heel. "We made our choices, and they made us." Solomon opened the barn window and climbed in. Tarkin vanished into the cool night air.

November 949 CE

Al-Bukhari squatted and looked at the ring in the palm of his hand, wondering. A shadow loomed over him.

"Are you the jeweler al-Bukhari?" said a young man, very pale, with wild reddish hair. A northerner, a Russian perhaps. His eyes glowed. In love, probably, al-Bukhair thought to himself. When the dead have been cleaned away, there is still time to love.

"I am." He stood. There would be time to think about the flames that would consume Aleppo. He did miss Bukhara dreadfully. . . .

"I came here to have you make a ring for someone important." The young Tarkin pointed at the ring al-Bukhari held in his hand. "I have heard of your skill, and know that you can do it. I would like a ring, if possible, very much like that one."

BENEATH THE SHADOW
OF HER SMILE

By the time I got to Bert, the sound of the shelling was sharp and clear in my ears. Someone was having an artillery duel down in the direction of Montauban. There were still some French units there, and it was close to the Somme, where trenches were damp and tempers short. I had heard it start when I was back in Amiens, lying in a bed at Madame Berthier's, but there it hadn't seemed to matter, coming as it did through a set of lace curtains.

The light of the declining sun shined the wrong way through the windows of the roofless houses. Before the War, people had lived in the town, then called Albert, but no one remembered those days. There was no one here now but the soldiers, and to them the place was called Bert, with a hard English *t*. Everyone knew Bert. French poilus shivering in the ruins of Fort Douaumont, at Verdun, pressed their crosses to their lips and thought of it. Russian conscripts drowning in shell holes at Aubers died whispering its name. German regulars on garrison duty along the Piave sang songs about it. For it was from this spot that the Golden Virgin tormented us.

Before the War, a huge gilded statue of the Virgin had stood atop the Basilica of Albert. She had proved a natural target for the German long-range guns located back toward Bapaume, though for a long time the tower suffered no damage. Finally one day a shell exploded just at the Virgin's feet. She toppled forward, slowly at first, then accelerating as she swung downward toward the earth . . . and stopped. And so she had hung there ever since, feet above her head, angled just past the horizontal, dangling precariously yet never falling. No amount of shelling had ever managed to get her to budge another inch. She was a miracle.

All of us, all the men of the War, were concerned about her, and about what she was trying to tell us. Theories abounded. Some held that she was throwing the infant Jesus down to the street, sacrificing Him before His time as an expiation to end the slaughter. Others thought that she was bent over in grief, for from her vantage point she could examine at her leisure the vast meat grinder of Somme sector. Or was she just trying to dodge the shells that flew past? To me it had always seemed that He had strayed somehow, and she had just leaned forward and gathered Him back up in her arms. His expression indicated that He wasn't sure whether to be pleased.

One thing was known by everyone, from the Channel, across Switzerland, and to the Adriatic: when she ceased to balance there on her tower and at last fell, the War would end. It was obvious that she would never fall. It was rumored that she was wired in place, with cables running down into the ruined basilica, holding her up, that German gunners were under strictest orders never to fire upon the tower, that she had indeed already fallen twice, but each time had been replaced by an identical replica, for High Command, which in the soldiers' mythology ruled both sides, had fattened on the nearly two decades of war that had ludicrously followed the assassination of a pompous Austrian archduke and had no desire to ever see it end.

Two American soldiers were guarding the front of the basilica, ostensibly because it was used as an artillery spotting post. They shared a cigarette, and I could smell its aroma out where I stood in the street. I considered my chances of hitting them up for some. Rather small, I thought. Nonexistent. There was still hostility between British and American expeditionary troops, lingering from the riots and mutinies of '26 and '27. Besides, I wore pressed cardboard boots with soles made from the treads of old tires, and my uniform was patched with bits of cloth that almost—but not quite—matched, while they looked like real soldiers, with polished leather boots and visored caps.

So I took a deep breath to catch the traces of tobacco smoke, glanced a last time up at the serene face of the Golden Virgin as she hovered over me, and made my way through the rubble to the far edge of town to join my company as it mustered after our liberty. The place was a dusty quadrangle that had once been a football field.

The quad was crowded with men, soberly lying to each other about the achievements of their liberties, but I saw my company standing at its usual spot, just at the corner of the military brothel, which stood where the goalposts had once been. The brothel had no name, only a number, although it was called a number of things, of course, by the men who sought release there. It was built of poured concrete, and its windows were narrow slits. Near the door was a sign detailing venereal disease symptoms in eleven languages. The main advantage of this was that it gave one the ability to say "painful discharge" in Czech.

It had been a long time since I'd lain on one of its rough stained pallets. I arched my back slightly as I walked, feeling the clean linen of Mme. Berthier's establishment on my bare skin, remembering. . . .

Toby had stayed out all night again. He'd been locked in the cellar the evening before to tend to his task, which was catching mice, but he'd thought of more important matters and I found him on the roof, smoothing his whiskers in male satisfaction, when I opened the shutters in the morning. He looked up at me and meowed.

"Toby," I hissed. "Get the hell—"

It was too late. Lisette froze in the middle of that charming childlike stretch and squeak with which she wakes herself, and looked out at the cat with her wide cornflower-blue eyes. She tossed her golden hair back and flounced over to the window.

"Toby!" she said, reaching out her hand. The cat rubbed against it and purred. "You know not to stay out like that. For that, you will stay out." She flicked him off the steeply pitched roof to the yard below, where Barbarossa, Mme. Berthier's mastiff, was waiting. I saw a yellow yowling streak go across the yard and over the fence. He never learned. That damn stupid roving cat never learned.

Lisette smiled at me, and kissed my earlobe. "Poor kitty," she said. "Poor kitty." She pirouetted joyfully. I took hold of her, and she giggled. I always wanted Lisette above the others, for she was so beautiful, and simple, in both her pleasures and her cruelties.

My hand explored inside her robe. "Bad boy," she said. "Bad."

"No, no. Good. Very good."

The door opened with a squeak of hinges. I turned. Standing in the doorway was a stout woman with dark dyed hair and a trace of a moustache, which she made no attempt to conceal. She slapped her hands together. The fingers were loaded with rings, which glittered in the morning light.

"Time to go, Mr. Beeman," she said. Her voice was deep, yet oddly unresonant. "Please release my Lisette, as she has other duties. We have a major of a Highlander regiment downstairs who wishes to see her." So, demurely, eyes downcast, Lisette walked past her mother and down the stairs, knotting her robe.

Mme. Berthier had several times described to me the event of Lisette's conception. It had happened when she was newly married, her husband at the front. She was walking home from church one day in autumn, the leaves turning, drifting down, and crunching beneath her feet, when she met her Fate in the form of a young Canadian officer who raped her. She remembered him vaguely, but with—as had gathered over the years—some measure of affection. He'd had golden hair like the sun, which Lisette had inherited. After hearing the enumeration of his physical virtues, I saw him as the sort of handsome lad that schoolboys get their first crush on. I was sure that the men in his unit had loved him to distraction. Her husband, whose name I never learned, was killed at the front shortly thereafter, and with a child to support, she took up a new profession. So Lisette had grown up on the edge of the War, eventually to work in her mother's establishment, which by the time I came there consisted of five girls in a large well-appointed house on a quiet avenue lined with plane trees. Aristocracy, in those times. They served good English breakfasts there. I went downstairs to eat one before I left.

"Welcome home, Dick. I knew you wouldn't be able to stay away. I'd kill a fatted calf, but I have a better burnt offering." The speaker was Frank Harris, who stood with our fellow NCO, Larry Pogue, leaning against the wall of the brothel. He was a tall, broad man, with the look of a hero, although of course being alive, he wasn't one. He reached into a pocket and pulled out a cigarette, which he waved at me. "American," he said. "From Virginia. At least that's what the sailor told me. Don't ask what I had to do to get it." I didn't have to.

"Take a puff, Dick." Pogue was shorter than either Harris or me, with sharp features and dark mystic eyes.

Although my body cried out for it, I tried to give the appearance of considering the offer judiciously, as if I didn't care. My act fooled no one, and I finally grabbed it. I felt better immediately.

Captain Totenham's ADC, Perkins, at last after much swearing got us all formed up for the march back to the main trench, where we would spend five days before moving back to the reserve trenches. The spot where we stood was already in front of some of our fortifications. The depth of our lines was nearly five miles. The military brothel itself, in obedience to regulations, had a Vickers .303 emplacement on its roof. The captain leaned sourly against the concrete wall, watching Perkins take roll. He had spent liberty in Paris, but it didn't seem to have made him any happier. The tap of his cane against his prosthetic left foot indicated impatience, and everyone was glad when Perkins got us lined up and the tapping stopped.

We marched down the Roman Road, which stretched from Bert to Bapaume, on the other side of the front. Nearly two thousand years old, it arrowed across the countryside but had been shelled so heavily that it was only suitable for foot traffic. We reached the end of the communication trench, which burrowed gradually into the earth, and turned into it.

As we marched, the level of the ground rising above our heads, I thought of Lisette. This liberty, in response to some idle questions of hers, I had spent a great deal of time telling her about my boyhood, of the times before, as the recruiting posters had it, the King had called me to war, while she lay back on the bed, whistling at the budgie to make it sing.

I told her about my mother, and the toy soldiers. I still remember the wooden box that held them and the splendid weight it had when they had all been carefully stacked inside. They were fragments of many of the family's boyhoods, and were all mismatched, all different colors, like meadow flowers. French cuirassiers, Russian uhlans, American bluecoats from their Civil War, red pantalooned Zouaves, long-coated foot soldiers from the army of Frederick the Great, roundhead cavalry, even one lonely Babylonian in skirt and headdress, carrying spear and shield. What pleasure those soldiers brought me! I would lose myself in arranging them, marching them in columns, charging them up the valley at Balaclava, holding Hougoumont against the French at Waterloo, pounding the insolent Swedes at Poltava, and saving Vienna from the Turk. My men were dashing and disciplined, even if some of them, particularly the soft lead ones, were missing arms, legs, and even heads. And my mother would call me in for supper, and I would not hear.

My mother made a mistake here, for she interpreted this boyish disinclination to quit a game as insolence, which was the one thing she could not bear. My scoldings were severe. One day she finally shouted in exasperation, "Stay then, with your soldiers!" and latched the door. I suppose if I had begged her forgiveness, she would soon have relented and let me inside to eat, but little boys can be more stubborn than mothers, and are seldom inclined to be wise. With forced gaiety, I picked up my men and went back to war. We fought battles beneath the kitchen window, made long retreats through rough country, then attacked again on the plain. War began to drag, the Seven Years' War stretching to eighteen, the Thirty Years' War to eighty. When one was over, another began. This went on, as the moon rose in the sky, illuminating the now ghostly soldiers, until the little boy's eyes grew weary and he fell asleep on the grass. Some unknown friend knocked on the door, and my mother came out and carried me inside.

We finally arrived at the main firing trench, the eight-foot-deep hole in the ground that was home. In front was a three-foot parapet of heaped earth, in back was a one-foot parados. The walls were supported by sandbags, corrugated iron, bundles of sticks, bricks, and stones. Repairs had to be continuous, else the sides of the trench would collapse.

Wire repair crews were sent out, and one group of men was set to extending a sap. We were going to build a new machine-gun post at the end. Those who were not thus employed retired, despite their weariness, to their gardens, which filled the area between the parados and the mortar emplacements with a tangle of bean poles and trellises. The various regiments that occupied the trenches in turn shared these gardens through a complex set of arrangements that had grown up over the years, and by now seemed eternal. I leaned back against the parapet, crossed my arms, and watched them. I could hear two soldiers chaffing each other, obscenely comparing the sizes of their cucumbers.

"Give it up, Dick. Plant a row of peas." Pogue stood next to me, mattock in hand. "A small thing, surely."

"I'm a soldier, not a farmer, damn you," I said sharply, startled by my own vehemence.

Pogue turned away, a slight smile on his lips. "Just a suggestion, Dick, just a suggestion." He clambered over the parados and headed toward his cabbages.

"Corporal Beeman?" said a timid voice. It was Private Willoughby. He was young, not more than fifteen, and had somehow blurred features, as if built hurriedly before the holidays. His watery blue eyes darted about in the light that escaped the entrance to the officers' dugout, and he seemed ready to bolt.

"Yes, Willoughby?"

"It's . . . it's . . . " He struggled to get the words out. "It's . . . I just saw the Yellow Man!"

Inwardly, I groaned. "Indeed? And where did you see this, ah, apparition?"

"Catfish Row. He was walking toward me with that face, all bloated, and the gas was pouring out of his mouth, just pouring out, Corporal, like smoke from a chimney. I could smell it! New mown hay. That means a German gas attack, doesn't it? Shouldn't we warn everybody?"

I sighed. "That won't be necessary. I'll go take a look. Catfish Row, you said?"

"Yes, sir."

"Don't talk about this to anyone else. Just stay here."

Trenches traverse to contain explosions and to prevent enfilade firing should the enemy gain control of any part of them. I headed down past Times Square and the Embarcadero. The trenches had previously been occupied by American troops, and none of us had found the energy to take down the neatly lettered signs that named the various traverses of the main trench. My universe was limited to the distance to the next bend.

The Yellow Man had made his appearance in the soldiers' mythology back in the twenties. He was someone who had been caught in a combined gas attack with no protection, but had somehow, by the dark of the moon, been transformed rather than killed. His skin was covered with blisters and open sores, his eyes were red and hemorrhaged, his flesh was rotting, his lips were a bright blue. He no longer breathed oxygen, but needed to inhale the poison gases for his survival. Thus, he was supposed to appear whenever a gas attack was imminent, so that he could breathe.

I turned the corner to Catfish Row. My eyes burned, and I smelled the faint odor of new mown hay. Phosgene, or diphosgene. I drew back, fingering the gas mask that hung on my hip. The moon had risen, and its light shined full into the trench. A few rats scurried about, but no Yellow Man was visible. The concentration did not seem serious, so I clipped on a simple nasopharyngeal filter rather than putting on the uncomfortable mask, and went forward. After searching around a bit, I climbed over the parapet into no-man's-land. Up and down the line I could hear desultory gunfire and see, here and there, the eye hurting, hanging glare of Very flares. The artillery I had heard earlier had fallen silent, their crews for the moment weary of war. I found it just beneath a clump of barbed wire. A gas cylinder. It wasn't rusted, although it must have been there awhile, and upon closer examination I found that it was made out of aluminium. Damn clever, these Americans, I thought, and twisted the stopcock shut.

I jumped back into the trench. In much of the same way as men see faces in rocks and tree stumps, and hear the approach of a beloved in every rustle of autumn leaves, so Willoughby had smelled the Yellow Man in the phosgene. I found someone to carry the thing off to a Field Ordnance Park, and headed back toward my home traverse.

Like a summer thunderstorm, a gunfight suddenly tore across no-man's-land. Everyone along the line joined in, shooting at nothing in particular, but making a great racket. Above me, human figures were silhouetted above the parapet, and I heard the thump of something being dumped into the trench, something about the size and shape of a human body. Another thump, softer this time, and a groan.

"Who's there?" hissed a voice. I made it out as Lieutenant Wallace's.

"Beeman."

"Good. Come give us some help while Jeremy goes to get a medic."

Jeremy King ran off into the darkness. Wallace had taken out a patrol, to investigate what the Germans were building a few hundred yards down the line. It looked to be a forward gun emplacement.

Hopkins was dead, a clean hole through his forehead. Smith and Calloway stood nearby, gasping, grateful to be back in the security of the trench. I heard moaning. Bending over, I saw Private Ackerman. His right leg was missing at the knee. The blood looked like black syrup as it spilled out in the moonlight.

I pulled off my belt, which was still real leather, and looped it around the stump of his leg as a tourniquet. I pulled it tight, and the bleeding stopped. After a moment, a Medical Officer and two stretcher bearers came and picked Ackerman up, to take him to the Casualty Clearing Station and thence to a Base Hospital, perhaps one in England. He'd be back in six months, with an artificial leg like Captain Totenham's. I looked in the direction they'd taken him and hoped he'd have enough sense to bring back my belt.

Pogue was waiting for me when I returned, whistling idly to himself as he cleaned the head of his mattock. The task absorbed him, and it did not seem that he noticed me.

There was something about Pogue that always bothered me. We were all superstitious, of course, and each had his own protective charm or set of ritual habits that he believed kept him from harm. Most of us kept believing in ours until we were blown to bits. I had mine. I have it still. A colored bit of rock shaped like the head of an ax, worn around the neck on a chain. Lisette gave it to me. She had found it, somewhere. Pogue's beliefs and talismans, however, carried the implication of having a significance beyond that of mere terror of dissolution, of being more religion than superstition. I didn't know why that disquieted me.

He looked up and smiled, teeth bright in his muddy face. "Yellow Man take a while to dispose of? I sent Willoughby to help with that sap; he seemed to be wanting something to do."

"Spot of bother. Hopkins got himself shot. And Ackerman left a leg in no-man's-land."

He sucked air between his teeth. "Too bad. They should have waited. Ah, well." He paused. "Have you heard how the end of the War will be signaled, Dick?"

I knew he didn't mean by wireless; or runner, or telephone, or anything like that. "I've heard the stories." The image had pursued me in dreams after I first heard about it.

"The firing of four black or dark blue Very lights."

Flares did not come in those colors, of course, and I remembered them, in my dreams, hanging dark and brooding over a nighttime landscape of tattered corpses where none remained alive to note that the War was over. My mouth was full of dirt and I could not laugh. "Why are you bringing this up?"

He smiled, a secret smile. "I have that Very pistol. I bought it from an old magic woman in Amiens."

I groaned. "First Willoughby and his damned Yellow Man, and now you have to go round the bend and start blathering on about old magic women and Very pistols. You've been taken, but the crone's got a line into a supply depot somewhere. You should report her."

"Might as well report the moon for being out after curfew. Settle down, Dick. Settle down. Let me tell you a story. A war story." He sat down in the earth with the air of a man sinking into his favorite armchair at home, in front of a fire.

"A war story," I grumbled. "Just the thing to calm my nerves." But I sat. It was cold and damp.

"There once was a man, quite a long time ago, a man of the land, who was called to war by his King. He was afraid, afraid of leaving his familiar place, and afraid of death on the field of battle, but he obeyed, and went, leaving his crops, and his land, and his home. He served well in the war. He had a quick wit, and a sense of order, so he became their equivalent of an NCO. When the war finally ended, he found that he did not want to return home. The slap of foreign hills beneath his sandals was a more pleasing feeling than the squish of his own soil between his toes. The work, he found, was easier, and more interesting, his men respected him, and his captains recognized him. He'd found a career for which he was suited.

"So he went to the capital, and lay a night and a day on the stone floor of the temple of the Goddess, she who made the plants to grow and the rain to fall and to whom all farmers made their prayers, and all soldiers likewise, for men wounded in battle will always call upon their mother. He beat his head against the stones and begged her to free him from his life of toil and allow him to continue at war.

"Women can be unreasonable, at least as men understand these things, and goddesses are no exception. Angered, for she misinterpreted his manly disinclination to quit what to him was an exciting game as insolence, she bade him to stay with his soldiers, if he wished, for his war was not yet over. So he picked up his spear and his shield and went back to the war, which had started anew. They sacked cities and forded streams; they made long retreats through the mountain passes and attacked again along the river. And he began to grow weary, for it seemed that just as the war was over, another began. . . ."

The earth *was* cold. I shifted uncomfortably, confused and irritated by Pogue's rambling. "What does this fable have to do with Very pistols?"

He yawned. "Not much, I suppose. Just a way of getting attention, a knock on the door. Let's just say that some of the soldier's comrades-in-arms were on somewhat better terms with the Goddess than he, and realized that it sometimes takes a third party to effect a reconciliation."

I didn't understand him at all. "And our friend the soldier?"

"Marches those hills yet."

I looked up at the bean poles standing silver in the moonlight. "Still beats farming."

He laughed, a short, sharp sound, almost a sob. "Stubborn, stubborn. Lucky his friends are just as stubborn."

I sighed. "How much did the bloody thing cost, anyway?"

"Twenty head of cabbage, ten kilos potatoes, one kilo peas, two dozen tomatoes. Most of my summer's production."

I don't know why I played along with his stupid game. "Why do the soldier's friends keep trying?"

"Because they know that eventually they will succeed." And he stood up, slung his mattock over his shoulder, and walked off down the dark passage of the trench.

Harris and I stared off at the enemy lines, trying to see what had been built there during the night. It was just after dawn. A mist covered no-man's-land, and there was a feeling of rain clouds coming off the North Sea.

We were standing at the end of the sap dug the previous night. The barbed wire surrounding us gleamed silver, unlike the older thickets guarding the rest of the trench, which had long ago rusted to a soft autumnal orange-brown color, looking more like hedgerows than like something that would tear you to shreds if you fell against it.

No-man's-land was a green carpet, vivid in the mist, which quickly swallowed the craters of exploding shells. It rained much in Picardy, and plants did well there, particularly when fertilized. No-man's-land at the Somme was probably the best fertilized area on the face of the globe.

The bodies that fell there vanished, but the equipment remained. I could see helmets, rifles, canteens, gas masks, even an occasional medal, once worn with panache in a frontal assault. Examining this detritus, I could trace the history of the War, like an archaeologist winnowing potsherds. There were the remnants of an experimental respirator, used in '28, the grinning remains of a skull inside it. Here lay a rifle with the stock made out of a brittle synthetic, 1931. Everywhere lay helmets. I could see one, German, with a brass spike on it, that must have been from before 1920. Another was gleaming beryl steel, of American manufacture.

Everywhere were the flowers of Picardy. Red poppies, yellow cabbage flowers, white cornflowers; for them there was no War. One helmet, overturned, served as a flowerpot and was full of a bobbing mass of blue cornflowers.

Harris peered through his binoculars and scowled. "Can't see a bloody thing. Could be a machine-gun emplacement. Could be the anchor point for a mechanical sapping operation. Could be a new cookhouse for the frontline boys," he sniffed, "though I can't smell any sauerkraut or borscht. Could be a new twelve-hole privy, in which case I vote for an immediate assault so that we can use it before it starts to stink. Let's go." He turned, and a rat squealed beneath his feet. He aimed a kick at it, cursing, but it hid behind some duckboards.

Back in the trench, life had settled into its faded routine. A gang was repairing the trench wall. Others were cleaning their weapons or attempting to write letters. Most were trying to sleep, though, curled up in funk holes dug in the walls.

I descended into the officers' dugout. Pogue and

Captain Totenham were in the NCO's dugout, discussing some operation that I didn't want to hear about, for I suspected I'd be hearing about it soon enough and I wanted to write a letter. Most of my immediate family somehow came to be lost in the years of war, but I had been thinking about a cousin, or perhaps second cousin, who had moved off to Liverpool or Manchester when I had been a child. He'd been mentioned at my house once or twice, though I didn't remember by whom. I had no one else to write to, and I thought that if I sent it off to General Delivery at those two cities, he might get the letter. I preferred writing on tables to balancing things on my knees and was hoping that the table in the dugout would be free.

Lieutenant Wallace was sitting at it, filling out a letter of condolence to the parents of Hopkins. He had a little book, issued to officers, open to the page that contained the approved phrases and adjectives for letters of condolence to the relatives of soldiers killed in action.

He looked up. "Beeman, I'm stuck here. Which would you say Hopkins was, gallant, brave, or intrepid?"

I remembered the hole through his forehead. "How, precisely, did he die?"

"He tried to jump me, and I was forced to shoot him with my pistol. He panicked, wanted to go back. Bloody bother, and my shot brought fire down on us. Tough luck for Ackerman, that."

I gave it some thought. "Heroic. Try heroic."

He peered at his book. "Hmmm . . . doesn't seem to be on the list, Beeman. Funny thing, that. 'Heroic' isn't here. Neither is 'bloody fool,' for that matter. 'Intrepid.' Good word, intrepid. A public school, rugger sort of word." He wrote it down, pleased with himself.

It took me less than five minutes to give up on the letter. I couldn't think of a thing to write, and I realized that I wasn't even sure of his name. I decided to try again some other time, and left the dugout.

Outside, the sky had clouded up and a drizzle looked imminent. I yawned, and realized how long it had been since last I slept. I looked around. Pogue and the captain were still in our dugout, and near me was a two-man funk hole with only one man in it: Willoughby. I pulled out my waterproof sheet and curled up next to him.

Sleeping, I dreamed. The land was green and fruitful. The corn was high, and date palms hung their heavy loads of fruit over the fresh-running irrigation channels. I ran across the fields, tripping over the uneven soil, hearing the sounds of her hounds close behind me. They dug in the earth, the men of that land, slowly and patiently, their faces shaded from the glaring sun by broad-brimmed felt hats. They did not heed my cries for aid, but continued to dig their earth, grinding the clods up. Some swung sickles, collecting the sheaves of corn. The land was flat, horizon to horizon, but ahead of me rose a steep hill, and atop it stood a tower. I ran up its side. It was covered with brambles, and my shirt tore, and I bled, but I continued to run, for I still heard the hounds, and she was still in pursuit of me. I tore free of the brambles and ran up the steps of the basilica, stopping directly beneath the Virgin. The American guards were gone. She looked down on me with a half smile, even as her hounds closed on me. Pulling a knife from my pocket, I started to lever at one of the bricks. I could hear the sharp crump of the German 88s and the return fire of French mortars. A strange broad-winged monoplane with English markings flew overhead, and as it banked away to the left, the pilot, in his clever enclosed cockpit, waved to me in greeting. The brick finally came loose. Someone tapped my shoulder, and Pogue was close behind me, wearing a wide-brimmed felt hat. He stretched out his hand. Between thumb and forefinger he held a pea. I paused a moment, my heart full of wild rage, but I heard the bay of the hounds ever nearer and at last, with a feeling of surrender, took the pea and thrust it into the opening left by the brick. The entire basilica creaked and groaned. The guns stopped. A pea plant emerged from the hole and crawled its way up the side of the tower. I looked up at the Virgin. Her expression was joyful, radiant. She leaned forward to gather me up into her arms. Then there was a rumble, and at long last she broke free of the tower and began to fall toward me. As she got closer, I saw that she wore Lisette's face. For a moment I was happy, then felt the sharp fear of being crushed beneath her. I cried out "Mother!" as her face rushed toward me. . . .

I awoke. Willoughby had huddled against me in his sleep, pushing me into the side of the funk hole. He was murmuring, "Mother . . . Mother . . . " under his breath, shivering. With a surge of annoyance, I shoved him over to the other side, where he remained. A light rain was falling from the sky. I let it fall on my face, trying to pretend that the tracks of tears were nothing but raindrops.

I stood up and looked at the sky. From the light, evening stand-to would be shortly. I heard the whistle of an incoming shell. Instead of diving into a funk hole and cowering against the wall, I looked up. It hit a few traverses down from where I stood. The blast thundered and cast a soldier into the air. He had his arms flung out, as if to embrace the sky. His body landed on the parapet, where it was stitched by machine-gun fire by a German who had no better target. A hand reached out and grabbed the body by an ankle, pulling it back into the trench. The firing stopped.

Captain Totenham walked up and told me that Pogue and I were leading a patrol that night. I said nothing.

The air in no-man's-land is thick and cloying, quite unlike the sweat and cordite stink of the trenches. The ground is soft, like dead men's flesh, which does, in fact, make up part of its composition. Every bump and dip in that terrain was familiar to us, but only familiar as seen at night, through a haze of fear.

Pogue strode on, past the huge old mine crater full of water. Willoughby hung back with me and looked as unhappy as I felt. We were to chuck a few grenades at the new German forward gun emplacement. It worried Captain Totenham, gave him trouble sleeping. Poor fellow. The wreckage of a German tank bulked to our left, and we angled away from it. It was about forty yards past that point that we ran into the German patrol.

They were as surprised to see us as we were to see them, I think, but there were six of them to three of us. Willoughby reacted faster than anyone, promptly turning and fleeing. I heard him cry out as the gunfire brought him down.

I dropped to the ground, reaching for my grenades. Pogue dove forward and rolled past the Germans. I saw a glint of metal as he reached . . . and fired straight up into the air. The Very pistol. "It can't go on forever," he called. "Good luck, Dick!" I raised myself up and tried to throw a grenade, but dropped it when a hot poker plunged through my shoulder. I tried to use my other hand to find the grenade, whose pin I had already pulled, but it was on the wrong side of my body. I rolled on my back to get at it, knowing I was dead. Above me, glowing in the night sky like holes to another universe, were four dark blue, almost black, spots, arranged equidistant from each other. I fought against it, but felt the darkness wash over me like a warm tide.

Bright sunlight pried its way between my eyelids. I turned my head to escape the glare, and felt an explosion in my shoulder. The pain shocked me awake. I was lying on the wet earth where I had fallen. The grenade I dropped had not exploded. What luck. Now I could just lie here until a German gunner decided to pump a few slugs into me to make sure I was dead. I lay there, squinting at the blue sky. The silence was total, preternatural. There was no gunfire, no explosions. Finally, unable to stand it, I raised my head and looked around me.

Fifty yards away lay the German trenches. Or rather, obviously, where the German trenches had been some decades past. There was no barbed wire, no gun emplacements, no parapet. Only a shallow depression, overgrown and eroded. The British trench, on the other side, was the same. Straining, I managed to stand up. I did a slow turn around, examining the peaceful, leafy country landscape.

It was then that I saw the corpses. It looked to be the result of a firefight. Five bodies, three in green uniforms, two in gray. I put up a hand to rub my forehead, and froze. The uniform I had been wearing for as long as I could remember had never been this shade of green, and had been tighter around the wrist. This uniform was just as worn, just as threadbare. But it was not the one I had been wearing last night. It was, in fact, the mate of those worn by three of the five corpses.

They lay scattered around the wreckage of a lorry overturned and still smoking. A blackened circle in the grass showed a petrol tank explosion. I walked over and turned one of the bodies over. Its placid, anonymous face told me nothing.

I heard the grind of gears and a laboring engine. Coming from the direction of what had been German lines was another lorry. I braced myself, although I was feeling so weak that there was nothing I could have done in self-defense.

The lorry had a white star on the door and a black man at the wheel. He looked at me, as if unsure of whether to stop. I was standing in his way, so he finally did. We stared at each other.

"Could you give me a lift to the nearest dressing station?" I asked, holding my shoulder.

"There's a field hospital near Albert," he said, with an American accent. "Hop in." I dragged myself into the cab with my good arm, and we started off.

"Trouble?" he said.

"Bit of a dust up. Nothing serious."

He grunted. "We should all be so lucky. Big battle, hear, at Boutencourt, on the road to Rouen"—he pronounced it "ruin"—"and it don't sound good. Damn Goddam. It's been a year since I got here, and I want to see Paree, and it don't look like I'm going to get to soon. Sheeit. Some big deal Invasion this turned out to be. Those that planned it aren't getting their asses shot off, you can bet on that."

"They never do," I agreed. Invasion? Were we so badly off here that we weren't even in Paris? Or were we fighting the French?

Ahead of us was the town of Albert, no longer Bert. It was the way it must have been before the War, full of small ugly houses of red brick. And—I looked hard. The basilica stood, and on top of it, proudly erect, was the Golden Virgin. A flight of monoplanes, which my comrade identified as Spitfires, roared by overhead on their way south. We drove through town, and he dropped me at the dressing station.

That was two weeks ago. I was treated by a doctor and billeted. No one questioned my right to exist. The War had ended here a long time ago and was called World War I, because World War II was here, and I was part of it, as a member of the invasion force that had crossed the Pas-de-Calais the previous year and now held most of the Artois peninsula, though there was talk of a German counteroffensive before winter. It was early September here too. September, 1947.

Pogue had achieved something, for I was, vaguely, starting to remember the ages of soldiering, in wars that always went on too long. I received my orders today. I am to report to the front, which is south of Amiens, along the western reaches of the Somme. From my cot, I can see the Virgin in her tower. She is smiling at me, but that tells me nothing.

They say the war should be over by 1949, 1950 at the latest. I can hear some of the hospital orderlies relaxing by digging in their gardens, just behind my tent. They are strengthening their squash poles, each thumping at his own squash with evident pride. Others are spading the soil around their parsnips. I roll over and look at them, catching glints of metal through a gap in the tent as they dig in the sunlight. One of them, wearing a broad-brimmed floppy hat, closely resembles Pogue. . . . I look at them and think, about thousands of years of his earnest advice, and his knock on the door. I should take a spade and join them. I really should.

Maybe then, Mother will let me come inside.

A DEEPER SEA

Jupiter Orbit, January 2033

The whale screamed in fear, the complex harmonics of its terror rumbling in the warm water around Ilya Stasov. He hung tensely in the null-g hub of the research space station *Jupiter Forward*. Stasov had concealed himself in an aquarium with the ecology of a Caribbean coral reef. He hung there, pulling water through his artificial gills, and listened to the whale as it screamed from the cold wastes of interplanetary space. The multi-colored fish surrounding Stasov had adapted to the lack of gravitational orientation, and floated with their dorsal fins in all directions, oblivious to the whale's cry.

The sperm whale screamed again. Stasov tightened himself into a ball, as if to escape the sound, then straightened and twitched a finger, calling on the imaging capabilities of *Jupiter Forward's* computer system. The space station orbited in Ganymede's trailing trojan point, and the whale floated near it. Instead of leaving the tank and going into space to confront the whale, Stasov brought the Jovian system into the water.

Banded Jupiter appeared in the aquarium like a sunken fishing float. A moray eel in a crevice watched it carefully, judging its edibility. Stasov imagined the chill of interplanetary space penetrating the tropical water. The dark-spotted sphere of Ganymede rolled among the sea anemones like a jetting snail. Stasov sucked hyperoxygenated water through his carotid gill attachments and looked for the cyborg sperm whale.

"Calm," he murmured through his throat mike. "Calm." He was linked directly to the whale's auditory centers.

The whale's image was still invisible in his view. Another finger twitch, and Jupiter shrank while Ganymede swelled. The water darkened in the tank, and the stars peeked through above the coral. The fish ignored these astronomical manifestations and went calmly about their business. The image of Ganymede grew to the point that Stasov felt himself flying over its rough surface. He no longer saw the tank in which he floated.

The sperm whale suddenly breached the surface of darkness and rose up out of Ganymede's invisible shadow. Fusion rockets burned blue along his length. Sunlight gleamed over the whale's great ridged bulk and glittered on the tessellations of the phased microwave array on his back.

But where was the goddam dolphin? "Weissmuller," Stasov said. "Speak to Clarence." Silence. "The whale needs your words." A longer silence. "Damn it, Weissmuller, where are you?" His left hand throbbed and he clenched it into a fist, as well as he could.

His only answer was the roaring hiss of Jupiter's magnetic field and the low murmur of the engineers as they checked the function of the whale's engines. Stasov keyed in more astronomical data. Ganymede shrank to a marble. The entire Jovian system now floated in the tank, satellite orbits marked, the computer giving him direct perception of their gravity wells sinking like holes in deep perspective. The space station of *Jupiter Forward* appeared in Ganymede's trojan point, a bright dot. The computer located the transponder on the dolphin's space suit and displayed it as a spark. Stasov looked at Weissmuller's current location and swore.

The dolphin had dived into Io's gravity well and been slingshot out toward Europa. Jupiter's plunging gravity well gaped before Stasov's eyes, and he felt as if he were being sucked into a whirlpool. He fought down a moment of terror. The dolphin's spark climbed slowly up toward him. Weissmuller always played things close to the edge. It would be hours before the dolphin could get back to *Jupiter Forward*.

Stasov examined Clarence's image, wanting to stroke the whale's back to comfort him. A trigger fish examined the hologram, seemingly surprised to see a sperm whale its own size, then darted away with a contemptuous flick of its fins. The real Clarence, desperately alone in space, of course perceived nothing of this.

Despite the immense modifications to his body, Clarence was still vaguely cetacean, though he now had vast, complex control planes to guide him through the Jovian atmosphere, making him look like a whale decorated with streamers as a float in a parade. Stasov spoke calming words, but he wasn't an expert in sperm whale dialect. That wasn't why he was there. The whale continued to send out echo-location clicks in the microwave band, unable to understand how he had lost consciousness on an island in the Maldives, in the Indian Ocean, and awoken here, in a mysterious place he had never heard of, a place of no water, no fish, and a dozen featureless spheres.

Irregular bursts of rocket appeared along Clarence's sides, spinning him. Data streamed into the tank, crowding the fish: fuel use, accelerations, circuit status. Voices muttered technical jargon. Stasov felt as he had when as a child, put to bed early, listening to the intent, incomprehensible adult conversation of his parents' friends through the closed bedroom door.

"Erika," Stasov said, keying another comm line.

"Director Morgenstern's line," a heavy male voice answered.

"Miller." Stasov hadn't expected the Security Chief's voice. But if he had him. . . . "Why is the dolphin running loose around Io?"

"There's something wrong with your comm, Colonel. You sound like you're underwater. You'd better check it."

Stasov kept one eye on the increasingly agitated whale. "I'm not a colonel," he snapped. "I hold no such rank. Please give me Director Morgenstern. We can deal with your dereliction of duty later."

"Dereliction, Colonel?" Paul Miller's voice had the lazy drawl that Stasov associated with thuggish political policemen and prison camp guards, whether they were American, Russian, or Japanese. "The dolphin wanted to go. My men aren't KGB officers." He chuckled. Stasov knew that sound well: the laugh of an interrogator putting a subject at ease before hitting him again. He'd heard it over and over during his months at Camp Homma. It had begun to seem an essential part of torture. "Should we have held him under physical restraint? That would be a treaty violation. Do you want me to order my men to commit a—"

"Damn it, Miller, quit babbling and get me the Director!" Stasov tried to conceal his sudden fear under anger.

"You just watch yourself, Colonel." Miller's voice was suddenly cold. "None of us are under your orders. It's a long way from Uglegorsk. The Director's busy. I don't have to—"

"Ilya," Erika Morgenstern's voice broke in. "What's the problem?"

"Cut all of the whale's systems immediately," Stasov said tensely. "None of the problems are on the engineering side. He's not responsible. Weissmuller's off somewhere around Io, and I can't handle the whale alone. I know it throws the schedule off. And the budget. But do it."

Morgenstern didn't hesitate. The hectic flaring lights along the whale's sides died and it floated, quiescent. "Done," she said. Subliminally Stasov heard cries of surprise and frustration from the engineers testing the vehicle. The vehicle. Clarence the cyborg sperm whale, hanging in orbit around Jupiter. He was there. Stasov could see him, but still wasn't sure he believed it. Test levels dropped to zero.

Stasov swam slowly to the tank's surface and edged out through the enhanced-surface-tension barrier that held the liquid sphere together, feeling the boundary as a line of almost painful pressure on his skin. He floated into the air, globules of water drifting off his body and reuniting with the large quivering sphere of the fish tank.

Once he had detached the carotid oxygenation connections, he drew a deep painful breath of the unfriendly air, reestablishing his ventilation reflexes. His diaphragm contracted painfully, having relaxed during his conditioned apnea.

A tiny fish flopped in the air, pulled out of the water along with him. Stasov shepherded it back to the tank. The cold air gave him goose bumps, and he shivered. He pulled himself over to an actual porthole and peered out at space. Clarence floated, surrounded by vehicles and swarming human beings, afflicting him as had the parasites that had clung to him in the seas of Earth. It would be hours before Weissmuller returned. Something had to be done. Stasov felt a twisting in his belly. It had been a long time since he'd tortured a dolphin. He knew that if he did it again, it would be his last act. But he could see no other way.

"Ilya," Erika Morgenstern said in exasperation. "You have to realize what these people think you are. What they call you—"

"The Shark of Uglegorsk," he finished. "You and I have been through all that. They don't understand anything."

Morgenstern stared at him with those efficient brown-green eyes that seemed able to see through both glare and darkness with equal ease. The first time he had seen those eyes they had spelled his salvation. He tried never to forget that. "You're the one who's not aware of anything. I have to balance two hundred fifty people from twenty countries aboard this space station, and turn in a job of research to boot. Hatred and fear aren't imaginary."

Stasov rubbed his maimed left hand and looked back at her. The room was in half darkness, as she preferred, giving her head, with its flat face and short graying coppery hair, the look of an astronomical object. She held court in an imperial style that would have dismayed her superiors at the UN Planetary Exploration Directorate—had they been permitted to know about it—guarded by acolytes like Miller, aloof, inaccessible, but aware of everything that went on aboard *Jupiter*

Forward. Stasov was sometimes startled by what had become of her.

"They should still be able to do their jobs," he said. "Or is your authority over them insufficient?"

She didn't flush—she had more control than that—but she narrowed her eyes in an expression of authority, to let him know that he'd gone too far. He stared back at her with the pale blue-eyed absence of expression that let her know that he'd been through worse than she could ever throw at him.

A hologram of Jupiter gave the room what light it had. The planet was sliced apart to show magnetic fields and convection cells, as if Morgenstern could as easily order a modification in the circulation of the Great Red Spot as she could in the air pressure of the storage lockers or the menu in the dining hall.

"We've come this far together," she said. "Since Homma. Now we're about to drop a cyborg sperm whale into the Jovian atmosphere." She shook her head. "I'm still not sure I believe it. But I can't risk the anger of the Delphine Delegation. They provide most of our financing. You know that. Miller's an idiot, but he's right. We cannot physically restrain an intelligent cetacean. It violates the Treaty of Santa Barbara." Her voice still had a trace of an accent from her native New Zealand.

"Articles twelve and thirteen," Stasov muttered. "Open Seas and Freedom of Entitles. Damn right I know it. Better than anyone else. And dolphins love the letter of the law. They think it's the stupidest thing they ever heard, but they use it whenever it's convenient. They can afford good lawyers."

"Exactly. I can't jeopardize the project. Not now. Not ever. The Delphine Delegation keeps us on a short enough financial tether as it is."

"Miller didn't oppose me because of the treaty," Stasov spat. "He did it because he thinks dolphins are wonderful innocent creatures, and because he hates me for what he imagines I did to them. There's nothing more terrifying than a sentimental thug. By letting him oppose me, *you* are jeopardizing the project. That's not just a machine out there. It's a perceptive being, trapped in a metal shell and hauled to a world he doesn't understand. He's going mad. Weissmuller's *already* crazy. Even for a dolphin. Look clearly, Erika. The project could end here."

She looked at him. He didn't have to say any more. Looking clearly was what she did best. It had taken her from an after-college job as a junior observer on a UN War Crimes commission to one of the most powerful jobs in the UN Planetary Exploration Directorate. And it had been the look behind Stasov's eyes, in the gardens of Camp Homma, that had given her the first glimpse of the direction to move in.

"All right," she said, finally. "Do what you have to."

"Do you mean that?"

"Of course I do!" she blazed. "I said it, didn't I? I'm giving you full authority, answerable only to me. Do what you want to your dolphin Messiah and his acolyte. Just get the project moving."

"Don't mock me, Erika," Stasov said heavily. "Don't ever mock me." He stood, raising himself up slowly in the low gravity. Director Morgenstern's comm terminal had been flickering constantly, and there were undoubtedly a dozen crises already piled up while she had chatted with her unpopular and essential Cetacean Liaison. "The project will move."

She eyed him, suddenly the more uncertain younger woman he remembered. "Ilya. What do you mean to do?"

"Don't ask me," he said, his voice dead. "I'll only do what's necessary."

Uglegorsk, October 2019

"You don't seem like a man who would be interested in stories, Colonel," Georgios Theodoros said as he stumbled up the wet stone steps, his long coat inadequate protection against the wind blowing off the Tatar Strait.

Colonel Stasov smiled, the third large star on his officer's shoulder boards new enough that he still enjoyed the novelty of the salutation, even from a foreign civilian. "It's not just a story, is it? It's evidence that what we are doing has been done before."

"I'm not sure that's true. It's all allegorical, allusive." Theodoros, a dreamy-eyed Greek with an ecclesiastical beard, stopped on one of the landings, affecting to examine the view, but actually to rest. There was little enough to look at. The sea before him was gray, with sharp-toothed waves. The thick clouds lowering over its obscured the boundary between sea and sky. This was nothing like the warm, dark Aegean where he did his delphine research. The island Sakhalin was a rough, hard place. That was why this Russian colonel with his pale blue eyes was so intense in his work. Though those eyes sometimes shone with the joy of a true discoverer, a look that had automatically led Theodoros to accept the other as a friend.

"No," Stasov stated decisively. "What humans and dolphins did during the reign of the Cretan Thalassocracy is significant to us here. That's why we brought you. Not just to hear stories. Thirty-five hundred years ago they developed the mental technology to deal with the problem. I believe you have brought the vestiges of that technology with you to Uglegorsk." He tugged at the binoculars he wore around his neck.

"They claimed to speak to dolphins," Theodoros murmured. "Perhaps they did." For years, no one had listened to his theories, and now that someone was willing to, he found himself somehow reluctant, uncertain of the consequences. The Soviets weren't interested in mere theories. They meant to act.

The research station at Uglegorsk sprawled out beneath them. Beauty being pointless against the cold rocks of Sakhalin, the station had seemingly striven for extreme ugliness, and succeeded in the Soviet manner. The metal huts, some of WWII Lend Lease vintage, were rusted and patched. Holding pens crowded the shoreline, their captive dolphins splashing and leaping. The base was dominated by the concrete vault of the dolphin laboratory, built with more recent American aid.

Theodoros's specialty was human-dolphin interactions during the second millennium BCE, a research topic too vague for delphine researchers and too practical for classicists and mythologists. So he had been surprised when he received an official invitation from the Vladivostok Oceanographic Institute to fly out to Uglegorsk to talk with Ilya Stasov. It hadn't been simply a polite facility tour followed by an hour talk, either. He'd been questioned intently for three days. A map of the Aegean Sea now hung in the main seminar room, the sites of Cretan cities marked on it, with a big star on Thera, the island that was the remnants of the great volcano whose eruption had brought an end to Cretan civilization. The Soviet researchers gathered in front of it to argue, arms waving, in their loud Russian. He and Stasov spoke English with each other.

The burly colonel sat down on a rock wall and stared off to sea. "Could you tell me the story, Georgios? Never mind how insignificant it seems."

Had the man really climbed up all this way for a view of various shades of gray? Through binoculars yet? Theodoros shivered and sat down next to Stasov.

"It took place on Delos, long enough ago that the Egyptians had no Pharaoh, and built with reeds. A singer lived on this island, a lyre player who had dedicated his life to Apollo and played to the sky and the sea. After a storm, the singer went down to the sandy shore to see what the sea had tossed up. On the beach lay a whale, sighing at the knowledge of his certain death. He cried thick, bitter tears.

"'Why are you here, brother?' the lyre player called. 'Why are you not off tossing the sea over your back, as the natural duty of whales?'

"'I have come to hear your songs,' the whale replied. 'Sing to me, while I die.'

"The singer sang to the whale for three days, while the birds wheeled and cried overhead and the sun rose and set and the whale's flesh began to stink. At the end of the third day the whale died. The man wept and sprinkled water on the whale's head, since dust seemed improper, and wished him good hunting in the world to which whales go, for he did not think that Hades had a place for him.

"He looked out into the sea and saw a dolphin dancing. The dolphin leaped and gamboled, but said nothing. When he saw the man on the shore he first ignored him, then slid up onto the shore.

" 'Do you wish to sing to your dead brother?' the lyre player asked. The dolphin said nothing. 'His soul needs your songs to speed him to the dark sea where he now swims.' Still the dolphin said nothing. 'He cries for the sound of your voice.' The dolphin remained silent. In a rage, the singer raised up his lyre and broke it over the dolphin's head. 'Speak not then, dumb beast, and go to your death unknown.'

"Blood came from the dolphin's blowhole and he cried out. 'Why do you torment me so?'

" 'To teach you the responsibilities of death and the songs that it calls for,' the singer said.

" 'I will hear you then,' the dolphin said. 'Teach me the songs, if you will not let me be silent.'

"And so the man taught the dolphin to sing the rhythmic songs of the ancients, those sung by shepherds at first light, by fishermen pulling in full nets, by priests to the brow of the impending storm. The dolphin took the songs and made them his own, adding the sounds of the sea.

"Apollo, hearing the songs, came down laughing, though his hands smelled of blood and corruption. He was an Asian god then, from Lycia, but was on his way to lead the Greeks.

" 'I have slain the monster, Typhaon, at Crisa beneath snowy Parnassus,' he told them. 'My Temple and wooded grove are to be there. Now that you are able to sing, friend dolphin, you will aid me. Find me my priests.'

" 'The sea moves,' the dolphin said. 'The land is solid. I will search.'

"The dolphin swam the seas until he saw a ship of Cretan priests bound for Pylos. He sang to them from the sea and they followed him, to that place beneath Parnassus that was, forever afterward, to be called Delphi, after the dolphin who had led them. Men and dolphins spoke from that time afterward."

Theodoros felt the warm light of the Aegean island die, and found himself again sitting on a cold stone wall above the Tatar Strait.

"It's there," Stasov said, pacing back and forth in front of Theodoros. "I know it is. But why did they stop talking?" His pale eyes stared at Theodoros as if suspecting the Greek of concealing something.

"The story doesn't say. My guess would be that it had something to do with the eruption of Strogyle, the great volcano on Thera. Whether it was the cause or not, that seems to mark the end of Cretan civilization. Once the men stopped talking, perhaps the dolphins did also."

"And have refused ever since out of sheer spite? Perhaps, perhaps. But I think there's more. The volcano . . . interesting . . . " Stasov continued to pace, then froze, staring out over the water. He put his binoculars to his eyes.

"What do you see?" asked Theodoros.

"I see a need for our work," Stasov said. He pointed. In the haze at the horizon Theodoros could barely discern a dark ship. "That's a Japanese vessel. The Americans have been allowing them to build armed cruisers. A mistake. The Japanese claim the southern half of Sakhalin, you know."

Theodoros had no idea why anyone would be interested in the place, but decided not to say so. "I don't think the Americans can do too much to stop them, Colonel Stasov."

"True enough. Though the Americans may soon find themselves in a war they don't want." Stasov paused. "Do the dolphins have a religion, do you suppose?"

"Colonel Stasov, I suggest that we should first learn how to talk with them, and only then worry about their religion."

"True, perhaps," Stasov replied, staring thoughtfully out to sea. "Though that may be the wrong way round." He roused himself. "Come down then. You can drink with us one last time before you leave. You have given me much to think about."

Theodoros, his stomach churning at the thought of another of the massive drinking bouts that, besides arguing, seemed to be the only form of entertainment at Uglegorsk, followed Stasov back down the stairs.

The vaulted dolphin research center was as huge inside as an aircraft hangar. The floor was always wet, and the air smelled of seaweed and iodine. Cables snaked across the floor with no attention to safety. Theodoros tripped over them constantly, even sober, while the Russians had no trouble even when roaring drunk.

The farewell party had spread among the tanks, as such events always did, as if the researchers wanted to include the dolphins in their festivities. Stasov and Theodoros found a quiet corner to finish their discussion. Stasov balanced a bottle of vodka on a signal processing box and handed the other a pickle out of an unlabeled jar. It seemed to the Greek that everything was pickled here: the cucumbers, the cabbage, the peppers, the fish, and the researchers. He tossed back a shot of vodka, took a bite of pickle, and grimaced.

Stasov chuckled. "You've learned to do it like a real Russian. The trick is to never look as though you enjoy it."

"I *don't* enjoy it."

"Ha. You are a real Russian."

The huge form of General Anatoly Ogurtsov loomed over them. "More of these damn foreign computers for you, Ilya?" He waved a stack of requisition sheets at him. "How can our budget support this?"

Stasov shrugged. "Sit down, Antosha." He poured the general a glass of vodka. "I need sophisticated array processors. Who else makes them but the Japanese?"

"Damn their yellow souls," Ogurtsov said, in ceremonial anathema. "They do make good gadgets. I hope we can buy enough to defeat them when we go to war." He sighed hugely. "That's all image processing gear. Why do you need it?"

"I think I know how to reach the dolphins," Stasov said. "Aural images."

"An interesting thought," Theodoros said. "What sort of images?"

"That's where I'll need your help. I'll need good sonic maps of the Aegean, and best guesses from oceanographic archaeologists on the conformation of the sea bottom at about 1500 BCE. Can you do it?"

"I think so." Theodoros was startled once again. When he had come here, to find the crude pens of inferior concrete already cracking, the drunken technicians, the obsolete foreign electronic equipment cadged or stolen from other research projects, he had been sure that he was wasting his time. Compared to the clean redwood boards and earnest college students of Santa Barbara or the elegant institutes at Monaco, this place was a hellhole. But somehow . . .

"We'll do it, you know," Ogurtsov rumbled. "Ilya will make sure that we do."

"General," Theodoros said. "I have no doubt that you're right."

The Aleutians, September 2022

The Americans had found it surprisingly difficult to defend their Alaskan frontier, but they fought viciously every step of the way. The assault of Kagalaska Island, supposedly a surprise attack, faced brutal resistance from its first moment. Such *desant* operations were new to the Soviet Navy, and they were only gradually learning how to handle landing assaults. The price of the lessons was high.

Long before his own ship came into range, Colonel Ilya Stasov was listening to the first casualty reports.

"Death, death, death," the dolphin keened. "The fuckers left me behind. Their lives have found completion. They're dead." Her voice came over a background roar, leaving it almost incomprehensible.

"Calm down, Harmonia," Stasov said, realizing that it was an easy instruction to give if you were out of the battle area. "What happened?"

" . . . exploding eggs. They don't listen to us anymore. You shark spawn, Stasov, you said they would listen!"

"It must be a new type of mine, Harmonia," Stasov yelled in reply, as the noise in his headphones increased. "Some new magnetic detector. We'll get the data—"

"Fish, fish. I won't go back until you give me a fish."

"You don't have to go back. Pull out now. We'll do a magnetic field analysis—"

"I want a belly full of fish for this, turd swallower!" With that, the line went dead. As it did, the landing ship itself thrummed, and the thunder of an explosion roared down the hatch from outside. He waited for the sound to die away, but instead it grew insanely louder, reverberating. It was the roar of the attack, and was not about to end. He raced up the companionway.

"Priblyudov!" he yelled at the comm officer over the noise. "The Americans have sowed the shore with a new type of mine. I've lost most of my first wave of dolphins. Send this info back to the *Novgorod.*" He waved a sheet of notes. The comm officer stared at him dully. "Hurry up!"

While Priblyudov stumbled to obey, Stasov plugged his earphones into the console and linked back up with his microphones. He stepped out onto the deck in the cold northern sunlight. Stasov stared in horror at the bare rock of Kagalaska, which loomed ahead of the long deck of the landing ship, wreathed in smoke. Rockets flared over his head and the 76-mm bow guns thundered at the shore. Below decks, he knew, a battalion of troops was gathered, with battle tanks and assault vehicles. Two landing ships had already hit the island. Stasov listened to his earphones.

The gray waters were covered with flaming oil. The dolphins, *his* dolphins, were strangling in it, their death cries cutting high above the rumbling of the engines and the crunching of propellers. The hazy arctic air was full of the sharp stink of oil and burning flesh. The other two landing ships had spilled their loads and the rocky shore ahead was covered with assault troops, swarming like isopods. Stasov closed his eyes, listening to the screams of death in his earphones. The thud of the American torpedo as it found the landing ship's unarmored side was impossibly loud, agony in his ears.

The ship slowed as if colliding with a sandbar, and listed. Stasov slid down to the railing, vaulted over it, and hit the water. He felt freezing water on his face, but his assault uniform instantly compensated, keeping his body warm. Another explosion, which he felt with his body, and the landing ship sank as if pulled under by a giant hand. Stasov stroked away to keep from being sucked down with it.

He pulled off his now-useless headphones and activated his throat mike. He called to those of his dolphins that had survived that far. Pitifully few.

Suddenly Stasov heard the call of a hunting orca, a killer whale that sped through the struggling forms of the drowning assault troops who had escaped the landing ship, calling, "Speak, food!" and devouring them when they did not reply. He came to Stasov. "Speak, food!" "I am Ilya Sergeiivich Stasov," he replied, insulting the orca by speaking in dolphin dialect. "Go fuck a walrus." It was amazing how quickly the ancient prohibition on conversation with humans vanished once it had been violated at Uglegorsk. The orca nudged him once, breaking several ribs, snorted "Spoiled food," and vanished into the polluted darkness.

The thunder of the assault lessened as the American troops were pushed back from the beachhead. The bodies of men and dolphins littered the shore, flopped on the rocks by the receding tide. A black line of oil and blood marked the highest rise of the water. Stasov climbed through the bodies. A rough road had been laid out and tanks ground up it. Bulldozers were already cutting out a landing strip. A few pockets of resistance were still being mopped up inland, but otherwise the island was in Soviet hands. Stasov made his way to the *desant* commander's temporary HQ.

"The American *Aegis* cruiser *Wainwright* is approaching in convoy from Kodiak," General Lefortov said. The whites of his eyes had turned yellow, and he looked like a dead man. The assault force had suffered numbingly high casualties. They were far from landbased aircraft, and the air cover provided by the carrier *Nizhni Novgorod* was insufficient to defend against an *Aegis* task force. "What can your dolphins do?"

"What's left of them?"

General Lefortov pointed his dead eyes at Stasov. He'd sacrificed enough of his own men to be indifferent to the fate of Stasov's precious dolphins. "We lost two attack submarines in the Bering Sea. The enemy advance is unopposed. What can you do?"

"Do?" Stasov said wearily. He thought about the

dolphins and equipment he had left. "We can sink it. It'll cost—"

"It might cost the war if we don't. Prepare your troops. I'll print up your orders."

"Yes sir."

Bataan, the Philippines, May 2024

Stasov slipped gently across the smooth wood of the porch into the hot butter of the Philippine sunlight. He moved slowly, his joints rough and unlubricated, as if he were a child's bicycle left out in the rain. The Japanese guards at the door of the barracks smiled at him as he passed, an expression he had long since ceased to try to interpret. Cracking dolphin communications had been easier. He had adopted a purely behavioral operant-conditioning model, letting blows, punishment cells, and food full of vermin modify his actions without the intervention of his conscious mind. He no longer tried to reason with the outside world, he simply responded to it. That let him keep his soul to himself.

They'd started feeding him well several weeks before, a signal of his imminent release. He had refused to feel hope. It was not beyond them to use the illusion of freedom to get him to betray himself. Yesterday they had allowed him an hour in a hot Japanese bath, and this morning they had dressed him in a rather elegant suit of blue silk. It was much too large, made, perhaps, to the measurements in his records from the start of his incarceration. His fingers had had trouble tying the knot on the tie, so one of the guards had delicately done it for him. It was not the regulation military knot he had been trying for, at least not of his army, but it would do. The high collar hid the scars on his neck where his carotid oxygenator had once attached. It wasn't until he actually walked out into the sun that Stasov began to think that he might be free.

Outside the barracks was a tiled patio where the camp's officers had often had parties at night with the local women. A woman waited for him there now. Not one of those dark-haired beauties that had been one of

Luzon's main exports for centuries, but a fair-skinned woman with coppery hair, the New Zealand member of the UN delegation to Camp Homma. She held a notebook.

"Colonel Stasov?" she said, standing. She was a plain-faced woman, strong. "My name is Erika Morgenstern."

They shook hands. "Not colonel," he murmured. "Not anymore." The hot sun made him dizzy, and the smell of the exuberant bougainvillaea that bloomed all around them seemed to clog his nostrils. His knees buckled and he sat down.

She watched him narrowly. "Are you in need of medical assistance?"

He shook his head. "No, certainly not. I have been . . . cared for."

"The Americans are unhappy about Camp Homma," she said, scribbling in her notebook. "Any information you can give the UN will be useful. Any violations of humane conditions."

He looked at her. "If I am being released, the time for Camp Homma must be almost over. The Japanese have a new empire to contend with. Including Sakhalin, I understand. American concerns are a minor problem." Stasov had been captured at Uglegorsk with the collapse of the last Soviet naval effort in the Sea of Okhotsk, by Japanese troops bent on avenging the atrocities of the Soviet occupation of Hokkaido.

The Japanese had chosen Bataan for their war-crimes detention camp, for they were displaying as much their victory over their American allies in the Pacific War as over their Soviet enemy. They named the camp Homma, after the Japanese general who had commanded the invasion of the Philippines in 1942, a deliberate insult to which the Americans were powerless to reply.

"Nevertheless," she said. "If you have been mistreated—"

"If I have been mistreated it is only just," he replied. "Americans make poor victors. They are too forgiving. The Japanese are more like Russians. They demand justice, and perhaps a bit more. Or have you forgotten that you are talking to the Shark of Uglegorsk?"

She looked startled. "Having a nickname is not a

crime. The Japanese have charged you with genocide and slavery, crimes you committed against the very species whose intelligence was demonstrated by your researches. These charges, however, are *ex post facto*—are you familiar with the term?"

"Soviet law is not very sophisticated, I'm afraid."

A Japanese guard brought them tea in graceful earthenware cups. With calm deliberation, Stasov poured the tea on the ground and let the cup fall on the pavement, where it cracked into pieces. The guard bowed expressionlessly, cleaned up the shards, and walked slowly away.

"What did they want from you?" Morgenstern asked. "What did they want to know?"

"They were curious about my work, my methods. My secrets."

"What did they learn?"

Stasov grimaced. "I learned more from them than they did from me. The Japanese have little sympathy for cetaceans. They murder them with less concern than even Russians. Their curiosity was purely practical. I told them little, and that little took them a long time to discover. I know what that's like. I've been on the other side of it. But they showed me that my life is not yet closed. I will continue living. That's no small thing to learn, and I should be grateful." The rustle of a rat in a palm tree made him jump. It took a moment for his heart to slow. "Are you a dolphin researcher, Ms. Morgenstern?"

"No. My interest is planetary exploration. Little enough use for that now, I'm afraid. After the Pacific War, the world's too poor to afford it."

He stared at her for a long time, long enough for her to worry that he was having some sort of traumatic stress attack. "That's an interesting point," he said finally, his voice betraying no particular emotion. "Interesting indeed. No, we can't afford it. But others might be able to."

Two days later they crossed Manila Bay to Cavite, where the Soviet delegation waited. Sea gulls spun in the hot, wet air. The water was glass smooth, with a long sickening swell. Suddenly, all around them, the ocean was filled with the flashing forms of dolphins. They leaped out of the water, occasionally clearing the boat itself. Stasov sat at the stern underneath the flapping Rising Sun and looked out at them.

The white-jacketed Japanese pilot accelerated and began to slew back and forth, though whether to avoid the dolphins or to hit them was not clear.

"Are they glad to see you alive?" Morgenstern shouted over the roar of the motor.

Stasov looked thoughtful. "Glad isn't the word. They know that something has been left undone. They will see me do it."

"Isn't something always left undone, Ilya? I don't understand."

"If something is always left undone, then no one would ever be allowed to die."

Morgenstern turned away from her incomprehensible charge and looked back out at the dolphins. Most of them were dark blue-gray, their smooth skins gleaming in the sun, but some of them had rough attachments on their sides, the cyborg modifications that made them machines of war.

"Those are Soviet military dolphins," Morgenstern said. "What are they doing in Manila Bay?"

Stasov shook his head. "None of my concern, now. Something for the Japanese and Americans to worry about."

"Why? Soviet forces have demobilized."

"They have. The Pacific Fleet is gone, the Japanese occupy Vladivostok, and there isn't a Red Army unit existing east of the Lena. But the dolphins aren't Soviet citizens, are they? And they have not signed any instrument of surrender." He sat back in his seat and straightened the knot on his tie.

They had talked little about dolphins over the past two days. They had, instead, spoken mostly of space exploration, of Morgenstern's hopes and dreams, as if Stasov had come into her life to rescue her. As if he and his dolphins could somehow get her into space.

She looked out at the dolphins sliding in and out of the

water and remembered the images from the TV: the flat burning shape of the Japanese aircraft carrier *Hiryu* at the Battle of La Perouse Strait and the vanishing prow of the *Aegis* cruiser *Jonathan Wainwright* as it failed to defend Kagalaska, both ships sunk by dolphins. The Soviets had been defeated, but the dolphins were still out there, and no one knew what they would do.

She looked at Colonel Ilya Sergeiivich Stasov, the Shark of Uglegorsk, and noticed that, for the first time since she had met him at Homma, he was smiling.

The Maldives, June 2029

Stasov clambered down over the slippery seaweed-covered rocks to take a look at the octopus trapped in the tide pool. It had come too near shore at high tide, probably in pursuit of crabs to eat, and been imprisoned when the water receded. Snails and sea urchins tumbled helplessly as the octopus whirled its tentacles. The red starfish and the sea anemones clinging to the rocks on the side of the pool went calmly about their business, ignoring the frantic interloper. Stasov reached in and prodded the octopus with his finger. It flushed dark with fear and irritation and huddled down between two rocks. The overturned sea urchins waggled their spines and slowly began to right themselves.

The waves slapped louder as the tide rose over the rocks, gleaming eye-hurtingly in the glaring sunlight. Here and there the water met momentary resistance from a ridge or a seaweed pile, but it rose inexorably over all obstacles, finally pouring into the tide pool and reuniting it with the sea. The octopus jetted and vanished in the direction of deeper, safer waters.

Stasov climbed back up from the water, away from the heavy iodine smell of the dark seaweed. Isopods, those marine pill bugs, scuttled madly under his feet amid the barnacles and black lichens at the upper reach of the tidal zone. Above was the rough, bare rock where the sperm whale lay baking in the morning sun.

Its smooth black bulk loomed above the rough rock like a dream of a living mountain, sharply outlined against the cloudless sky. It had leaped from the sea sometime during the night and smashed itself on the land. Without help it would be dead by noon. Staring up at it, mesmerized, Stasov tripped over a stretch of the limp tubing that now crisscrossed the island. A firm hand grabbed his elbow and held him.

"We're ready to pump," Habib William's wheezy voice said. "Tubes are soft now, but under pressure they're like tree trunks. Get one of them wrapped around your leg and you got some trouble. Not to mention one leg fewer." Williams was a short, skinny man with a bald brown head. His white suit was cut with precise jauntiness, and he carried a flowered Japanese parasol. He peered at Stasov with narrow, obvious suspicion. "Now tell me. Why are we here?" He reached down with the parasol's crook and flipped the switch that was the only external feature of a satiny ovoid the size of a desk. It hummed, and seawater filled the tubing. Water sprayed out of hundreds of nozzles, played rainbows in the sun, and ran down the whale's sides.

Stasov gazed at him, pale blue eyes as featureless as robin's eggs. "We're saving a whale," he said. "That's your job, isn't it?"

Williams scowled. "It is. Cetacean rescue for the Indian Ocean. Fine, a respectable occupation, pleases my mother, though it means I can't get home much. I know my profession. What I don't know is why I, and Marta and Jolie and Ahmed, are *here,* on this tiny rock in the Maldives. The water is as clear and calm as I've ever seen it. There hasn't been even the hint of a storm in a month. Halcyon weather. This time of year we sit in a garden in Colombo and play cards. Marta usually wins. She claims it's skill."

He walked around the perimeter of the spray, stepping over the streams that now flowed in the cracks down to the sea. Stasov followed. On the other side of the whale were the two heavy-lift helicopters that had brought the rescue team from Sri Lanka. Next to them was Stasov's own aircraft, a tiny military surplus helicopter, its red star dimmed by sun and salt. Stasov thought of the red starfish in the tide pool. That helicopter had fought in the Aleutians, but its star now seemed to have an aquatic rather than a military character. Things did manage to change, sometimes. Ahmed and Jolie had set up a crane that curled over the sperm whale like a scorpion's tail.

"Then, this morning, the sun comes up, and the Indian Ocean sea-search satellite tells me there's a giant parmacety lying on the rocks in the middle of the ocean like a toy some god's child forgot. It happens. I've seen gams of whales beach themselves and pods of dolphins bash themselves against cliffs until the water is red. Sperm whales do reverse brodies and drop themselves on islands to die. I don't know why they do it, but I'm used to it. What I'm not used to is getting to the scene at top speed and finding Colonel Ilya Sergeiivich Stasov lying next to the whale, wrapped in a blanket, listening to the whale die."

"I hold no such rank," Stasov said sharply. His large hands tightened on each other. "The research vessel *Andrei Sakharov* has been in the Maldives for the past two weeks, not half an hour's flight from here, at Ihavandiffulu Atoll." Stasov had trouble pronouncing the outlandish word. "And she has been my station for two years."

"Oh, has she?" Williams said with heavy sarcasm. "And aren't you afraid you'll be sunk if you venture into the open sea? The sea has become a dangerous place, these days. I would assume for Soviet ships more than anyone."

"We've had no trouble." Stasov took a breath. "I heard a call on one of our hydrophone buoys. Two weeks ago. A deep call, out in the Arabian Basin. If you play back your recordings, you'll hear it. Three humpbacks, in close chorus. A simple call. It said, 'The Bubble Is Rising.' It was a call to prayer. So I am here."

Williams stared at him, incredulous. "Are you serious?"

"Absolutely." Stasov lifted his suntanned, high-cheekboned face to the sky. "The Bubble Has Risen."

"Bullshit." Williams restrained his temper with a visible effort and turned away.

Stasov shook his head, knelt, and folded up his blanket. "The whale is dying. You want to play militia officer, interrogate me and throw me off your island.

Understandable. But while we argue theology, the whale's mass is slowly crushing its lungs. Don't your people have the respirator ready yet?"

The cetacean rescuer jerked his parasol shut, snapping several of its delicate wooden ribs. Stasov followed him to the crane. Williams carefully removed his white suit and finally stood, in paunchy dignity, wearing only a pair of red bikini shorts. Stasov also stripped. The two men stepped onto the crane and were lifted up to the whale's back, which was warm and smooth under their bare feet. They were immediately soaked by the spray that played over the whale.

Williams pulled the crane's respirator nozzle over to the whale's blowhole, located asymmetrically on the top left side of the snout. He stimulated the proper acupressure points with an ultrasonic probe, anesthetizing the sensitive blowhole. He then inserted the nozzle and adjusted the suction cups that held it firm. A signal to Ahmed, and a rush of air inflated the whale's lungs.

"We can give him a breath of air, but we're going to lose him," Williams said. "A lot of damage down below where you can't see it. He must have done a world record jump, from the looks of it. Cracked ribs, organ ruptures, internal hemorrhaging. A mess. Is this poor dying thing your Bubble, Stasov?" He snorted in disgust. "Dolphin superstition. Another of their mass of stupid lies."

From the whale's back the two men could see the whole stretch of sea surrounding the island. Countless white splashes broke the otherwise calm water. Dolphins, hundreds of dolphins, were dancing in the sea. They surrounded the island out to the horizon. Williams stared at them, his face twisted with disgust.

"We've heard many lies over the past few years," Stasov said, sweeping his arms at the dolphins. "The nature of dolphin Revelation isn't one of them."

"Are you asking me to accept the religion of those thugs?" Williams said. "Are they here to kill us? You." A sudden look of realization swept across his face. "They want to kill you. For what you did to them at Uglegorsk, and after."

Stasov shook his head slowly. "They know that I'm to live, for now. And when it is time for me to die, they'll let me handle it myself. Dolphins are capable of an elementary politeness. No, Mr. Williams, they are here to witness the rising of the Bubble. The Great Whale swims beneath the surface of reality, and the buffetings of Her flukes are the swirls and eddies of our lives. A sweep of Her fluke has thrown this sperm whale out of the sea. God rises to breathe. When She does, all will change."

"No, Stasov, I don't buy it." Williams looked as if he wanted to pace, but there wasn't room enough on the whale's slick back. "You pretend not to believe it, officially, but you know that the dolphins have been at war with the human race since the end of the Pacific War. They sank the cruise ship *Sagittarius* off Martinique. They've cut through the hulls of fishing vessels. They've killed swimmers in the open water. It's been random murder."

"Murder?" Stasov asked. "War? The actions of insane beasts? Which is it?"

"You've played your legal games all the way along. That's how you escaped punishment, and the way they will, too."

"The evidence that they've actually killed anyone is ambiguous."

"Ambiguous!" Williams's face turned red. "Colonel Stasov, pain and death are not ambiguous."

"That's quite true," Stasov said seriously. "I know. But whatever has happened, the Americans and the Japanese have been forced to negotiate at Santa Barbara, recognizing dolphin rights. As they should have done years ago, at the end of the Pacific War."

"This is your doing, damn you! You tortured them. Your cetacean research station at Uglegorsk ranks with Dachau and Auschwitz. I watched them die at Kagalaska. I was there."

Stasov breathed slowly. "It was a war. A war for survival." His voice was calm, almost dreamy. "But next time you give your diatribe, use some of our own Soviet concentration camps, such as Vorkuta and Kolyma, instead of those German ones. My grandfather died at Vorkuta. It lends a nice symmetry." So Williams had been at Kagalaska. Had he watched his comrades' blood crystallize on the blue rime ice and felt despair when the *Wainwright* sank?

"You tortured them and now you accept their faith?" Williams asked.

"I didn't know I was torturing them," Stasov said softly. "I didn't know. But without understanding their faith, we would never have been able to communicate with them at all."

"We'll talk with them at Santa Barbara. But you, thank God, won't be there."

"No. I am forbidden. I am a war criminal." Stasov shaded his eyes. Was she finally there, at the northern horizon? He watched as the huge white shape of the *Andrei Sakharov* pulled itself over the edge of the water. From this distance she looked pure, almost Japanese. Her rough welding and patched cables didn't show. "We want the whale, Mr. Williams." His voice was distant. "We intend to take it over from you."

"What?" Williams followed Stasov's gaze. His face hardened when he saw the ship with the red star on its prow. "Damn you, you can't have it."

"Is that your choice, Mr. Williams? The *Sakharov* is equipped with the full complement of systems for keeping the whale alive. It will die otherwise, within hours. You know that."

The *Sakharov* had once been an Aleksandr Brykin-class nuclear-submarine tender with another name, and had loaded sea-launched ballistic missiles into their launch tubes, missiles that, fortunately for the human race's survival, had never been fired.

"Better dead than in your hands," Williams shouted.

Stasov gestured, taking in the dolphin-filled sea visible from the whale's back. "The dolphins don't seem to agree with you."

"Fuck the dolphins! They probably want to haul the whale into the ocean so they can rape it." He ran a hand over his scalp, gaining control of himself. "No. I can't do it. It will imperil the treaty negotiations at Santa Barbara." He smiled, pleased at this legalistic solution. "If we turned a whale over to Colonel Ilya Sergei—"

"I'm glad you take so much trouble to pronounce my entire name," Stasov said icily. "But who is being

legalistic now? Unless we intervene, the whale will die."
He paused, in wonder at the threat he was about to utter.
He had long ago resolved to put the military behind
himself. "The *Sakharov* took on a platoon of Russian
troops when we resupplied at Karachi a week ago. We
are taking them to Oman. I think they would be willing
to assist us in saving this whale's life."

Williams stared out at the approaching ship. "You
don't give me any choice," he said stonily.

"Choice is usually an illusion."

Off Hokkaido, September 2030

The aerobody had developed a noticeable list to star-
board and vibrated vigorously, as if drilling through air
suddenly solid. The airship's pilot, Benjamin Fliegle,
took a slow sip of the steaming green tea in his stoneware
cup and set it back in its heated, gimballed holder on the
control board. The sleet was heavy outside, and the
windshield wiper, inadequately heated, stuttered under
a thick layer of ice. Fliegle, his small shaven head
perched on top of his orange saffron robe like a potato on
a pumpkin, leaned forward and pounded on the windshield with his fist. The wiper tossed a chunk of wet ice
and moved more smoothly. The aerobody tilted peri-
lously, and he grabbed the wheel. "Pesky thing," he
muttered.

The rear hatch opened and admitted a figure in heavy
insulation, as well as a blast of wet freezing air.

"How does it look?" Fliegle said.

"Not bad," Olivia Knester said as she stripped her suit
off. "Just noisy. I'll overhaul it in the shop when we get
back to Kushiro, but it won't give us any trouble." Now
naked, Knester also pulled on an orange saffron robe.
She was a chunky middle-aged woman with extravagant
curled eyebrows that tried to compensate for the shaved
skull above them. "However, Benjamin . . ."

"Yes, Olivia?"

"The engine isn't buying your theories about the
virtual identities of reciprocating parts. It will not 'wear
into perfection,' it will wear into junk. Keep the crank-

case oil full. Until we achieve satori and leave the Wheel, we must keep it lubricated." She turned to Stasov. "Put on your suit. We should find the proper pod of orcas soon. Benjamin, it's time to start listening."

Fliegle dropped the aerobody's altitude to fifty feet and cut back the engines until they moved at twenty miles an hour. A lever on the panel released the hydrophone. As Stasov pulled on his wetsuit, Fliegle put in his earphones and leaned back in his seat with his eyes closed. The altitude continued to drop.

"Benjamin!" Knester said sharply.

The nose went back up. "Sorry."

Stasov put on his fins, fitted underwater lenses into his eyes, and snugged the oxygenator onto the valves on his neck. Then he attached the microphone to his throat, strapped the transducer and signal processor to his chest, and activated the bone conduction speakers behind his jaw hinge. Orca speech included frequencies from 5 Hz to 80 kHz, far beyond the range of human hearing. His equipment compressed and processed the information so that he could communicate.

Sitting on the rocky peninsula of Shiretoko Hanto, communicating with the notoriously touchy orcas, had left the esoteric Buddhist monks of Yumeji Monastery unconcerned with human things. Fortunately this attitude encompassed Stasov's own past, so he had received evenhanded treatment. The monks reassured him. Everyone wanted to escape the Wheel, but everyone was bound to it. Death, in the dolphin view, was the only possible escape, an escape the Buddhists did not permit themselves. Stasov found himself more dolphin than Buddhist.

"I hear him," Fliegle said. Knester nodded at Stasov, and the double bay doors swung open.

He stepped out, tucked, and fell through the gray and vaporous air, then smacked painfully into a cresting wave. As the water closed over his face, reflexes drilled into his autonomic nervous system took over. His diaphragm ceased to inflate his lungs, in a conditioned apnea, and he began to derive oxygen from his carotid gill connections.

He listened to the chatter in his earphones, sorting

signals from noise. A long descending note rumbled, found the resonant frequencies of his joints, and intensified until his entire body was in pain. An orca's shout could break bones, rupture internal organs, and fill the lungs with blood. The orca's voice died away, then sounded deeper, and he was suddenly filled with unreasoning terror. Orcas' voices could kill, or they could stimulate a fear response, pump adrenalin into the human bloodstream, and race the human heart. Cetacean tricks were old to Stasov. Somewhere inside his mind a stopcock opened, the dark waters of fear drained, and he was calm again.

"Greetings, Stasov," a cool voice said. It used the sliding tones of the simple orca dialect reserved for speaking to children, or humans. The voice was familiar. Where had he heard it before? "Thou hast words to speak. Speak them then, for thoughts must be herded and swallowed, lest they escape to the open sea." Of course.

"It is a long way from Kagalaska, Bottom-Thumper," Stasov said, using the slightly contemptuous nickname this orca had earned for his childhood habit of bumping the hulls of Japanese fishing boats. "I trust your hunger has been stayed?"

"My hunger is infinite. But thou art still spoiled food. I must content myself with swallowing the minds of men, leaving their bodies to the sharks and fishes."

"Are you still chasing prime numbers?" Stasov asked.

"I am. I taste the fins of the Goldbach Conjecture. Soon I will sink my teeth into it. It shall not escape."

Bottom-Thumper was a highly respected mathematician, both among humans and orcas. Dolphins, on the other hand, had no interest whatsoever in mathematics. "Your prey weakens," Stasov said politely.

"Do not seek to distract me with minnows. Let loose thy desires and get thee from my sea!" The thunder of Bottom-Thumper's voice buzzed in Stasov's ribs. He hung alone in darkness, only the speed of Bottom-Thumper's replies indicating the orca's proximity.

"The Bubble Has Risen," Stasov said. "We have the Foreswimmer, the whale that signals the coming of God's Echo. We want to take him out of this sea, and let him swim in the deeper waters of the planet Jupiter. I ask you to allow this and to make the proposal in your negotiations at Santa Barbara."

Absurd and makeshift, it somehow all fit together, the only way Stasov had found out of the trap he had placed himself in. Unfortunately, it involved putting himself here in the black water, making a request that could cost him his life. Cost him his life much too soon.

"Do I hear the echo of thy guilt, Stasov?" the orca asked. "I detect its ancient fleeting shape in thy voice. Thou art foolish, as men are wont to be. Thy crimes were necessary and thus were not crimes at all. Thou may live or die, as thou thyself choose. Does an orca need to tell that to a human?"

"Is this prey then released to our jaws?" Stasov asked formally, ignoring the orca's reasoning.

"It is," Bottom-Thumper replied. "But ye humans know not the swift current that has seized you. We shall provide a guard to windward: who will be the Echo of God."

"The Messiah," Stasov said in shock.

"Thy term, inadequate and misleading, but it will do."

He had expected the orca to insist on providing an intelligent cetacean as escort to the sperm whale, whose intelligence was about that of a great ape, but had not expected the Messiah himself. It all made sense, though. It all fit together. "We will make the proper arrangements. It will not be easy. We have never taken a cetacean into space before. For an orca—"

"Not an orca! The voice of God echoes without speaking, and the Echo is not an orca!" Bottom-Thumper was suddenly in a high rage, his syllables ragged like fish with their heads bitten off. The orca spoke in an odd grammatical tense that was used either to describe dreams, or to make statements so true they were apodictic, such as 'all things die' or 'before my conception I did not exist.' Stasov could barely follow the grammar.

"Watch your rectum," Stasov said in dolphin, recalling the insult he had made to Bottom-Thumper when they first met in the bloody waters off Kagalaska. "The walrus is still awaiting your pleasure."

The orca went silent for a long moment. "I should have eaten thee then, Stasov, in that swarming evil-tasting sea. But my belly was full of men. For the last time, I fear. Thou hast the Foreswimmer, a wounded sperm whale ye wish to lift to Jupiter, a planet none of us sea dwellers has ever seen. God's Remora must accompany the whale, for the Time of the Breath is near. Go now to the Aegean Dolphin Sanctuary. There is thy goal. And much good luck may thou and all thy fellow humans have with whom thou will find there."

And then he laughed. And laughed. And *laughed,* a sound like an immense train at a grade crossing. Razor-edged, their thoughts suffused with blood even as they reasoned their way through the most subtle philosophies, bitter thinkers on the end of all, dispensers of justice and death, orcas laughed long, hard, and often. Bottom-Thumper's laughter stopped.

"Art thou willing to pay the price?"

"I am, whatever it is." Stasov could not slow the pounding of his heart.

"Float out thy limbs and remain still. Well met then, Ilya Sergeiivich Stasov."

Stasov relaxed his arms and legs and floated spread-eagled. Suddenly, silently, the smooth shape of the orca sped by, thirty feet long, black, powerful, and vanished again.

The pain was as sudden as the smash of an ax. Stasov twisted his body in agony and managed to activate the buoyancy harness. It righted him and carried him to the surface. He spit water, gasped in the cold air, and was finally able to scream.

The aerobody floated overhead in the pewter sky, a blunt-nosed wedge with two propellers flickering aft. It turned lazily around and drifted over him, buzzing like an immense insect. A harness lowered and scooped him up delicately. The sea opened around him. He looked down. Scarlet drops of blood fell past his dangling feet, the only flecks of color against the gray of the sea and sky. A six-foot-long hooked dorsal fin cut the surface of the water. The orca's head was just visible, water flowing over it in a smooth layer. Bottom-Thumper spouted once and vanished.

Knester was ready with salve and bandages. "Such accuracy," she said admiringly. "He charged a price only a human could pay."

"Damn him," Stasov said through clenched teeth.

"Don't be such a baby. A wound like this is a compliment. Usually an orca will smash you with a fluke, toss you in the air, or puncture your eardrum by shouting when making an exchange, to show his contempt. A blood price is a genuine honor, but usually involves death or maiming for life. The spinning of the Wheel is beyond our knowledge, so I can't guess why he thought you deserved such delicacy."

"We're old friends," Stasov said. She was right. It wasn't every man who was charged a blood price by an orca and ended up losing only the last two fingers on his left hand.

St. Petersburg, February 2031

Erika Morgenstern forged grimly up the street into the teeth of the wind. Huge rafts of dirty ice thrust out of the Neva River, revealing black water beneath a quickly freezing scum.

The dark granite blocks of the embankment held the elegant Baroque city out of the greedy water. Despite the cold, she paused, to marvel at the golden spire of the Cathedral of SS. Peter and Paul as it rose above the frozen city.

Ilya Stasov was housed in an eerily beautiful eighteenth-century red-stucco building with white pilasters, vivid against the snow. Two guards in bulky greatcoats, rifles slung across their shoulders, checked her papers before unlocking the door.

"You have been meeting at the Institute for Space Research?" one of them asked, a friendly youngster with straight flaxen hair sticking out from under his fur cap. "That is good. We have long waited for the Americans to ask for our help. We are smart, but poor."

That wasn't quite it, of course, and she was from New Zealand, not America, but Morgenstern wasn't about to argue with him. Instead, she smiled back. "Yes. We're going to Jupiter." She wasn't sure she believed it herself, but the agreement had been signed just that morning.

"Together, ah? That's the only way to go so far." He opened the door for her and saluted.

The hall was dark, and like all Russian hallways smelled of cabbage, this time with an overtone of frankincense from the icon lamp that glowed in the corner.

Typewriters clacked somewhere in the rear. She only belatedly identified a low moaning as a recording of a humpback whale call. A silent, suspicious woman, her hair tied severely back, led Morgenstern up the stairs to the front of the house.

Stasov greeted her with a formal triple cheek kiss. She held on to him for a moment longer. He had put on weight since Homma, but was still thin. "It is good to see you," he said. "Have you succeeded?" His hair was shaved close, like a swimmer's. He looked tired, and had circles under his eyes.

"Yes," she said. She thought about the years of effort that had finally brought her here to St. Petersburg. "We're going. In principle. As to your idea about our finding . . ."

The silent woman brought two glasses of strong tea. Stasov sweetened his with a teaspoon of blackberry jam. His left hand was no longer bandaged, and he held his glass with his thumb and first two fingers. "It is not a joke. The Delphine Delegation will provide the funding, as they have agreed at Santa Barbara."

"But why? To haul a maimed sperm whale off to Jupiter? It doesn't make any sense!"

"I have told you, though you choose not to accept it. It marks the arrival of their God. If you don't understand that, of course it doesn't make any sense."

"God save us from religion." She felt a deep sense of frustration. "I feel like I'm being financed by some dotty maiden aunt who wants her Pekinese to see Jupiter."

He tapped the rim of his glass with his spoon. "This

maiden aunt will have billions of dollars in reparation money from the Santa Barbara agreement. That money is as good as any other. It is the only way you will succeed."

"I understand that. But I don't have to like it."

"None of us have to like what we have to do." A bell rang in the next room. "Excuse me," he said. "That's Vladivostok." He walked out, slumped, his limbs heavy. He looked infinitely tired.

She glanced around as she listened to his low voice on the phone. The room was packed with papers. Diagrams and maps covered the elaborately figured wallpaper. The lion-footed desk was covered with strip charts and sonograms. A small bed, severely made in a military manner, was the only clear area. A heavy red folder lay on the desk. In a mood of idle curiosity, Morgenstern flipped it open. 'Minutes—Santa Barbara negotiations,' it said. The date was yesterday's. She flipped through. Every day of the negotiations, supposedly kept under rigid security, was there, extensively marked and annotated in Stasov's angular hand. She closed the notebook and sat back down in her chair.

Stasov's voice continued. She listened to it, but couldn't make out the words. After a moment, she realized that he wasn't speaking English or Russian. He was speaking a dolphin dialect. The . . . person on the other end of the line was not a human being.

"Did the dolphins fight a war with us?" she asked when he returned.

"With whom?"

"Don't be coy with me, Ilya!" she said heatedly. "Did they sink ships, those veterans of yours?"

"Until the Treaty of Santa Barbara is signed, the war between human and cetacean will continue, as it always has. It's simply that recently the struggle has been a trifle more even. That's all I will say."

"What do you have to do with Santa Barbara?"

He glanced at the red folder. "I'm not permitted to have anything to do with Santa Barbara. But I like to stay informed."

"How do you hold all this in your head? The whale

you might have started another war when you took it from the Indian Ocean people by force."

"I had to do it," Stasov said. "There was no other way. It's a step on the way out."

"Did you see all this, when we met at Homma?"

"I saw the sun. I saw freedom. I saw that I still had to live. I felt my redemption, but did not yet see its shape. There are still a number of things I have to do. Some of them frighten me."

"Did you see me, Ilya?" she asked, with a feeling of constriction in her throat. "Have you ever seen me? Or just what I can do?"

"I saw you, Erika. But I saw myself as well. Don't try to force me into a position I do not hold. You understand better than anyone what it is that I'm after."

She sighed. "You don't look well, Ilya. Do you sleep?"

"Poorly. Nightmares."

"Of course," she said. "Homma."

"No," he answered. "Uglegorsk."

The Aegean Sea, April 2031

The cliffs rose up a thousand feet above the water, encircling the twenty-mile-wide harbor like protective arms. Whitewashed villages clung to the cliff tops, glinting in the morning sunlight. The sky was a vivid cloudless blue. Stasov leaned against the mast, feeling it warm on his back. The *St. John Chrysostom* creaked serenely across the still water in the harbor. His guide, Georgios Theodoros, silently trimmed the boat's bright sail. It billowed out in the breeze, and they began to flop over the water. Soon they had emerged from the bay of Thera onto the open waters of the Aegean Sea.

"They call it the Temple of Poseidon Pankrator," Theodoros said. He rested easily at the stern of the boat, bearded face turned to the sun like a cat's, eyes half closed while he kept one arm over the tiller. "Poseidon, Ruler of All. Wishful thinking, attributing ancient supremacy to the Sea God. He ruled the sea, and horses. Not much else. But the Temple is the only structure this near which survived the eruption of the volcano

Strogyle, that black day four thousand years ago, so perhaps Poseidon took it back to his bosom." That eruption had left behind the harbor of Thera, which was the immense caldera of the collapsed volcano.

It had been years since Stasov had seen Theodoros. The Greek had aged gracefully, gray appearing in his beard. He had gained a certain unpleasant notoriety due to the association of his theories with Stasov's infamous work at Uglegorsk, but he showed no hurt or anger. In his home waters he was quite an eccentric. Though the regulations governing the Aegean dolphin territories prohibited the use of noisy motor-driven vessels, they certainly did not require the hand-built wood hull blackened with pitch, the dyed woven linen sail, and the watchful painted eyes on the *St. John Chrysostom's* prow.

"I never guessed what it would take," Theodoros said. "All my studies, and I never understood."

"I never guessed how much it would cost," Stasov replied. "But without you I would never have figured anything out."

Theodoros looked out over the sea. "It may have been a mistake, Ilya. But of course that's absurd. We had to discover their intelligence. If only . . ."

"If only they weren't a contemptible, corrupt, sexually perverse bunch of braggarts, cowards, and fools?" Stasov snorted. It was now proverbial that the more one studied dolphins, the more one disliked them. "Why didn't your ancient sources mention that?"

"They mention it, but obliquely. The humans of that era were perhaps not much different, and didn't see that it deserved much comment."

"But how did *they* figure it out?" Stasov asked in wonder. "That was four thousand years ago! They had no sound generators, no signal processing laboratories. How did the men of the Cretan Thalassocracy learn to speak to dolphins?"

"You've got it backward. I think dolphins learned to talk from humans, being too pigheaded to think of something like that on their own, just like the unlettered Greeks learned civilization from the Cretans."

"Learned?" Stasov said. "Or were compelled to learn?"

"Did the ancient Cretans enslave dolphins to guide their ships into dangerous harbors, assist in salvage operations, and scout out enemy defenses? Most likely. I doubt, however, that they felt any great guilt at having done so."

"But still." Stasov hit the wooden gunwale with his fist. "To sail out in a ship like this, dive into the water, and learn to speak to an animal. It's incredible. The equipment we used, the time . . ."

"Don't underestimate your own achievement, Ilya. In ancient days, remember, the dolphins had not resolved to be silent. Breaking that resolution was the difficult thing."

"Difficult," Stasov said, eyes downcast. "That's one word for it."

Theodoros ignored his companion's sudden gloom. "And we were all closer to nature then, and the gods. Remember that story about the lyre player, the whale, and the dolphin that I told you back at Uglegorsk? A whale was more than a whale. He was the Foreswimmer, he who comes before, the First Bubble that rises from the spout of God to foretell the coming Breath, the new incarnation. The dolphin over whose dim head our singer broke his lyre is the Echo of God, or as others have termed him, God's Remora, Her humble, material associate, the Messiah. And that brings us here."

"Whatever happened to that dolphin?" Stasov asked. "After he guided the priests to Delphi."

"Did he die, his task finished?" Theodoros shrugged, looking closely at Stasov. "The story doesn't say. Dolphins perceive the universe by sensing sounds they generate themselves. This makes them arrogant, as if they define the universe, and their final arrogance is their belief that they can finish what they have to do, find closure and die, achieving completion. Fortunately humans, dependent on the world outside themselves, are incapable of such a self-satisfied attitude."

Stasov turned away. "After four thousand years, they tell me, the Messiah has been born. The orcas are angry that he is not of their number but otherwise don't seem to find it much of a matter for comment."

"Why should they? He is a material Messiah, immanent, not transcendent. A money changer. A Pharisee. Even dolphin theology is crude and stupid."

That made Stasov smile. "At last we've found your pet peeve, Georgios. Lack of theological rigor."

"Don't laugh, you're the one who has to deal with it. So you want to push these lazy, incompetent creatures to the Time of the Breath. Why?"

"I shattered their silence, and now I forever hear their voices. If I bring on the Breath, and they reach their new incarnation, perhaps I can find peace."

Theodoros looked sorrowful. "You won't, Ilya. You never will. Peace is only within. But here we are." He dropped sail and the boat stilled. No land was visible. A buoy marked the shallows where the Temple lay. "Into the sea with you. Seek the Messiah. I will await your return here." He smiled sunnily at Stasov, who sat, motionless, staring at the smoothly shining water.

"You have to face them," Theodoros said. "You have madly driven this far. How can you stop?"

"I can't. I always want to, but I can't." Stasov put on his fins and slipped into the water. Dolphins commented to each other somewhere in the distance, but the water around him was empty. He swam toward the voices, recognizing them. Bottom-Thumper at Hokkaido, and these three here. Who else?

In a few moments he came into sight of the Temple of Poseidon Pankrator. Buried by volcanic ash and millennia of bottom sediment, the Temple had been lost until a sounding survey detected a density anomaly. After negotiation with the Delphine Delegation it had been cleaned and restored. A forest of the distinctive Cretan columns, wider at the top than at the bottom, held up a roof edged with stylized bull's horns. Everything had been repainted its original bright polychrome, the columns red with green capitals, the bull's horns gleaming with gold. The Temple was used as a symbolic site for formal human-dolphin negotiations, since it had been from the men of the Cretan Thalassocracy that dolphins had first learned the habits of speech.

Stasov swam slowly over the old sacred precincts, tracing out the lines of the religious complex of which the Temple of Poseidon Pankrator had once been the center. The rest of the ruins had been cleared of debris and left just as they were. In front of the Temple was a large open area. This had once been the Sacred Pool, where dolphins had swum to pay homage, with the sullen sarcasm that must even then have been part of their personalities, to the humans' anthropomorphic version of the Sea God.

Three dolphins swam fitfully around the Temple. The sun probed through the water and gleamed on the ultrasonic cutting blades that made up the front edges of their flippers and dorsal fins. Their sides were armored and their bellies packed with superconducting circuitry. They turned and swam toward him in attack formation. Phobos, Deimos, and Harmonia. A coincidence, that those three had survived. The children of Aphrodite, wife of the cuckolded artificer Hephaestos, and Ares the War God. Fear, Panic, and Harmony, the contradictory emotions of Love and War, with a healthy assist from sullenly impartial technology.

"Colonel!" Deimos said, and the dolphins stopped, awaiting orders. They would still obey him, he knew. If he commanded them to cut Theodoros's boat apart, they would do it without a moment's hesitation, despite the treaty violation it would entail. His authority over them would always exist, for they knew he had the power to change the shape of the world, a power that caused them agony and terror.

Stasov ran his maimed left hand down Deimos's side, feeling the scars and machinery. In the war's second year Deimos and a dozen of his fellows had preceded a run of Soviet attack submarines from Murmansk through the perilous sea gap between Greenland and Iceland, where the enemy had placed his most sensitive submarine detection technology. Packed with equipment that made them appear to all sensors as Alfa-class submarines, the dolphins had drawn ASW forces away from the real Soviet attack. Five of the nine submarines had gotten through, to provide a useful diversion of enemy forces from the main theater of war in the North Pacific.

Deimos alone of his comrades had survived, and been decorated with an Order of Lenin.

"I am not a colonel," Stasov said. He was tired of saying it.

"What are you then?" Harmonia said. Her artificial left eye glittered at him, its delicate Japanese optics covered with seaweed and algae. "An orca that walks?"

"An orca with hands," Phobos agreed. "A good definition of a human." He was the largest of the three and had gotten through the war miraculously unscathed. "We know what you want. You want God. That's why you're still alive."

"Why the hell do you care?" Harmonia made a thrumming noise indicative of disgust. "Why should we?" Her eye kept twisting and focusing at nothing. She had lost the left side of her skull during the landings at Kagalaska. Her job had been cutting free mines with her ultrasonic fin blades while suppressing their magnetic detection circuitry. At Kagalaska the dolphins had encountered a new model. Stasov had never figured out how Harmonia had managed to survive. "Why have you dragged us here to do this? I'm bored."

"He wants to hurt us more," Deimos said. "This way he can drive *all* of us. He will use the Remora like a narwhal's tusk. He will pierce us. Isn't that true, Colonel?"

"It's true," Stasov said. "But it doesn't matter. It has no effect on the validity of my request."

"Stop knocking a dead body around with your snout," the massive Phobos said. "Save logical games for the orcas, who like them. They bore us."

The three dolphins' voices sank through the water like lumps of lead. Each phrase seemed a deliberate effort, but that did not silence them.

"I'm not playing games," Stasov said. "I am serious."

"But why do you care?" cried Harmonia.

"I do. I always have."

Phobos swam up and knocked Stasov aside as if he were a vagrant piece of seaweed. Three chevrons, now dark and tarnished, marked his dorsal fin, one for each of the American submarines whose destruction had been attributable to his skillful use of his sonic and magnetic detectors. He had also helped sink the American *Aegis* cruiser *Wainwright,* saving the landings on Kagalaska.

Even now, his side bruised, Stasov felt that same surge of gratitude that had overcome him when he watched the cruiser sink into the North Pacific. "Answer her question," Phobos said. "Why do you care?"

Harmonia did not allow Stasov to answer. "We certainly don't. God talk is stupid."

"God will rise when She wants to," Deimos said. "We can't push Her flippers with our snouts."

They circled Stasov like mechanical murderous sharks.

"Tell us why this matters to you," Phobos roared.

Would they slice him apart with their ultrasonic blades, these decorated veterans of that heroic, futile war, and stain the clear water with his blood? He felt like a man returned to the grave of his comrades, only to have their bony hands reach out from death to pull him beneath the surface. He would welcome their cold touch, because he knew they had the right.

"It matters because it has to happen," Stasov said. "It is necessary."

The dolphins hooted contempt. "You always do what is necessary, Colonel," Deimos said. "You tortured us until you ripped the voice from our throats—because it was necessary. You took away our bodies and turned us into mechanical sharks—because it was necessary. You killed us in your incomprehensible human war— because it was necessary. Now you come to tear us from the womb of our sea and throw us into the cold deeps of space *because it is necessary?*"

"Eating is necessary," Harmonia said. "Fucking is necessary. Breathing is necessary. Death is necessary. You're as stupid as a sea turtle that fucks in the sea and then climbs out into the air to lay its eggs where the land dwellers can steal them. I'm sure the turtle thinks it's necessary."

"You're like a shark maddened by the smell of blood," Phobos said, suddenly quiet, "who eats and eats and can't stop until its belly bursts. Won't you ever have your fill of us, Ilya Stasov?"

Crying under water seemed so maddeningly futile. He

reached his arms out to them, a meaningless gesture. But what could he give them? An apology? A confession?

"You are right," he said. "I need to do it so that at last I can rest. I can try to forget what I have done to you."

"Rest," Deimos said. "A human word." Dolphins slept with only one hemisphere of their brains at a time so that they could always keep swimming. They could never stop, because they had to breathe. "Why should we grant it to you? The Treaty does not require it."

"And if the Treaty does not require it," Phobos added, "we will not do it. Name us the proper articles or leave."

"Brothers," Harmonia said, suddenly quiet. "Stasov wishes to die. He cannot until he is finished."

"Yes," Stasov said. "Give me your Messiah. And let me die."

Uglegorsk, June 2031

It was the scene of his nightmares. The tanks were now empty, the floor dry, the electronics long since packed up and discarded, but the high vault of the laboratory still contained all of the pain and terror that Stasov could imagine. From the platform where he stood, the pattern of tanks on the floor looked like an ice cube tray in an abandoned refrigerator. The vault's concrete was cracked and aging, the color of long-buried bone.

Stasov held tightly to the thin metal railing, though there was no danger of falling. Even empty, the building whispered. The Japanese had long ago given up on the idea of turning the Uglegorsk station into an atrocity museum. It was too far from anywhere, and the torment there had not involved blood or physical torture but pain too subtle for a human to see. They concluded that the museum would have been utterly unvisited. So it had lain empty, until Stasov's irregular request for a last look at it.

The Japanese had been extraordinarily polite and cooperative, and had left Stasov to wander on his own through the ruins. Perhaps, Stasov thought, it was because they knew he could punish himself more effectively than they had ever been able to.

Suddenly something thunked on the metal stairs. Stasov shivered. Was the place really haunted? The thunk became regular, and Stasov heard the heavy breathing of someone pulling himself up the stairs.

A large figure loomed out of the darkness. "Ilya," he said. "It's been a long time."

"Antosha!" Stasov embraced the massive Anatoly Ogurtsov and kissed him. He hadn't seen the general since the middle of the war. Veterans of Uglegorsk never spoke to each other, even if they lived in the same town. The slightest word would have shattered the icy barriers they had set up around that time. Stasov suspected he knew why the other was there. Ogurtsov would ask a question, eventually. Stasov only hoped that he would be able to answer it.

Ogurtsov stepped back. His right foot was a prosthetic. When he noticed Stasov's attention, he slapped it with his cane. "Not an orca, unfortunately," he rumbled. "Nothing appropriate like that. A single bullet through the knee at Unimak. An ordinary soldier's wound." He reached into his jacket and pulled out a vodka bottle. He pulled the stopper out with his teeth and offered it to Stasov. "To old times."

"To old times," Stasov responded, and took a swallow. He almost choked.

Ogurtsov chuckled. "Now don't insult me, Ilya. I make that stuff myself. An old man's hobby. Flavored with buffalo grass."

"It's excellent," Stasov managed to choke, tears in his eyes.

"Have you lost your taste for vodka?" Ogurtsov laughed. "I remember," he gestured with his cane at the tanks below, "how we sat, you, me, and that Greek philosopher, Theodoros, and unriddled the ways of the dolphins. The drunker we got, the more sense we made of their myths and their gods. And we figured it out."

"And we did it. We tortured them until they spoke."

Ogurtsov regarded him warily. "How were we to know? How should we have realized the incredibly strong response of the cetacean brain to the sense of sound? The aural illusions we generated for them tormented them, drove them mad. It's as if those optical illusions you find in children's books drove humans to extremes of agony."

"We didn't know," Stasov whispered. "For months, years, we tortured them with illusions of moving sea-beds, of impossible echoes. Their absolute faith in their senses broke them like dry sticks in our hands."

"It was a long time ago," Ogurtsov said. He put his arm around Stasov's shoulders. "Let's get out of here."

They climbed down the stairs and walked among the crumbling tanks. "Remember the first time one of them spoke?" Stasov said.

"Ilya, please—"

"Do you remember?"

Ogurtsov shook himself. "Of course I remember." He paused by a tank and looked in at its cracked and stained bottom. "There were four of us. You, me, Sadnikova, and Mikulin. Mikulin died last year, did you know? He tripped and fell down in the snow. He was drunk. He froze to death.

"I can see it. Sadnikova stood over there, her hands on the signal generator. I stood here, you next to me. Mikulin on the other side. It was our final, most sophisticated sonic pattern. The eruption of Strogyle and the sinking of the sea bottom. We'd spent months on it. We played it for that one we called Kestrel, because he swam so fast. I don't know what—"

"He died in the Battle of La Perouse Strait."

"So he got his wish at last." Ogurtsov grabbed onto the edge of the tank. "We played the illusion. And he cried out—"

" 'Let—me—die,' " Stasov said through clenched teeth. "That's what he finally screamed. 'Let me die!' " He shivered. "That's how we began to talk."

"We never listened to what they said, you know. We made them talk, but we never listened. We've never understood why they want to die."

They walked through the rest of the building silently. At the back door they stopped. The sky had its usual high overcast. The *Sterlet,* the boat from the Vladivostok Oceanographic Institute, floated just offshore, its gaily fluttering red flag the only spot of color against the sea and sky. It was the vessel that would take Stasov to Vladivostok, finally back in Russian hands. From there he would go to Tyuratam, and from the spaceport there to Jupiter.

"They fought a war against us, didn't they?" Ogurtsov said. "And most of the human race never really believed it. The slimy aquatic bastards."

"Yes," Stasov answered. "They did. They sank ferryboats, pleasure craft, fishing boats. Whenever they knew they wouldn't get caught, whenever events would be confused. Terrorism, plain and simple."

Ogurtsov shook his head. "We trained them well. Phobos probably sank more than his share. He was a mean one."

"I don't doubt it."

They went down to the water and strolled along the rocky shore, letting the waves lap against their feet. Ogurtsov maneuvered easily over the rocks, occasionally kicking a loose one with his prosthetic foot. He looked at Stasov. "I've talked to people in St. Petersburg. You've gotten everything. Everything we hid. Why do you want it?"

Stasov did not return his glance. The question had finally come. "I don't know what you're talking about."

"Ilya!" Ogurtsov took his shoulder, his hand massive. Stasov stopped. "You've cleaned out the black files, the ones the War Crimes Commission was always after. Circuit diagrams, sonic structures, echo formats. All the ways we generated those sonic images, and the effects that they had. The recordings of dolphins in pain. All of our results." He shook Stasov's shoulder. "I thought most of it had been destroyed."

"No," Stasov said. "We never throw anything away. You know that, Antosha."

"No one knows that stuff exists. The Japanese suspected, the yellow bastards, but they couldn't get their hands on it. They tried hard enough to open you up."

"They tried. I learned more from them than they did from me."

"Why do you want that stuff? After what we've been through? We never wanted to have anything to do with it, ever again."

"I don't *want it,*" Stasov said. "I've never wanted it. But I need it."

Ogurtsov stopped, as immovable as a mountain, holding Stasov in his grip. "Ilya, I feel guilty. We all do, each in our own way, some, I grant you, more than others. But we try to forgive ourselves, because we didn't know what we were doing. What gives you the right to think that your guilt is more important than anyone else's?"

"I know what I have to do, Antosha. That's all. I'm not trying to compete with you."

Ogurtsov dropped his hand, letting him go. "Do it then," he said, his voice tired. "Do it and be damned."

Jupiter Orbit, January 2033

Weissmuller pumped his way toward *Jupiter Forward.* His entire body ached with fatigue. He'd never swum so far before, and he couldn't stop to take a rest. That was all right. The universe was really not such a big place after all. Surgically implanted physiological indicators buzzed into his bones, frantically warning him that Jupiter's magnetic field was about to give him a radiation overdose. The medical personnel at *Jupiter Forward* had warned him strictly. He belched in contempt. What was the problem? Humans were always afraid of all sorts of things they couldn't see or hear. The problem of ionizing radiation was too bizarre and subtle to interest Weissmuller. It could be taken care of. Humans liked solving things like that. That was what humans were for.

Though he accepted it as his due, Weissmuller's spacesuit was a marvel. It followed his contours closely. Since dolphins cannot see upward, the head dome was clear on the underside of the head only, revealing the slyly grinning jaws. The suit circulated water around the dolphin's body while hugging it closely to prevent bruising his tender dolphin skin. The microwave array thrust up between the oxygen tanks on either side of his dorsal fin.

Myoelectric connections to Weissmuller's swimming muscles operated his suit rockets, so that his motions in space were the same as they were in the water. The powerful movements of his tail operated thrust rockets; his fins fired steering rockets. A velocity-dependent retro-rocket simulated the resistance of water, slowing him if he ceased to thrust with his tail. He was kept stable by automatic sightings on the fixed stars, which washed around him like sea-foam.

Weissmuller felt a resonant self-satisfaction. All the way down to Io and back! Jupiter and its satellites floated around him like diatoms. His echo-location signals told him that Ganymede and Jupiter were each about five kilometers away, since the microwave signals took seven seconds to get to them and back. He knew that the distance was actually much greater, but the illusion was powerful, giving him the feeling that the Jovian system could have been dropped into the Aegean Sea and lost. Even the most distant satellite, Sinope, seemed a mere hundred twenty kilometers from Jupiter.

"I fuck you, Jove!" he shouted, and shrieked in delight. He felt an erection and cursed the human engineers who had not designed the suit to provide him a release for it. He hunched, trying to rub it against something. No good. The suit fit too well. Humans had hands, so they could masturbate. Their one evolutionary advantage. He wanted a female to assault, but there wasn't one for millions of kilometers.

He thought of a shark he and the rest of his pod had killed. The dolphins had violated it repeatedly, contemptuously, then sent its body spinning into the depths, cursing it as it sank. The thought gave him a warm glow. And that sailor, who had fallen off his fishing boat near Malta! Humans were poorly built, and Weissmuller still fondly remembered the way the man's ribs had cracked like brittle coral against his snout. Had there been witnesses, of course, the dolphins would have ignored him, or even saved his life by pushing him to shore, the sort of grandstand behavior that so impressed humans. But it had been night and the man alone in the sea. How he had struggled! One of Weissmuller's brothers still bore scars from the man's scaling knife, making him a target for mockery.

Weissmuller's lust was now an agony. Could he ever

violate Jupiter the same way? Could even the humans, through one of their massive incomprehensible devices? Damn them for this insulating suit!

He distracted himself by thinking of international securities markets. The flows appeared as clearly in his mind as the currents in the Cyclades, which he had maneuvered since youth. What a roiled and complex sea the humans had invented! Capital flowed from Japan the way fresh water pours from an iceberg. The money fluid washed back and forth, rising here because of the hectic warmth of success, roiled and turbulent there because of an opposing flow. His investments, concealed under a variety of front organizations like clever hermit crabs, were doing well. It was another sea where Weissmuller could swim. No other dolphin could. But then, no other dolphin was God's Remora. He could eat the morsels from Her jaws.

Ahead, finally, was *Jupiter Forward*. Exuberantly, Weissmuller did a polyoctave Tarzan yell that stretched up into the ultrasonic. He arched gracefully around the space station—and whipped his tail to brake. The vast bulk of Clarence, the cyborg whale, floated beyond it, a tiny human figure just above the whale's head. Ilya Stasov. Weissmuller fought down the urge to turn and flee. He was bone-tired, and the radiation alarms were becoming actively painful. Besides, what could Stasov do to him? After all, he was the Messiah.

"Ah, Weissmuller," Stasov said. "Thanks for coming back. Find anything interesting?" Aided by computer voice synthesis, he could speak almost as well as a dolphin. Weissmuller found his speech slightly menacing, as if the dolphin words concealed orca teeth.

"None of your business," he said sullenly. "Bugger off."

"I'm afraid it is my business." The tone was mild. "You must talk to Clarence."

Weissmuller approached the whale. Microwave echo-location was useless at this range, since the click and its return overlapped, but the clever humans had installed a processor that gave the dolphin a calculated synthetic echo. The human-modified sperm whale was now huge, much larger than even blue whales had ever been.

Weissmuller had never heard a blue whale. They had vanished long before he was born.

"Don't threaten me! You can't. Article Fifteen of the Treaty of Santa Barbara. I'll tell the Delphine Delegation and they'll replace you. See if they won't."

"Don't be an idiot, Weissmuller. They won't replace me."

Weissmuller twitched irritably, setting off random bursts of fire from his rockets. He knew they would never replace Stasov, no matter what the human did. Stasov had continued to live when he should have been dead, because his tasks were unfinished. The thought of what completion would mean frightened the dolphin. "I won't do what you say, I don't care what—"

"You must talk to Clarence now, Weissmuller. He's in terror. He doesn't know where he is. He needs your help."

"Fuck you!" Weissmuller shrieked, and buffeted Stasov with his powerful tail. The man sailed off helplessly, tumbling until he managed to regain control with his own clumsy maneuver rockets.

"You float like a jellyfish," Weissmuller called. "A sea urchin!"

When Weissmuller had been young, he'd heard a story about ghost voices, about long-dead whales whose last calls had echoed around the seas for decades, refracting through thermoclines, sucked into the depths by cold subsurface cataracts, resonating through abyssal trenches, to finally rise up and moan their long-sunken words to the hearing of a terrified dolphin. When Stasov finally spoke, he spoke with the voice of a ghost.

"When I first did this, I had no idea of what I had done. Now I understand. It is . . . necessary. Forgive me."

"Forgive you? Feed me, and I'll forgive you. Ha ha." While orcas and humans laughed, dolphins expressed their pleasure more in the way an elderly pervert snorts at short-skirted schoolgirls.

Suddenly, Weissmuller heard the wide sounds of the sea—the clicks, groans, wails, chitters, and thumps of the aquatic obbligato. Ranging far away were the overlapping calls of a gam of humpback whales and the sharp slap as one of them breached and fell back in the water. Nearer were the loud thumps of a school of the tiny fish humans called sea drums. He was afraid. This sea was far away. The dolphin pinged out a tentative echo-location signal.

The echo returned. Bottom was a mile down, past an ill-defined thermocline. There was a set of three submerged volcanic peaks, one with a coral atoll around it, some twenty kilometers away. Nearer was a seamount that made it to the surface, creating a tiny island. Weissmuller knew the place, though he had never been there. The dolphin language had a word for every place in the sea, a word that is a schematic of the echo that the place returned, a sort of physical pun. An intelligent dolphin could carry a map of all the world's seas in his head like an epic poem.

Weissmuller was near the Maldives, in the Indian Ocean. He could hear the shapes of the distant whales as well as those of the fish that swirled around him. He pinged out a stream of signals. They returned, bearing their load of information, the details of the terrain, the sizes of the schools of fish.

With that, the pain began. His mind knew that what he heard was not real, but the part of his brain that processed the information was beyond conscious control. He felt a growing panic.

He heard the terrified call of a sperm whale. It was alone and had lost track of its gam in a storm. Weissmuller ignored it. The fears of the huge foolish whales were none of his concern. It called for help. He yelled at it to shut up so that he could hear that marvelous all-encompassing sea.

Suddenly, the bottom moved. The dolphin felt a primal terror. The sea and its creatures moved eternally, but the land always remained steady. When the bottom of the sea became unstable, everything ended.

He was no longer in the Maldives. He swam the Aegean, and could sense the landmarks of the Sea of Crete as they had been four thousand years before. This was where it had started and where it had ended. The water roared and the bottom shook, marking the destruction of the only universe intelligent dolphins had ever known. Panic pierced through him. The bottom of the sea rippled like the body of a skate, and his mind dissolved in agony.

As the sea bottom rippled it lost its contours, becoming as smooth as the back of a whale. And indeed that was what it was. The floor of the sea had become a whale that thrust powerfully beneath him. Her spout could blow him to the stars.

"Ah, my Remora," a giant voice spoke, using the dolphin language but not sounding like a dolphin or an orca. "The parasite on God. I should rub you off on the barnacled hull of a human ship and leave you to sink to the bottom of the sea."

"No!" Weissmuller screamed. "You can't! I am your Echo. I know it all. All! I have done my duty. I know how humans work. I know their money, their markets. I can defeat them. I can achieve our destiny. You know me!"

God's back rose up toward him, and the edges of the sea closed in. The surface of the water above him became solid. Weissmuller heard his own echoes returning faster and faster, with improbable clarity. And he would be unable to breathe! He was trapped. He was going to die.

"I know you," God's voice said. "You are a coward and a fool."

"No! Forgive me! Forgive—"

The walls closed in around him and then vanished, leaving the vasts of space. Weissmuller keened desperately and flailed around in terror. "Stasov!" he shrieked. "Where are you? Let me die!"

"You know me," Stasov said quietly.

"I know you! You changed the world so we would speak. You tore the voice from our throats! Your teeth gave us birth. Oh, it hurts. Life hurts!"

"It always hurts. You are the Echo of God. The thinking races of the sea have raised you up here so that you may pull them after you. You will hurt most of all. Or so you will believe." Stasov paused. "I'll never forgive you for having forced me to do this. Instead of completion I end with the knowledge that pain is never finished."

"A human problem, not mine," Weissmuller said. "I

will talk to the whale." Then, plaintively: "I'm sorry I went to Io. I feel sick. Ilya?"

Stasov silently activated the whale's voice. Clarence promptly sounded an elaborate and specific call.

Weissmuller shook, panicked. "It's a death call, Stasov. A death call!"

"What else do you expect?" Stasov said coldly. "Do you think that you're the only one who wants to die? I've heard that call before."

Stasov had once watched a gam of seven fin whales get chased for three days across the South Atlantic by two cooperating pods of orcas. It was a vicious, hard pursuit. Finally the fins, tired and spent, sent a call to the orcas, who stopped pursuing immediately and waited. The fins gathered close together and talked to each other while the orcas swept around them. Finally, one fin whale emerged from the gam and swam out to the orcas. The whales had decided among themselves which was going to be eaten. The orcas tore that one to pieces and let the others swim away unharmed.

"Clarence wants to negotiate his death with you."

"What do I say to him? I don't know what to say!"

"Tell him he has to live. To live and suffer. Just like the rest of us."

One of *Jupiter Forward's* spinning rings was filled with water, providing Weissmuller with a place to live. He could swim around and around it, leaping into the air at those points that engineers had raised the ceiling, and feel almost at home. No solid place intruded. There was nowhere for a human being to stand, so Erika Morgenstern and Ilya Stasov floated in the water. Morgenstern hated this, as an affront to her dignity, but there was no way to compel the dolphin to visit her office.

"What did he do to you, Ilya?" she whispered. "I haven't seen you look like this since . . . since we met."

"It's what I did to him that matters," he answered, his voice flat.

"But what—"

"I had to do it *again.* What I once did all unknowing, I just did with full understanding of what it meant."

The dolphin appeared around the curve of the ring,

skimming the water toward them. He had learned to use the low gravity and the Coriolis force of the spinning ring to extend his leaps. He hit the water with his belly, splashing them, and vanished. A moment later he nuzzled the Director's crotch. She gasped, then, having been briefed by Stasov, reacted by driving her heel into the dolphin's sensitive blowhole. Weissmuller surfaced and keened in pain.

"Stop it," Stasov said. "It's what you deserve."

"Screw you, Madame Director," Weissmuller said. In air his breath was foul with old fish. He moved his head toward her, and despite herself, she ran her hands down his smooth sides. He wriggled. "Did you buy Vortek like I told you?"

Her hands stopped. "Yes."

"And?"

"It's up seventeen in the past month, damn you! How did you know? How could a dolphin possibly know anything about the technical knowledge market? And more importantly, why did you tell me?" She pushed him away.

"I wanted you to understand that I'm not just kidding around. I know where the tuna school. Believe it."

"What are you talking about?"

The dolphin was silent for a long moment. "About one kilometer south-southwest of Portland Point, in the sea off the island of Jamaica, is the wreckage of the *Constantino de Braganza,* a Spanish treasure ship out of Cartagena, sunk in 1637 by a Dutch privateer as she tried to flee to the safety of Port Royal. We heard it happen, but we didn't know what humans were fighting for. It carried three tons of gold bullion, another ton and a half of specie, and an equal amount of silver, all of which now lies on the bottom, along with the bones of men." He spoke almost tonelessly, as if reciting a long-ago lesson. "Given the rights of the Delphine Delegation in such matters, I think it might be possible for us to assist you directly, Madame Director Morgenstern. If you agree to assist us. We know where the ships lie. We remember."

"You mean the goddam Treaty of Santa Barbara gives the dolphins—"

"Full salvage rights," Weissmuller interrupted gleefully. "Anything that went down more than fifty years ago. Article Seventy-seven and sections one and two of Article Seventy-eight. You thought your technology gave you the advantage. Ha. You forgot about our memory. It's long. Longer than you ever dreamed. Humans think they're so smart. Big joke."

She turned to Stasov. "You must have known. How did you allow them to swindle us like this?"

He stared back at her and did not reply.

"All that money," she murmured. "All that money . . ."

"We want to make a deal," Weissmuller prompted.

"What are you offering me?" she asked.

Weissmuller twitched and wailed suddenly, as if he were a mystic in a trance. "Full control of the next project! Not subject to restrictions, regulations, and the need to resolve conflicts between various entities. I'm the first dolphin in space. I won't be the last. Not by a long shot. We want to escape, and we need the hands of humans to do it. Humans must carry us to the stars. I hate it! Our destiny, in the hands of *humans*. All I can do is pay you. There's a Venetian galley off the coast of Dalmatia, full of gold. It sank in 1204. I hope you rot in Hell." He twisted and disappeared into the water.

"They aren't the ones who want it, Ilya," she whispered. "I don't know why, but *you* want them to go to the stars. That's why you helped them with the Treaty of Santa Barbara."

"That's true," he answered simply.

"I've known it since I visited you in St. Petersburg and saw that folder, as I suppose you meant me to. It was just part of your expiation." She swallowed. "Just as I was another. You tried to show me, but I never listened. I had no idea how little I meant to you."

"Erika, I had no choice. I had to make up for the evil I had done. I've explained it to you before."

"Is your guilt the most important thing in the universe? Is everything you've done since I found you at Camp Homma justified by it?"

They drifted apart in the water as if physically pushed by her intensity.

"I needed to reach an ending," Stasov said. "I needed to find completion."

She stared at him, suddenly frightened. "And have you?"

He shook his head slowly. "Nothing is ever complete. But I reached my ending before I left Homma. I realized that when I tortured Weissmuller, with the full knowledge of what I was doing. I'd always had that knowledge. I'd always known. I ripped their minds apart so that we could conquer some rocks in the North Pacific. I tormented them to satisfy my curiosity."

"No," she breathed. "No. You never knew."

"Perhaps I didn't know they could speak. But I always knew they could suffer. And as long as I live, they *will* suffer."

"They'll suffer even if you don't live."

He looked at her for a long moment. "True. But that will be none of my concern."

Stasov floated in space, the great form of the whale in front of him.

"Ilya," Weissmuller said, his voice large and hollow. "I have done all that I had to. We can float now, humans, dolphins, and orcas, on a great sea of cash. With that money we can swim to the stars. It's hateful! I feel more disgusted than I ever thought I'd be."

"Yes," Stasov said. "The Time of the Breath is upon us." Jupiter loomed above him, through some odd error of perception, like a heavy fruit ready to fall. Clarence drifted quiescent, singing a simple song to himself, almost a lullaby. His physical systems had been checked, and Weissmuller had managed to calm him down, finally doing the job that most humans believed he had been brought to do. Stasov alone knew that he had been brought to lead his people forth from the sea.

Looking at the dolphin and his massive companion, Stasov had a sudden image of dolphins, grinning faces at the front of the bodies that were their ships, slipping through the spaces between the stars, gamboling amid the debris of the cometary Oort cloud that surrounded each star, whipping, in tight formation, over the frozen surface of a neutron star, and finally plunging through a planet's warm blue atmosphere to fall hissing, red-hot, into the alien sea, there to swim and play as they always had. When the time came to move on, they would blast with a roar back into the infinite spaces that had become their second home. Humans, more sedate and deliberate, would follow after in their own ships, dolphins leaping in their bow waves and guiding them to a safe port.

Morgenstern would, he knew, continue the task that had driven her since youth, even though she had discovered that her passion had been used by another for his own purposes. Neither she nor the dolphins had seen any reason to pull cetaceans into space, but Stasov had decided.

"What happens to the Remora once his God breathes?" Weissmuller said. "What happens to the Echo once God has located what She is after? What am I now?"

"Nothing," Stasov said. "And less than nothing."

The countdown was reaching its conclusion, and Clarence's rockets prepared themselves to blast.

"Then let me die! I can go with Clarence and sink into the endless seas of Jupiter. I've done what I had to."

"No," Stasov said. "You're still necessary to others. It's my turn to die."

"You selfish shark spawn!" Weissmuller shrieked. "You've played with us, ripped us apart, driven us to our destiny, and called up *our* God to help you create the echo that *you* want to hear. You always get your way! I say I will die and there isn't anything you can do about it!" He thrust his tail and his rockets flared. "I won't stop at Io this time!"

Stasov had expected this, and was already straddling the dolphin, as if riding him through the sea. He manually stopped down the oxygen flow until Weissmuller was suffocating. The rockets died, and the dolphin shuddered beneath him.

"Ilya," Weissmuller said forlornly. "I fear the net. Humans caught us when we followed the tuna, suffocated and killed us, thoughtlessly. They didn't realize that when we listen we do not think, and are thus easily captured. You tortured us with false echoes and woke us up. Are you going to haul us to the stars in your nets? Won't you ever leave us alone? Won't you ever stop tormenting us?"

"There's only one way to stop. I see that. You don't have to tell me."

"Do you think death will stop you? The pain is always there. Damn you!"

Stasov drifted near Clarence, until the surface of the whale suddenly changed from something next to him to something beneath him. He found the point of attachment and tied himself to it.

With smooth thrust, fusion flames blossomed around Clarence's midsection. Clarence sang a journey song, one full of landmarks in a sea that he would never hear again. Could he invent new ones for the deeper sea of Jupiter?

Stasov rested against the gravity created by Clarence's acceleration.

He would never hear Clarence's new songs.

Soon he would sink into the deepest sea of all.